Nikola Scott started her career in book publishing before she became a writer herself a decade later. Her acclaimed debut novel, *My Mother's Shadow*, was translated into over a dozen languages and became a long-running bestseller in Norway. Her other novels, *Summer of Secrets* and *The Orchard Girls*, were also published widely around the world. Nikola lives in Frankfurt with her husband and two sons.

By Nikola Scott

My Mother's Shadow
The Orchard Girls
Summer of Secrets
The Life I Stole

The Life I Stole

Nikola Scott

REVIEW

First published in Great Britain in 2023 by
HEADLINE REVIEW
An imprint of HEADLINE PUBLISHING GROUP

1

Cataloguing in Publication Data is available from the British Library

ISBN 978 1 4722 6083 3

Typeset in 12.25/14pt Garamond MT Std by Jouve (UK), Milton Keynes

Printed and bound in Great Britain by Clays Ltd, Elcograf S.p.A.

Headline's policy is to use papers that are natural, renewable and recyclable
products and made from wood grown in well-managed forests and other
controlled sources. The logging and manufacturing processes are expected
to conform to the environmental regulations of the country of origin.

HEADLINE PUBLISHING GROUP
An Hachette UK Company
Carmelite House
50 Victoria Embankment
London EC4Y 0DZ

www.headline.co.uk
www.hachette.co.uk

For Jim & Sharon

A note on the correct form of address for surgeons

In the UK and the Republic of Ireland, surgeons are traditionally addressed as Mr (Mrs, Miss or Ms) rather than Dr. This is said to go back to the time of barber-surgeons, when physicians were academic men, holding a medical degree, while most surgeons were craftsmen, trained on the job. With the rise of the voluntary hospitals in late-eighteenth-century England, the public perception and status of surgeons began to match that of physicians, and in the early nineteenth century, formal qualifications for surgeons were put into place.

To this day, surgeons keep the title of Mr (Miss, Mrs, Ms), as a badge of honour that highlights their heritage.

One

'Let's make a dash for it, quick!'

Heavy raindrops were thumping the ground and a growl of thunder heralded a more serious downpour. Dodging passers-by, I pulled Isobel down Fleet Street, turning the corner towards the dark wooden doors of Finley & Smith's Bank. In the ante-room, dimly lit and deserted, we paused for a moment to catch our breath and shake the rain off our coats.

'Now, we don't have a lot of time,' I said, pushing damp curls out of my face and trying to bundle them more neatly beneath my hat. 'You show them the paperwork, tell them about your parents' car accident . . .'

Isobel had been folding her umbrella, but at that, she pressed her lips together and looked over my shoulder to where the interior of the bank was dimly visible through the glass doors. 'Oh Agnes, I don't think I can,' she said in a choked voice. 'It's still so difficult to talk about them without . . .' Her eyes were already welling up with tears. 'They'll all be looking at me and . . .'

'No one will be looking at you,' I said soothingly. 'People come in to fetch things from their safety deposit boxes all the time.'

Isobel was clutching the sodden scrap of black lace she used for a handkerchief when her face suddenly lifted. 'Agnes, you do it. Just say you're me. You're so much better at this sort of thing.'

I assessed our reflections in the ancient mirrored panel. At first glance we did look rather alike, both of us slight and fair, both dressed sombrely in deference to Isobel's recent bereavement. But where Isobel was shy and neat and pretty, I was skinny and a bit scrappy-looking after years of rationing and running up and down stairs with a coal scuttle. And even the mirror couldn't disguise that Isobel's gown was a nice chequered cotton with a slim belt above practical but well-made leather pumps, while I was in a simple dark grey dress and cardigan that befitted a maid.

Isobel fidgeted next to me, her pleading eyes hollow and dark-shadowed.

'All right,' I said quickly. 'Give me your gloves, quick, before someone comes, and your coat. Pull mine all the way down over your dress, like so. Perfect.'

In seconds, I had belted Isobel's good coat tightly around myself, buttoned up her gloves and straightened my own coat around her thin figure. I ran a practised eye over both of us and gave her a reassuring grin. We'd done it many a time over the last weeks as we packed up the McIntyres' house, weathered the funeral and a myriad of other painful errands, because Isobel, shy and kind and absolutely devastated after her parents' deaths, was struggling with any reminder of them and constantly on the verge of tears.

'Perfect.' I reached to tousle her hair into something less formal while simultaneously trying to neaten my own unruly curls.

'What do you think we'll find in the safety deposit box?' she whispered. 'Mother never mentioned it. Probably full of useless ancient paperwork.'

'Or treasure.' I gave my hat a last tweak, then nudged her encouragingly. 'Just think, it could be full of gold or lovely diamonds.'

Handy as well as lovely, I thought to myself, because Isobel's inheritance was modest to say the least. At least my wages were paid through to the end of the summer, after which I'd need to find a new position. As for Isobel, there was a small trust paying for her education – a summer course in France, then a place to study at King's College, Durham, in the autumn – but after that she'd have to find some additional means of supporting herself.

'Wait, my bag,' she whispered. Her mother had given it to her, a sturdy leather satchel ready for student life and monogrammed with her initials, *IAM*. I slipped it over my shoulder, gave Isobel my own battered handbag and reached for the door. She held me back, her small hand light on my arm. 'Thank you,' she said. 'For everything. I know the last few weeks . . . well, I haven't been much help, have I?'

'You've been grand, Iz, and it's not been easy.' I squeezed her hand, then straightened and fixed an authoritative smile on my face. 'Now, let's go and get you some treasure, shall we?'

'My deepest condolences, Miss McIntyre.' The bank clerk looked from me to the small black key to the papers I'd fanned out across his desk.

Feeling Isobel lean forward automatically at the address, I gave her a surreptitious kick on the ankle and nodded archly. 'Thank you, very kind.' I was careful to make my voice cool and crisp, erasing any trace of the faint accent that sometimes still crept in, even though it had been years since I'd left the East End. I thought I was doing rather well – I certainly was enjoying myself – but something about us seemed to have piqued the clerk's interest, because he gave me a long, searching look.

'You found this among your parents' personal effects, you say? It says "Bellingdon" here.'

'Yes, the Bellingdons . . . er . . . were my mother's family.' I shifted a little, trying to find a more elegant way to sit in Isobel's coat, which was a little fuller than mine, and to my immense irritation, I felt myself flushing slightly under his scrutiny. Ignoring the way the chapped skin around my nails snagged at the soft insides of Isobel's gloves, I summoned the icy hauteur I'd

3

watched Isobel's mother use on delivery boys, piano teachers and shopkeepers alike, and fixed him with an equally cool stare. I'd faced much worse than fussy, middle-aged Mr Bristow, who had combed a few strands of hair over his bald pate and was now leafing through the papers for the third time.

'If you'd be so kind. We're in rather a hurry.'

I rose without waiting for his answer, waved for Isobel to follow suit. Behind us, I heard Mr Bristow finally shuffle together the papers and clamber to his feet, and allowed myself a small smile.

'It's one of our older boxes,' he said as we walked into the back. 'The stairs are steep, Miss McIntyre, so do watch your step.' His tone was polite now, and I felt a small thrill at being at the receiving end of the kind of courtesy he would never have extended to me as a maid. 'Will your,' he gave a small, discreet cough in Isobel's direction, 'girl wait here perhaps?'

'Of course not,' I said curtly. 'She'll accompany us.'

He kept up a polite patter on the way down the staircase, which was steep and dark and not nearly as fancy as the marble-clad front area of the bank. A spiderweb of cracks covered the dark walls, some of the bigger gashes roughly patched up with mortar. Not a surprise, perhaps, given that half of London was still in a state of disrepair after the Blitz. I accidentally brushed against a loose piece of plaster and a small cavalcade of rubble scattered down the stairs, making him break off mid sentence. I fought a brief, visceral urge to turn around and scrabble my way back up towards the light. A memory pushed in, of the very last night I'd spent in London, my mother and I crouching in an underground space much like this, faces upturned to listen for the Germans, flinching at every impact.

Another piece of plaster skidded down the stairs and hit the bottom with a loud thwack. My heart beat hard in my chest. My mother had loathed the public shelter, so we'd not gone there a lot. *It'll be a light one, Agnes. The Germans don't care about little old us down here, I promise.* She'd sewn a special cover for her work table, like a large tent with a nest of blankets inside. She'd play games with me in the velvety darkness, singing and murmuring and telling stories to keep the roaring and thumping outside at bay. Sometimes the air raid warden discovered us in time and marched us down the street, forcefully pushing us into the cramped space of the public shelter as the siren faded.

The grit slid beneath my feet. Mr Bristow was waiting at the bottom of the stairs, his eyes liquid black in the flickering light of the wall sconce. Could he see into that dark, shuttered place at the back of my mind, where Mum and I clambered reluctantly into the least desirable corner of the shelter on Bell Street, my mother giving next door's nosy Mrs Hayes her most brilliant smile as we squeezed past feet hastily pulled away from *that Crawford girl* and her good-for-nothing mother?

But when I drew closer, making room for Isobel to step off the stairs behind me, I saw that Bristow's eyes were fixed on the cracks in the wall, and a fine bead of sweat glistened on his upper lip.

'Careful,' he said abruptly, jerking his gaze away and motioning us along. 'The old boxes are all the way in the back, I'm afraid.'

Isobel was already obediently walking in the direction he indicated, but I hesitated.

'Brings back some memories, doesn't it?' he said.

'It certainly does.' I gave myself a push. I was no longer ten and cowering in the dark beside my mother. I was twenty, and the war was long behind us. The light from the sconces flickered, throwing large jerky shadows on the walls and ceilings as I strode quickly ahead of Bristow and Isobel, past walls lined with safety deposit boxes, heading through an archway towards the back. Just a few more minutes and we would be above ground once more, hopefully with Isobel's treasure in hand.

I blinked and turned, wondering wildly if my mind was playing tricks on me, taking me back to the droning of enemy
planes, the rat-a-tat of the anti-aircraft guns weaving into my
mother's voice. But no, there it was again, a strange low rumbling sound, a subterranean groan as if the earth itself was
coming alive, was—

'Agnes!' Isobel's voice was shrill with fear. 'Oh my God,
Agnes! What is *happening*?'

Whatever it was, it happened very fast, even as I turned back
towards her, unsure where I was going because direction was no
longer possible with the whole space – yes, the vault itself –
moving. The light danced violently as the walls shook and
trembled, then something collided with my back, so hard that it
propelled me the last precious metres into the vaulted space. I
screamed. Lying there on the ground, I screamed on and on,
simply to feel the air in my lungs, because as long as I could do
that, I was still alive, I was still here, I was—

Darkness.

Two

I came to slowly, my limbs reaching for consciousness before my mind did, my hands scrabbling at rubble. Dust everywhere. My eyes gritty . . . my eyes . . . I tried to blink, sluggishly at first, then faster, but I couldn't penetrate the solid wall of darkness.

It came to me in a single great rush then, the memory of the roar, like the earth itself had contracted and heaved out boulders and bricks, plaster and metal.

Panic, sharp acid in a roiling stomach, battled against the urge to struggle, to burrow up into the light. With a massive effort, I forced myself to lie still, to feel my heart beating. It was quiet now, so still the silence was loud in my ears. But I could hear, and I could move, could wiggle my toes, which meant – I struggled up – that my legs were working, they were just trapped under something. Clutching the strap of Isobel's leather bag, which was – absurdly – still around my shoulder, I felt scratchy wool tweed on top of my lower half. Limp and motionless, Mr Bristow didn't budge, not even when I groped for his wrist. It was then that I suddenly remembered.

'Isobel!' I shouted, jerking my fingertips away from Mr Bristow's non-existent pulse and pulling my legs out from under him. 'Are you there? Anyone? Help, HELP!' The darkness closed tightly around my shout, extinguishing it immediately.

Then a groan, a small one, a few feet away from me.

'I'm coming, stay there.' I swept my arms ahead of me to feel for her amidst the rubble. It seemed to be strangely alive; there were things fluttering in it – paper, I realised. And metallic things, safety deposit boxes perhaps, or – I made a strangled noise when I felt tines – a fork? The things rich people kept in bank vaults.

'Stick your hand up and move it about.' I swept the floor more urgently, scattering what felt like pearls ahead of me.

'I don't think I can.' Her voice was fainter now, but closer, too, and I shuffled faster on my knees. 'Something's fallen on me, and . . . it's *in* me . . .' Her voice was muffled by a spluttering fit of coughing.

'I've got you.' Frantic with relief, I felt along her body for her hands, found one and gripped it. 'I'm here. Don't worry. Don't worry a bit.'

She gave another strangled cough, and I knew without a shadow of a doubt that there was a great deal to worry about.

'Mr Bristow, is he . . . What happened?'

'He's dead.'

She gave a muffled gasp of horror, and I bent over the sound. 'The building must have collapsed, or part of it. It still happens, I read it in the paper. Structures damaged in the war, no one realises where . . . But you, Izzy, where does it hurt, where?'

'Everywhere,' she said, with some difficulty.

Giving her a reassuring pat on the shoulder, I bit back a gasp when I felt a piece of metal sticking out of her side. She twitched, gave a stifled moan when my hand caught on it.

'I've got something around my throat,' she rasped. 'Get it off me, Agnes, get it off . . .'

I felt for her neck. 'Your scarf, hold still.' Keeping hold of her hand, I fumbled for the small knife I always kept in an inside pocket of my dress and sawed at the fabric. I tried to draw strength from the way my fingers folded around the metal of the knife, warm and reassuring, then slipped it back into my pocket.

'There, all better now.' I tried to make my voice firm. 'Now we just need to wait for them to dig down and free us.'

'But will they?' she said in a small voice. 'Poor Mr Bristow.'

'I'm sure they're already shifting boulders and digging. It was probably a good thing we were down here when it happened; the foundations protected us. And he wrote my name – I mean yours – in the ledger, remember? Then there's all this treasure to protect!' I guided her fingers along the fork. She made a sound that sounded almost like amusement, and I was glad all of a sudden that I couldn't see the damage to her body, because without it, she seemed fine, might still make it if only they found us soon.

'Hellooo! Hellooo! Help!' I shouted. 'Down here, down . . .' I broke off, suddenly realising I was using up precious air we might very well need as time wore on.

'Just think, Iz.' I stroked her arms to stop her shivering. 'Think of all the exciting things happening tomorrow! France, here we come!'

'France,' she said faintly.

She was to do a summer course there before starting medical school up north in the autumn, all organised by Mrs McIntyre, who had been so excited about her daughter's academic future that it was almost unbearably ironic she would never see it come to fruition. After the accident, Isobel hadn't wanted to go anywhere much at all, but she was doing what she'd always done, which was following her mother's wishes.

But then: 'I want you to come to France with me,' she had announced a few days after the funeral. 'Otherwise I'm not going.'

'Don't be silly, the course is paid for already,' I'd said. 'And I have to find a new position.'

'It's bad enough that we'll be split up at the end of the summer,' she said with the stubbornness shy people often displayed when least expected. 'Me swanning off to uni while leaving you to work in some poky job. You're coming.'

'No one else will have a maid with them,' I protested. 'What'll I do?'

'You're not really a maid. Well, not in that way. So, sit in the sun. Swim. Read. Help me with organic chemistry.'

It might be a good thing, I had thought as I sorted out the McIntyres' rented house in the school grounds. Give me a bit more time to think about my own future. I'd been sent to live with the family when I was ten, an evacuee from the East End during the London Blitz, and stayed on when my mother was killed during an air raid. Isobel had attended whatever private school her father was teaching at, while I went local. I was lucky, really. None of the other maids I knew had stayed on beyond fifteen, but Mrs McIntyre placed great store on education and I had a knack for sciences, could remember anything at a single glance. At my last school, nice Miss Lewis had even suggested that I should try for a scholarship at university. Sciences or education. It had sounded like something out of a dream: a life that included books and the solitude to study them, where I was no longer a mostly-maid-sometimes-companion living with a borrowed family but could carve out a place of my own. An impossible dream for someone without money or family, perhaps, but dreams, last time I checked anyway, were still free.

'Agnes?' Isobel's voice was a faint wet hiss.

'Wine and handsome Frenchmen charming everyone in sight.' I spoke quickly to cover my fear at the sound of that hiss. 'All perfectly respectable, of course – your mother wouldn't have had it any other way – but enough to make you feel giddy and pretty in that maroon tea dress she bought you. And then,' I paused dramatically, 'student life. Living in digs with other girls, cramming together for exams and lectures and—'

'Can I tell you something, Ag?' Isobel's faint whisper interrupted me. 'I was never . . . so keen. It was Mother . . . she wanted it . . . more than me, I think.'

'What?' I turned towards the sound of her voice, surprised. 'Of course you were keen, and you worked so hard, Iz.'

'Isn't that just like me,' she said, a little bitterly. 'Diligent to the last. I . . .' She coughed painfully. 'I never quite knew how to tell her.'

I digested this, thought back to all those glorious hours we had pored over her books together. I didn't need any of it for my own schooling, which was so much more modest than hers, but she appreciated the help and I loved it anyway. I was better at the sciences; she liked ethics and philosophy, was brilliant at Latin. We'd always kept an ear cocked towards the corridor for her mother's footsteps. At first she'd seemed to like me well enough, Mrs McIntyre, had even been impressed with my school work. But as I got older, she became strangely volatile and unpredictable with me, harsh even. And anyway, all hope had rested on Isobel, a solid, imperturbable mantle of expectation that left no room for anything but acquiescence. You couldn't have stemmed the tide of Mrs McIntyre's plans if you'd wanted to.

'I think she . . . Mother would have loved to . . . Her father was a doctor, remember, and his father before him, right here in London. She always said it was in our blood . . . our duty to keep . . .' She broke off, her breathing broken and strained, and I clenched my fingers around hers.

'Why did you never tell me?' I said to distract her.

She was silent, then she said, awkward and halting, 'I always . . . I mean . . . So churlish not to, when you . . . wanted so badly . . . would have been so good. I tried to persuade Mother to help you, but money . . . there wouldn't have been enough and . . .'

I felt her fingers slip from mine and let them go, staring into the darkness and remembering the day Isobel had got her acceptance to King's College. Mrs McIntyre had been uncharacteristically expansive, toasting everyone in sight. *I won't forget this moment for as long as I live*, she kept saying, and I knew that I, too, would remember it for ever. The smell of flowers on the sideboard; champagne, furiously protected all through rationing, pearling up the insides of the glasses I was handing out; shy Isobel forced into the limelight, blushing furiously.

Later, I had gathered up glasses and dishes in the empty drawing room. At the sight of the letter, still sitting in pride of place on the side table, I had felt something rush through me, something that wanted to burst out and shout to the world that it wasn't just Isobel's, that it was mine too; *that Crawford girl*, a poor evacuee, living in someone else's house on the fringes of a life she didn't really belong in. And if the great cogs of the universe had been calibrated just a hair's breadth differently, then *I* might have received that letter.

I was surprised the glasses on my tray didn't shatter with that rush, which I'd have loved to say was generosity and pride on Isobel's behalf. I *was* pleased for her, really I was. She'd worked so hard. But it was uglier than that, baser, this jealousy, this rage at the futility of it all. This hopelessness. Because of course it did matter whose name was on the letter, and it did matter that I was exactly who I was.

'Well . . . won't be . . . going anywhere now.'

I started guiltily at the rasping hiss. Isobel was my friend. She had crept into my room when news of my mother's death had come, had talked to me and listened, had included me and never, ever treated me like a servant.

'Yes, you will.' I leaned over her to find her hand again. 'All right, so we'll skip France, you'll be in hospital for a while. I'll visit you loads, though, and sneak in some biscuits and grapes, and read to you, some light reading from *Gray's Anatomy* to get you in the mood—'

'Agnes!' Her fingers had suddenly tightened around mine, surprisingly strong, and her rasp was louder. 'You'll go. You'll go *for* me . . . Take my place at university.' She ground out the words with a laboured hiss.

'What? But how could I? *You'll* be there.'

'Don't be a fool,' she hissed. 'I'll be long gone . . . but if you make it . . . you go.' Her voice was faint, a soft exhale of words.

'Isobel, you're mad, I couldn't possibly do that. And anyway, you're going to be fine. You hear me, you'll be *fine*.'

'Do it,' she said, and for a moment, if you discounted the dust and the grit and the almost palpable cloud of terror gripping us both, she sounded like she really would be fine. 'You deserve it. You've been . . . We were always . . . you and me . . .' Her voice grew fainter.

'Isobel, no.' I was shouting now. 'Please hang on, don't leave me here, please . . .'

Frantically I felt her chest, her throat, my hands sticky and warm with her blood, searching for a breath, the flutter of a pulse. With a choked gasp, I scrabbled backwards, away from her dead body. That she should die like this when she'd only ever tried to be good, and that she should leave *me* down here, trapped, all alone . . .

'Help!' I howled. 'Help! *HELP!*'

My words were swallowed by the impassive wall of darkness, along with my rage and terror, until there was only a strange sense of emptiness. I crawled back towards her and, taking a deep breath, let my fingertips coast gently across her cheeks, sweeping away dust and grit, before finally closing her eyes. There was a roaring in my ears, of fear and grief and loss, and I reached for her hand and gripped it to keep myself from falling apart.

'Help!' I whispered. 'Please.' Then, more loudly, 'PLEASE!'

Silence. I sat for a long time in this strange space between life and death, unable to let go of Isobel's hand, thinking about her and us, our shared past, my future, *her* future that never would be.

Take my place. You'll go for me.

I frowned, shook my head, as if she could still see me. 'You're mad, Izzy,' I said softly. 'It would never work.' Then I sat up straight and shouted for help, again and again, and the more my voice was swallowed up by dust and grit, the louder I shouted, as if trying to convince the nothingness out there that I refused to give up.

And then it happened. Faint and mumbling.

'Hello? Is someone down there? Hello? Mr Bristow? Miss McIntyre?'

'We're here,' I shouted, and jumped up, brandishing Isobel's bag towards the ceiling. 'I'm here. Help, help me, please.'

Three

Over the last three years, London had burst into life, much like the television sets that had cropped up in shop windows everywhere, drawing crowds of onlookers. However, bomb craters and building works were still very much in evidence as the bus slowly crawled past a half-crumbled house at the end of a row, with bombweed climbing around boulders that stuck up like gappy teeth. Suppressing a shiver of memory, I looked away from the cracks running across the facade and checked my watch for the tenth time.

'Excuse me, what is the hold-up?' I asked the conductor.

'Oh, it's only the young queen herself, innit?' he said cheerfully. 'Can't hold up royalty, can yer?'

'When do you think we'll be at Thamesbury Hospital?'

'Should be on our way momentarily, miss. Don't you fret, visiting hours aren't for a while yet; just been there to see my mam yesterday, and—'

The bus jolted forward and he fell up the aisle mid sentence, his ticket machine clanking against the seats as he caught himself. I got up and stood at the back, ready to jump off the moment the hospital came into view.

I wasn't going there for the visiting hours, of course, although I didn't blame him for assuming that. He couldn't know I was here for my first day as a doctor. Well, strictly speaking, a medical student, less than halfway through my training, but someone well on her way to being a doctor anyway. If the bus ever got a move on, that was. I leaned all the way out, my curls straining to

15

join the slipstream as at last the hospital loomed ahead, larger than life behind its ornate wrought-iron gates.

'Miss!' The conductor gave a scandalised shout. 'Get back inside now.'

But we were scheduled to be in the gallery to watch our first list of operations this morning, and under no circumstances could I miss it.

'Sorry!' I called over my shoulder, and jumped.

His outraged spluttering faded as I caught myself at the edge of the street and started running.

The head porter was on the phone, but he gave me a conspiratorial wave from the lodge and pointed to the right. 'Best hurry,' he mouthed. 'Up two flights and to the right. Theatre 4.'

'Thanks, I know!' I waved back as I sped past. I'd spent almost all of yesterday trying to figure out the building. As a teaching hospital, Thamesbury was big and bustling to start with, but navigating the many corridors, wards and operating theatres was made infinitely more complicated by the fact that the main building had been badly hit during the war. As elsewhere across the city, rebuilding had been slow, which meant that wards had had to be cobbled together, sometimes forced to share space with each other, accommodation for doctors and nurses was at a premium, and any and all rooms were drafted in for storage and utility.

I dodged a group of workmen carrying ladders towards the Tomeyne Wing, which had been almost completely destroyed during an air raid and was still hidden under scaffolding. Despite my hurry, I allowed myself one moment of pure, unadulterated thrill at the sight of doctors, nurses and orderlies hurrying back and forth beneath the glass dome of the entrance hall. As of today, I would be part of it all.

I made it to the corridor leading to Theatre 4 with a minute to spare, skidding around the corner and almost colliding with the back of a small group of people clearly headed for the same place as I. At the helm was a rather heavyset man, his baldness offset by an untidy salt-and-pepper beard. Dr Everett Carlisle. I'd seen his picture in *The Lancet* and knew he was one of the best-known consultant surgeons at the hospital. He was accompanied by, I guessed, his registrar and house surgeon, an anaesthetist, maybe a senior student or two. A tall, dark-haired young man brought up the rear.

I eyed the distance between myself and the door to the theatre, behind which I was supposed to be waiting with the other students, and realised there was only one option. Jabbing a stray pin back into my hair, I darted forward and silently fell into step with the very tail end of the group. Startled at my sudden appearance, the tall young doctor frowned, obviously trying to place me. I had just a moment to notice that his eyes were an unexpected greeny-blue below his shock of untidy dark hair, before he quickened his step and followed the group through the door.

Inside, a door to the right led to the theatre area. One of the other men opened it for Carlisle, while I discreetly broke away to the left and the small auditorium, where raised seats gave a view through a glass partition into the theatre.

Breathing hard, I sank down on the only available seat, at the back.

'You never walked in with *them*?' The skinny young man next to me, whose red hair glinted in the fluorescent light, looked at me with round-eyed shock.

'Bus took for ever,' I whispered back, craning to see the activity behind the glass.

Surgeons and assistants were emerging in lightweight white cotton clothing to scrub up and don gowns, caps and masks. In the theatre itself, the scrub nurse had been laying out and checking over her instruments while the anaesthetist was tending to the patient. Over in the preparation room, Everett Carlisle was reading a chart, his hands held aloft. Privately, I had to admit to being a little disappointed. The way he'd been described – a

Fellow of the Royal College of Surgeons, with a private practice on the side, and part of the committee advising the minister on the nationalisation of the health service – I'd expected a tall, God-like figure, gliding around in charge of life and death. Instead he was heavy-jowled and scowling, his bald pate gleaming beneath his cap. His eyes seemed almost comically large behind his spectacles as he finished reading, then summoned the tall, dark-haired doctor to his side with a brief nod.

'Can you imagine being in there?' The red-haired student next to me didn't sound all that keen.

'That'll be a long while away,' I assured him.

'Father says we'll be up to our elbows in blood and guts from here on.' He flushed, as if suddenly aware of possibly offending my delicate sensibilities. I watched the tall doctor nodding at the consultant, and refrained from saying that it took quite a bit – and certainly not blood and guts – to offend my sensibilities.

Behind the glass, the preparation was winding up. Carlisle had proceeded through to the operating theatre and seemed dissatisfied with the arrangement around the table, then the way the patient's abdomen was being prepared. He was everywhere at once, talking to the scrub nurse, checking in with the anaesthetist, then rounding on another nurse, who was covering the patient in sterile towels.

'Not like that, Nurse.' Someone had turned on the tinny loudspeakers rigged outside the glass structure, and Carlisle's voice suddenly boomed across the gallery. 'Cross-wise, please.' He strode back into the preparation room, where the dark-haired young doctor was the last to scrub arms and elbows. 'Are you trying to wash away your sins, Grey? Glove up, please, we've got a lot to get through today.'

'What's your name?' the red-haired boy next to me asked.

'Quiet, please, students.' Another young man had popped through the door into the gallery and was now fixing us with a threatening stare. He was rail-thin and a little stooped; stalking up and down the shallow steps next to us, he reminded me a bit of a stork. 'I'm Harry Jenkins, one of the housemen. No talking, laughing, smoking or any other nonsense during the operation. If you must ask questions, I will answer them at the end. Better yet, don't ask them at all unless you want to burden your fellow students with an embarrassing display of personal inadequacy—'

'Welcome, new students.' Mr Carlisle's amplified voice cut across him. 'First on today's list is a routine appendectomy. Patient is a thirty-five-year-old woman, brought in this morning with abdominal pain. In good health otherwise. Abdomen is a little swollen. It should be a straightforward procedure, performed under my close supervision by my houseman, Mr Grey.' He nodded at the tall, dark-haired doctor, who was standing ready next to the patient and frowning down at her. It was a little hard to make out from here, but he seemed . . . nervous?

Everett Carlisle gestured for the nurse to rearrange something on the instrument tray, then turned to the anaesthetist. 'May we begin?'

'I'm Iain,' Red Hair muttered as the young doctor stepped up to the bed, holding out his hand to the theatre nurse. An expectant hush fell over the hall. 'Two i's. And you?'

I had said her name a thousand times over the last three years, thought of her a million times more. I'd studied photos to make sure I looked like her, I'd learned to copy her handwriting in letters back to school chums. Every now and then, though, it still brought me up short. I thought of the cracks I'd seen in the bombed-out house I'd passed on the bus earlier, realised I was still clutching the leather bag monogrammed *IAM*. Its hard surface was no longer new and shiny but scuffed and moulded to my side after carrying my books for the past three years. With a slow, soft exhale, I slid the bag off my lap and on to the floor, then turned to Iain with a smile.

'Nice to meet you, Iain. I'm Isobel. Isobel McIntyre.'

Four

'More to the left, Grey, and down. There . . .'

For several minutes, apart from the soft clinking of the instruments, short, muttered exchanges between the nurses, and the occasional question in the direction of the anaesthetist, Everett Carlisle's voice was the only thing we heard. Even muffled by his face mask, it punched through the loudspeaker, a staccato stream of commands that brought him closer and closer to the young doctor, until the area around the patient's abdomen felt quite crowded.

The students in the gallery were standing now, eyes fixed on the operating table, but being much shorter than everyone else, I couldn't see anything. Slowly, silently I climbed on to my wooden seat and crouched there, rising gradually higher until I was a good head and shoulders above everyone else and could finally make out the exposed square of abdomen on the operating table.

Grey's eyebrows were drawn together in concentration, dark shadows like smudges under his eyes, his mask moving in and out in time with his breath.

'Swelling there. Press lightly. That's right. Here, gentlemen, you can clearly see the obstruction – yes, there.'

The others leaned in, crowding the young doctor further. Gripping the scalpel, he scrutinised the opening and advanced on it again.

'Slow down a little. Wait, not like that.' Grey seemed to have made a choice Carlisle didn't agree with, because he gestured to the theatre nurse for another scalpel. Grey muttered something under his breath, but Carlisle shook his head, leaned over the abdomen. I craned my neck, noticing that the consultant, so heavy-footed earlier, had begun moving with an unexpected lightness and finesse the moment he'd got hold of the scalpel. I stretched higher to see what Grey was doing wrong, but my movement seemed to alert him to our presence on the other side of the glass. He glanced up at the gallery and spotted me towering on my seat. Something creased his eyes, whether surprise or irritation I couldn't tell; he had already flicked his gaze back down to watch Carlisle.

'Finish up, please, Grey. Students, I hope you were able to see clearly how the procedure should be performed.' He kept his eyes fixed on the young doctor's hands. 'Next up we have a perforated duodenal ulcer.

The list was done. Harry Jenkins, the stork-like houseman who'd been lecturing us in the gallery, got to do an abscess (and didn't fare all that much better than Grey), Carlisle's registrar the ulcer. All around me students were packing up with excited whispers. Below, a porter had taken the last patient up to the ward, the theatre was being scrubbed down, and the doctors emerged in dribs and drabs from the partition door and left. Jenkins perfunctorily answered a few students' questions, his replies mostly consisting of irritated entreaties not to waste his time, before sweeping out in a very credible imitation of Carlisle that was only slightly marred by the anaesthetist forcing him to break his stride in the doorway.

'Lunch, then that hygiene seminar,' Iain said with a sigh of relief.

A blonde boy pushed past. 'Exciting morning, eh, miss? Coming, Iain?'

A girl walking down the steps behind them threw me a shy smile. She was serious-looking, with thin, frizzy hair cut quite short, and was holding herself almost unnaturally straight. I wondered if she was making an extra effort to blend in with the men around us. Smart of her, perhaps, because we – me, her and a couple other girls I'd seen in the gallery – did seem to be in the distinct minority. Medical schools had to take a certain percentage of women these days, whether they wanted to or not, and I'd seen a few female doctors out in the hospital itself as well. But their presence had felt oddly jarring, as if a group of girls had suddenly been admitted to an all-boys' boarding school, somewhere steeped in archaic traditions that took itself very seriously and only reluctantly allowed intruders on its hallowed grounds.

I watched Iain and the blonde boy – I heard Iain call him Benedict – vanish through the door along with the rest of the students, but for some reason I felt the urge to linger. It was a momentous day, after all, the first operations we'd seen up close. I was watching the nurses scrub down the theatre on the other side of the glass and thinking through the particulars of the ulcer operation when I suddenly heard footsteps.

A second later, tall Mr Grey emerged, looking a bit dishevelled and somewhat irritated. He stopped short.

'Ah. The latecomer. And, if I'm not mistaken, the girl from the back row. I can't seem to get this bloody mask off, and the nurses are all busy prepping the theatre for the afternoon list.' He turned and gestured at the ties, which he'd somehow managed to tighten right around his neck like a noose. 'Would you mind?'

He was restless, filling the small space by the door with so much energy that I took an involuntary step back. He wasn't gangly like the stork-legged Jenkins, but rather rangy, in an impatiently graceful kind of way. He was still wearing the white T-shirt that surgeons wore beneath apron and gown. It had rucked up a little from his efforts at twisting round to catch the ties of the mask, revealing – I swallowed – a bit of skin at his lower back. The only men I'd ever been close to had been in suits and ties, at the most in shirtsleeves at uni, never practically *en déshabille* like this man. *Fast girls fall fast*, Mrs McIntyre used to

22

say, disapproving of midnight parties, women wearing trousers and, I'm sure, men in T-shirts with bits of skin showing.

The sun flooded through the high windows, turning his profile into a sharp silhouette as he looked back at me over his shoulder, his eyes sparking impatiently. 'Do I need to pull rank?'

'We're not in the military,' I said, nettled and yet somehow goaded into stepping forward again. 'So no, I shouldn't think so.'

'Well, seeing as you're at the bottom rung of wherever we do find ourselves, miss, I'm above you and I—'

'Can stop calling me miss now,' I said.

'Miss Student,' he amended grudgingly. 'Oh, come on, I've still got to change. Please?' He grinned suddenly and pushed a hand through his hair so that it stood up even more. 'See, I've got manners, and I won't call you miss again, I promise.' He sagged at the knees invitingly, and before I knew it, I had the ties of the mask between my fingers. I was so close that I could see the small nick on the edge of his jaw where he must have cut himself shaving this morning, noticed that his skin seemed smooth otherwise, almost luminous. He was trying hard to be still, but I could feel him wanting to move, the muscles on his back bunching close to my hands.

I forced myself to look away just as he said, without turning round, 'And I'll have you know that when I need someone's pity, I will ask for it.'

I was surprised into an honest answer. 'I wasn't pitying you.'

'Yes, you were. I could see it on your face all the way up in the gallery.'

'If you must know, I was wondering if anyone can think clearly when someone else is talking non-stop at them. That was all.' I was close enough to catch his scent, fresh and sharp and clean, a mix of disinfectant and cigarette smoke and something else – peppermint? It made me flush, the fact that I even noticed, and I spoke a little more sharply than I'd meant to. 'Did you see your own insecurities reflected back at you, perhaps?'

'I did not, but thank you very much, Dr Freud.' He twitched impatiently as I tried to tug the knot free.

'What were you doing when he told you to stop?' I asked.

'Inverting the stump of the appendix. He didn't like that.'

He looked over his shoulder at me, a faint echo of his earlier grin creasing his eyes, turning them greener than before, and I found myself smiling back before I got a hold of myself. He was just one of those public-school boys I'd met by the dozen these last few years: clever, charming, confident. Cheerfully able to wheedle anything out of anyone. He indicated the back of his mask. 'Any luck? Sister'll have my hide if there's one missing.'

'She won't if you stand absolutely still.' Briskly I extracted my silver pocketknife and sliced through the ties, handed him the ruined mask.

He looked down at it, then at my hand. 'What on earth is that?'

'A knife, of course.' I was about to stow it back in my pocket, but he was faster and plucked it from my palm. Turning it over in his fingers, he examined the mechanism by which the blade locked into the wooden handle, huffing when he accidentally nicked himself and a fine line of red appeared across the ball of his thumb.

'Expecting an imminent attack, are we?' he enquired.

'I just keep it with me for luck.' I tried to take it back, but he held it out of my reach.

'Oh look, there's something etched into the handle. Is it a face?' He leaned in to show me, and his scent filled the narrowing space between us, crisp and clean. I didn't have to look, though, I knew the etching by heart.

'It's a daisy,' I said. A tiny round face, two dots above a smiling mouth and miniature petals fanning around.

'An odd sort of talisman for a girl.' He was so tall I had to look up at him, noticing as I did that in the slanted sunlight from the high windows, his eyes were now a clear green. For a moment I was unable to look away, he was so glorious, so much *there*.

'It was my mother's, actually,' I heard myself say.

The knife had never been far from Mum's hand, almost an extension of it as she unpicked seams to reuse the fabric, the blade a blur of tiny perfect strokes. I looked away, tried to swallow the words back in. Isobel's mother had been a housewife, wielding nothing more lethal than a letter opener. I couldn't afford to be careless.

'Won't she mind?' he said curiously.

'She's dead.'

I went to retrieve my bag, and when I returned, he was holding open the door for me.

'I'm sorry,' he said quietly.

'Yes, well. It happens.' I pushed past him. 'Goodbye, Mr Grey.'

'Actually, it's just Grey.' I looked back over my shoulder. 'They don't want to confuse us, you see.' He was swinging the ruined mask round his finger, cocking his head a little to the side.

'Us?'

'Grey Carlisle at your service,' he said, giving an oddly formal little bow. 'As you can see, you're not the only one who's inherited a sharp instrument from a parent.'

Five

The lecture hall was full when I arrived, so I stood at the back. Over on the other side I spied Iain and Benedict horsing around with a few other students, Benedict saying something outrageous that had the rest roaring with laughter. A few rows over was the girl with the wispy hair. She smiled when she saw me, gave a small shrug at the space next to her as if to apologise for not keeping me a seat. *No worries,* I smiled back, and settled against the wall, looking down at my notebook with its notes on today's operations. I felt for my pen but instead found my knife again, touched the smooth, worn metal.

Daisy. That had been my mother's name, Daisy Crawford. There was a little daisy on every item of clothing she'd ever made, a tiny, laughing flower-face squeezed into an inconspicuous place. She loved knowing that a part of her walked out into the world hidden in the folds of a skirt or the inside of a sleeve. She was like that. Different, living by her own rules, the good-for-nothing seamstress from Bell Street. And her daughter, scrawny and clever, in clothes that were too bright, too well made for wartime austerity, when she should have been keeping her head down and blending in. Like two peas in a pod, *those Crawford Girls.*

'Agnes's father is missing in the Far East.'

Mum rarely said more than those eight words, unusual for her given that embellishing things was her bread and butter. 'He's missing presumed dead,' she sometimes expanded when I, rather than nosy Mrs Hayes from next door, asked her if he'd ever come back so we could be like all the normal families. 'And we're perfectly normal, Agnes.'

Not to Mrs Hayes, apparently, who the very next day twitched her skirt away from me in such an ostentatious way that she startled me into stumbling over, grazing my knee. She bustled away on a muttered swell of words I didn't quite understand but that almost certainly included *the gutter*, *respectable neighbourhood* and *all very well for some*. It was one of many such encounters – women crossing the street when we appeared; whispers and disapproving sniffs in the queue at the butcher's – and I realised very quickly that one crucial piece of information was missing from those eight words. He might be my father, but he wasn't my mother's husband.

'I'm saying it like it is,' she said when I broached the subject, and for once she wasn't smiling or warm. 'Your father *is* missing; he *is* presumed dead. It's devastating. That's what they should be saying.'

'But Mum—'

'You're not to let those old biddies get to you, Agnes, I've told you.'

Something about my face, questions wanting to tumble out, and worries as well – about children following me home from school calling me names, about the butcher's wife giving us the worst gristle for our coupons – made her pull me into a hug. 'They're just jealous, darling. They don't have what you and I have: a place to make things beautiful, big dreams to live up to. And each other. That's the most important thing. Me and you, always.'

She had set herself up as a seamstress, but her dream was one day to be a famous designer. *Not just for wealthy people, but women like you and me, too. I'll find a way to manufacture my gowns and dresses cheaply enough for ordinary people to buy them. One day, Agnes.*

That day had always been far off, though, and my earliest memories were of Mum working off and on at the factory before she quit every time, hating the shift work. Then she did any other odd jobs she could find to pay for the single shop-cum-room we rented from old Mrs Beadle, with the lavatory out the back. At night we dragged a mattress in front of the stove to sleep, but during the day it was a proper if shabby shop, a small sign outside proclaiming: *Daisy Crawford, Dressmaking and Tailoring*.

I loved sitting in a corner over my books, watching her work. An ancient Singer, Mum's most prized possession, stood on a long, scratched table, next to a chipped mirror. Her pincushion was in pride of place, a brightly coloured felted armband in the shape of a daisy, with pins sticking out of its white and yellow face. There were boxes of fabric scraps, buttons, threads, and all the little bits of pretty she was always foraging for around the neighbourhood. Shiny feathers perfect for dolling up hats, round glass pebbles she'd found in the rubbish outside the bottle factory, silver foil and tiny ribbons that had littered the street after a doll-maker's shop had been hit during an air raid. She might not know how to cook a proper tea – in fact she often forgot about meals altogether – and she didn't wash the windows on Tuesdays like the other women on Bell Street. But any old rag became beautiful under her hands, and any dress spectacular.

When she didn't have enough work, she turned her mind to the room, using scraps of paper, fabric and paint to cover the shabby, water-spotted walls with colour. She hung old pieces of string across the ceiling, knotted all over with tiny buttons and pieces of glass encased in webs of stitches, until it was like living in an oscillating rainbow bubble that shimmered so brightly it almost hurt your eyes. She would tell stories while she sketched new designs, cutting out miniature versions from newspaper, tiny bodices above doll-sized skirts, just to see how they looked.

Sometimes, watching her study a piece of fabric with a thoughtful frown, I pictured all that beauty jostling inside her, colour and glitter and glitz dying to burst out on to the brown-grey streets of the East End, where business had been slow for as long as I could remember, even though my mum was a whizz at making do and mending. *She can mend anything,* I'd tell women earnestly, pressing little cards into their hands featuring drawings Mum had done along with the shop's address and a list of services. *She's ever so good, I promise, she'll make it prettier than before.* But we were too far from the nice areas, where women might still have afforded to hire her, and around here everyone did for themselves as much as they could.

Some business came our way, yes, and friendships, too. The bedridden spinster living two doors down asked Mum to make her nightgowns and thick socks when we went round to see if she needed shopping done. Mum made tea and dresses for the factory girls who pressed their noses against our shop window on their way home, ogling the sketched designs on the walls. Then there was the butcher's assistant, who was as relentlessly bullied by the butcher's wife as we were; the rag-and-bone man, whose winter coat was falling off him in tatters but who always held scraps of fabric aside for Mum; and old Mrs Cooper, who minded her four grandchildren during the day and often couldn't cope, so the grandchildren came and ran riot in our shop.

Others, however, the kind of women who might have money to spare for proper clothes, dresses and coats, didn't like the missing elements in the Burma story and were deeply suspicious of all the colour and life that surrounded Mum like a halo. They didn't like that she often wore trousers out on the street, that she'd never married anyone else and settled down properly with a gaggle of children, at least *pretending* that she was trying to be like the rest of them.

As I got older, I worried constantly about the lack of money in the little tin on the kitchen shelf, the fact that despite her big dreams we lived hand to mouth, with nothing left over by the end of the week. But she wasn't deterred. 'Just another step in the road,' she'd say as she patched stacks of threadbare sheets for a small hotel on Willcox Street, or sewed hundreds of buttons on an order of uniform jackets. 'It takes time.' She'd hold up a winter coat a neighbourhood woman had dropped off – with the distinct air of doing us a favour – which Mum had spent a lot of time on trying to make less *brown*. 'You've got to keep at it. It *will* happen, I promise.'

I nodded. I could never not agree with my mother's conviction that you could make your own future, but secretly I could see evidence everywhere that that *wasn't* the case, that no matter how much you tried to claw your way out of poverty, it would keep a grip on your ankle and pull you right back at the first opportunity. And even if she seemed impervious to what people said about us, I felt, all the time, that slow, imperceptible seep of shame lapping at the threshold of our shop, an itchy, grubby oddness, like we were two pieces of grit stubbornly grinding our way through the neighbourhood.

A loud squeak suddenly cut through my thoughts, and I looked up quickly to see that the lecturer had arrived. He opened the blackboard with a flourish while simultaneously dropping an armful of books on to the desk, setting some of the front-row students to help lay out props for his lecture. Below me, the restless, joshing crowd of students slowly settled and a hush fell over the room. As I started to scribble notes, in handwriting I could never get to be quite as neat and small as Isobel's, I suddenly wondered what my mother would make of the rows of students below me. The boys indistinguishable in a variety of dark suits, only occasionally broken up by a daringly coloured tie; the few girls in practical dresses and skirts. I pictured her diplomatically suggesting a panel to flatter the frizzy girl's narrow dress, or adding cuffs to the boy three seats down, who looked like he was drowning inside his suit.

Sometimes a girl I was friendly with at school, Mary, came back to the shop with me and Mum taught us the basics of sewing, because *keeping oneself clothed is one of life's great skills*. Colour would splash across her pattern table as she turned an old dress into culottes, the same kind made by Elsa Schiaparelli, a famous fashion designer in Paris. And then she told us tales of a princess in trousers, not waiting for someone to bring her missing shoe, but opening up a shoe shop, where her wicked stepsisters worked as drudges until their dying days.

Mary seemed to love it, and I was glowing because she was seeing my mother how *I* knew her to be, fun and warm, not eccentric and different. The very next day, however, Mary's mum came round holding the purple culottes between two fingers, telling Mum she'd forbidden her daughter to visit again. *Unnatural this is*, I heard her say. *Keep away from us.*

That night, I watched Mum from my mattress, sitting at her work table and staring down at the culottes, her hands idle for once. Eventually she got up and checked on the blackout curtains, and in the light of the small oil lamp I saw her face, unsmiling and etched with shadows and lines. For the first time ever, she looked defeated.

In the years to come, I wondered if that was the moment when she'd started to care what other people were saying, because shortly after, she did, for once, what she was told. Since the beginning of the war, the authorities had been evacuating children from the inner-city districts – Operation Pied Piper they called it. Mum had always refused to be separated from me, until the day a bomb took out the house next to us, and two of the factory girls were killed in a raid on the docks. It was irresponsible and foolish to keep me here any longer, Mrs Hayes said. And Mum, who never listened to anyone, was suddenly nodding, in the grip of a fear that was, like much else about her, immovable and uncompromising. I was to leave the following week. A place had been found for me up north, with a family called McIntyre. I'd help around the house a bit. There was a daughter, she said, who would be good company, and Mr McIntyre was a schoolmaster teaching at a fancy girls' school. *Just think, books until you've got them coming out of your ears, Agnes.* And the moment the war was over, I'd be back with her. *The minute Mr Churchill says we're done, I promise, I will be waiting for you at the station.* I refused, I argued, I shouted, but she collected my warmest clothes and undergarments, a coat made from all manner of scraps, thick socks. It was fixed and I would go.

She'd pressed her knife on me the night I was put on the train. 'I'll feel happier if I know you're armed,' she'd said, nudging me to get me to smile. 'And the daisy'll keep you company.' She never cried, so it might have been a trick of the light to think her eyes were strangely bright. But I'd been too upset to look closely, could barely embrace her in farewell, because I didn't want to go, hated her for making me, couldn't bear to think of her returning to our rainbow flat, where she'd be sitting under our kitchen table at night, alone . . .

Balancing my notebook in one arm, I reached to touch the knife in my pocket with my other hand. For a moment I smelled the wet fog of an early London morning, the steam whistle shrill in my ears, children and parents crammed on to the platform. I wished, very much, that I hadn't mentioned her to Grey Carlisle. He would never know who my mother really was, of course, but it had made me feel uneasy nonetheless, the way he'd held the knife in his hands, stroked the little daisy face. As if somehow, by talking about her, I'd brought her here, into my Isobel world.

To reassure myself, I glanced down at my navy skirt, straight and unfussy, my cardigan the same as everyone else's. And then another thought strayed across the back of my mind, and I wondered suddenly what my mother would make of me now, the daughter she'd taught to sew purple culottes amidst the grey-brown of the East End.

Six

I'd best stay out of Grey's way, I thought, and make sure to keep my mum's knife hidden from now on. It wasn't all that difficult, given that we barely seemed to stop running between the hospital, lectures and theatre demonstrations, which left us little time to study, let alone have cosy chats with tall young doctors who were related to the most eminent consultant at the hospital. In the second week, we were split up into smaller groups to shadow various consultants on the wards. The rather complicated-looking rota assigned *McIntyre, Isobel*, along with *Mallory, Iain*, *Mertins, Benedict* and *Moore, Susan*, to report to Mr Carlisle's 'firm' – the group of doctors attached to a consultant – on one of the male surgical wards.

Consequently, the following day saw us rushing down the hall towards Ward III for Everett Carlisle's rounds. Benedict, red-eyed with tiredness – out late over the weekend, he said, and could people please keep their voices down – was lagging behind, while Susan, the frizzy-haired girl I'd loosely befriended since the first day, was chivvying everyone along anxiously, and Iain seemed mainly relieved not to be close to open abdomens. 'I don't like surgical,' he confided as we strode along. 'GP material myself, like my dad. Just trying to get through what I absolutely must. You?'

'Haven't completely made up my mind,' I said. 'But I like surgical.'

'Any surgeons in your family?'

'Yes,' I said. 'My . . . well, my grandfather.'

Or rather Isobel's grandfather, Mrs McIntyre's father, who

had been a thoracic surgeon called Hector Warren Bellingdon. 'He worked here for a spell, actually, he—'

I broke off when I spied the tall dark-haired figure of Grey Carlisle standing just outside the ward and waving us forward impatiently.

'We're not late, are we?' Susan asked breathlessly.

'Yes, you are.' Harry Jenkins, the hint of a stoop rounding his narrow back so we could see the top of his thinning hair, had detached himself from a group of doctors to join Grey in the corridor. 'Rounds are about to begin, and as Mr Grey and I have the unenviable honour of keeping an eye on you, I beg you not to do anything stupid. At other hospitals, students might be observers only at this point' – he emphasised the word 'observers' to make it clear that this would have been his preferred option as well – 'but not so at Thamesbury. In the first year of your clinical course, you're expected to work certain hours on the ward, pitching in wherever the doctors, sisters or staff nurses tell you to. No matter how dirty, how lowly. Nothing is too small to provide a learning opportunity. *You* are the lowest—'

'Easy, Jenkins.' Grey rolled his eyes at him. 'Come on, you lot, let's get you into the ward.'

Grey's face had brightened briefly in recognition when he saw me, but he was already striding ahead and didn't say anything more. So much for worrying about staying out of his way, I thought, a little disgruntled. House officers apparently weren't in the habit of acknowledging individual students more than necessary, let alone wasting a second's thought on previous conversations about mothers and knives.

Jenkins was still issuing instructions. 'No one wants a student to sprout half-baked learnings from the back bench, so don't ask questions unless absolutely necessary, and never, *ever* interrupt the consultant—Oh, I'm sorry, sir . . .' He turned, oozing reverence, as Everett Carlisle himself came around the corner.

I had worked out most of the hospital structure by now, the various medical and surgical wards and other specialities, as well as the consultants and senior hospital medical officers who led them, each firm supported by a staff of house officers, registrars and students from all rungs of the training ladder. It didn't take the other doctors' reverence and Jenkins's continued bowing and scraping for me to fully grasp the intense jostling for space up that ladder. There were far fewer spots at the top than aspirants below it, and even with many students set to go into general practice or move elsewhere in England, there were still a lot of candidates determined to outdo each other on the way up.

Carlisle stomped past, giving Iain and Benedict a fleeting look of assessment while entirely ignoring Susan and myself. We followed him through the ward doors as he resumed a conversation with his registrar seemingly *in medias res*, all the while impatiently wagging his finger for a stack of papers one of the housemen was holding. He said something to Jenkins, then nodded briskly at Grey. Curious how neither of them openly acknowledged the relationship between them. To the contrary, Carlisle's expression had acquired a hint of steel, while Grey seemed to become silent and watchful, as if he was trying to stay well below the radar. I wondered how you could not be openly proud of someone like Grey, who wasn't terrible-looking, I supposed, and who seemed clever, too, judging by the discussion I could overhear now.

Silence had fallen across our little area as Carlisle read through the stack with the same intense concentration I'd noticed in the theatre.

'Let us begin, Sister,' he finally said.

The ward sister, a small, efficient-looking woman, fell into step with him as he strode into the ward.

'Come *on*,' Jenkins hissed to us.

*

Ward III was a long Nightingale ward, with rows of beds along each wall. Cool, clear light from the tall windows lit up silver bedsteads polished to a gleam. The patients themselves seemed strangely small, tucked in between hospital corners with their eyes towards the advancing group of doctors. The ward was rather full, the beds close together, but even that didn't mar the impression of uncompromisingly sharp angles and crisp cleanliness. I'd already heard about Sister Veronica, who ran the ward with terrifying efficiency and was feared by nurses and doctors alike. Even the wheels on the beds were all turned at exactly the same angle, I noticed. I'd been on a few wards as a student, and once in a small cottage hospital when I'd broken my leg as a girl, but none had been as uncompromisingly white and – well – cold as this. It made me feel oddly wary, and keeping my head down a little, I followed the group of doctors towards the first bed, notebook poised.

It didn't take me long to make several crucial discoveries about Everett Carlisle, and to understand exactly how he had become who he was. He was as impatient and exacting as I'd seen him in the operating theatre, and the way he towered over the patients, glowering at them through his spectacles, froze most of them in fear. His delivery of diagnoses was brutally honest – I noticed one of the other doctors cringing as Carlisle told a patient about a cancerous biopsy when the unspoken rule was to shield the patient from all but the mildest aspects of the truth. At the same time, he treated each and every case with a focus that missed nothing, let no detail slip, allowed for absolutely no mistake.

He was particular to the point of neurosis about the ward. This ranged from the positions of the other staff (Iain and Benedict were instructed to stay opposite him, while Susan and I were at the very back of the group behind him) to the exact size of the opening between the curtains and the way the bandages were stacked on the trolley, keeping Sister Veronica in perpetually anguished humiliation because she and her staff couldn't but fall short somewhere. He didn't seem to care or even notice the human behind the ailment (or indeed the human behind anyone; within minutes he'd made Harry Jenkins flush so red with mortification at having mislabelled an abscess that he seemed on the verge of tears). But in his brusque, slightly angry way, he treated each case as if it was his personal responsibility to go into battle against it.

I had assumed it was arrogance that had made him take over some of the operations in the list I had watched in the gallery. I didn't think so now. He wasn't above gathering information or details he might be missing, was constantly barking questions at the ward sister and other doctors, roping them in for second opinions and assessments. Once, to Sister Veronica's horror, he even asked a terrified patient if he had noticed anything particular about the smell of his neighbour's urine. He was also quite good at including the senior students, explaining a diagnosis here, asking a question there.

The moment he'd amassed enough details, however, he cut everyone off in midstream and waited for the whole ward to be suspended in total silence before making his final pronouncement. I didn't want to like him; I *didn't* like him, to be honest, because he seemed harsh and rigid, detached from anything but the case. But the further down the row of beds we progressed, the more I found myself desperate to become a part of it all.

Yet while by the end of the week, Iain and Benedict had managed to get an occasional nod or question from Everett Carlisle, Susan and I were no closer to even a flicker of acknowledgment than when we started. It wasn't that he was insulting or dismissing us; there was none of the irritation and downright antagonism my presence seemed to bring out in Sister Veronica, for example, none of the patronisingly paternal indulgence of some of the other doctors. For Carlisle, we simply didn't exist at all.

*

On top of consultants' rounds and operations, writing up our notes and keeping up with the rest of our coursework, we medical students were assigned time blocks on the wards, where, under the ward sister's supervision, we were to apply ourselves in whatever capacity was needed. Technically this meant opportunities to get to know ward routines, see patients and cases up close, shadow doctors in their day-to-day work. In reality, however, given that we weren't allowed to do any patient work without a doctor present, it meant that we were often scurrying about doing whatever Sister Veronica thought fit. The nurses, including Staff Nurse Willow, were a nice bunch, always happy to share advice and warn of Sister's imminent approach and generally glad of an extra pair of hands, but Sister Veronica lived up to her reputation in every way and seemed to consider our presence a burden she didn't deserve.

Iain and Benedict were roped in to help lift patients, wheel them down for X-rays and move the heavy screens, while Susan and I were set more feminine tasks: helping with meal trays, tea rounds and vases – all flowers had to be taken out of the ward at night, as Sister Veronica felt strongly that they used up valuable oxygen – and, of course, the inordinate amount of cleaning that seemed to fill nurses' days. Bedpans and Winchester bottles, bowls and kidney dishes, soiled sheets and linen. Sister clearly meant this to be degrading – she occasionally surged past me on a swell of mutterings about spoiled madams and needing to get one's hands dirty – and as the days wore on, I got the sense that she somehow projected on to me her rage at whatever Carlisle had criticised that day.

I'd not been a maid for nothing, however, and it would take a lot more than the sluice to throw me off. Susan was faring less well. When she stumbled over the edge of a patient's bed one day, jarred a newly stitched wound and caused the man to yelp in pain as blood seeped through the bandage, Carlisle's large, protuberant eyes swivelled in her direction, unnerving her so much that she fled in panic. Hating myself for wishing that she'd work a little harder to keep the side up, I sat her down over tea and buns afterwards to cheer her up. But with each day that passed, she seemed more overwhelmed than before and perpetually close to tears, fumbling even the simplest task, until she stopped coming altogether and we heard she'd left.

This, for some reason, caught Carlisle's attention. When he was given the news, his eyes lingered thoughtfully on the back row, as if Susan's departure had answered a question he'd found puzzling to begin with and was now relieved had been resolved in the way he'd anticipated. I tried to catch his eye, determined to show him that the question had *not* been answered, thank you very much. But he'd already looked away and was beckoning Sister Veronica to his side for the next patient.

It was customary for students to be assigned individual cases during their clinical course and shadow them from beginning to end. When Jenkins reminded Carlisle of this, he nodded absent-mindedly, his eyes on a chart, then assigned Benedict the prostatectomy in Bed 4. Iain, who'd been mostly hiding in the back, got a tonsillectomy in Bed 9. I, meanwhile, was assigned the hernia repair in Bed 16, which turned out to be an older man called Mr Salinger, who absolutely refused for me to witness his examination by Carlisle's senior houseman, Mr Tallard.

'I won't have my privates looked at by a woman, Doctor,' he groused loudly. 'I have rights, it's not moral.'

Sister Veronica appeared at the bedside like a wrathful angel.

'I'm going to sort it out, Mr Tallard,' I said hurriedly, trying to avoid being overheard by the patient and Carlisle. 'Sister, please don't—'

But the man gave another loud, theatrical huff, and before I could hold her back, Sister Veronica had marched over to Mr

Carlisle, asking, in a voice reverberating with righteous indignation, if I couldn't be moved elsewhere because I upset the quiet of her ward.

'Maybe maternity?' she suggested with a meaningful look in my direction.

'I said, I'll make it work,' I hissed. I had nothing against maternity, but had always disliked the way women were automatically lumped in with midwifery.

Carlisle looked up distractedly, eyeing my white coat as if struggling to put my presence into context. Then he shook his head and told Sister Veronica that if students couldn't deal with a simple assignment, they might find another occupation where their skills would be more suitably applied. And before we could say anything else, he had waved Tallard to his side to discuss something with him.

'Bad luck, McIntyre,' Benedict said sympathetically as we walked out into the corridor.

'Try and make it up from the chart,' Iain advised. 'Father says the most important thing at this stage is just to stay out of trouble and hope for the best.'

'Oh really,' I said savagely. 'And how can I hope for the best when I'm either washing bedpans or stuck in the back row?'

Iain shrugged good-naturedly. 'It's just the way it is, I suppose. Hey, where are you going? You'll be late—'

But I had turned on my heel and was striding back into the ward.

'I'll just have another look at the chart for Mr Salinger,' I told Nurse Baker as she hurried past with the tea trolley.

'Course, miss.' She gave me a cheerful smile, adding in an undertone, 'Good luck with that one.'

'Forgotten your handbag?' the old man said, his eyes on his newspaper. It was a *Daily Herald* and rather thin, I noticed, only a few well-thumbed pages at best. All the same, he licked his finger with an exaggerated flourish to turn the page, making his neighbour grin appreciatively.

I waited calmly for him to look up, and when he did, his smug expression slipped a bit and he tucked his blanket more firmly around his legs. 'Don't even think about it,' he muttered, reaching for his cigarette packet and laying it across his knees.

'Wouldn't dream of it.' I plucked the chart from the back of the bed and quickly started copying its contents into my notebook. Mr Salinger watched me, then suddenly bent forward and snatched the chart out of my hands. 'That's private information, that is,' he said mulishly. 'I have rights.'

I looked down at the long smear of ink across my notebook, then back up at him. To his obvious discomfort, I was smiling broadly as I bent to pick up the newspaper pages that had slid to the floor. 'I have an excellent memory, Mr Salinger,' I said. 'And I'll be back.'

Seven

I arrived at the hospital early the following Monday morning to check the rota on the noticeboard outside the main office. As the hospital was overfull and in disarray until the Tomeyne Wing was finished, the schedule was always changing, depending on where staff was needed and what consultants were on duty. *McIntyre, Isobel* was still very much attached to Everett Carlisle's firm, however, although how I'd ever be able to progress anywhere else when I was perpetually staring at people's shoulder blades from the back row, I didn't know. I wondered what Sister Veronica would say if I started bringing a small box to stand on.

Pondering the technicalities of that, I walked down the administrative corridor, studying the portraits lining the wall. I liked it up here, seeing the people who had come before me, all with their own specialities, their own passions. No women doctors had made it up on to these walls yet, however – not that they were all that common in the floors below either. Maybe I should take Iain's advice and work harder to blend in with the men around me? I gave my frill-less blouse and plain black skirt a wry smile, my hair gathered so tightly at the back of my neck that I had a perpetual headache. There wasn't much else I could do about my appearance to be more like them, unless it was trousers, of course. So much more practical when hanging across the sink in the sluice, but most likely destined to make Sister Veronica keel over in shock, and then where would I be?

I was squinting up at a bushy-bearded surgeon posed in front of a shelf holding a hammer and a saw with ominously reddish teeth when someone came belting around the corner and ran straight into me.

'Ooof.' Grey Carlisle doubled over, then straightened. 'So sorry,' he said breathlessly. 'What are you doing here? You're not worshipping at the altar, are you?' He gestured to one of the nearby portraits, and I jumped slightly when I saw, right next to the bushy-bearded surgeon, an enormous oil painting of Everett Carlisle. Big, crusty whorls of paint made it seem almost three-dimensional, his hand holding a scalpel level with my ear.

'Good God!' I took a big step back, then forward again when distance seemed to make the painting even more forbidding.

'Tsk tsk, where's your respect?' Grey laughed, then shrugged off his coat and started rummaging through the inside pockets. For once, Everett Carlisle seemed to be looking directly at me, but the painter hadn't quite managed to capture the intense focus that seemed to look right through you at the same time, unless you did something extraordinary – or extraordinarily stupid – to pique his interest. He had, however, captured the impatient scowl, as if both painter and viewer were wasting Carlisle's valuable time.

'What's he like at home?' I asked, curiosity winning over my plan to squeeze in a large pot of tea and an iced bun in the cafeteria before my day started. 'Is he as . . .' I chose my words with care, settling on 'formidable?'

Grey looked up from his coat, glanced at his father and turned his back on him. 'Exactly the same. You should have seen him at parents' day at Edgewood. He once got the most popular teacher there sacked for not teaching us the correct way to dissect a frog. I never lived it down. Here, can you hold this a second?' He shoved his bag at me and I slung it over my shoulder, remembering the day my mother had come to school with me to talk to Mr Thomas, I'd asked to sit with the more advanced pupils and read ahead of my class. He'd confiscated my precious tattered copy of *Introduction to Science* instead and thrust the primary school primer into my hands so hard it had left a bruise.

I'd thought I was going to wait outside while she spoke to him, but she shepherded me in ahead of her, pressing a wrapped parcel into my hands as we went. 'Mr Thomas, I think there may have been a misunderstanding. Agnes would like the chance to explain how much she enjoys your teaching, and how keen she is to sit with the older children.'

I'd given it my best, embellishing my admiration for his lessons, smiling a lot and finally handing him the package. By the time we left, Mr Thomas had cracked a smile (unheard of) and returned *Introduction to Science* (even better). Next day, I sat reading peacefully, while he sported a beautiful scarf in dark navy made out of a set of old curtains Mum had salvaged from a bombed-out house.

'Edgewood, what's that?' I asked.

'Boys' boarding school down in Surrey. Carlisle men have gone there since William the Conqueror.' He was still rummaging through his coat. 'Where's it got to?' he muttered, his hair standing on end. I pictured him at school, young and full to the brim with all that energy. He'd have been as effortlessly excellent at academic subjects as he was at hockey and rugby, or whatever else they played at fancy schools like that. And all the while his path had been laid out before him, smooth and wide open, his acceptance of that fact casually entitled, mildly exasperated even.

'William the Conqueror went to Edgewood?' I asked, smiling a little.

'Well, records are a bit patchy on that score, if you must know.' He looked up and winked at me. 'But public opinion – my father's – is that if he could have gone anywhere, that's where he would have chosen. Aha!' He finally drew out a small, rather battered-looking envelope, folded in half. 'I'm glad I ran into you, actually, because there's something I wanted to give you.' He snapped the envelope at me. 'Here.'

'For me?' I eyed it warily.

'Who else do I have the pleasure of chatting with on a deserted corridor next to a life-size portrait of my father?'

'It's never from *him*?' I breathed with a mixture of hope and awe.

'Of course not,' he said impatiently. 'It's from my mother.'

'What?' I was so startled that I took the envelope. 'What on earth do *I* have to do with your mother?'

He sighed. 'Let's move along a bit, shall we?' He jabbed his chin meaningfully at his father before herding me down the corridor, back in the direction I'd come from. 'I'm not totally sure he'd approve, even if your grandfather *is* Hector Bellingdon.'

'Approve of . . . ?' I asked, confused.

Grey was striding along, one step to each of my two, and I had to run to keep up.

'The fact that my mother seems to know you.'

I stopped in my tracks, so suddenly that my shoes skidded along the linoleum with a sharp screech. 'She *knows* me?'

Given Isobel's background, the fact that her grandparents had lived in London, her grandfather a surgeon here, it wasn't at all unreasonable that she would catch someone's attention in the medical community. Reasonable and yet terrifying. My worst nightmare, really. 'I . . . I can't imagine . . .'

Already my mind was spooling through all the contingency plans I'd come up with and finessed over the years. Stick as close to the truth as possible, say as little as necessary, be on your guard at all times. I closed my mouth with a snap, looked down at the letter, willed my brain to rake through any mention of a Mrs Carlisle.

'How does . . . I mean, *how* does she know me?' Even to myself, my voice sounded forced with the effort of being casual.

'It's not a secret, is it?' he said, amused. 'Well, you know Father. One-track mind if there ever was one. He tends to talk about his work ad nauseam, never leaves the hospital behind. He wasn't talking about you per se.' He held up his hands quickly. 'He doesn't approve of female students.'

'And?' I said.

'I happened to mention that Jenkins and I were looking after the younger students, now that we're almost finished. My mum likes that kind of thing, human interest, gossip, you know. And then, I don't quite know exactly how, your name came up.'

'My name came up,' I parroted.

'Are you going to repeat every single thing I say?' he asked. 'It wasn't just you; it was also your, erm, slightly unfortunate friend, you know, the one with the hair . . .'

'Susan,' I said, absently worrying at the flap of the letter.

'Right. My mother felt badly for her, knows Father too well. Anyway, one thing led to another, and all of sudden it transpired that she knew your mum.'

'My mum. Of course.' I nailed a smile on my face. 'Sorry, Mother just never mentioned it.'

He said something else in reply, but I was looking down at the piece of paper in my hand. Words jumped out here and there.

Diana . . . grew up together . . . funeral.

Oh God.

I felt my fingers curl around the edges of the letter, forced myself to keep them straight.

Dear Isobel,

I hope you don't mind my getting in touch like this. I was a dear friend of your mama's. Diana and I grew up together in London, then sadly lost touch when she moved away. I cannot tell you how sad I was to hear of your parents' accident, and how sorry for your devastating loss. The funeral was a lovely, dignified gathering, but of course it's the weeks and months that follow that are the hardest. I didn't come and introduce myself, thinking you probably had enough to cope with that day without fielding convoluted explanations of who I was. I wrote to you afterwards, only to learn that you'd left for France.

Imagine, then, how thrilled I was to gather from Grey that you're now living in London, and not only that, but connected with him and my husband! What a wonderful coincidence and lovely surprise. I can only think that fate has brought us together. I'd love to take you to tea at the Ritz, my treat, so we can maybe get to know each other a bit. I'm aware from Everett how terribly busy medical students are, so do let me know what time and date would suit you and I'll make sure I'm free. I so look forward to seeing you and await your response.

Ella Carlisle

Tea.
Tea at the Ritz.
Tea with Mrs McIntyre's old childhood friend.
Who'd been at the funeral and seen me there. Seen *both* of us there, Agnes *and* Isobel.

Eight

The letter crackled slightly in my pocket as I turned off busy Westview Road and wove my way through smaller streets towards my lodgings, walking past houses and shops, my back warm from the September sun.

A gaggle of children were pressing their noses against the window of a shop, where a television set held pride of place. A nurse cycled by on a bicycle, her black bag balanced precariously on the handlebars, and two women chatting on the footpath hastily stepped out of her way.

Of course, I couldn't meet Ella Carlisle, that much was clear. I'd have to write and politely (but firmly) decline, on the grounds that I was too busy (which was true), and say that I would get back in touch later that term (never). And hadn't Grey said his father wouldn't approve? That alone settled it, didn't it, and would have to convince Grey as well, should he push his mother's invitation in some way, because I so obviously didn't need anything else to aggravate Everett Carlisle.

The women returned my greeting, although one of them glanced curiously at me and I realised that I was gripping my pocket around the letter so hard it bunched up my coat. I quickened my steps, relieved when my lodgings came into view.

The detached Georgian house stood at the very end of a cul-de-sac, tidy rows of terraces sweeping towards it like pupils lining up for the headmaster. It was owned by Mrs Schwartz, a large, square, Jewish widow, who bustled about the place and played her baby grand piano at all hours. The house seemed rather grand at first approach but was unexpectedly and cheerfully ramshackle and messy inside. Creaking parquet, windows that clattered with draughts, and mismatched furniture lovingly dusted by Katia, Mrs Schwartz's sister-in-law, who grew vegetables and herbs in the overgrown garden round the back.

I'd heard two women talking about Mrs Schwartz's lodging house after trudging round cheaper digs on the Fulham Road, where students piled in two and three to a room. They were the obvious choice, but were so tiny and darkly wallpapered and small-windowed that I couldn't bring myself to sign up. Not just because they were cramped – a bit difficult for me ever since the vault – but because they were so densely inhabited. I'd done well as Isobel so far and thought it wise not to subject myself to too close a scrutiny from others.

Mrs Schwartz mainly rented rooms to musicians from Eastern Europe, but the moment she'd heard I was going to be a doctor, she had taken a shine to me and marched me up to the tower room, a little turret right at the top of the house overlooking the street. There she stood, her hands folded across her considerable black-clad bosom, her expression smug as if she knew that seeing this, surely I couldn't say no.

I didn't. Despite the price, despite the fact that I'd probably be better matched with a young, bustling student community, there was something about Mrs Schwartz's house that reached for me the minute I stepped across the threshold. I loved eating with the other lodgers, mostly old Polish musicians who sat in the drawing room drinking black coffee and cloudy brown schnapps in tiny glasses, arguing in rapid-fire Polish at all hours and filling the rest with their music. Then there was Mrs Schwartz herself, who had stood guard over my studies since my first day at the hospital, when I'd come home late, dazed and exhausted. She switched from heavy-handed Dvořák dances to mellow Chopin sonatas while I worked, and berated the tradesmen for ringing the bell too long. And Katia, heavy eyebrows knitted together in concern at my scrappy physique, was constantly pressing food on me. *A table is not blessed if it has fed no scholars*, Mrs Schwartz would say in her guttural Yiddish-laced English, and Katia, who had no English at all, beamed next to her.

But most of all, I loved that no one here seemed to care at all about where I'd gone to school and who my family was, whom I knew and whom I didn't. I didn't have to constantly watch my accent or modulate my vocabulary; it didn't matter that I was a woman in a man's world. Instead, they asked how my days had gone, clustering around to hear stories of students and patients, demanding sequels to particularly exciting bits.

Izabella, they called me, a runaway up-and-down lilt that emphasised *bella*, instead of *Isobel*, a word that always sounded a bit brusque, like it was trying to swallow itself. In here I was neither Agnes nor Isobel, but *Bella* or *Iza*, whose arrival was greeted with a chorus of huzzas and entreaties to sit and chat, until Mrs Schwartz impatiently shooed me upstairs with stern instructions to work hard. A little later, Katia's heavy footfall could be heard as she deposited a plate of food outside my door. It made me feel comfortable, yes, and welcome. But most of all it made me feel safe. For the first time since the night in the vault, perhaps the first time since I'd left the East End and my mother, I was able to exhale properly, all the way from the bottom of my stomach, my shoulders dropping away from my ears, my belly softening.

Now, as I extracted my large wrought-iron key from my bag, the ground-floor window was flung open and Mrs Schwartz's head appeared.

'There you are, we were wondering. Everyone's already eaten, but Katia will bring you dinner in the garden. Evening air and plants are especially good for the brain. Go now, shoo, before the soup is cold.'

She disappeared as quickly as she'd come, and moments later, the piano started up, a bracing march that chivvied me around the corner and on into the garden, where Katia's famous chicken soup with *kneidlach* was steaming gently on the wooden table. The monotonous staccato of a typewriter came from one of the rooms above, where Jaroslaw, a former journalist at one of the Polish underground presses, was working on a biography of famous resistance fighter Witold Pilecki. Down here, the evening sun flooded the back garden with the last lingering warmth of the day, and the air smelled of the late roses trying to survive the onslaught of Katia's runner beans and cabbages.

Mrs Schwartz, now accompanied by someone with a clarinet, switched to something soft and sad as I ate my way through Katia's *holishkes* – stuffed cabbage rolls – the bowl of soup, and a dumpling swimming in vanilla-scented custard. This was another new thing for me: seemingly endless supplies of food. Not just the novelty of it after years of rationing, but the matter-of-factness with which I was fed, the focus on the exact level of my consumption, the gruff disapproval at my continued scrawniness despite all their efforts. I smiled to myself as I wiped the bowl clean with the last piece of bread, because if I finished, Katia would be wringing her hands that it wasn't enough, and if I didn't, her face would fall at the fact that I hadn't enjoyed the food. I had got Marek to teach me 'the food was lovely' in Polish. *Jedzenie było dobre.* I said it softly into the garden, where the light faded into shadows. I emphasised the *dz* as he'd said to, and rolled the *r*, and was just feeling that I was doing Iza quite proud when the letter crackled in my pocket again.

I sat up straight, my shoulders tight. Slowly and extremely reluctantly, I reached for it and laid it on the table in front of me, staring at the dainty signature in the half-darkness. *Ella Carlisle.* Devastated at losing her friend before they'd had a chance to rekindle their friendship, glad of a second chance with me. And the thing that worried me most: *The funeral was a lovely, dignified gathering . . . I didn't come and introduce myself, thinking you probably had enough to cope with.*

I pictured a slim woman to match the handwriting, a gentler

version of her son's impatient ranginess, perhaps, elegant and understated in a black dress. I frowned, trying to remember someone watching us across the small crowd that had attended the McIntyres' funeral, but the day had been a blur of misery and horror. Isobel was frozen in shock, unable to attend to anything, so without any other family to step in, I was the one who led the charge. On the way to the church, I had suddenly been struck myself by an almost physical blow of terror at what *I* would do when I left this place, this sort-of-home. So we'd kept close to each other all that day, Isobel and I, one propping the other up.

The service had been surprisingly well attended, actually, given that the McIntyres, always following Mr McIntyre's postings, never stayed anywhere long enough to put down roots. But the turnout from the school had been decent, and the accident had garnered a lot of sympathy and goodwill from the community. Even if Ella Carlisle had come down the line to shake our hands and murmur condolences without introducing herself, would she have known for sure which one of us was the daughter and which the maid? Unless Mrs McIntyre had regularly sent her old friend photos of Isobel. Unlikely, I decided, if they'd lost touch ages ago. And yet, what if she'd asked someone, what if a guest had pointed out Isobel, what if she *knew* . . .

I couldn't chance it, there was no way. Walk towards Ella Carlisle through a crowded tearoom, watch her look of pleasure and anticipation change to confusion, then to disbelief and finally horror. She would surely call the police, and I would be convicted of fraud and theft. She'd most certainly tell her husband, and if I wasn't already in prison, I would be expelled from Thamesbury straight away. Maybe Carlisle would make it public even, have me walk down the beautiful marble staircase through a crowd of doctors, nurses and students, wide-eyed with the scandal of it all, the arched dome ringing with their whispers at my disgrace, nurses' habits twitched out of my way, people shrinking back.

Never would I work in the medical profession again – or, really, any job that needed a reference and a clean record. Instead, I'd be *that Crawford girl* once more, who'd got no better than she deserved.

No. I funnelled the word into the fragrant evening air, a long, soft hiss of determination. I had put too much into this already; I wouldn't let that happen. Above me, Mrs Schwartz had paused in her playing, then resumed as my thoughts strayed back to where it had all begun, that moment in the darkness when Agnes had become Isobel.

Nine

We had both been covered in dust and rubble, our faces smeared with grime, Isobel in my coat, me holding her shiny new leather satchel. When they finally brought us back up to the light, I'd been shaking so much that the doctor didn't even try to make head or tail of my gibberish, but fixed up my scratches and injuries and, before I could object, gave me something to put me to sleep. When I came to in the hospital the next day, Isobel's bag was sitting next to the stack of her clothes folded neatly on the stool beside my bed, and the first thing I heard through the woolly pounding in my head was the nurse addressing me as Miss McIntyre, offering me a cup of tea, asking who they should ring for me.

Part of the bank's facade had collapsed, she told me, made unstable by undetected damage to a load-bearing wall during the Blitz. 'I'm ever so sorry about the other girl, Miss McIntyre, what a devastating tragedy,' she said, patting my hand and smoothing my blanket. 'Was she a friend?'

She couldn't have known what it was that made my eyes fill with tears, my throat constrict so I could only nod and turn away: Isobel's death most of all, yes; our devastating last hours together in the vault; but also a visceral horror at myself, which made me want to leap out of bed and run to wherever they kept the dead bodies, dig up 'Agnes Crawford' and fix what I'd done.

I could have admitted it right then, of course. But the nurse was gone before I could speak. During the days and weeks that followed, I talked myself in and out of it a hundred times. I hadn't killed or harmed anyone; to the contrary, I'd been trying to *save* a life. And who was in charge up there anyway, who had dropped us both into the great scales of the universe at Finley &

Smith's Bank and decided, on a whim really, who would live and who would die? What was fair about lovely, kind Isobel's life being wasted, just like that, her future destroyed, her smile, her gentleness gone? And hadn't Isobel herself been the one to suggest this as the way forward. She had practically *ordered* me to take her place at university. *You go.*

So I went. I walked out of the hospital as soon as they let me, found a cheap, nondescript boarding house. I fielded paperwork and questions as swiftly as I could, organised a discreet burial for 'Agnes'. Then, dodging newspaper reporters and other officials, I escaped to an anonymous seaside town in Wales, where I spent the weeks until September walking along windy beaches, trying to put myself back together in some way and stop shaking every time darkness fell and I was forced back into my small hotel room, with the walls closing in.

No, I didn't say anything. Because the truth was that beneath the devastation at Isobel's death, the sadness that seemed to have lodged itself permanently inside me, making my eyes prickle and my face hot with misery, there was also something else. A small flame of hope. A promise of freedom. I didn't like feeling that, like I was glad of her death in some way, but it just kept flaring, this wonderful, heady frisson of excitement and possibility.

I repeated our conversations back to myself like a rosary of redemption, not just the one in the vault, but earlier ones too, when we were girls. Her whispered encouragement, sitting up together at night or curled over a book, when we unpacked boxes, walked around yet another new town: that life would turn out all right for me too, that as soon as she was settled somewhere, I'd come and live with her, maybe assist her, or become a nurse. I wanted to keep her close through those memories, but I also wanted to shore up my increasing conviction that she was actually right there with me, that she would do everything she could to help me master this.

For a long time, I was convinced I would be found out; got up every morning sure that this would be my last day as Isobel McIntyre, that someone would show up on my doorstep at any moment. *Agnes Crawford. We've been looking for you. Please come with us.*

But, unbelievable as it seemed, I got away with it. And I kept getting away with it, every day putting a little more distance between myself and what had happened in the vault, between myself and Agnes Crawford. Isobel had no other family, nothing to inherit other than her name and the money put aside by her parents to get her through university. Whatever had been in the safety deposit box had been lost in the collapse, and in any case, the bank was not a place I'd ever return to. The McIntyres had moved too often for her to form deep bonds with anyone, which had been partly why she and I had grown so close. As far as her schoolmates and former neighbours were concerned, she had gone to France, then on to university, and I was able to field any correspondence that cropped up along the way.

As for Agnes, well, any friends Mum had left behind would assume I was still with the McIntyres or working elsewhere. The very thing I'd once found so claustrophobic about the East End – that you rarely broke free of what you were meant to do – would now come in handy. It wouldn't occur to them that I wasn't in service, or a shop girl, a teacher at best, because they'd never in a million years think that someone like me would take the kind of leap I had and make a proper go of it.

I recalled how Isobel had spoken, the way her voice had gone up at the end of each sentence, as if everything had been a question. The way she'd dressed her hair, pulled back or in soft waves at the nape of her neck; how she'd walked – slower than me, tripping a little as if unsure. I practised her handwriting by filling a secret notebook with every single thing I could remember ever hearing about her, her family, her childhood, the timeline of their moves, the places they'd lived. I made contingency plans for every eventuality, rehearsed safe things to say when I slipped up, until even I sometimes felt like I was actually her.

Yet there had been close calls, many of them. The time I stuttered my way through an exam, betraying that my Latin was rudimentary at best, even though Isobel's application had boasted of her distinction. The fact that I failed my first set of exams altogether, had to redo the year. The friend of the McIntyres who wrote to invite me for the holidays, ringing to say that they'd even send me the train fare, doing it again the following Christmas, making it almost impossible for me to rebuff the invitation.

And the biggest, closest one of all. Rose Bellerby, an old chum excited to start at Durham, and how thrilling to see dearest Isobel again. Could they find digs together? She'd be there in September, late August if she could get away, and couldn't wait for Isobel to show her the best spots . . .

It had taken all my ingenuity and desperation to weasel my way out of this. I'd made up a family emergency that had forced me to relocate to London in the middle of medical school; applied to school there, roping in anyone I could think of to help, until I'd finally got a spot at Thamesbury to continue the clinical part of my studies. Ironically, it had been Isobel who had helped me with this once more – it had been mention of her grandfather that had seemed to open this final door, because Hector Bellingdon's name, though he himself was long dead, still carried a certain weight around here.

I'm so sorry to miss you, I wrote to Rose Bellerby, a surge of relief threatening to derail my neat penmanship, *but I'm sure I'll see you soon*.

It was almost entirely dark now, the sounds of the neighbourhood and the last song of the blackbird in the undergrowth muted by velvet shadows. Upstairs, I heard Mrs Schwartz close the lid of the baby grand with a soft thud, then her footsteps clacked out of the drawing room and faded down the hall. A moment later, a light came on in the window above me, spilling brightness across the garden.

We were one now, Isobel and I. She was all around me, like a heavy cloak that hid my old self from sight, squashing Agnes right down until sometimes even I forgot she was there. Only every now and then did something – a colourful dress swishing into a tea shop; a snatch of song, a thread of a story, the brackish smell of the river – slip past my Isobel shell, with a piercing stab that felt aching and strange, that made me want to unpin Isobel's hair and rip off the demure, dark clothes she wore and sit with my mother under the table, drinking tea and making up stories as the night air filled with crashes and thunder. I never did, though. I never slipped. I pulled Isobel tightly around myself and pushed forward, safe in the knowledge that this was where I belonged now, in this shiny new life of mine.

Ten

These days, however, my shiny new life was starting to show a few blemishes, mainly because Everett Carlisle continued to stonewall me so successfully that I couldn't really get anyone else to take me seriously either. The nurses were kind, with one of the third-years whispering that Sister Veronica was a baptism of fire for everyone, and I shouldn't take it to heart. I didn't really care that the ward sister showed me less and less respect as time went on, continuing to slip in tasks usually reserved for first-year nurses. I'd be out from under her beady eye as soon as I was rotated on. What I minded was always being relegated to the back of the group during rounds, where I couldn't see and had to surmise from the muttered conversation around me what was happening; and I also minded, very much so, having to listen to the others discussing their cases while all I had on my books was cobbled-together notes from the chart and a lot of *I won't let this woman see my privates.*

Two days later, I decided that while I might not have a beautiful navy scarf made from curtains to hand, I could give it my best try nonetheless.

'Mr Carlisle?' I had waited for him at the corner, planning to make my case as quickly as I could in the few yards that separated us from the entrance to the ward. He'd been glued to some papers in his hand, and when I spoke, he jumped a little and looked irritated. I did have his attention now, although perhaps not quite in the way I'd hoped.

'Is there a message?' he said curtly.

'No, sir, and I didn't mean to startle you.' I spoke quickly, conscious that I'd already wasted three strides down the corridor. 'Could I have a word?' In the interests of time, I didn't wait for him to agree. 'The patient I'm supposed to be shadowing is refusing to be shadowed, and I was hoping you might assign me someone else.'

I moved ahead and turned as if to engage him in a proper face-to-face conversation, but all I managed was to force him to stop so as not to run into me. His eyes, enlarged and bulbous behind their spectacles, narrowed.

'Miss,' he said, infusing the single syllable with enough doubt to make it clear he couldn't be bothered with my name, 'I've assigned you a patient; it's not up to me to make that case yours.'

'He'd prefer a man,' I cut in. Better get to the heart of things. 'But I'm sure there'd be someone else who wouldn't mind having me, maybe the kidney patient in Bed 8? I'm not picky, I just want to work, and I could easily take on several cases now to make up for lost time . . .'

To my dismay, Carlisle was moving again, forcing me to shuffle backwards towards the group of men behind us.

'You want to work?' he repeated, his tone mocking.

'Yes,' I said, holding his gaze, then tacked on a quick 'Please, sir.'

'They all do. Girls like you, they come here full of ambition, vow eternal commitment. And what do they do? Eh? You tell me, Miss Clever-Clogs.'

'Er, they work hard?' I said before I could help myself, then quickly added, 'If they're given the chance, sir.'

'They fall,' he said curtly. 'At the first hurdle. Look at the other girl. Two weeks in and she's done. Took up another student's space, someone who might have gone on to do real good, change the face of medicine even. And if it's not the actual work, then it'll be a romance or marriage, wanting a family.'

I opened my mouth, closed it again.

'Nothing to say to that, is there?' he said, not mocking now, but almost conversational. He was already reaching for the stack of case notes in Sister Veronica's hands, but for a moment he turned back. 'It's not up to me to help you stay, especially not when I already know it's unlikely you will. Do you think you'll only get to treat female patients from here on? That you can run for help every time it gets difficult? Not how it works, miss, not how it works at all.'

I was reasonably sure that not just Sister Veronica but everyone else – including Mr Private Parts, who couldn't possibly know I'd been talking about him but who looked insufferably smug nonetheless – had heard my exchange with Everett Carlisle. At least Grey was nowhere to be seen, although Harry Jenkins more than made up for his absence. His stream of whispered rebuke at directly addressing a consultant only ground to a halt when Sister Veronica sent me to deal with bedpans in the sluice for the remainder of my ward duty.

I would show him, I would show everyone, if it was the last thing I did. I'd become a surgeon, a consultant, the most eminent consultant surgeon there ever was, I'd be at this very hospital until the end of time, until they had to wrench the scalpel out of my ninety-year-old liver-spotted hands, and even then I'd come back to haunt Everett bloody Carlisle . . .

'Here you are.' Grey Carlisle came closer, peered at my face. 'Are you quite all right?'

'Couldn't be better,' I said curtly. I directed the sprayer towards the bedpans, hoping it would make him leave.

Undaunted – to his credit, I had to admit – he came closer still, shook his head at my red, chapped hands. 'You know, the probationers should really be doing that. But I suppose if Ward Sister—'

'What is it with you men and bossy women in authority? Some kind of public-school complex?'

Ignoring my comment, he reached to twist the nozzle of the sprayer to direct it better.

'Look, I know Father can be quite gruff and all, but if you just keep your head down and do what he says, it *will* get better. Look at my abscess operation day before yesterday. He didn't take over once, and that only took me, what, four years?' He smiled encouragingly.

'Keep my head down?' I twisted the sprayer back to its original position. 'Everyone's favourite modus operandi around here. But *I'm* not afraid of him.' The emphasis hung in the air, barely there but enough to wipe the smile off Grey's face.

'I just thought I'd come and cheer you up a bit,' he said coolly. 'Part of my role, unfortunately, to prop up flailing medical students.'

'I'm not flailing.' I turned to him for the first time, and the sprayer moved with me, making him step back a little. 'Or I won't be for long, at any rate. You all think I'm just here to play, that in due course – sooner rather than later, if your father had his way – I'll realise I'm better off as a nurse or a midwife, or better yet, leave the medical profession altogether. But I've gone to great lengths' – at this, I flicked my eyes away from him and back to the sink, because I really didn't want him to see just how great those lengths had been – 'to get here, and I'm not giving up. So you'd better get used to having me around. And for the record, I think he's right. Your father. About male patients. I do need to find a way to make them trust me. And I will, you just watch me.'

He didn't immediately reply, but when I glanced at him, I saw to my surprise that while his eyes were still flashing in annoyance at my earlier slight, there was something else there too, something that looked – my heart gave a strange hitch – like grudging respect. For a moment we stood there, a fine cloud of rainbow-coloured mist around us. I was the first to turn, abruptly, directing the sprayer back at the bedpans.

'Mother told me you wrote saying you didn't have time to meet her,' he said.

Oh. Yes. Between Carlisle, the hernia and Sister Veronica, I'd momentarily forgotten Ella Carlisle and her dangerous invitation to the Ritz.

'It was very kind of her to invite me,' I said, 'but with my coursework, rounds and the work here on the ward, I really am too busy.' Even to my own ears it sounded a bit rattled off, and I gave the bedpans a particularly noisy spray to distract him from it. I could feel him staring at me; then, to my amazement, he started laughing.

'I can't believe it.' He leaned back against the counter and crossed his arms, eyeing me in an infuriatingly amused way. 'You *are* a coward, Miss McIntyre, regardless of what you say. You don't want to go because I said my father wouldn't approve. Not quite so blasé after all, are we?'

'I'm *not* a coward,' I said heatedly, accidentally flinging spray across us both.

'Of course, I don't blame you.' He shook the water off, then held up his hands in mock innocence. 'Father *wouldn't* approve of Mother socialising with anyone more emancipated than a tea cosy. But since, according to you, you're not afraid of anything . . .'

'I'm not,' I said through gritted teeth, even though there were a few things I *was* afraid of, very much so. 'I'm just—'

'Busy, yes. You mentioned it.' He nodded faux-seriously, his expression smug.

'Oh, be quiet.' I was about to follow this up with a few more choice expressions, and possibly the sprayer again, when a figure suddenly appeared in the doorway. 'Miss *McIntyre*! Whatever are you doing?'

While Sister Veronica gave me the inevitable dressing-down, Grey stood next to the rubber sheets hung up to dry with a benevolent expression that made me even more furious, barely able to meet Sister's outrage with enough humility to get me off the hook.

'You . . .' I rounded on him the moment she'd bustled back into the ward. 'I want you to take it back.'

'What, that you can't stand up to Sister any more than us boarding-school boys can?'

'That I'm a coward. Take it back.'

'I won't,' he said flatly. 'Not until you've done my mother the courtesy of having tea with her. The Ritz, too; I should have thought any starving student would jump at the chance of cucumber sandwiches and scones. You'll see her anyway at the Bonfire Ball, so it'll be embarrassing if you've turned down her invitation.'

'Bonfire Ball?' I took a step back, fury suddenly laced with unease. 'What are you talking about?'

'The hospital always holds a big ball in November, has done for decades,' he said. 'To bring in a bit of extra money for building works and such. Technically, fundraising activities aren't allowed any more under the NHS, but Father put in a good word with the ministry, so they can have the ball one last time to coincide with the reopening of the Tomeyne Wing.'

'But why would *I* see her there?' I was vaguely aware that I sounded rude, but I couldn't help it. 'I'm not going.'

'Yes, you are, Cinderella,' he said smugly. 'It's traditional for all staff and students to attend. I guess it's kind of like the servants' balls of old, you know.'

For a moment I was tempted to say that no, I didn't know, and that I found his casual lord-of-the-manor entitlement and people putting in good words with the ministry more than irksome.

'Attendance is mandatory, or at the very least highly advisable. People from the royal colleges – professors, former surgeons and physicians – will be there, along with students and staff. And my mother is on the organising committee. So really, as I said, it would be very awkward if you saw her there for the first time after rejecting her invitation, wouldn't it?'

Awkward. I suppressed a sudden hysterical urge to laugh. Yes, it would be awkward indeed if Isobel McIntyre was pushed forward for introduction and Agnes Crawford discovered in her place. Oh God . . .

He was still looking at me expectantly, but instead of delivering a pithy comeback, I said, 'Why is this so important to you?'

The smug smile faded from his face. 'It's important to her,' he said eventually, 'so it's important to me.' He straightened a stack of metal dishes on the counter, lining up the edges exactly. 'If you must know, she's been a bit low lately, and I'd like to see something give her a bit of a lift.' He paused again, gave the stack another small tweak, then added, 'She has some health troubles.' He was still looking at the dishes, but I saw his face twist. And all of a sudden, he wasn't blithe and jokey and confident, but quite young-looking and a bit anxious. 'She was so excited when she discovered you. I think she felt badly about never making up with her friend. So I'd like to help. I want—'

But we would never know what he wanted, because Sister Veronica had swept back in, asking shrilly if we were quite finished before, in short order, dispatching Mr Grey to assist Mr Tallard with the wheezing lung in Bed 4 and me to stay behind and help Nurse Jameson scrub soiled sheets.

At the door to the ward, he said, 'How about a bargain, Miss McIntyre? I'll help you with Mr Salinger if you have tea with Mum. An inguinal hernia in exchange for cucumber sandwiches, eh?'

At this, I had to smile. 'I'll get there myself, but thanks anyway.'

Sister Jameson had come in and got started on the sheets, humming to herself, but I stood just inside the door and looked into the ward. Mr Salinger was sitting up in bed, the same tattered newspaper still on his bedside table, playing with his now-empty cigarette pack.

'Do leave some for me, Nurse, I'll be back in a moment.'

'No worries,' she said good-naturedly. 'Sister's over in her office. I'll keep an eye on her, but better make it quick.'

I darted out of the ward and down the back stairs to the ground floor, where a small kiosk sold newspapers, cigarettes and chocolate. I bought a pack of cigarettes and some matches, then looked through all the newspapers until I found a copy of the newspaper Mr Salinger had been reading, the *Daily Herald*, at the very back. It was a few days old.

'Let you have it for half-price,' the kiosk man said.

'Get away with you,' I said, pretending to be scandalised. 'No more than a third. As it's old news and all.'

Back upstairs, I waited for Sister Veronica to emerge from her office and head towards Gynae IV. Ideally, the gynaecological ward would have been closer to the women's surgical, but due to space restrictions, it had spilled over on to our corridor and was separated from Surgical III by a cluster of side wards as well as private rooms, the kitchen, linen cupboard and other store-rooms. Once her habit had swept out of view, I drew myself up, straightened my coat and tucked my hair back into its bun before stepping out into the ward, where Nurse Baker was just approaching Bed 16.

'I'll take this from you, Mr Salinger,' she said cheerfully, bending to lift the heavy glass Winchester bottle just as I popped up next to the bed.

Salinger eyed me. 'Not you again.'

'Now play nice, Mr Salinger.' Nurse Baker clucked her tongue and winked at me.

'Yes, do, Mr Salinger.' I peered at the Winchester bottle. 'Seems all right, doesn't it?'

The nurse laughed, but Mr Salinger looked scandalised.

'It's not right, the way you carry on, miss. And you can't do anything to me without the doctor present.'

'I won't, don't worry.' Throwing a look over my shoulder for

Sister Veronica's whereabouts, I perched on the side of his bed. 'I come with a peace offering.'

'And I'll get you a nice cup of tea.' Nurse Baker bustled off.

'Hm.' Salinger eyed the bulging pocket of my coat.

Slowly, for maximum dramatic impact, I withdrew the newspaper, then the cigarettes, before finally adding the matches. I fanned all of it out in my hands and waved it enticingly. 'A bargain, Mr Salinger. Entertainment in exchange for your acquiescence.'

'Sister says they frown on smoking in the wards,' he said, his hand already creeping towards the cigarette packet.

'It's just her, they don't elsewhere; everyone does it. But I can find you a wheelchair and take you out for a smoke whenever you want. They have a nice bit of corridor back there with a view over the road.'

'Hm.' He nodded. 'Fancy them having the *Herald* in a posh place like this, eh? Nurse brought me some of the other papers, but they're just not the same.'

'It's a few days old,' I said apologetically. 'But better than yours, I'm sure.'

'Mine's from last week.' He sighed. 'My daughter's meant to visit, but she's . . . I think she's got too much on.'

'Would you like to send her a note, maybe? I could post it for you.'

'Nah, I don't want to be a bother,' he said bashfully.

'You? Never.' I chuckled and laid the paper on his bed. 'So, have we a deal? No more shouting and carrying on? Answering a few questions and letting me have a look at . . .' I cleared my throat delicately, 'things?'

'Nothing too personal,' he grumbled, already ripping the top off the cigarette pack.

Out of the corner of my eye, I suddenly noticed Everett Carlisle walking back through the ward from the direction of the private rooms. He'd been in conversation with someone, but now turned and watched my interaction with the old man.

'I'll try to contain myself.' I patted Mr Salinger's arm. 'But I can't promise anything. I'll go and find you a wheelchair.'

Much later, I found myself down in the cafeteria, where, over tea and enough iced buns to prop up anyone's flagging courage, I wrote to Ella Carlisle to let her know I could see her at the Ritz at 5 p.m. on Tuesday, if it suited her, and thank you for the kind invitation.

I posted the letter quickly, before I could regret it, which I did, of course, the moment I heard the *thunk* of the envelope hitting the inside of the postbox. I stood there, my hand on top of the box, and wondered if I'd just made the biggest mistake of my life.

Eleven

The Palm Court at the Ritz was like something out of a fairy tale.

Prettily set tables and ornate chairs were arranged beneath the decorated ceiling; a chandelier lit up the delicately painted walls. Above the murmur of conversation there was the gentle plinky-plank sound of a piano and the burbling of a fountain, and black-and-white-dressed waiters glided past to deposit étagères holding tiny sandwiches and cakes, tea trays and other accoutrements.

Standing by the entrance as I waited for someone to guide me into the warm, scented interior, I saw a woman feeding perfectly cut squares of ham into her handbag, from which the head of a tiny dog protruded. A mother and daughter leaned in, laughing over tea, their hair clearly freshly set and beautiful under their hats, and an old woman dressed all in black was drinking something frothy from a wide glass flute.

I'd been jumpy with nerves, foreboding filling my mouth with a sour taste of fear every time I'd pictured this moment. Again and again I had to force myself not to check whether my dress hung straight and my hair was still curling tidily under my hat. I'd been to the ladies' room at the Lyons around the corner already and knew that nothing about me could possibly give away my hammering heart and hands sweating inside their gloves. I knew how to do this, I kept reminding myself, almost angrily; after all, I'd lived with Mrs McIntyre, who had been a stickler for etiquette, for years.

All the same, tea at the Ritz was a bit more upper-class than hosting local ladies at a rented house on school grounds. So a few days ago, I had found myself nipping across to the warren of used bookshops around Leicester Square, where kind Mr Brown at Rare Books and Antiquities pulled out something called *Manners and Etiquette for the Young Lady*. It seemed a little prim – the cover showed a woman smiling demurely – but he'd said it would see me safely through anything life threw at me. I hadn't told him that life was about to throw at me a woman I'd never met, and quite possibly the arrival of the police or Everett Carlisle (hard to say which I was more anxious about). Mr Brown must have known something was up, however, because he'd nodded kindly, saying, 'Never let them see your fear, my dear, that's more important than anything you'll find between the pages of a book,' and bowed me out of the shop with my brown paper package.

I had infinite faith in all things found between the pages of a book, however, and after spending precious hours studying fork arrangements, the correct way to address one's elders, how to sit down when quality was present and how to take your leave gracefully before you became a nuisance, I felt ready to go into battle.

On an impulse, I had picked up a small, colourful feather from Katia's vegetable bed this morning and stuck it in my hat. Looking around, it seemed a rather paltry version of the other ladies' sweet little pillboxes with netting, satin cloches and tilt hats, but it had reminded me of foraging for pretty bits with my mother, the way she could use anything to make something, and so had seemed a good omen for the afternoon. Now I leaned back a little to catch the flutter of iridescent blue in the mirror. All would be fine, I told myself firmly. Just stick as close to the truth as possible, neutral subjects only, and deflect attention away from myself at all other times.

A throat was cleared next to me, and I turned quickly to see a moustached man in an impeccable black suit staring down at me.

'I'm Isobel McIntyre. I'm here to meet . . .' I paused. Was she a Mrs? Or – surely not – a Lady? 'I'm here to meet Ella Carlisle,' I settled on.

The maître d' sketched a reverent bow at the name, his voice suddenly several degrees warmer. 'Of course, Miss, er, Mc-Intyre. It's this way, please, if you'll follow me. William, why are you dawdling, take Miss McIntyre's coat, now!'

He set off at a swift trot, weaving through the tables, and I followed him, my heart beating hard in my chest as he headed for a table where a woman sat alone. She was quite clearly waiting for someone; the table was set for two. I only had a moment to notice that she didn't look much like her son – where Grey was all sharp angles and rangy impatience, she was petite, wispy almost, her eyes round as a child's in a thin, friendly face – before panic flared anew. Hot and paralysing, it drowned out all rational thought. I couldn't do this, I'd be arrested, marched out of here like a criminal. Think, Agnes, think fast, do something, *anything* at all . . . Was it too late to turn and run, make my excuses? Yes, it was too late, because Ella Carlisle had risen and was already coming towards me, her hands outstretched.

'Isobel! How lovely.'

From somewhere above me, I watched myself extend my hands and let them be squeezed, saw the smile on my face, the nod as I stepped up to the table. The light of the chandelier caught the small mother-of-pearl buttons on my dress, and I heard myself speak, sounding absurdly normal and strangely foreign at the same time. 'Lovely to meet you, Mrs Carlisle, and thank you very much for the invitation.'

'Not at all, I'm so looking forward to our chat. Thank you, Morton.'

'Of course, ma'am.' Morton bowed himself away from the table, a waiter materialised, and in the ensuing kerfuffle of being settled in chairs and draped with napkins, I was able to hide the overwhelming surge of relief that had rushed straight to my knees. Tea appeared almost instantly, along with sandwiches and cakes.

'You must try some of these scones, they're the best in London.' She spoke fast, and I noticed that she too seemed nervous. 'And the jam is lovely. William, I think we'll need another fork, and the Oolong, not the Ceylon . . . There, that's better. Sugar?'

She chattered on, and hardly daring to believe it could be this simple, I cautiously relaxed. When I caught my reflection in one of the mirrored panels, my feather a tiny hint of blue, I felt a rush of thrilling triumph. It *was* that simple, apparently. I was safe. And not just safe, but I was having a scrumptious tea at the Ritz, of all things, like it was the most natural thing in the world for me to be here with a lovely lady in a silk dress. I smiled as the dog passed on the way out, its little head lolling out of the bag, and its owner smiled back.

'Er, won't you have anything?' I'd realised a beat too late that Mrs Carlisle had fallen quiet and was looking at me intently, her own plate empty. 'These scones really are delicious,' I added, slightly unnerved again. 'Raisin are my favourite. Why don't you have one, or perhaps a cream bun, or—'

'Oh, I don't have much of an appetite,' she said off-handedly, 'not like you students, certainly. Students need brain food, that's what I always say to Grey. I love nothing more than when he comes to dinner and Cook can feed him up properly. I tell Everett all the time not to work him so hard.'

It was a slight stretch for me to marry her warm, easy use of Carlisle's first name with the frowning, barking man I knew from the ward, but at least she'd stopped looking at me and was talking again, her hands fluttering around her plate. I busied myself with my scone, thinking to myself that she could do with a few of those cream buns, the way her skin stretched across her thin hands like paper.

'I wanted to say first of all,' her voice had suddenly become a bit choppy, and I looked up quickly, 'how sad I was to hear of your mother's death.' Her hand was trembling, making her teacup clatter against the saucer, and forgetting that I was going to keep my distance, be neutral and deflect, I reached across to catch a spill of tea with my napkin before it could spoil her dress. She smiled gratefully. 'Diana and I, we were such good friends at one point. I wrote to you afterwards, but you'd already left and . . .'

Relief rushed in again. I really and truly was safe.

'. . . Anyway, I'm very glad to meet you now, because it makes me feel' – she flushed and shrugged a little self-consciously – 'like Diana isn't gone altogether. I won't monopolise you,' she hastened to add. 'I know you're busy. But I hope you'll allow me to look after you a little. I'm sure Diana would be happy to know that someone is there in the background. I know I would be if you were my daughter and all alone in a big city.'

It came at me then, sharp as an arrow, this unexpectedly kind, lovely thing to say, cutting straight through the triumphant thrill of my charade. The gold rim of my plate blurred in front of my eyes and something very painful seemed to be lodged in my throat. Quickly I tried to gather my Isobel armour around me again, but Ella's smile was reaching for me across the table, her brown eyes warm on mine. 'Death is so final,' she said softly. 'And your mum's so particularly cruel.'

The room felt blurry at the edges, the words 'your mum' strangely warbled. Yes, of course she meant the car crash. So cruel. And Mrs McIntyre's death, so final. And I was meant to be grieving all that, I was meant to be Isobel – I *was* her, I *was* grieving – but oddly, and helplessly too, because I rarely thought about it if I could manage it, I remembered whom I was really grieving for, my own loss that had also been so particularly cruel, so very final.

A few weeks into my stay at the McIntyres', news had come that a V-2 had taken out a whole chunk of Bell Street, and that Mum, with all her talk of they-don't-care-about-little-old-us, had died under our kitchen table. The pain was like nothing I'd ever experienced. For all my childhood, I had been a part of her, slept next to her, helped her feed fabric through the Singer. Had listened to her stories, helped her forage for beautiful things, fallen asleep to her songs. She had stitched herself into my very essence and I into hers, so that her death felt like a physical severing, like someone was cutting her out of me with her little silver knife, unpicking us stitch by perfect stitch, until I was left lopsided, reeling, the gaping loss so huge I didn't think I would ever recover.

'I still dream of her, dying in screaming agony, flames swallowing her up,' I heard a hoarse voice whisper, and started when I realised it was mine. 'All alone when I should have been with her. I left her behind, I should have been there to save her—'

I came to with a start, saw Ella Carlisle staring at me across the table, two red spots on her cheeks, her eyes brimming with tears, and with a momentous effort forced myself to stop talking, pressed my lips together to prevent anything else escaping. I had never talked about my mother's death. Isobel had sometimes crept into my room at night, having heard me scream through a nightmare, had straightened the mess of twisted sheets and sat with me, patted my back, wiped my face, whispering and soothing in the darkness. But even then I'd not been able to talk about it.

I felt a hand touch mine and recoiled, then relaxed as Ella grasped my fingers. 'I'm sorry, Isobel, so desperately, desperately sorry.'

I blinked at the name, then felt a sudden, unaccountable stab of something hot and burning. Rage. But also longing. And regret, an odd, singing kind of sorrow. Because even if I'd wanted to now, I could never talk to anyone about my own grief or my memories, not when I was supposed to be grieving as someone else. Involuntarily my mouth opened again, but Ella had turned to a passing waiter.

'Another scone for Miss McIntyre,' she said in a choked voice. 'The raisin ones, please.'

Twelve

I ate my scone in a strange, fierce silence, worried that if I stopped chewing, I'd say something careless. What had I been *thinking*? I couldn't afford to lower my guard, not here, where I was at my most exposed since Rose Bellerby, risking everything in the throes of some long-forgotten memory.

'I suppose she . . . I mean, did Diana ever . . .' Ella Carlisle had spoken abruptly and a little awkwardly, and it took me a beat to realise what she was asking. I swallowed the rest of my mouthful. Careful now, Agnes.

'She didn't mention you to me,' I said. Hurt flickered across her face, and I added quickly, 'But that doesn't mean anything, you know. She didn't talk much about her life in London generally.'

It was true, I really hadn't heard Mrs McIntyre talk about London at all. She was only ever looking ahead, to the next posting, to setting up house, making sure Isobel's schooling was sorted. She had been a restless sort of soul, trying to fill her days with her daughter and her charity work and her ladies' luncheons, and I'd often thought that if ever there had been someone who would have benefited from working, it was her.

'How did you know her?' I asked, keen to divert attention away from me again.

'We grew up together.' Now she did reach for a scone, found the cream, the jam, the little knife that seemed to exist solely to spread jam on scones. 'Across the road from each other in Chelsea. We were best friends for years, despite being so different. I was taught by a governess, stuff for ladies, you know, while she went to school. She was terribly clever, as you know. I couldn't have thought of half the things she did. But of course, even though she would have loved to, she couldn't go all that much further. It just wasn't done for girls back then, university or higher education. And in any case, for Hector Bellingdon it was all about Alexander. Only son, you know, the golden boy. Your grandfather had such high hopes for him.'

I put my fork down. 'You knew Alexander?'

Isobel and I had sometimes secretly speculated about Diana McIntyre's older brother, who had died as a young man, just before Isobel was born. Isobel was convinced the siblings hadn't been close, because her mother never talked about him. But I had noticed Mrs McIntyre pause by his photo every now and then and gently touch the frame, her face softening before she moved on, restless and hard again. Privately I'd wondered whether he had anything to do with the fact that she could never quite settle, or that she so often seemed angry with life.

'He was older than we were, of course, but we spent time together.' Ella's earlier softness was gone. She was stabbing clotted cream at the scone's surface, but only managed to make it come apart in a mess of crumbs, jam and cream.

'Were you there when he . . . died?' I picked my words carefully, because I didn't have enough information on Alexander to be sure what Isobel would have been expected to know.

She set down her fork, her thin hands looking almost skeletal. 'No,' she said. 'I wasn't. Diana and I had fallen out by then. It was just after she got married. She refused to speak to me, see me even.' Her voice was hard and a little too loud, and I stared at her, opened my mouth to ask more questions just as Morton sidled up and silently removed her plate, averting his eyes delicately from the mushy mess.

'Can I get you anything else, Mrs Carlisle?' he enquired.

'Maybe a clean plate,' I suggested when Ella gazed around slightly hectically. 'And might we have a little more hot water, please?'

76

'Of course.' The maître d' backed away. 'Straight away. William!'

'I've managed to shock Morton.' She forced a laugh. 'If I'm not careful, I won't be allowed back.'

'I'm pretty sure that even if you came to set the place on fire, Morton would bustle up with a box of matches and help you light them, Mrs Carlisle.'

Her face relaxed a little. 'Oh please, won't you call me Ella? Mrs Carlisle was Everett's mother, and . . . well, let's just say I very much hope the similarity ends there.'

To my relief, she laughed quite naturally, and by the time Morton had returned with the plate and more water, she had changed the subject. She asked about my studies and professors, talked about the Bonfire Ball, about her naughty twin daughters, away at boarding school, about life as a surgeon's wife. I wondered if I should dig for more information about her rift with Diana, and possibly about Alexander, to add to my secret notebook. But I didn't want to risk betraying myself, and either way, there was little opportunity to interject anything, as Ella's chatter came determinedly fast, her cheeks flushed and warm.

'I've long resigned myself to being married to Everett *and* the hospital, although he's very strict about never mentioning specifics about any of the patients. From what I hear, he is quite the force of nature there. I do hope he hasn't steamrollered all over you. He's still getting used to times changing,' she went on before I could come up with something diplomatic. 'It makes him nervous, see, the modern world, when he's used to how things have always been done.' She finally drew a breath, her face still flushed, her eyes bright.

'Did you, er, mention that we were meeting today?' I asked cautiously.

'I did.' She frowned, then added, 'Although I'm not sure he heard me properly, he was rushing off.'

I nodded, relieved that I wouldn't have to field Everett

Carlisle's annoyance at my invasion of his private life, and so almost missed her suddenly adding:

'I thought he'd be interested, actually, because he knew Diana too.'

I sat up, my back very straight. 'Your husband knew M— I mean, he knew Mother?' I realised I'd sounded a little too shrill, and bit the inside of my lip.

'Well, he was a young doctor, just starting out, when Hector Bellingdon was already well established. But they lived in the same neighbourhood . . .'

Too close, I thought, a little wildly, too close to me. I needed to get out of here, and soon.

'. . . and when Hector Bellingdon – I mean when Alexander— Oh! Grey, darling!'

I turned sharply. Grey Carlisle stood behind Morton. His hair was wet and he brought with him a smell of rain.

'Were we expecting you?' Ella enquired.

'I had an errand to run and thought I'd stop by, see how you two are getting on.' Bending to kiss his mother on the cheek, he took in her breathless demeanour, the blobs of jam and tea on the tablecloth next to her cup, and then my slightly stricken expression, which I quickly rearranged into something neutral.

'Actually, I had better be going, Mrs Carlisle . . . Ella.' I started rising from my chair and Morton darted forward. 'But it was a lovely afternoon, thank you.'

'Oh, already?' She sounded disappointed, but Grey nodded. 'I'll find you both a taxi, shall I?'

'I could have got myself home just fine.' Ella gave a small huff of annoyance as she got to her feet. 'You make me sound like I'm a hundred years old.' She flashed me a conspiratorial smile. 'The Carlisle men still think women are made of glass. But of course *you* aren't, Isobel. All the things you've been telling me, about school and working. Oh, to be young again now, what I might do with my life. I could have been a politician, you know.'

She nudged me. 'I'm quite good at getting people to do what I want.'

'I don't doubt it for a minute,' I said, and she gave an unexpectedly naughty bark of laughter. I liked her, I realised suddenly, to my slight discomfiture. I really quite liked her. Maybe, if things had been different, she might have become what she wanted: a motherly friend to a lost girl. All the same, I was profoundly glad that the afternoon was drawing to a close.

I nipped to the powder room, then took my time walking back to the foyer, hoping it would mean that Grey and Ella were about to depart when I rejoined them. No such luck.

'Grey, you really didn't need to check up on me.' They had their backs to me and Ella was fussing with her gloves. 'I *am* taking care of myself, I promise you. Your father's on at me night and day, too.'

'You look so tired. Father said he made you an appointment with Dr Brookes for next week.'

'He did.' Ella sounded irritated. 'Even though I've told him countless times that I don't want to see Dr Brookes. Isn't there anyone else?'

'Brookes is the best, Mum, truly. You've got to go.'

'Of course I'll go. Your father is most insistent. But I am not happy.'

They'd been speaking in hushed voices, Grey scowling with the effort of convincing his mother to do whatever it was he wanted her to. I was just hanging back, trying to decide whether to slink back into the Palm Court, pretending I'd forgotten something, when Morton swept in through the door.

'Taxi's just coming now, ma'am. And a separate one for Miss McIntyre?' He looked past them in my direction and they both turned.

'Oh, we can drop her off on the way.' Ella smiled at me, clearly relieved to extract herself from her conversation. 'You said you

79

live in Pimlico? Grey, go and wait for the taxi outside.' Beneath her rosy flush, she did look tired now, perhaps even a bit glassy-eyed.

'I'm sorry to hear you've been unwell,' I said after a slight pause. 'Only I couldn't help overhearing . . .'

'Oh, that.' She made a show of peering out into the gloom beyond the glass doors. Grey was standing there chatting with the doorman.

'He worries about you,' I said, watching him offer the man a cigarette, holding out his lighter for him.

'I wish he wouldn't.' She frowned. 'He's got so much on, constantly on duty, up at all hours.'

'Probably comes with the job – worrying, I mean.' I peered out into the evening too, as if our conversation was just a casual exchange. 'What's the reason for his concern?'

The corners of her mouth quirked up. 'You're a curious kind of person, I noticed that earlier.'

I waited, letting the silence grow a little. I'd noticed that people tended to fill an empty space if you let it go on long enough.

'Pain,' she said after a while. She didn't look at me, just gestured at her stomach, then, hesitating, towards the lower end of her torso.

I nodded. 'Who is Dr Brookes?'

'An old friend of the family, obstetrician at Guy's.'

'Ah, I see. And you don't . . .'

'No. Don't get me wrong, I'm not squeamish, really. You can't be, living with a doctor. But even I have my limits. It would be so awkward to lie on his table in the morning and then sit across the dinner table from him at night. However, Everett insists, and now he's made that appointment.'

'You could always see another doctor,' I suggested. 'A woman, even. There are plenty of very good female obstetricians.'

She choked out a laugh and turned to me. 'I'd like to meet the person who dares tell Everett Carlisle that his wife is being treated by a lady doctor.' She caught herself just in time. 'I'm sorry. I'm sure you're doing brilliantly. As I said, he sometimes has a little trouble keeping up with the times. And anyway,' she said in a final sort of way, 'he's given me something for the pain and it's already helped me so much. I'm actually feeling quite bouncy these days.'

Ella was quiet on the drive back, and so was I. Grey's valiant efforts at conversation – about the disgraceful state of London's streets, the recent bouts of fog, and the young queen Elizabeth – filled the taxi as houses glided by outside the window, the streets less bustling the further away we got from Piccadilly. Only a few more minutes and I'd be home, where the lodgers, my books and Katia's savoury *kugel* would be waiting. We were turning down towards the river now, drawing up at a row of tall houses on Chelsea Embankment.

'Oh Isobel, stay inside. The taxi'll take you home, Grey is going back to the hospital anyway,' Ella protested as Grey helped her out.

'Thank you, that's very kind, but I'll walk from here,' I said firmly, already on the street.

'Well, if you're sure . . .'

'Very much so, it's only a little further. Now, goodbye and keep well.' I injected a very audible note of finality into the farewell, and her face fell, only to brighten again immediately.

'Oh, I've had the most splendid idea,' she said delightedly. 'Grey, we must ask Isobel to the dinner on Saturday, don't you think?'

'The fundraising dinner for the Bonfire Ball?' Grey sounded a touch doubtful. 'I wonder, would Father be all that keen, I mean that one of his students . . .' But at the sight of his mother's enthusiasm, he nodded quickly. 'Of course, Mum.'

'Oh, it would be lovely. Do say yes, Isobel.'

No. Under no circumstances.

'It would be a chance to hobnob with other doctors,' she added enticingly. 'Connections are so important; those consultant posts are very hard to come by.'

True enough, and equally true that I'd need all the help I could get to keep up with the other students, who had the distinct advantage of being male and in possession of a plethora of uncles and fathers with practices and connections, while I just had dead Sir Hector. But a whole dinner, up close with Everett Carlisle, who'd known Diana, known her family? See, there it was already, the slip-up. *My* family. I had to stay in character. Others there would have known the Bellingdons too, might have kept in contact with Diana, seen a photo of Isobel even. And yet, wouldn't it be the ultimate proof that I could do it?

'Do say yes,' Ella said. 'Let us spoil you a little.'

Her eyes were warm on mine, her smile reached for me the way it had at the Ritz, and I pressed down any lingering misgiving. She'd just keep asking, she'd wheedle and charm, would be kind and inviting. There was nothing for it. I would chance it.

'Thank you very much for the invitation,' I said. 'I'll be there.'

Thirteen

Mrs Schwartz had got into Shostakovich today. The floor of my room vibrated with her energetic playing as, late on Saturday afternoon, I surveyed my dress options for a dinner party that would include a fancy house on the river, a group of doctors who knew Isobel's mother and grandparents, and the potential for things to go very, very wrong.

Between hospital and coursework, I'd been rushed off my feet since the Ritz, with no time at all to think about what to wear. So it would either have to be a tea dress I'd made myself for student dances, or a long navy gown that Mrs McIntyre had bought just weeks before she died.

Isobel had stood on a little platform in Botts department store while I guarded the packages and parcels we'd amassed in preparation for France and university life. Mrs McIntyre had just settled on the classic navy-blue dress, the bodice structured and high-cut, with a simple long skirt. Isobel, who had never been particularly fussy about clothes, had cocked her head at herself in the mirror.

'What do you think, Agnes?' She had turned to where I was sitting in the corner. I'd been miles away, thinking of ways to dress up my blouse and skirt without spending a fortune, and wondering how empty the house would be once Isobel was gone.

'The green one is beautiful,' I said. 'The waist is so tiny, and I love the huge skirt.'

The shop girl had nodded vigorously, but Mrs McIntyre had pursed her lips.

'I think we'll go with the navy. It'll take you anywhere, darling.'

Smothering a slightly hysterical laugh at the thought of what Mrs McIntyre would say about the 'anywhere' on offer tonight, I tried to make the navy dress swish a little. I pictured myself walking into a room full of beautiful people, a room where Grey Carlisle would be raising his eyebrows at me in that laughing, mocking way he had. The dress moved sluggishly against my hand, settled back. Mrs McIntyre hadn't believed much in swishing, favouring muted colours and severe cuts. To be fair, in the years after the war it had been a struggle to put together any kind of wardrobe, fun or otherwise, but even when rationing had finished, she hadn't deviated much from her conservative, pragmatic approach to clothing, talking about *fashion plates* and *fast girls* as if one inevitably led to the other.

I let the dress go and watched it settle silently on the hanger, remembering a much earlier day than that afternoon in Botts. I was ten, had just arrived at the McIntyres' carrying my small suitcase filled with clothes made by my mother. Bright fabrics had erupted into the dark, sparsely furnished attic room like a colourful sandstorm, lighting it up with colour and verve and cutting momentarily through my homesickness. Mrs McIntyre had held up my coat with its rainbow padding. It had been made almost entirely from scraps, but cleverly so, creating a quilted pattern, and was cut at such a jaunty angle to just above the thigh that you didn't really notice how patched together it was. She had gingerly fingered the hem of a pair of wide-legged trousers embroidered with an intricate pattern of little pecking birds and stitched-on flowers, before dropping them back on to the bed with a moue of distaste.

It came out often, that moue of distaste. When I spoke without being spoken to and said exactly what I thought. When I left the house without expressly asking for permission, like I'd done back home. When I was trying to teach Isobel the polka and Mrs McIntyre came upon us careening around the room and laughing uproariously, Isobel wrapped in my tassel-fringed scarf

84

like a Hungarian peasant. When I told stories about bold prin-
cesses and wicked fairies and shoe-shop-owning Cinderellas.
Other things, too. Once, I had involuntarily reached for Mrs
McIntyre's hand during church; stupid really, but 'Abide with
Me' had pushed a hot ache behind my eyes, and I was suddenly
missing my mother so much I thought I would die. Without
looking, she had removed my hand and placed it back on my
lap, nodding at Isobel, who sat with her legs crossed at the
ankles, hair nestling tidily against the collar of her dress.

Quite the free spirit, she'd say, referring to what she called my
'antics', with another one of her moues. *Little girls should be seen
and not heard, did your mother not teach you that?* At ten, I couldn't
understand why she didn't seem to like me, I could just feel it:
that same whiff that had often followed me and Mum in the
East End, the slow seep of shame, the hint of dirtiness. Being
different, which had never mattered when I was with Mum, but
which made me feel gritty and itchy now under Mrs McIntyre's
cool, appraising gaze and her views on what was proper and
just-so. I stood out like a sore thumb here, this scrawny East
End evacuee with her outlandish clothes. *Trousers*, I'd heard Mrs
McIntyre mutter to one of her cronies. *Trousers!*

She didn't throw Mum's clothes away; we were in the midst of
rationing, after all. *I can make my own clothes*, I told her. *Mum taught
me, I just need a bit of fabric.* But the fabric she gave me was dark and
utilitarian, and bit by bit, muted shades and conservative shapes
replaced my mother's bright garments. Isobel and I stopped dancing the polka, and news came of my mother's death. Then one
day I sat in church in navy and grey, hands folded, ankles neatly
crossed, and realised that I'd allowed Mrs McIntyre to shame all
my mother's colour and life right out of me.

I gave the navy a vicious poke. Well, she'd done me a favour
really, hadn't she? Her disapproval of Agnes had been an easy
guidepost for how to become Isobel, and she'd given me a ready-
made costume to wear to boot. I'd never changed much about

85

Isobel's wardrobe. Of course I'd tweaked it, had made myself a new blouse, turned a collar, repurposed a skirt. But it all tended to fit in with what she had worn, almost as though dressing like her gave an extra layer of security to my masquerade. Or maybe it was simply superstition; that the moment I started deviating from her, I would lose it all.

Tonight it was even more important than usual to keep Isobel's mask in place, to be quiet and blend in, to observe rather than stand out. And yet – I closed my eyes and saw a burst of bright fabric, tiny stitched birds and cheeky flowers skipping by in a whirl of colour – for once it might have been nice to wear something less like her and a little more like me.

Mrs Schwartz suddenly leaned into the keys as if to tell me to stop wallowing in silly nostalgia, and I quickly pulled the navy dress over my head. Isobel had been a year younger, but we'd been the same size, so it settled easily around me now. Tweaking the sleeves into place and smoothing down the skirt, I closed my eyes, spared a quick thought for the girl who'd smiled at me from a platform in Botts department store, then stepped in front of the mirror.

A pale, slim woman was looking cautiously back at me, hair gathered in a soft bun at the nape of her neck, eyes wide and unblinking. I looked shy and a little unsure and quite serious, and – I felt a mixture of triumph and unease – more like Isobel than ever. I watched the young woman in the mirror dip her head as she picked up the little hat that matched the dress, and a pair of gloves, and had to blink away a strange rush of unreality as department-store Isobel crept into the mirror in front of me and the dress, *her* dress, rustled against my legs. Then I shook myself, tossed a few things into my handbag, clamped it under my arm and left without looking at her again.

'Izabella?' Mrs Schwartz called from the drawing room as I walked past, mentally running through my notes on Mrs

McIntyre's extended family, which seemed to develop more holes the closer I got to the dinner party. 'Come in and be admired.'

'Oh, Mrs Schwartz, I'll be late.'

'Very fashionable, then,' she said serenely. 'Come.'

The lodgers, crowding around the table as usual, politely rose to their feet at my entrance, while Jakob, now the one behind the piano, launched into a fanfare. At Mrs Schwartz's beckoning, I turned, raised my arms and tried to make the skirt twirl.

'It's . . . nice,' Marek ventured.

'But quite, well, quite simple, no?' Mrs Schwartz moved her head slowly from side to side to take in the navy in all its muted glory. 'Very blue.'

'I suppose so.' I looked down at it and shrugged.

'You look beautiful,' said Jakob gallantly. 'Magdalena, let the girl go, do.'

'Yes, she doesn't want to hang around with us old codgers.' Jaroslaw had fetched the tray of schnapps glasses from the buffet, along with the bottle. 'Well, it is a celebration, isn't it?' he said at Mrs Schwartz's look of consternation. 'Izabella painting the town and all?'

'Hardly painting the town,' I said, hoping Mrs Schwartz wouldn't pick tonight to decide that she should act as my chaperone. 'Just the home of a doctor from the hospital, very well known. Everett Carlisle. He's having a small gathering, all doctors.'

She nodded gravely, as if she had expected no less of me. 'But I do think it needs a bit more.' She disappeared down the hall. 'Katia!' I heard her call.

Jaroslaw held out a little glass, and I had to laugh. 'Have one on me, please. I need my wits about me.'

Mrs Schwartz's heavy footfall came back down the hall, followed by Katia, who smiled and pretended to swoon when she caught sight of me, then plucked a stack of fabric from Mrs Schwartz's arms.

'*Szal.*' It unfolded in a flash of rich green satin, and I saw that it was embroidered all over with intricate patterns of vines and trees, birds and animals, in silver and gold thread. Katia shook it a little, and the fabric shimmered and shone in the light, the creatures moving as if they were coming alive in her hands.

'A stole.' I was unable to take my eyes off it.

'A gift,' Mrs Schwartz said softly. 'For my father. He was supposed to conduct *Peter and the Wolf* in '39 – Prokofiev, a very new piece then, Russian, beautiful, modern. But . . .' She ran her finger across the tiny snapping creatures that I now realised were wolves. 'He was arrested shortly before. Katia saved this when he and my brother . . .'

She fell silent, and she and Katia draped the stole around my shoulders, muttering softly among themselves. The lodgers settled on their chairs again, humming their approval. Jakob played a haunting tune on the piano.

'Peter,' Mrs Schwartz said with a nod at the melody. 'About to go into the woods.' She ran her hands down my arms to smooth the fabric, her grip warm and firm as she reached around to pull it straight. For a moment, oddly, I found myself leaning into her touch.

'Oh, play the wolf, Jakob,' Gregor begged. 'It's my favourite.'

'Just because you play the horn. We need something cheerful. The bird, Jakob. She's meant to go to a party.' Jaroslaw got up and stood by the piano to tap out a rhythm while Katia pinned the stole carefully in place with a brooch elaborately decorated with vines. When she stood back, I saw her put her hand on Mrs Schwartz's shoulder and squeeze it.

The tassels slithered against my skin and I caught one of the silky fronds in my hand. The vivid green and gold shone against the navy of the dress, deepening it like the Northern Lights illuminating a midnight sky. I thought about my plan to slip into the party and blend into the background, observe and be quiet. Be Isobel.

Jakob was playing another melody now, this one lower, more threatening. The wolf creeping forward in discordant minor keys as if ready to pounce. I pushed away a rush of goose flesh prickling up my arms and smiled at Mrs Schwartz and Katia.

'I love it, thank you.'

Fourteen

Three large red-brick houses stood along a stretch of road called Chelsea Row. Each facade was differently constructed and decorated, but they shared the same kind of brickwork, patches of green framing stately entryways; like siblings, I thought, different versions of one and the same person. The Carlisle residence, the one on the left, was narrow but stretched three storeys high, with beautiful cornicing and a turreted gable and tall windows through which light spilled out on to the footpath. A man in a butler's uniform beckoned me inside and I stepped across the threshold, looking around in wonder at the tiled entrance hall, the portrait-lined corridor, the magnificent upward sweep of the stairs.

I could hear a babble of conversation and barks of laughter. The butler arched an eyebrow in the direction of Mrs Schwartz's stole, but I shook my head and drew the gleaming fabric more securely around my shoulders as he led the way down the corridor.

The party was crowded, much more so than I'd expected. At least twenty people were dotted around the long drawing room, some obviously there for their wealth, others perhaps to represent the illustrious part of the medical world. Among the latter I recognised Dr Quintrell, an instrumental figure in the recent poliovirus research, who was talking with an older man, both with dignified wives by their sides. An ancient-looking man with a bushy beard, not unlike the portrait with the bone saw in the hospital's administrative corridor, was deep in conversation with a younger doctor I thought I'd seen on one of the medical wards. Thrill skittered through me at the prospect of talking with these people, of being, as Hector Bellingdon's granddaughter, a bona fide part of it all. But then I gave myself a hard mental shake, reminding myself to stay on my guard. They might have known the Bellingdons, were about to throw a shared memory at me that I would be expected to know about. No matter how much I wanted to be a part of things, I couldn't afford to slip up, not for a single moment.

'Isobel, so lovely that you could come, I'm so glad!' Ella Carlisle was suddenly there, petite and pretty in a rose-coloured gown, nipped in at the waist and flaring out beautifully, with miles of satiny tulle in the skirt. She looked a bit tired, I thought, and her eyes were overly bright in her thin, powdered face, her skin both flushed and pale at the same time. But her smile was as warm as it had been last time I saw her. 'Everett is running late, so we're not even close to dinner. But let me introduce you round. Ah, Sophia . . .'

An older woman, stately in purple brocade, with many jewelled combs in her hair, advanced. 'Lovely do, Ella dear, although a bit too much rabbiting on about the National Health Service for my taste. I only hope I won't be seated anywhere near that young man over there.' She pointed at the Thamesbury physician still in animated conversation with the bushy-bearded old man. 'He can't stop talking about it, such a bore.'

I refrained from saying that the National Health Service certainly wasn't as much a bore to ordinary people as it might be for people hung with jewelled combs and living in houses like these, and nodded politely.

'And all the last dahlias in your garden were blown over last night. I had a peek through the back window – you really must do up that room, you know. You should have your gardener—'

'Sophia,' Ella cut in, 'I'd like you to meet Isobel McIntyre. Diana's daughter – Diana Bellingdon, remember?'

Now, I thought wildly, as Sophia thrust her face right into mine, the jewelled combs bobbing up and down, it would happen *now*. My heart was beating so loudly, I thought surely she could hear me. How stupid, how infernally short-sighted to risk it all . . .

'Goodness, so it is!'

I exhaled a long, slow breath.

'Melanie, come here!'

I couldn't have asked for a better person to introduce me than bossy, bullish Sophia, who had my arm clamped under hers and was holding court with my story.

'Hector Bellingdon's granddaughter, remember? Tall, frightfully clever.'

'Hector Bellingdon operated on my father, saved his life, you know.'

'Goodness, what a small world. And how lovely for you, Mrs Carlisle.'

'Brookes, Brookie! Come and hear this.'

As more people joined – wives, mostly – Sophia fleshed out my family history for the benefit of those who hadn't known the Bellingdons, which was highly convenient for me, not least because I wasn't required to say much at all. 'Lost everything in the crash of '29, poor as church mice, had to let go of the house and pretty much everything else.' She leaned in, people murmured and swayed, and I nodded gravely, busy storing away new snippets of information. 'And then of course that other horrible business . . .' She paused for dramatic effect.

Horrible business? Involuntarily I found myself leaning in along with everyone else, was about to ask a question when a hand was suddenly clamped around my wrist and Ella tugged me away sharply.

'I need to whisk her around before dinner, which is late – I do apologise – because Everett's been held up. Don't mind Sophia, she's a frightful gossip,' she added as she towed me towards the bushy-bearded man. Wondering what the gossip actually was, I looked back over my shoulder to where Melanie and Sophia were whispering with the man called Brookie.

'Is that Dr Brookes, the specialist you're—'

'Hush,' she said, a hectic flush blooming across her cheeks. I didn't blame her for not being keen to be treated by any of the doctors here; it would be like being examined by an uncle. 'There, Lady Edith is lovely, and her husband, Sir Fensby, has been at the Royal College of Surgeons for ever. And there's Mr Payne. His niece is here too, somewhere, I think in the winter garden. He'll be a good one for you to meet.'

I met them all and it was glorious: Dr Quintrell and his conversation partner, Mr Payne, a retired surgeon from Guy's. The bushy-beard Sir Fensby and the younger physician he'd been talking to, Dr Smethwick, who'd bored Sophia about the NHS. Some squinted a little doubtfully when Ella told them I was a student, but they soon warmed up, not just at the chance to talk about their specialities but, of course, at the mention of the Bellingdons.

'Old medical family,' Mr Payne said portentously. 'It stays in the family, you know, it's in the blood.'

In the blood, was it? I refrained from rolling my eyes. I'd always found the old boys' network a bit irritating: the way it sorted everyone into belonging and not belonging according to rules only understood by those on the inside. Quintrell and Payne were nodding at me encouragingly, however, and I realised with a small cringe that I was currently coasting very happily on the very same kind of nepotism myself.

'I'll do my best to live up to it,' I said quickly, keen to change the subject. 'What I actually wanted to ask you, Mr Payne, is your view on accessing a strangulated hernia. I'm shadowing a patient on the male surgical ward, and—'

Startled, old Payne peered at me as if seeing me properly for the first time 'Surely that's not something they teach women?'

I frowned, a little surprised. 'Of course they teach it. Why wouldn't they?'

'Well,' he gave a small huff of disapproval, 'I know we're supposed to be going with the times, but women's sensibilities are so very different, their constitutions so delicate . . .'

'I don't think anyone who's seen Miss McIntyre on the ward could call her constitution delicate.' An amused voice came from behind me. Grey Carlisle had drifted over with a group of younger people. 'Or seen the kind of weaponry she keeps on her person,' he added in my ear.

'Which she is sorely tempted to use on several someones at the moment,' I muttered darkly.

Mr Payne was now lecturing a girl in red about the glass of champagne she was holding. She nodded, but I noticed her fidgeting, as if she was going to run and drink it anyway the moment his back was turned. Her dress was different, very modern, the skirt draped so cleverly around her legs that she seemed to be floating atop a ball of scarlet tulle. It was something that Mrs McIntyre would mostly definitely have called 'loud', and I smiled to myself in sudden recognition; it was something my mother might have made.

'You scrub up nicely,' Grey said. 'Emphasis on nice, not on scrubbing up,' he added quickly. 'Which is to say, you look nice.' He cleared his throat. 'Normal, anyhow.'

'Maybe you should stop while you're ahead,' I suggested. 'Did you think I was going to show up in a white coat covered in blood? Although maybe I should have,' I added with another dark look at Payne. 'Keep people on their toes, you know.'

'We appreciate your restraint.' He smiled and, relaxing cautiously, I smiled back. He must have had a good night's sleep for once, because his face was bright, the curve of his mouth softer than at the hospital, where he always seemed a bit guarded. His eyes, a darker green in the low light, held something a little unnerving, and unexpectedly I felt my heart hitch slightly.

Relief, I told myself firmly, to be on the up when I'd feared I might be going down, thrilled to find my place here after all, Payne's view on my delicate sensibilities notwithstanding. And yet this was different from the adrenaline of a narrow escape; it was lighter and brighter, zinging up and down my back, and even though I wanted to step away, I didn't. Madness, really, in a room filled with illustrious people, where I needed to be on the lookout, to be gazing up at Grey Carlisle, who was staring back at me as if we were locked in a contest.

'And how are you enjoying the evening, Mr Carlisle?' I said, making my tone light and mocking.

'Very much, Miss McIntyre.' He raised his eyebrows.

'Oh, do call her Isobel, Grey.' Ella suddenly appeared next to us, looking flustered. 'Where could your father possibly have got to? Cook is about to have a fit of the vapours. Mabel, dear, there you are, so lovely you could come.'

It was only then that Grey broke away, and I found myself standing in a cluster of young people: the girl in red tulle, an assortment of men, and finally the girl whom Ella had addressed as Mabel. Everything about her was soft and pretty, her hair gleamed in neat waves, her dress was elegant and obviously expensive.

'This is Isobel, she's a student at the hospital,' Ella said to the group. 'Grey, make the introductions, please. Oh, wait, I see Clarke. I'm sorry, I've got to nip over to make sure he calms Cook down.'

She disappeared to talk to the butler who'd opened the door to me earlier, and Mabel stepped into her space, came to stand close to Grey. Her eyes flicked up and down my navy dress in subtle assessment, lingered on Mrs Schwartz's stole, then she slowly laid a hand on his arm.

'We wondered where you'd got to, darling. Nice to meet you, er, Isobel, was it?'

'Yes. And you.' My words tripped into each other, crowding

out whatever had been zinging across my skin just seconds ago. 'Lovely,' I added irrelevantly.

'You'll know Harry Jenkins?' Mabel waved a casual hand in his direction.

'Miss McIntyre.' Jenkins inclined his head in what he obviously felt was a gracious acceptance of my unexpected appearance at such an illustrious do.

'And this is James, and Bobby.' Two young men, rather mischievous-looking, and identically impeccable in dark suits, bent over my hand.

'We call them the evil twins.' The girl in scarlet tulle skipped forward, her skirt bouncing cheerfully. 'And since no one introduced me . . . No, don't splutter, James, I know you were ogling poor Isobel. Don't mind him, Isobel, truly. Mrs Carlisle was very kind to include us tonight, even though we don't know a saw from a scalpel. My uncle is a fellow at the Royal College, and I've practically grown up with Grey, so I guess maybe that's why. Anyway, I'm Louisa, but everyone calls me Lulu. And I like your stole, it's *fabulous*.'

'So is your dress,' I said, leaning in to inspect it more closely. 'Are those inverted pleats?'

'Yes, clever you.' She gave a little twirl and watched as the dress fanned out, retreated. 'No one needs to know that I had a moment of ghastly realisation in the car and just *knew* I looked like a puffball.'

'Not at all. A puffball's a mushroom,' I said. 'Bulbous, white and lots of spores . . .' Aware of pretty Mabel shifting next to me and the young men looking at me as if they'd just come across a strange insect circling a lamp, I forced myself to stop. 'I think you look like a lovely cloud at sunset.'

Lulu gave a small gurgle of laughter and nudged Grey. 'I like her.'

'Yes, I rather thought you would.' Grey smiled and turned away, and we didn't look at each other again.

Fifteen

Grey and Mabel were perfect for each other. She teased him just the right amount, knew what to say to all the old doctors, batted her eyelashes in a way that could only be called expert. And Grey, seemingly the only man in the room under thirty-five who wasn't covertly watching her lean and laugh and pout prettily, clearly held her in his sway.

I'd asked how they knew each other, but only half listened to her answer – something about a cricket match gone awry in the park and a silly friend being late – as I tried to figure out why it felt so strange to think of Grey Carlisle having a girlfriend. Although if I had, I'd have probably picked someone exactly like her: soft and feminine, her impeccably cut dress moving as if it was an extension of her in a way I'd never achieve in a million years, whether in Isobel's dress or any other.

I watched them too – it was hard not to; they were so striking a couple that they drew the little group of young people around them like a centrifugal force. Lulu was talking a mile a minute, while Harry Jenkins, I noticed, was watching Mabel with a hungry expression.

'Er, Mr Jenkins, what did you think of the prostate surgery last week?' I cut through Lulu's chatter, feeling that maybe he needed saving from himself.

'Admirably performed,' he said, a little absent-mindedly. 'Medicine's making such strides.'

'Oh, that's right, you're a doctor too.' Lulu gazed at me with round-eyed wonder. 'They don't often come in the female variety, do they?' She gave a huff of laughter, then, 'How terribly clever you must be, don't you think, Harry? Harry?'

But Jenkins was back to staring at Mabel and, I decided, beyond help. 'If you'll excuse me, I'm going to powder my nose.'

I found a fancy little washroom the size of a large cupboard under the stairs, and had just stepped back out into the corridor when I heard a familiar harsh voice from the front door. 'I'm terribly sorry, Ella. Please give everyone my apologies. I'm just going up to change. Won't be a moment.'

Footsteps came towards me, headed for the stairs. Quickly I tried to duck back into the loo, but it was too late. Halfway up the stairs, Everett Carlisle caught sight of me lurking in the shadows below him.

'What on earth are *you* doing here? Ella!' He gestured towards me, 'Since when do we invite my students to my house?'

Ella turned and saw me. 'Oh, you're impossible, Ev. I did tell you. She's Diana's daughter, Hector Bellingdon's granddaughter?'

'Ah. Right.' This seemed to bring him up short, and he looked at me, actually *looked* at me, as if seeing me for the first time. 'You've got some big shoes to fill,' he said, still brusque but not quite as dismissive any more, before disappearing up the stairs.

I should have been happy, ecstatic even, that we were now in the stage of shoes needing to be filled, which I hadn't been anywhere close to before. And I *had* built my entire application around Isobel's grandfather precisely for this kind of thing. Everyone used their connections, didn't they? All the same, a small part of me wished that what he saw when he looked at me wasn't just Hector Bellingdon's granddaughter, but me, as myself.

'Well, I suppose the roast'll keep a little longer.' Ella sighed and shepherded me back down the corridor. 'Doctors' wives have to have a lot of patience, that's all there is to it. You'll see.'

'I won't be a doctor's wife, though, will I?' I said, my mind still on Carlisle's expression. Then I smiled at her. 'At least, I'm not planning on it.'

'Give it time.' She laughed easily, then linked her arm through mine. 'Actually, now that we have a few minutes until dinner, there's something I wanted to show you.'

Walking ahead of me, she opened a door that brought us into a small private sitting room. Lined with bookshelves, it was comfortably crowded with knick-knacks and books, and a small bureau covered with paper. Picture windows overlooked the garden, a sweep of lawn lit in patches from the streetlights below.

'What a pretty little room,' I said, looking around.

'It used to be my mother's. Now, where did I put it . . .'

'Your mother's? You grew up in this house?'

'Yes, sad to think just how far I've gone in life, isn't it?'

Ella rummaged a little hectically behind the sofa, and I kept out of her way, moving over to the one wall without shelves. It was crammed with framed photos and small painted portraits, and a variety of clear glass frames containing carefully pressed flowers that hung suspended like gossamer. In the middle was a wedding photo of Ella and Everett. Everett sat in a chair looking serious, and Ella, impossibly young and small, stood with a hand on his shoulder. I lingered over a picture of Everett decked out in some kind of sporting outfit – rugby, perhaps? There were lots of pictures of cheeky-looking twin girls, and many more of Grey at various stages: a baby with watchful eyes; a little boy hanging over the edge of a pond sailing a toy boat; astride a horse, long legs dangling down; a teenager in a dark gown. It gave me a small hitch of envy, watching a whole family's life played out in such detail as if watching them on a stage.

'You're such a tease.' Mabel's voice came through from the drawing room, which, I realised, was just on the other side of a door at the far side. I leaned in to examine a photo of Grey behind a piano, his hands poised on the keys, and wondered what Everett Carlisle thought of Mabel. He probably approved of whatever occupation she had; something charitable or chic, like working for a respectable ladies' magazine. *She* wasn't elbow-deep in bedpans, that was for certain.

'Here it is,' Ella said. 'Clarke must have tidied it away again.' She held up a large photo album, old-fashioned and stiff, each page featuring black-and-white photos on thick paper. 'Now, I hope this won't make you sad, but I thought you'd like to see it anyway. It's just lovely.' Riffling through the pages, she stopped to tap on a picture. 'This was taken just before Diana's wedding.'

I leaned over the album and swallowed back a small, startled noise when I saw Mrs McIntyre. She was young in the picture, her mouth not yet as set as later, her face smooth and unlined. She held up a carriage clock, grinning at the photographer. I didn't think I'd ever seen her grin like that.

'My mother was her godmother, and because Diana's family . . . Well, they were hard times then, and Diana was at our house a lot. That's me.' She tapped the next picture. In it, Diana had her arm around Ella, who looked young and lovely, head turned away to smile at someone outside the picture.

I turned the page and recognised, with a start, the young man from Diana McIntyre's mantelpiece. Her brother, Alexander.

'Alexander was there too?' I said it casually, as if I knew all about him.

Ella looked at him, her finger poised above the picture but not tapping this time. 'Yes, he was around,' she said. 'He was finishing his residency, with excellent prospects of being taken on. Nothing but the best for Hector Bellingdon's son, of course.'

The photo I remembered had been a formal portrait, stilted and cool. This was a snapshot, filled with movement and laughter, Alexander's head tilted up to look at the camera. He was brandishing something at the lens, a roundish shape.

'Is that a ball?' I peered at it.

She smiled. 'A vase. Alex swore it looked like a rugby ball and threatened to throw it. Almost gave Di a heart attack, because it was a wedding present from the Royal College of Physicians.'

'Did it break?' I asked.

'Of course not,' she said. Now she did touch his photo, though not briskly as before; instead she rested her finger on it briefly in the way Mrs McIntyre had done with the framed portrait on her mantelpiece. 'Diana caught it. They were both good at sports.' There was a hitch in her voice, then she tapped a larger photo at the bottom of the page more forcefully. 'Here she is in her wedding dress. Doesn't she look like Diana the Huntress?'

I nodded. Mrs McIntyre rising like a Valkyrie from the stiffest, straightest wedding dress I'd ever seen was familiar territory for me, because she'd kept a similar portrait on the mantelpiece wherever we'd moved. I bent closer, then suddenly froze, blinking rapidly.

'She'd had a few fittings already, but she still wasn't happy with the back of the dress – she had quite particular tastes – so I said bring it here for Silkie to have a look at it. At that point they weren't all that well off really, couldn't afford all these alterations she wanted . . .'

But the sound of Ella's voice had grown muted and woolly in the background, as if someone had taken a blanket and tossed it over both of us. Because right there, in the photo in front of me . . . But it couldn't be, surely not . . .

Ella had broken off in mid sentence, perhaps noticing that something was amiss. 'I'm sorry,' she said. 'I can see how painful it still is. I didn't mean to be thoughtless. Shall we leave it for now?'

I could feel her thin shoulder bumping mine as she patted my arm, but I didn't pay her any attention. I wasn't even looking at Mrs McIntyre, who wasn't yet a Mrs but still Diana Bellingdon. My eyes had snagged on something else entirely. A young woman crouching at Diana's feet, holding the hem of the train. Her hair was pinned back beneath a cap and she was half turned away, but there was something so achingly familiar about the way her back was rounded, one hand cradling the fabric, the other reaching for a pin. In the photo, her pincushion was nothing more than an irregular blob on her wrist, but my mind rushed to fill in the details, saw the bulbous round of a felted yellow daisy stitched with eyes, the green armband embroidered with leaves and a tiny butterfly on one side.

'This girl,' I said, keeping my voice steady with enormous effort. 'The seamstress. Who . . . who is she?'

Ella looked confused, then bent to inspect the photo more closely. 'She wasn't a seamstress,' she said, and her voice was curt. 'Silkie was a maid.'

'A maid?' I asked faintly.

'Yes, she worked in our house. She was around the same age as Diana and me, a little older maybe. And . . . well, we were friends, the three of us. Best friends, actually, even though she was a servant.' There was something brittle in her voice now. 'Here, take the picture, why don't you, it's ever such a lovely one.' Her voice was still hard, though, and she scraped at the edges of the photo impatiently.

'Silkie?' I said. 'That was her name?'

'We called her that because she was mad about clothes. And so good at sewing too, could make anything look—'

'Beautiful,' I finished woodenly. 'I don't know why she, why Mother . . .'

But the word swelled in my mouth, filled it with a sour, sharp taste. There was a strange whooshing in my head and I didn't hear Ella's reply, my hand automatically reaching for the picture she'd detached from the album.

Because there she was, clear as day. The woman kneeling at Mrs McIntyre's feet was my mother.

Sixteen

It wasn't possible. A trick of the eye, an illusion. My mother couldn't possibly be a maid called Silkie in a photo album belonging to a woman I'd only met a few days ago. My mother was called Daisy, and she'd lived in a small, shabby shop on Bell Street. She couldn't have known Diana McIntyre and Ella Carlisle.

Well, yes, said my mind, stupidly logical at all times, of course she could. My memories of leaving London were rushed and hazy, a child's recollection at best, but I had always assumed that my placement with the McIntyres had been chosen by the government. But what if it hadn't been? What if Mum had known Diana McIntyre – stop being stupid, Agnes, of course she *knew* her; wasn't she right there on her bloody *knees*, pinning up her hem? – and had asked her to take me in as a favour? Then what, in turn, had Diana McIntyre known about us, about me? And how had *I* never known this, that Mum had once been a maid for a fancy family, living in a beautiful house on the river only a few miles as the crow flew from what would become our home in the East End? She'd so rarely talked about anything in her past, only ever looked to the future, so bright, so full of possibility: *Any day now, Agnes, we'll be out of here, you and I, together* . . .

By the time we'd gone through to dinner, I felt winded with confusion. Mercifully, I had been seated next to Harry Jenkins, who got stuck into the wine and didn't require me to do much more than nod at his monologue and move pieces of cold fish around my plate as a brand-new, much bigger worry suddenly occurred to me. I was fairer than Mum, but I shared the curly hair that sprang up rebelliously when least convenient, her slightly slanted eyes, the stubborn curve of her mouth. Would Ella – I could hardly wrap my mind around the irony of it all – recognise me as the daughter of her maid, her old friend?

I caught her eyeing me with some concern and quickly hitched a smile in place. My face felt warm and thin, almost see-through, as if every facial expression, every twitch or gesture, might give me away in new and unforeseen ways. I pointed to my plate and mimed enjoying the smoked mackerel, which still sat there, its fins glinting slightly, its tiny eye dull in the light from the candelabra. She seemed reassured, and smiled back before dipping her head to listen to something her neighbour was saying. Studying her out of the corner of my eye, I tried to picture her young and slender, exclaiming at Diana's dress, laughing with her, with my mum.

Someone materialised next to me and deposited something new on my plate that looked like meat suspended in jelly.

We were friends . . . Best friends. It did explain why Mum had sent me to the McIntyres in particular. But what it didn't explain was why Diana McIntyre hadn't treated me like you would a friend's daughter, a *best* friend's daughter. Not like someone whose presence brought forth a constant whiff of distaste, and whose independence and difference had to be systematically ironed out of her, like the sharp pleats on Isobel's school skirt. I frowned down at the meat wobbling on my plate, and something bitter and itchy made me shift in my chair. For Diana McIntyre, clearly friendship couldn't really cross the class divide. She had obviously felt beholden enough to Silkie to keep me on, but not enough to make me an actual part of the family. And I – unknowingly, ironically – had gone on to become exactly the same sort-of-maid-sometime-friend to Isobel as Mum seemed to have been to Ella and Diana, a relationship that might have been a true friendship if it hadn't been stretched too thin across all the things that separated us.

The smile on my face was starting to feel frozen, and I took a bite of jellied meat instead, regretting it immediately when the gamey taste flooded my mouth.

'Lovely dinner, isn't it?' Sophia's friend Melanie, on my other side, had been deep in conversation with an older man for most of the meal. Now she turned to me.

'Yes, quite lovely.' I made vague pointing motions at my mouth, where the gel-like meat lump was refusing to move. Hoping she'd just turn away, I reached for my water glass, found it empty. Grey, sitting opposite me next to Mabel, was watching me with a small crease between his brows. A girl with a serving platter passed behind him, and he leaned back, whispered something to her. A moment later, she came round the table and refilled my glass. Mabel leaned in to ask him something, and he nodded and replied, throwing me a last glance out of the corner of his eyes as I drank gratefully.

The water was clean and cold. It washed away meat and bile and made me feel marginally more in control. I couldn't think about this properly now; I needed to get back to what I'd been doing before. Stay calm, deflect any questions, gather information. Even if that information was suddenly a whole lot more than just the tools to play a role, even if it was about my mum, and her friends. Light glinted in the profusion of jewels and headdresses and I felt another spike of bitterness. Best friends, eh? While we'd been living hand to mouth in the East End, Ella had been here, amidst all this luxury. While Diana McIntyre was hosting polite socials with local ladies and pursing her lips at my clothes, my mother had been killed sitting under her sewing table in a small, shabby dress shop.

I kept looking determinedly down at my plate as the main course was served, then dessert, but eventually I had to rejoin the conversation.

'How wonderful for you to be here tonight.' This time it was Sophia, leaning across the table towards me. 'I wondered, though, is it painful, after your grandfather . . . I mean . . .' She lowered her voice and inclined her head meaningfully. 'I mean, his sad end,' she said in a stage whisper. Three more people now downed tools and were looking at me expectantly, and I wrenched my thoughts out of my mum's past and into the story I was meant to be living right now.

'They were hard times,' Melanie said to no one in particular. 'And losing a child at any age is unbearable.' Almost everyone was silent now. Across the table, Ella had laid her fork down and was staring at her plate. 'It's no wonder that he . . . I mean, that he had lost hope. It must have been so difficult. Not just for Hector, but for all of them. Do you remember how close Diana was to Alexander? She just adored him, two peas in a pod, those two.' She looked at me not just compassionately but curiously as well, and I knew I'd been silent for far too long.

'I was ever so sorry about your parents' accident,' Lulu piped up suddenly, before I could speak. 'I'm sure Mrs Carlisle has a lot of memories to share. It must be lovely to hear about your mum's youth and such.' She nodded wide-eyed encouragement at me.

Come on, Agnes, say something, *anything*. You're supposed to feel something for Hector Bellingdon; he was your grandfather, for heaven's sake. Poor man must have committed suicide, judging by the pained looks of those around us, ruined by the crash of '29. Alexander Bellingdon, the golden boy, dead, Diana touching his picture as she moved past . . .

'We've not had a chance to catch up properly.' I pitched my voice low, hoping it would convey the gravity they were expecting.

'Yes, they're keeping Isobel very busy at the hospital,' Ella said, quite obviously as keen to change the subject as I.

'A nurse, how nice.' Melanie smiled indulgently. 'Do you remember helping out in the Red Cross during the war, Sophia? I always fancied I might go on—'

'I'm not a nurse,' I cut in, my head suddenly clear, because this was the only thing that made sense to me at the moment. 'I'm going to be a doctor. A consultant,' I clarified, feeling that that particular aspect of things might have been ambiguous in my earlier conversational round.

'Golly,' Sophia said faintly. 'Well . . .' She cast around for something to say, settling on 'We're all looking forward to the Bonfire Ball, aren't we, John?'

'Very much.' The man on her right was chasing pieces of meringue around his plate with a tiny fork.

'I can't believe it's the last time they're having it,' Mabel said disconsolately. 'It's been on the social calendar for decades. I feel like fewer and fewer grand events are happening these days, like it's all falling apart.'

'Hardly falling apart, when the hospital will finally have a new wing,' I said before anyone else could answer, but out of the corner of my eye I saw Dr Smethwick nod vigorously.

'Times have changed with this nationalisation of health care,' said the ancient Sir Fensby.

'And for the better,' Dr Smethwick said briskly. 'Even you must agree it's a good thing not to battle on many fronts but to have a unified system that is easy and free for all patients.'

'We've had national insurance before; patients were cared for just fine,' Fensby grumbled. 'Now we have gatekeepers, mountains of paperwork. Policed all the time, no longer masters of our own fate. Medicine has become . . .' He coughed and reached for a glass of water.

'It's become accessible to all, not just those who are able to afford it,' I said. And then, out of nowhere, I suddenly said a lot more things, perhaps prompted by the ghost of my mother in this very room, the vast chasm between her and these people, between them and me – the real, deep-down me. 'Surely medicine is not a privilege but an essential. It cannot be that good care is only available to those who are able to pay for it, while less fortunate people are reduced to cramming into clinics.

Affordable medical care is a basic human right; it's needed to stem maternal and infant mortality rates, it's vital in order to keep our society progressing, improving—'

I was interrupted by someone clearing my plate. There was a long beat of uncomfortable silence. Grey opened his mouth, and at the far end of the table Everett was straightening up threateningly, but Melanie beat him to it.

'Well, the old ways are changing for sure.' She smiled indulgently. 'These days the hospitals are all pushed together into huge complexes, getting bigger by the minute and—'

'As they must. The new Tomeyne Wing will allow for better patient care, less cramped wards elsewhere,' I said crisply. 'Finally enough room for maternity, obstetrics, gynaecology—'

Lulu smothered a gurgle of laughter, and I felt my sweaty back connect with the gilded chair. Had I really just said the word 'gynaecology' at a fancy dinner party?

'Gentlemen, why don't we break away for a smoke.' Everett Carlisle's voice was choked. 'Ladies.'

Seventeen

If I had achieved one thing at dinner, it was to thoroughly frighten people away from any further conversation with me. While the gentlemen stayed behind for cigars and, no doubt, a good chunter about me, the ladies went upstairs to freshen up, most giving me a careful wide berth. I followed them slowly, stopping on the landing to look down into the hall. My adrenaline and rage had drained away, leaving behind a coil of nerves and confusion in the pit of my belly.

'Isobel.' I turned around and saw Ella Carlisle. 'Listen, I wanted to apologise. I shouldn't have shown you that photo in such a hurry before dinner when I knew people might talk about her, and about your grandfather's death, and it would all feel too casual. I didn't realise quite how interested people still were. I'm sorry.'

The ladies were now coming back out on to the landing, flowing around us towards the stairs.

'No, *I'm* sorry, Ella,' I said quickly. 'For being stroppy and saying all those things in front of your guests. I certainly didn't mean—'

Just then, mortifyingly, a burst of laughter floated up and a hissed '*Gynaecology!*'

I flushed, but Ella gave another one of her unexpectedly naughty chuckles. 'They're doctors, for heaven's sake, it shouldn't come as a shock to any of them. It's just the fact that it's a woman saying it. As for the wives, Sophia's been dying to be on the committee for the ball, insufferable old windbag that she is. Serves her right to be put in her place a bit.' She gave another whoop of suppressed laughter, so mischievous that I found myself actually smiling as she started down the stairs. Halfway down, though, she suddenly stopped, clawed forefinger and thumb around her right hip, stooped over with a wince of pain. Alarmed, I reached to help her, but she waved me away.

'I'm fine,' she said, almost angrily. 'I was in the garden earlier, too much kneeling and carrying buckets.' She showed me her scuffed palm, a scratch on the underside of her wrist. 'Wrestling with my roses. Don't tell Everett. He's already cross because he thinks I've been overdoing things with the Bonfire Ball committee. But I've been working on it for so long, I simply can't let go of it.' She winced again and dug her fingers into her hip in a gesture that seemed to have become an automatic response to frequent pain. 'I've got to go,' she said abruptly, and without another word, she hurried ahead.

I followed more slowly, and when I reached the door to the small sitting room, I could see her standing inside, massaging her lower abdomen. Glancing quickly around, she took a small brown bottle out of her reticule and shook some drops on to her tongue, before squaring her shoulders and disappearing from sight. A few moments later, I heard someone say her name as she rejoined the party in the drawing room through the connecting door.

The post-dinner alcohol seemed to have loosened things up considerably. Conversation and laughter drifted out into the hallway, more raucous than before. I watched the party through the half-open door. Sophia, jewelled combs now listing a bit, was regaling two other women with a story about, of all things, the London Zoo. Jenkins was nodding sycophantically in all directions while keeping a close eye on Mabel and Grey. Everett held court in one corner, taking a spellbound audience through something that sounded like a kidney surgery, clearly as used to commanding attention in a social setting as he was in the operating theatre. They all seemed so sure and bright, so utterly confident of their place in life.

Leaning against the door jamb, I took the photo out of my bag. When I became Isobel, I'd sewn my only picture of Mum into the lining of my suitcase and put Isobel's framed photo of her parents on display wherever I lived. It had been difficult anyway to hold on to memories of my childhood, because there had been no one to talk to about Mum, no one to remember any details of our life together. Even more so as Mrs McIntyre had so persistently discouraged me from being the person I'd been before, had wanted me to be more like Isobel so that I wasn't an embarrassment to her. And once I really had become Isobel, I'd always known there would be no way back. I'd never regretted my choice, because what I'd got in exchange had been everything I'd ever wanted, and everything Mum would have wanted for me. Pushing all my memories into the lining of a suitcase had been a small price to pay.

But now she'd shown up here, of all unlikely places. I traced her rounded back with a finger, lingering on the blob of her daisy pincushion. It tugged at me, the shape of her, memories and stories lapping like the colours of the rainbow at the edges of my mind, and for a moment I wanted nothing more than to crawl right inside the photo, see my mother's face turn away from Mrs McIntyre's hem and light up with a smile. *There you are, darling girl, I've had the most brilliant idea. Come see.*

I held my breath until the pain faded, then studied the grainy fabric trailing on to my mother's hands and wondered whether somewhere outside the sepia-coloured edges of this photograph had been . . . well, had been my father, too. Had he called at the kitchen door on Silkie's day off to fetch her for the pictures or a dance, pretty in a dress she'd made herself? I traced the rough edges of the photo. I had stopped asking about my father very quickly, because she never elaborated on who he had been. And because it was one of the few things that seemed to make her sad, that brought out something in her that wasn't with me and in our life together, but in the past, where she still seemed to be waiting for him to come back for her. It was in the involuntary twitch when the postman clattered by outside, the way she always sat facing the door, that tiny quiver of expectancy, that vibration of a hope that was never fulfilled. I didn't feel anything for him, if I was honest, had little curiosity about his identity, his death. His absence was so absolute, such a given, and my mother's presence so larger-than-life that she more than made up for it. But one thing I did hate about him: that he had made my independent, storytelling, bursting-with-beauty mother wait for him when he had abandoned her. Abandoned us.

And now he was hovering around the edges of a part of my mother's life I'd known nothing about. A part that would eventually include – I bit the inside of my lip – her falling pregnant. Who had he been, and how had she come to be in the East End, alone?

Ella might know, I thought suddenly. If they'd been friends, she'd have known *him*, wouldn't she, could probably tell me.

A shout from the drawing room jolted me and I almost dropped the picture. But of course I could never ask her about any of this. What was more, I would have to be extra careful from now on not to betray any connection to Silkie at all, lest some long-forgotten likeness triggered a memory for her. I was no longer my mother's daughter; I could never be her again. I belonged to Diana McIntyre now, I was Hector Bellingdon's granddaughter, was respectably, safely upper-middle class, far, far away from Bell Street.

'There she is, the new asset on London's dinner party scene!' Laughter erupted into the corridor as Lulu tumbled out, followed by Mabel, Harry Jenkins, James and Bobby, all chattering nineteen to the dozen. 'Why are you lurking in the hallway when we're about to go dancing?'

I just managed to slip the photo back into my handbag before Lulu was next to me. 'The Vanderbilt's just opened again, first time since the war. Come on!'

The hall rang with laughter and voices as coats were collected and taxis requested, and I suddenly found myself face to face with Grey.

'I think I might bow out now,' I said. 'I shall see you at the hospital, I'm sure.'

'When we treat women on the new gynaecological ward?' he suggested.

'At the very latest then,' I said in a dignified way. 'Goodbye.'

But he held me back by the elbow. 'I wondered – are you quite all right, Isobel? You seemed a little . . .' he groped for a word, 'strange at dinner.'

I made a slightly strangled sound.

'Preoccupied,' he amended, then hesitated and added, 'Was anyone . . . I mean, did anything upset you?' His voice was low; not jokey or bantering, but like he really wanted to know, and for a fleeting second, I had the absurd urge to tell him.

'Grey? James is getting the taxi now,' Mabel called from the hall, now dressed in a shiny rose satin coat that made her, if possible, look even prettier than before.

'Coming.' He quickly dropped his hand from my elbow and took a step back, but he was still frowning a little. His contours were lit sharply by the bright chandelier behind him, but the angular symmetry and clear-cut lines of his face were softened by the shadow of the stairs. 'Sure you're not desperate for a proper night out?'

'Oh, do come,' Lulu shouted from the front door. 'The Vanderbilt's the most wonderful place in the world, truly.'

Part of me strained towards the lovely cool night air rushing in on a swell of river smells, wet leaves and darkness. But Grey was still smiling slightly, and jabbed his chin towards the others. 'I'll need someone to help me corral that lot.'

I had to smile myself when I saw Lulu waltzing Harry Jenkins round the hall while Bobby did his best to trip them up. Mabel, however, was walking back toward us.

'Grey, darling, are you coming?' she said lightly, looping her arm through his. 'And you too, of course, Isobel,' she added after a long second, her mouth set in a careless smile. 'Lots of lovely single men at the Vanderbilt.'

The two of them joined the others by the door, laughing at Lulu and Harry, calling out to the taxi driver. Mabel looked back once to where I still stood in the corridor, and I saw her smile to herself, her eyes glinting a little.

'On second thoughts, I think I will come,' I suddenly heard myself say. 'Let me just say goodbye.'

Eighteen

'Oh Vandy, it's so good to be back.' Lulu clasped her hands in ecstasy. 'It's been too long.'

The Vanderbilt Bar had suffered heavy damage during the war and, judging by the masses packing into every available space around the bar and the small round tables, it had clearly been much missed in the last few years. At first I'd felt the familiar panic at descending underground, especially given the bar's history. But the air was perfumed and smoky, the walls hung with deep red velvet drapes to cover raw concrete so that it seemed like we'd stepped through a door into the *Thousand and One Nights*. Low lights from the wall sconces caught on slinky gowns and satiny chiffons, diamonds nestled against décolletages and wrists. The dance floor was full of people, limbs entwined, faces close, and up on stage, a young man was crooning into a microphone.

Grey's friends spilled into the bar, greeting chums left and right. It took me a moment to rise above the drab navy-ness of Isobel's dress and my lack of sleek, interesting hair. Then someone pressed a pink drink into my hands and someone else prodded me forward and relieved me of my coat, tossing it on to a chair nearby, so I fixed a determined smile on my face and plunged into the crowd after them.

'Isobel!' A voice suddenly cropped up next to me and I turned to see Iain. His shy, goofy grin was so familiar that I felt a flush of relief, which must have made my greeting a lot more effusive than usual, because he seemed quite delighted.

'Iain, how nice to see you. Of all the bars in London . . .'

'Well, we did say we were going to be here, didn't we?'

Now that he mentioned it, I did remember a conversation about a night out on the town, organised, no surprise there, by Benedict, but I'd been too preoccupied with finishing up my final report on Mr Salinger, who'd been discharged the day before, to pay much attention.

'I thought you might—' But the rest was drowned out by Benedict.

'Huzza, you made it, McIntyre – and you're not covered in pus and blood for a change. Oops, sorry, didn't see you there, sir. Er, *and* Dr Jenkins, now will you look at that.' He sketched a deep bow at Grey and Harry Jenkins, which was derailed half-way down when he caught sight of Lulu and swayed in an enormous pretend swoon.

Harry Jenkins gave a haughty huff, which Benedict used as cover to sidle up to Lulu and introduce himself. Iain said, a little stiffly, 'I didn't realise you knew Dr Grey that well. You never let on when we're at the hospital?'

'I know his mother a bit,' I said. 'Well, my . . . that is, my mother knew his' – I was momentarily derailed by the absurdity of this statement – 'and she invited me over tonight. So I came with them.'

'Ah.'

'Grey is quite nice, actually,' I said, a little defensively. 'When you're not surrounded by blood and gore,' I added to lighten the mood. But Iain seemed put out, as if my arrival with Jenkins and Grey set me apart from him, and not in a good way.

'Come, ogle Solly with us, Isobel!' Lulu had appeared. Part of me wanted to explain to Iain how exactly it had all come about, but I gave him a casual wave instead and let Lulu tow me towards the stage, where Solly, of Solly and the Heart Brothers, was still hugging the microphone, eyes sparking, his teeth a flash of white. As he smouldered down from the stage, you could practically hear hearts breaking across the dance floor.

'Wonderfully dishy, right? Good thing I'm spoken for.' Mabel was right next to me, and her smile was a little more friendly than before as her eyes followed Iain's retreating back. 'As long as Lulu behaves herself.'

'I'm never able to really,' Lulu said cheerfully. 'And we'll get to talk to him, because Grey knows him,' she told me importantly. As if on cue, Solly spotted Grey and waved as he finished up the song.

'Let's get the boys to find you a dance partner, Izzy,' Lulu shouted over the applause. 'And then we'll have some fun.'

Our group swelled. Iain was nowhere to be seen, but Benedict continued to try his luck with Lulu. Harry Jenkins was covertly eyeing Mabel, who hung on Grey's arm, chatting with a group of friends they'd met. They all seemed to be working either in politics, the Foreign Office or, quite possibly, a gentlemen's outfitter, because they were identically sharply pressed and slick. A few had pretty girls with them, others were obviously scouting for entertainment. Lulu was holding court, her wicked asides making me dissolve in helpless laughter, while I was, if not constantly swept off my feet like Lulu and the others, in perfectly reasonably demand as a dance partner. The light caught Mrs Schwartz's stole, the music fizzed in my veins and I found it easier and easier to push the earlier part of the night, the strange coincidence of the photo and what it might mean, out of my mind.

Several dances later, I fell into a chair next to Grey. Mabel was now dancing with one of the sharply dressed boys; Lulu, finally, with Benedict, all the while managing to converse with James and Bobby *and* keep her eyes fixed on Solly.

'Someone's well into letting their hair down.' Grey nodded at my head with a chuckle. Quickly I reached for a nearby glass, gave my rounded reflection an exasperated huff and started tucking curls back into my chignon.

'I quite like this loose version of you,' he observed. 'At the hospital you're always so . . .'

'Determined?' I kept my eyes on the reflection in the glass. 'A valuable addition to the ward?' I smiled to myself, wondering what Sister Veronica would say if she could see me now. Or indeed – I set the glass back down a little harder than necessary – Mrs McIntyre. She had allowed Isobel a small sip of champagne every now and then, but had been very clear on alcohol's otherwise devastating effect on girls' morals. I looked up to realise that Grey's eyes were fixed on the edge of my jaw, where a curl had started surreptitiously creeping forward again.

'A bit buttoned up,' he said. 'On your guard. Unless you're armed with a sprayer and fighting with me in the sluice, of course. It's another compliment.' He held up his hands laughingly when I opened my mouth. 'In my charming, roundabout way. And while we're on the subject . . .' he hesitated, 'I wanted to thank you.'

'Thank me?'

'Yes, for going to the Ritz, and tonight. Mum was so happy that you did.' He tossed back the remaining half of his drink.

'I was so sorry to hear she's unwell,' I said quietly. 'She told me about it,' I added when he looked at me in surprise.

'You must really have disarmed her,' he said. 'It's been like pulling teeth getting her to talk about it at all. But you ask a lot of questions, I noticed that about you.'

'It comes in useful.' I gave him a half-smile, then said, serious again, 'What do they think it is?'

'We're still investigating. I think she's been feeling unwell for a while, but it only came out a couple of weeks ago. We ruled out most renal and gastroenterological issues, a variety of infections. Not much left now except for . . .'

There was a long pause. I met his eyes and saw it there, but neither of us seemed to want to say the word out loud. 'Cancer,' I finally said, pushing it out almost reluctantly.

He exhaled a long, careful breath. 'Dr Brookes has been away and only got back this morning, otherwise he'd have done the biopsy already.' He bit the inside of his cheek, fiddling with his empty glass. 'I'm glad she mentioned it to you, because I worry that she's constantly holding back about how bad it really is.'

'Like she's trying to shield you?'

'Perhaps, yes. Or shield herself maybe.'

We fell silent, then I said, 'I think you should send her to see a female doctor. It would make her more comfortable, get her to open up.'

I thought he'd dismiss it out of hand, but he nodded. 'There's an obstetrician, Mrs Fatima, over at Wandsworth Hospital, who is supposed to be very good.'

The music had swelled into something jaunty and bright, too bright for what we were talking about.

'What about your father?' I asked.

'What about him?' Grey said tetchily, then he sagged back. 'He's worried, which of course translates into coming at everything with a battering ram. He absolutely insists Brookes is the one, but maybe I'll talk to him about Fatima.'

Silence fell, and when I looked at him, I saw that his eyes were fixed on something far away.

'I can tell she's afraid,' he said in a low voice. 'She's been so different lately, you know. Going through all her things in the house, her papers and photos. She thinks I don't notice, and I'm barely there, to be honest, so I don't have much of a chance to ask her. But whenever I am, there's something kind of frantic about her rummaging and organising and rushing round. It feels like . . .' he paused, then, almost furtively, as if it were a shameful secret, 'like she's putting her affairs in order because she thinks she might not be around much longer.' The words came out in a rush and he didn't look at me as he gripped his glass.

I stared down into my drink. Putting her affairs in order. I didn't know her well enough to tell, but now that he said it, there definitely was something reckless about her mood, a bit erratic, rushed, urgent. Maybe that explained her sudden interest in Diana, too, in making her peace with whatever had happened between them.

Grey shifted next to me, his eyes still fixed on his glass. I hesitated, then leaned forward and put my hand on his arm. 'They're making advances in cervical cancer treatment all the time, you know.'

'Maybe, but survival rates, whether from the cancer or the treatment, are . . .' His voice petered out, and I saw his throat move as he swallowed.

'I know,' I said, a little helplessly. I did know. 'But don't give up hope until you absolutely have to.'

He pushed his hand through his hair in a jerky, almost angry way.

'Thank you,' he said, a little awkwardly. 'You're really nice to talk to, you know that? Mum, well, she just bats it all away, the concern and questions, unless she's well and truly cornered. Father doesn't like talking about it either, and anyway, he's conditioned to see the worst, which doesn't leave all that much room for lovely things like hope. For a medical family, we don't seem particularly well equipped to deal with all of this.'

A small fanfare from the stage cut him off, and a scruffy man, his hat at a rakish angle, slid behind the piano. A smattering of applause greeted his arrival, which he acknowledged with a bashful grin.

'Adam,' Grey said. 'Always late, drives Solly mad.'

Solly didn't look all that mad, but he did give a deep, exaggerated bow when Adam's fingers started racing up and down in a flurry of notes. Grey's eyes lit up and he leaned forward, as if inhaling the sound, then he suddenly got to his feet and held out his hand.

'Come on, let's dance.'

Nineteen

Grey was quite different to my previous dance partners, who'd attacked each song with determination and a steady prattle of practised chat. He had a fluid elegance and an impeccable sense of rhythm, so that only the smallest pressure was needed to tell me where he'd turn next. I was a little guarded at first, following him carefully, but bit by bit I was swept up by the music, my hair coming loose again as we twirled and wove around other couples.

'Where did you learn to dance like that?' he shouted over the music after he'd flung me away and collected me again. The song was winding down, a few more twists and turns until we came to a standstill at the edge of the dance floor.

'You're not so bad yourself,' I said breathlessly, gathering my hair and fanning the back of my neck with it. 'They teach you at that fancy school?'

He laughed and waved to a waiter. 'You won't believe it, but my mother taught me.'

'Ella?' I laughed. 'You Carlisles are full of surprises, truly.'

'She loves going dancing.'

'With your father?' I bit back another laugh as I pictured gruff, bespectacled Carlisle swinging Ella round the dance floor.

'He's quite good,' Grey said reprovingly, then laughed again. 'I think it's the one condition of their marriage. She keeps his life running smoothly, and he takes her dancing on a regular basis . . .' He broke off. 'Not so much lately, maybe.'

I took his arm. 'Hope, remember? Come on, I think we have one more in us before we have to find the others.'

It took me only a bar or two to realise that it was a much slower number than before. But before I could pull away, we were on the dance floor, Grey's hand light in the small of my back. The notes dripped from Solly's trumpet like honey, and every now and then I heard Grey humming. The gentle vibration travelled along our arms where it met that strange, secret thrill I'd felt in the drawing room. It was the music, that was all, the velvety sound that seemed to be funnelling directly into the small space between us. His grip on my hand tightened a little, as if he too was aware of just how small that space was. But when I looked up, I saw that he had his eyes closed, his lashes feathering across his cheeks, his shoulders relaxed as he moved in time with the music.

'You play the piano, right?' I said abruptly, suddenly keen to be back in that cool, crisp world we usually occupied together.

'A bit.' He didn't open his eyes.

'A bit well, or a bit decent?'

'A bit I don't get to play nearly enough.' Now he did open his eyes, looked down at me. A small frown had appeared between his brows. 'Again, so many questions, Miss McIntyre.'

'Your parents have a piano at their house, though, couldn't you—'

'No,' he said curtly. 'Father doesn't think—'

'There you are!'

We twitched apart at the sound of Mabel's voice. Her smile was as brilliant as before, her skin now delicately flushed, and if she was put out that I was dancing with Grey, she didn't let on. Still, bit by bit I found myself shunted sideways as she threaded her arm through his, and we were soon joined by Bobby and Lulu and the others, then – I bit back an involuntary sound, because he was even more magnificent in the flesh – Solly himself.

''Lo, Grey.' He grinned and pumped Grey's hand. 'Fancy filling in for Adam for a bit? Late to start with and already wants a break.' His voice was like liquid caramel, warm and fluid, and he was as tall as Grey, so for a moment all was long legs and broad shoulders. I couldn't blame a gaggle of adoring girls for inching closer.

'I've been trying to persuade Solly to play at your birthday party.' Lulu melted against Solly, who deftly melted the other way, bumping into Harry Jenkins, who was quite obviously trying to decide who to disapprove of first.

'No can do, lovely, I'm away.'

'It'll be a bit of a stuffy do anyway, to be honest,' Grey said. 'Not your scene at all.'

'How can you say that,' Mabel gave him a playful punch, 'when Lulu and I will be there?'

'Must run.' Solly boomed a laugh. 'Fuel up. See you up there, Grey?'

And just as quickly as the cluster of people had formed, it disbanded. Solly loped away, Grey was pulled into a conversation by Mabel, Lulu consoled herself for Solly's rebuttal by forcing Jenkins to fetch her another drink. Over by the bar, Iain and Benedict were rabble-rousing with some other medical students. I thought of joining them, of being swept up in the familiar banter about body parts, the morgue and Sister Veronica's ferocious ways. But it was as if dancing with Grey had opened something up that I'd managed to keep happily closed for the last few hours. I could feel it jostling for attention at the edges of my mind: Ella and Diana, my father and my mother, wanting me to try and make sense of what had happened back then.

It took me a moment to retrieve my coat and evening bag from our table and make my way to the exit. I had just reached the door when the trumpet gave a triumphant squeal behind me. Solly had returned to the stage; Solly and – I turned all the way round – Grey Carlisle. He slid easily behind the piano, half bowed at the crowd and made a show of flexing his fingers and rolling his shoulders. Then, without warning, he narrowed his eyes and leaned forward, and a rush of notes came scudding down the keys.

He didn't sway and dramatise like the other musicians — in fact he moved very little — but what he played and *how* pushed a sting of tears into my eyes; not sadness so much, but yearning, loose and liquid, hope chasing happiness. Loss. Blinking furiously, I tried to watch the dancers, people clapping and cheering, Mabel dazzling and graceful, Lulu singing along happily, her red dress moving about her as if it was alive. Grey had slowed now, taking his time over the turns and swirls of the melody, and I felt a squeeze of nostalgia so painful it took my breath away.

It had always been dark in Mum's shop. We were on street level, and more often than not, fog hung above, wet and yellow with smoke, drizzle or rain turning the greyness of the houses even greyer. But on sunny days, there was one short hour in the late afternoon when the sun came through the two gables opposite. Light would fill the room, find the sketches on the wall, the strings of buttons and glass draped across the ceiling, a rainbow of colour that moved and undulated in the breeze from the open door. Rainbow hour, she'd called it, and the moment it happened, we would down tools and dance. She had taught me all the ones she knew, her dressmaker's dummy in her arms to show me the steps, or holding a dress by the sleeves and twisting it, throwing the skirt up in a flurry of fabric, until the room spun in a glorious kaleidoscope of colours.

A shoal of notes skittered down the piano now, like bright minnows darting through sunlit water. I knew the audience was packed with people; I knew that Grey was playing to a crowd. But in that moment, it felt like he was speaking to me alone, as if we were continuing our conversation about dancing and mums and memories. Someone pushed past me, laughed an apology, momentarily obstructed my view, and when I could see him again, Grey was looking out into the crowd. His eyes swept from side to side, nodding a greeting to someone off to the left. And then they suddenly found me, all the way across the dance floor, and he smiled and raised a hand in farewell.

Twenty

'Sister, see that the patient's bandage is changed immediately; the ends need to be properly secured.'

Sister Veronica looked like she'd have quite liked to say that the bandage was fine – it looked fine to me too, to be honest; Sister's standards were exacting to say the least – but instead she scratched an irritated note on her pad.

Carlisle was standing over the patient, a very young man who was holding his arm cautiously, so much so that it seemed to almost hover above the blanket, I noticed.

'Well, what are you waiting for?' Carlisle demanded, still looking at the boy's arm. 'Where are all your nurses?'

'You asked for them not to clutter up the ward during rounds,' Sister Veronica said through gritted teeth, 'but we'll have it done the moment you're finished.'

Ignoring her, he looked around and then, unbelievably, lifted his fleshy finger and pointed it through the wall of bodies.

'You. Undo the bandage and give us an assessment.'

'Sir?' I said, so startled that the word came out muffled.

'Sir!' Sister Veronica repeated, scandalised. 'She is *not* qualified, nor allowed—'

'Who is in charge here?' Carlisle enquired coolly, but Sister Veronica, obviously feeling that desperate measures were needed, had already summoned a nurse. 'Nurse Baker! The trolley, please.'

All around, patients were now sitting up in bed to watch. Nurse Baker came hurrying towards us. Carlisle took the trolley from her and impatiently shoved it in my direction. Heat rushed across my back as everyone turned to look at me, but it wasn't until I saw Carlisle's eyes, cold with annoyance, that I realised that this was his revenge. He hadn't forgiven me for speaking up and talking back at his fancy dinner party.

Out of the corner of my eye, I saw a tall shape moving round to stand directly opposite me. Grey's face had the same impassive expression he always wore when working in close proximity to his father, but his chin jabbed towards the trolley. I gripped the handle, making metal kidney dishes and trays clank loudly, and the sound cut through my nerves. Not looking at anyone, refusing to be rushed by Sister Veronica's impatient huff, I disinfected my hands and picked up the scissors.

'It's all right.' I smiled at the young man, who was eyeing the scissors with a worried expression. 'This won't hurt a bit.'

'That's what they always say, Doctor,' he whispered, flushing a little.

It took me by surprise, and I realised it was the very first time I'd been addressed as 'Doctor'. I straightened up and nodded calmly. 'I'll do my best, then. May I see the chart?'

Avoiding Sister Veronica's icy glare, Nurse Baker darted forward and held out the chart. It told me that a long, deep incision had been made on the inside of the right arm, following an older abscess extraction that hadn't healed properly.

'Does it hurt here?' I asked as I started slowly cutting away the bandage, taking care to keep well away from the incision.

'It hurts up there,' the boy gritted out. 'I can only sleep if I lay it up like this, so it doesn't touch anything else.'

'You're clever to do that,' I said as the skin came into view. 'It doesn't help a wound to be rubbed up and irritated—' I broke off in surprise when he flinched and gave a yelp. 'Surely this shouldn't hurt yet?' I said, frowning.

'We cleaned and changed the wound last night, as instructed,' Sister Veronica said forbiddingly.

Ignoring her, I turned the arm over very gently. 'Tell me

where it hurts especially,' I encouraged the boy, but he glanced at Sister Veronica and pressed his lips together.

'There must be inflammation somewhere,' I said, more to myself than anyone else. There was whispering behind me, but I ignored it, studying the incision from every angle. It looked neat enough, a long cut that had been stitched together perfectly, and part of me took a moment to admire Carlisle's handiwork. The skin around it was red and a bit inflamed, which was normal as far as I remembered from my classes. Slowly I ran my thumb up alongside the incision, listening to the boy breathing faster and faster.

'May the nurse now bandage it back up?' Sister Veronica enquired crisply.

'No.' I bent over the arm again. 'I think something's not quite right here, sir.' I was watching the boy's face as I got to the top. 'I wonder if you need to open the incision again.' Someone gasped, and I realised I'd just told a consultant what to do. But since I was already in it, I turned to Carlisle. 'See?' I pressed a little more firmly than I had before, and the young man screamed, his body bowing almost double as he tried to twist away from me.

'Miss, whatever are you doing?' hissed Sister Veronica, alarmed. 'Sir, really, this has gone on long enough, I must insist . . .'

But Carlisle's eyes were intent on the wound, and he was already motioning for me to step back. In a matter of seconds, a screen was wheeled into place. Nurse Baker stood ready with a tray as he perched on the edge of the bed. Grey and the registrar were conversing in low mutters. Carlisle hadn't told me to stay, but neither had he sent me packing, so I remained where I was, for the first time able to watch him work right up close. He didn't speak to the patient save for one or two brief questions, but he picked up the young man's arm with surprising gentleness. Like me, he kept his eyes on the boy's face as he felt carefully along the wound, watching where he started breathing fast.

'Inflammation starts exactly here. We do need to open it back up,' he said tersely. 'Bandage it up, Nurse, and we'll put it on the list first thing.'

There was a moment of heavy silence, then Sister Veronica gestured at Nurse Baker, and the rest of us filed out from behind the screen to join the others. Keeping my head down, I took up my customary place at the back as we proceeded to the next bed. Carlisle held out his hand for the notes; silence fell, but a muffled noise from the boy being bandaged behind the screen made him glance up. He frowned, seemed to recall himself, then turned until he found me at the back.

'You'll be shadowing the incision in Bed 4 as of now, Miss McIntyre,' he said brusquely. 'I shall tell Professor Forsythe to expect a full set of notes by the end of the week.'

Twenty-One

The week had been busy and increasingly chaotic. A steady intake of new patients filled the wards almost to breaking point, made worse when a water pipe burst on one of the antenatal wards. Already Surgical III was being forced to share space with the gynaecological and maternity wards, an uneasy alliance that was made more fractious when the additional beds from the waterlogged antenatal ward had to be accommodated on our floor.

Meanwhile a bout of stomach flu had swept across the hospital, taking out so many people that the remaining staff had to work double and sometimes triple shifts, with some of the residents on duty for eighty hours or more. Many lectures and classes were cancelled, so that medical students could pitch in wherever needed.

The additional beds in the Tomeyne Wing were now so desperately needed, the wards so cobbled together and the chaos for the poor nursing staff such that Matron, quite obviously at breaking point, was rumoured to have stormed out and dressed down a group of bewildered construction workers before she was escorted back in and given a restorative cup of tea by one of the night sisters.

Everett Carlisle had been held up on the ward by the aftercare of a complicated tonsillitis when an orderly brought up yet another bed. He handed it off to a slightly harassed-looking Nurse Jameson, then turned towards Carlisle. 'Excuse me, sir, they need someone down to help out in Casualty, urgent.'

'Try next door,' Carlisle said without looking up. 'We can't spare anyone here.'

'I tried four wards.' The orderly started withdrawing, wisely in my opinion, because now Carlisle did turn to him and he didn't look pleased. 'They're short too.'

Carlisle sighed and pinched the bridge of his nose, then his eyes fell on me, restocking a tray in the corner. They narrowed speculatively, then he nodded as if he'd made up his mind. 'She goes.'

After a moment of startled hesitation, I practically threw myself forward in my rush to comply.

'What are you waiting for?' Carlisle demanded when the orderly shifted from foot to foot.

'It's only, I'm thinking they'll not want a girl student. Begging your pardon, miss.' The man bobbed his head courteously at me.

Everett Carlisle made an exasperated noise. Already turning back to the patient, he said, without looking up again, 'Grey, you go too and keep an eye on her.'

I was fairly certain Grey had been on his feet for the better part of two days, and he opened his mouth perhaps to say just that, then obviously thought better of it and turned on his heel without a word.

'You have a lot to answer for,' he said as we rounded the corner, skirting a nurse hurrying the other way with a stack of blankets. 'I was about to knock off, you know. After forty and a half hours, and yes, I counted.'

We had reached the very back of the building and were following the orderly down seemingly endless flights of stairs.

'But just think how exciting a finish this'll be to your day,' I said bracingly.

He laughed and held open a door for me. 'You do know that Casualty is considered purgatory, right? It's where house officers and medical students go to die.'

I could hear noise at the end of the corridor, voices and shouting, a door slamming.

'Medical Siberia.' He shook his head. 'But you asked for it.'

He pushed open the double doors under an ancient, rather dilapidated sign, *Accident and Orthopaedic Receiving Hall*, then beckoned me inside with a flourish.

'Oh, Doctor, good. I need a bit of help here.' Inside a cubicle, a nurse was bending over a man who reeked of gin and had huge gashes across cheek and shoulder. 'This patient needs stitching up, and once you're finished, the woman over by the door needs a look . . .'

Casualty wasn't large, but it was busy and, it became clear as the night wore on, rather haphazardly organised and distinctly understaffed. Patients brought in from a ramp at the back were assessed and treated down here, or else sent up to wards or operating theatres. Through the melee of voices and ringing phones wove the sharp, acrid smell of disinfectant, along with blood and other, baser smells: unwashed bodies and dirtiness and wet wool. Nurses hurried back and forth with trolleys and trays; here and there I saw senior medical students assisting a house officer.

The registrar on duty glanced briefly up at Grey, then dispatched him to tend to the drunk.

'Friday night,' he said, already turning back to the woman who'd tipped a scalding kettle over her hand. 'And fog setting in. Nightmare.'

'What's on Friday nights?' I asked Grey, who was smiling his thanks at the nurse proffering a tray. He hesitated, and I had the impression that he avoided trading a look with the nurse.

'Pay day,' he said. 'People out in the pubs, getting into accidents. Brawls. That kind of thing.'

Casualty might not be popular among the hospital staff, but in less than an hour down here, I had got closer to patients than in all the last few weeks put together. I cut away clothing and helped bandage sprained limbs. I held vomit buckets and hands, took pulses and blood pressure, wiped up blood and a bottle of gin that had slid out of the drunk's pocket and shattered on the floor. But more interestingly, for the first time I worked not just in close proximity to but actually *with* Grey. He had a very different style to his father. He moved through cases quickly and efficiently without seeming rushed, as focused as Everett Carlisle but more detached and so less intense.

'Shave that spot, exactly there, then slowly around the gash. If you can't see the wound clearly, then creep your way forward, like so. You can be quicker about it, Isobel, it's a razor, not a scythe.'

'Hold still, please,' I told the drunk.

'I'd do what she says, she's the one with the blade.' Grey leaned in. 'Swab. Press. Although maybe let go of his neck a bit,' he added with a grin. 'Here, move over, I'll do the rest.'

When he was finished, both of us sagged back against the gurney at the same time. The patient peered at the bandage, then lay back and closed his eyes.

'We don't make a bad team at all,' Grey said, nudging me. 'Small hiccup when you tried to strangle him, and we've probably imbibed at least one gin fizz each via the vapours alone. But well done.'

A little later, several victims of a road accident were brought in. One of the Casualty house officers was summoned to the operating theatre, and a student had to leave after accidentally slicing open his thumb, meaning the rest of the staff were even more harried than before. I stuck to Grey, and as the hours progressed, it felt as if the room was becoming smaller, pushing the two of us closer and closer together as we worked our way through beds and patients. I listened to him and watched his hands, held bowls and instruments, swabbed and bandaged and even – utterly, utterly thrillingly – under his gimlet eye stitched up my very first, admittedly tiny, gash.

At some point, however, our paths diverged. I had come back from emptying some buckets and he'd been called into one of the side rooms to confer with Mr Hughes, a senior registrar who'd been drafted in from obstetrics and gynaecology. I was just looking around for him when two orderlies brought in a young woman on a stretcher.

'Oh, Doctor, can you take her?' one of them shouted in my direction. With a rush of pleasure that for the second time in a week someone had actually called me Doctor – unwarranted, granted, but thrilling nonetheless – I ran to help the nurse fetch a bed. By the time we'd wheeled it through, Mr Hughes was looking down at the woman on the stretcher. She was in her early twenties, maybe, and pregnant. Her dress was bunched up around her legs and she lay sideways, hunched over her midsection. She refused to straighten, forcing them to lift her on to the bed with her body in a strange rictus curl.

'Anyone with her?' Hughes enquired briskly.

'One of the neighbours found her at the bottom of the stairs in a faint, rang it in. Thought she must have fallen down the stairs.' The orderly's voice was matter-of-fact enough, but it didn't need the doctor's glance at the woman's left hand for me to understand.

'She might have taken her ring off, sir,' I said quickly. 'Women often do when their hands swell in late pregnancy, don't they? It'd be altogether natural.'

Hughes frowned at me over his spectacles. 'Who are you?'

'I'm a student sent down to help, sir.'

'Well, I'll be sure to ask for your opinion especially next time, Miss Student.' He jotted something on a chart. Across the room, someone called his name. 'But since you're here, help Nurse Jones get her dress off.'

'Here?' the nurse said. We were standing just inside the doors out to the ramp, where ambulances arrived and departed.

'Move her to that corner over there until we know where

she'll go. Find a screen if you can.' Hughes scratched something on his pad. He was hoarse and impatient; his eyes were red-rimmed with tiredness.

We wheeled her into the corner.

'I'll try and find a screen,' Nurse Jones said. 'If you could cut her dress? Across there, like so, careful around the arm where the blood is.'

The dress, well-worn to start with, was badly torn, and in order to get to her arm, I knew we'd need to cut it all the way across the chest. Still, I swallowed a little when I saw the embroidery at the front, the little ruffles running down the seam. She'd obviously been dressed up for something, something that – I swallowed again as large bruises on her legs and stomach area came into view – had gone badly wrong. I cut slowly and carefully, then unbuttoned the rest and covered as much of her as I could with a sheet. She had her eyes squeezed tightly shut, as if she could block out the indignity.

'What's your name?' I asked, bending over her and gently extracting the last part of the dress.

She winced and bit her lip, then murmured faintly, 'Lily. Lily Collier.'

'That's pretty.' I folded up the dress as the nurse reappeared.

'Screens are all in use,' she said apologetically. 'I've sent someone to find us one. Let's get her in a gown, then.'

We wrapped the girl carefully in the gown. She was obviously in pain, but stayed silent throughout, her teeth gritted, her eyes still shut tight.

'Can you tell us what happened?' I asked. 'Or would you prefer to wait for the doctor?'

'I'd like to leave,' she whispered. 'I didn't mean for them to take me, I only—' She moved and gasped as her wrist was jostled. 'Please, miss, let me leave. I did nothing wrong.'

'Of course you didn't,' I reassured her. 'We'll get you sorted in no time.' As I carefully laid her wrist down by her side, I met

Nurse Jones's slightly anxious eyes across the bed. She jabbed her chin sideways and we moved out of earshot.

'Listen, you're new down here, so I'll just . . . Well, it's Friday night, isn't it, so things are usually bad.'

'Pay day,' I said.

'Yes, pay day. But not just for men out in the pubs. It means enough money in the tin for all sorts of *things*. For something like . . .' She gave a discreet but pointed look at the woman's belly. 'And when it goes wrong, then we have to take 'em in. But they don't like it here. It's a crime, for starters, and it's not . . . Well, all I'm saying is, you won't want to go on and on about it in public—'

'Shall I get you some tea and crumpets?' Hughes was back, glowering at our hushed huddle. 'Or will you kindly assist me in the examination?'

A few moments later, he looked up from the patient. 'Wrist is only sprained, needs to be bandaged,' he said. 'Nurse, tend to the bruises and scratches until Mr Grey is free to do the wrist. So, miss. Tried to fall down the stairs, did you?'

The girl had kept her eyes closed throughout, teeth pressed together against the pain. Now a dark flush stained her cheeks and her lips quivered. 'No,' she said. 'It was . . . I was trying to . . .'

He waited for an impatient moment, but when she couldn't seem to find the words, he turned away, gestured for the chart. 'Never mind. Least said, I suppose.'

'Sir?' I spoke tentatively. The nurse, who was gathering bandages and ointment from the trolley, cleared her throat warningly. 'Doesn't it look more like she's been . . . I mean, those bruises on her legs and belly . . . like she's been beaten up?'

Hughes raised his eyes above the chart.

'Maybe she made it home after she was attacked, then fainted there,' I added quickly. 'It *is* possible. I promise you, Lily – Miss Collier – nothing will happen to you. Just tell us who did this to you. Was it a man?'

There was another beat of silence, then she flushed more deeply.

'I think you have your answer,' Hughes said coolly. 'Story as old as time. Believe me, we've seen them all and more. As for you, remind me of your name again, please.'

'Isobel McIntyre.' I swallowed. 'Why?'

'Because I'll be making enquiries as to why a student is allowed to interfere with a case like this. What firm are you attached to?'

'Mr Carlisle's,' I said, gritting my teeth.

'Right. He'll be hearing about this.'

'Isobel?' Grey Carlisle was suddenly next to us. 'What's going on?'

'She's offering her opinions where they're not needed,' Hughes said curtly, turning away to finish writing up the notes.

Grey took in the girl in the bed, me still holding the heap of her ruined dress. He hesitated, then picked up the edge of the sheet and tucked it more securely around her before turning to Hughes. 'I'm sorry to hear it, sir. She's been a good help so far.'

'Very well, just see she doesn't get loose again.'

'Why on earth are you examining this woman out here, Mr Hughes?' An older woman with a salt-and-pepper bun under her cap had drawn level with us.

'There wasn't room anywhere else,' Hughes said distractedly, turning as another nurse approached with a question. Lily Collier opened her eyes and flinched a little when she saw so many people crowding around her bed.

I patted her hand. 'It'll be all right, don't worry,' I whispered. 'Just another moment and you'll be made comfortable.'

'The screen in Room 2 is free now, Nurse,' the older woman said. 'I'm going out with the Flying Squad in a moment, but would you like me to have a quick listen, Mr Hughes?' She turned to Lily. 'I'm the midwife, love. Now, whatever happened to you?' Without waiting for an answer from anyone, she'd pulled out a Pinard horn and bent over the girl's belly to listen.

'Fell down the stairs,' Hughes said, sounding weary now. 'Although the lady student and I disagree on this.'

'I . . .' I started, but on reflection decided not to make things worse for myself and stayed silent as the midwife palpated along the bottom part of the belly one last time.

'Baby's fine, miss,' she told the girl kindly, then straightened and gave the doctor a long look. 'Doesn't look like she fell down the stairs to me either; more like she got a good beating.'

For a moment there was silence, then Hughes flushed a deep, angry red. Nurse Jones, ostentatiously busying herself with dragging the folding screen closer, kept her eyes carefully averted.

'Then maybe you can find her a wedding ring,' he said through gritted teeth. 'And a husband to pick her up while you're at it. Mr Grey, be so kind as to see to the wrist.' And in a flash of white, he stalked off.

Twenty-Two

Grey was leaning over the young woman's arm while I cleaned blood off her scrapes and Nurse Jones saw to the bruises on her legs.

'Thank you, miss,' the girl said when Grey and the nurse had gone. 'For being kind.' She was flushed and sweaty after her ordeal, her wrist laid carefully atop her chest. They'd given her something for the pain and her eyelids were drifting shut.

'A good night's sleep and you'll be all right,' I said, carefully tucking the blanket around her.

'I don't know,' she said faintly. 'Nothing about this is all right really.'

My gaze slid to the empty fourth finger on her left hand. I knew that women sometimes bought themselves a ring so as not to make their situation obvious, cheap tin that turned the skin beneath a sickly green. Mum and I had once ventured to Woolworths, where she'd stood and looked at the selection for a long while, then abruptly turned and left.

Nurse Jones returned to wheel her away, and I patted the girl's arm, picked up the bundle of her clothes and went to find Grey. He was talking to the midwife in one of the side rooms.

'Keep her up on the ward for a week, Doctor,' she was saying.

'I can do a few nights, Mrs Smith, but they're at breaking point upstairs. If she's fit to leave, she'll be better off coming back to outpatients for a check-up.' Grey scribbled something on the chart. 'Or seeing her GP.'

'Oh, just for a bit, Grey,' I said quickly. 'She looks like she could do with a warm bed and a square meal.'

'We're not really a boarding house,' Grey began, then he stopped and gave me a tired smile. 'I'll ring up to Sister.'

'She really wouldn't say what happened?' Mrs Smith asked once he'd gone. 'She's not bolshie enough to be a prostitute, that's for sure,' she added.

'Yes, and too clean, I think.' I was studying the remains of the dress. When I looked up, I caught her eyeing me curiously and flushed a little. I'd sometimes seen prostitutes out and about, but it was probably not all that common for someone like me to know what they actually looked like. 'I wonder,' I said quickly, 'if she was trying to talk to the father, to try to . . . well, change his mind perhaps.'

She nodded, then sighed. 'He's not likely to, if that's how he responds.'

'Probably better off without him then,' I said, suddenly fierce. 'If you get beaten up every time you ask for something. Really she should report him.'

'It wouldn't improve things for her, and anyway, if she refuses to even talk about it to us, there's little doing.' The midwife sighed. 'You'd think that after two world wars, the women's vote and television, we'd be a little more tolerant of the reality of ordinary people's lives.'

'Where will she go when the baby comes, do you think?'

'The convent. The workhouse if she's unlucky, but they'll take the babe if she's not careful.'

I frowned. I'd seen my fair share of things in the East End, and heard rumblings too, but I had already spoken too carelessly. I wouldn't do it again. Mrs Smith seemed to feel the need to address my frown nonetheless. 'The baby carries the shame of the mother, that's what people think, so the earlier they're separated, the better. *I* don't think that,' she added when she saw the frozen expression on my face. 'But I've worked in all sorts of places where people do. They think the baby's blood is tainted somehow because it's born out of wedlock. Dirty like her, you know.'

'People's blood sure has a lot of work to do,' I said tartly, 'if it's meant to hand down looks, talent *and* moral stains.'

She stared at me for a moment, then chuckled. 'Quite. Well,' she grew serious again, 'maybe the father will come round. It is very hard to do this alone.' There was a shout from outside and she turned. 'I know the community midwives; I'll ask them to keep an eye on her. And maybe I can come up with something. Can I leave you to deal with those?' She nodded at the bundle of clothes in my arms. 'Probably only fit for the incinerator now, sadly.'

She left, but I didn't make any move to follow her. Instead, I leaned against the steel table and thought about Mum. She must have been dismissed from service the moment her pregnancy had begun to show. Had she begged my father to stay and make an honest woman of her, like Lily had, putting on her favourite dress to persuade him to take me on? I folded Lily's dress, straightened the sleeves so the stitching lay smooth and bright, imagined my mother on a gurney, eyes closed against the whispers. But at that, I felt a smile tugging at the corners of my mouth. She might have been dismissed and poor, but she wouldn't have given a fig about the doctors' words or the nurses' sidelong glances. She'd have tipped up her chin and asked them to please be careful with her best dress. I wondered what it would take to make others, young women like Lily, find that same strength to stand up for themselves. I found I was stroking her dress harder now. I'd hold on to it. Maybe there was still hope.

'You're a student, you said?' The midwife was back.

'Yes, just started my clinical course. I'm on duty on Ward III. But I'm only helping out,' I added hastily. 'I haven't done any patient work at all, other than cleaning things up.' I squirmed when I remembered Mr Hughes asking for my name, and wished I had done something down here worthy of reporting to Carlisle that hadn't involved making trouble.

'Maybe you *should* be doing more patient work,' the midwife said. 'What're you thinking of specialising in? General practice?'

'No, definitely not. I think . . . I'd like to be a surgeon.'

'Nothing like lofty dreams, eh? Here, help us get the Flying Squad ready, why don't you?'

Without waiting for my answer, she hustled me into a store cupboard where a nurse was balanced precariously on a stool, angling for a stack of blankets on the top shelf.

'Mrs Smith, the van's just back now, ready to be restocked,' she said as we entered. 'Oh good, you brought help. All quiet for the moment, but this week's been such a nightmare, and now fog too.' She jumped down and tossed the teetering stack of blankets into my arms without a word as Mrs Smith disappeared with a trolley. 'Would you mind terribly handing me those – yes, all those.' She jabbed her hand at a shelf and I collected bandages and packets of dressings and set them out on the counter.

'The Flying Squad?' I asked.

'It's an obstetric emergency service. Thamesbury covers part of the East End, Mile End, Stepney, Limehouse. They get called out for postpartum complications. Well, mostly postpartum – haemorrhage, retained placenta, obstructed labour and so on – but people call in all sorts of childbirth emergencies as well. The squad try to do as much as they can on the spot, blood transfusion, resuscitation and such, but an ambulance stands by if they need it.'

She broke off to count out the items as she packed them, then motioned for me to start stacking the equipment on a trolley.

'Our squad's a bit unique in that it doesn't drive out only for calls but takes enough equipment to do several cases in one go. Helps out the community midwives. Babies just keep on coming, don't they, regardless of the fact that everywhere's short on staff. We know a thing or two about that, right?' She grinned and jabbed her chin from her own tousled uniform to my white coat covered in all manner of unspeakable stains. 'Maybe you can step in sometime? We take an obstetrician, sometimes an anaesthetist. Mrs Smith goes a lot; she practically created the squad. And they always have a nurse and a student. Usually obstetrics or midwifery students, of course, but—'

'But we take all sorts.' The midwife had reappeared. She took hold of the trolley with the equipment and started bumping it down the ramp. The nurse and I followed with the rest. 'I'll ask for you upstairs, shall I? Ward III, you said?'

Oh no. Go back to the East End?

'That's terribly kind, Mrs Smith,' I said hurriedly.

'Watch out!' someone shouted as an ambulance pulled into the yard.

'But I'm not in obstetrics, and I'm really quite far down the line. I couldn't possibly . . .'

Mile End, Stepney, Limehouse. Without waiting for my mouth to come up with a solid excuse, my mind had already darted around the corner by the butcher's and on down cobble-stoned Bell Street towards the door of the small, shabby shop . . . But I couldn't. I couldn't risk anyone remembering Agnes Crawford, putting two and two together, creating unnecessary trouble. The shop was destroyed, Mum was dead and my old life there was gone.

'All right,' Mrs Smith said easily. 'Hang on to the trolley for a mo, though. You can do that, right?'

It took two people to push the equipment across the yard. From the right appeared a registrar I'd seen around on the third floor.

'Let's get moving, we just had our first call,' he said briskly. 'The fog'll delay us, but we'll flag down the first policeman we see and he can guide us. Nurse Reeds, all present and correct?'

'Yes, sir.' The nurse was slightly out of breath as she lifted the last of the equipment into the van. It had clearly been repurposed into an ambulance: the faint letters spelling *FISHMONGER* shone through the white paint, and when she threw open the door, there was a hint of the sea.

The midwife was already behind the wheel. Sticking her hand out of the window, she gave me a wave. 'Ta ever so for the help, miss.'

Twenty-Three

'You'll be happy to hear we're done.' Grey Carlisle emerged from the back door, trudged down the ramp and fell on to the small wall next to me. He pulled out a battered cigarette pack and perfunctorily offered it to me before lighting one and taking a deep drag.

'Lily Collier was transferred to the ward?' I asked.

He nodded. I looked towards the gate, thinking of the Flying Squad rattling through the darkness towards the East End. Did my mother have to go to the workhouse or the convent, or any of the other places where unmarried mothers went? I tried not to imagine what exactly she'd had to do to claw her way out of wherever she gave birth to me.

Grey's cigarette gave a sharp hiss. Even with the rush, even hollow-eyed with tiredness, he had the well-fed, wholesome look of someone who'd never had to claw his way out of anywhere. I wondered about his childhood, a little boy in shorts, taken to the park by Nanny to feed the ducks, safe in the knowledge that the world was spread out before him for the taking. It'd been the same for Isobel. Diana McIntyre had been fierce about many things, but none so much as getting Isobel into higher education, preferably where she could follow in her grandfather's footsteps.

Surreptitiously I ran my hand over the small bulge of the silver knife in my pocket and remembered my mother occasionally bringing home books for me, ancient, tattered volumes on all sorts of subjects, from philosophy to chess. They'd lived in a crate in the corner, carefully put away each night until I knew them by heart and she sold them on in exchange for something else, something that might mean I would not be forced on to the path *I* had been set by life and circumstance.

'I was glad you were there today,' Grey said suddenly.

I stopped thinking about Mum and felt a rush of pleasure. 'You were?'

'I liked working with you. And the way you talk to the patients, make them feel at ease. Like that unmarried mother, you—'

'Don't call her that.' My voice was so sharp he turned, surprised. 'We don't know what happened to her, we don't know her story.'

'All right, the pregnant patient with the bruises,' he amended easily. 'But that's just it, you knew what to say. She trusted you.'

I thought about this. 'I think we forget that a lot of them have never been to hospital,' I said. 'The closest to an institution they know is the workhouse, and if someone goes in there, they rarely come out. No wonder they're afraid when they end up in this strange-seeming place, strangers towering over them spewing a lot of medical jargon.'

'Interesting view you have of our profession.' He chuckled, then stretched out his legs with a long-drawn-out groan. 'I've officially been on these feet for forty-eight hours without sitting down once. I might not get back up from this lovely little wall; I think I'll just sleep here. We'll be back tomorrow anyway.'

'Count me out. I want my bed,' I said, suppressing a yawn.

'You'd leave me here on my own? The lone half of Team Carlisle–McIntyre?'

'I could always find you a wheelchair.'

'Now that would be heaven,' he said dreamily, and when I looked over, I saw that he'd closed his eyes.

Fog was swirling around the lights at the end of the Casualty ramp and clung to the muted orbs of the street lamps outside the gates. It wasn't the usual yellow pea-souper, more like being inside a gossamer cloud of air that had turned into a silky mist. There was a small overhang above our wall, so we were quite well protected, and the occasional cold breeze was soothing on my warm face.

'You know,' Grey, eyes still closed, extracted another cigarette, 'I'm sorry about what I said earlier, about you being sent to purgatory. I'm beginning to think that Father knew.'

'Knew what?' I blew gently into the fog and watched it swirl and eddy around us.

'That you'd be good. No one wants to be in Casualty, yet here you are, positively thrilled. You're thrilled by everything, in fact, even the bedpans. I think he's beginning to see that.'

'You mean it?' I searched his face.

'I'm not sure it's quite the blessing you think it is, having his focus on you.' Grey grinned, then sat up, drew his coat around him more securely and lit his cigarette. 'I'm also thinking that he'd probably have loved to have a child like you.' He gave me a wry half-grin. 'If—'

'If I was a man?'

'If you got your principles a little more under control. And yes, if you were a man. My father is nothing if not predictable.'

'Well, good thing he has you, then.'

'Yes. What a wonderful thing.' Grey smoked in silence for a while. 'I'm not sure I'm going to be much of a credit to him, to be honest. I'm not *thrilled* enough, I don't think. Tell me about being thrilled; maybe I can pick up a few tips.'

I watched the little orange dot of his cigarette hiss against the fine mist. 'I just always wanted this.'

'That's it?' he said, incredulous. 'We've been through blood, vomit and tears together tonight, and you give me "I always wanted this"? Come on, McIntyre, you're so good at asking questions. Now it's your turn. Tell me.'

'Well,' I took a breath of wet night air, cigarette smoke and disinfectant, 'it feels like a humming. Inside you, you know. Something that becomes your whole field of vision, that fills all of you until nothing matters but doing the thing you love most of all. You can't not do it,' I added. 'You have to.'

He slowly lowered his cigarette and stared at me. 'You feel all that in *there*?' He pointed his cigarette at the hospital rising behind us, faint squares of light twinkling through the fog. 'Really?'

'Do you remember those books, the Home University Library series?' My eyes followed the tendrils of fog shrouding the gate through which the Flying Squad had long disappeared. 'My mum found me one on science, *Introduction to Science*, by Professor J. Arthur Thomson.' I wrote it into the air with a bit of a flourish. 'I was nine,' I added. Grey made a small noise next to me, but I was back in Mum's workshop, the Singer chattering in time with me sounding out the words. 'It was like a door into another world, filled with things I didn't quite understand but would come to in time. From that moment on, all I wanted was to go through that door, to belong in a place like this. It took . . . it took a while, but now that I'm here, there's no going back, ever. And down here in Casualty, it somehow feels like I'm closer to that feeling. Closer to people the way they really are, not just cases tucked into Sister's perfect hospital corners. It feels human down here. Real.'

I fell silent, because I suddenly wondered whether I also felt closer to myself – the real me – down here. Upstairs, despite my best efforts to blend in, I always seemed to be chafing against Sister Veronica's perfectly white ward and the way things were done. Tonight, for just a few hours, I had become part of the rush, had blended into the urgency without having to constantly worry about keeping my mask in place or figuring out the rules, judged only on how I worked under pressure. But then I remembered Mr Hughes and sighed, because I most certainly had been chafing against the way *he* thought things should be done. Who was I trying to fool anyway? I might have dragged Agnes up by the boot laces when I became Isobel, but here at the hospital,

Miss Lady Student was yet again a piece of grit in the system, although now for a whole different set of reasons.

'If you can feel all that after a night working in Casualty,' Grey said, sounding a little awed, 'then I definitely need to work much harder on being thrilled.'

'It'll come, once you're out from under . . .' I jabbed my chin in the direction of the hospital. 'Once you can go your own way, find the kind of medicine that suits you.'

'My own way, eh? They've got that one worked out already. Mum is desperate for me to eventually take Father's Harley Street practice off him, with the bonus that I'd stay close to home. And of course I want her to be happy because . . . well, who knows what's going to happen, and meanwhile, *he* just wants me to be him, keep the Carlisle legacy going, preferably in a place where he can boss me around until he retires. Which will be never, because he'll live for ever, obviously.'

'But what do *you* want to do? Come on, Carlisle,' I said in a credible imitation of his earlier swagger. 'We've been through gin, body parts and razors together. Tell me.'

He tossed his half-smoked cigarette into the dark space beyond the ramp. 'It's not nearly as worthy a contribution to the human race as yours.'

'All right.'

'And it requires a bit of thinking outside the box. To dream big, if you will.'

'I'm good at dreaming,' I reassured him. 'Tell me.'

'I'm thinking about enquiring at the London Conservatoire. They have auditions next year, in June.'

'The piano?' My shock was unflattering, I knew.

'I know, it's not something a self-respecting Carlisle should be focusing on,' he said, now a little defensive. 'But if I was free, if I could just wake up one day and do exactly what I wanted, it would be that. It's always been that. Started at Edgewood – which by the way is a place you want to be good at rugby or die trying. I made some extra money selling stuff out of Mum's care packages, then paid to have secret lessons in town with the choirmaster. Spent more time in detention than I cared for – the housemaster thought I had a lady friend, see – and I had to beat up a few of the boys when they found out the truth and started calling me a sissy, but it was worth it. And Father never knew a thing. Boxing champion by day' – he held up his hands in mock awe – 'secret pianist by night. Of course, *he* made me stop boxing before too long. Said it would be dangerous for my hands. My "most important tools".'

He said it mockingly, obviously expecting me to smile, but I didn't say anything for a long moment, my mind going back to a crate of old books in the corner of a shabby shop. What would it have been like to have someone like Everett Carlisle fighting your corner, pushing you, clearing the way for you?

'I suppose I can see his point,' I said. 'To have all this,' I waved my hand at the hospital behind us, feeling cold, damp air against my fingers, 'to be good at this and instead—'

'He's not here to hear you, you know,' he cut in, annoyed now. 'There's no need to toe the line.'

'I'm not toeing the line,' I said. 'But you're being handed everything on a plate, Grey, *everything.*'

'Good to know whose side you're on,' he said coldly, and started getting to his feet. 'I thought you of all people understood about dreams. I'll see you in there, shall I?'

But I took hold of his arm and pulled him back down. 'Oh, don't sulk just because someone is asking an uncomfortable question. Sit down and tell me about the piano. Would you play with Solly?'

He made an impatient sound. 'No, of course not. That was just for fun,' he said stiffly, then lost some of his stiffness when he grinned and closed his eyes in apparent ecstasy. 'Although it would be pretty amazing, I'm not going to lie. Touring around the country and all. No, Sol's got his group all set, and anyway,

I want to study it properly. Classical piano, play concerts, teach in the meantime.' He leaned back against the wall and tapped his fingers on his knees. 'If I'm even good enough. I might not be, I suppose.'

'Don't fish,' I said kindly. 'Of course you're good. You're very good.'

He turned a little pink. 'You really think so?'

'You almost made me cry at the Vanderbilt,' I said encouragingly. 'But . . .' I paused, 'I also think you'd make a brilliant doctor. Working with you tonight was amazing. If that's you not being one hundred per cent thrilled, I don't know what you could go on to do if you were all in.'

I started getting to my feet, wincing when every single one of my joints protested.

'What you said earlier,' Grey said from behind me. 'The humming, like nothing else matters in the whole world.' He wasn't looking at me but at his long, slender fingers tapping out a gentle pattern on his leg. 'The only time I truly feel that is when I play the piano.'

The sound of a church bell tolling midnight drifted through the fog, a strange, unearthly sound coming from nowhere. He lifted his head, listened carefully until the last chime had finished.

'Well, there you go. Twenty-six years old and not a great deal wiser, eh? It's my birthday today,' he added when he saw my questioning look.

'I thought it wasn't for another couple of weeks. Aren't you having a fancy party?' Ella had sent me an invitation a few days ago.

'Which I hope you'll be attending.' He too had clambered to his feet, with a series of pained groans. 'No, today, in exactly three hours, is when I first saw the light of day.'

'And you're celebrating it with me, at the back end of Casualty, being dripped on by the fog. I'm truly touched.' I smiled. 'If I'd known, I would have rallied the nurses round to sing.'

'Oh, don't. I hate fuss. Although,' he nudged me lightly as we walked up the ramp to the door and came to a stop, 'maybe a little fuss is in order after all. Who knows what exciting things the year will bring?'

'May it bring you all the happiness you deserve, Grey,' I said, suddenly feeling oddly breathless. 'And that you get to do more things that . . . that thrill you.'

Something sparked in his eyes at the word 'thrill' and he opened his mouth, just as a lorry drew up at the ramp, the sharp grating sound of the tyres cutting through the strange tension that had bloomed between us. He shifted, gestured towards the door.

'After you,' he said, his voice a little hoarse. I turned quickly, keen to be away. As I stepped through it, he said from behind me, 'You'll come to the party?'

'I . . . Yes, if I'm free,' I replied, a bit flustered.

He smiled, a sudden, swift smile, and pushed his hand through his hair, making it stand on end, his eyes the bluest green I'd ever seen.

'Good.'

Twenty-Four

It was a beautiful autumn. The parks were full of people making good use of the last sunshine, the streets were busy. At the hospital, time seemed to blur. Working on the wards; standing in the gallery for hours to watch operations. Rushing between the hospital and the library. Slumping tiredly over textbooks at night until even the most serious ailment became mere black squiggles on white.

I worked in Casualty once more but was careful not to put a toe out of line. I tried even harder to impress Everett Carlisle, pouring all my energies into the cases on the ward, including my new patient in Bed 4, the young man with the infected incision, who was well on the mend and perfectly happy to talk to me.

I routinely fell asleep over Katia's heaped helpings of *cholent* or matzo ball soup, and had, mercifully, very little energy left to think about the photo and my mother. Maybe the memories would fade, I thought, if I worked harder and kept my head down. Maybe in time my mind would turn to the future again, rather than feeling this strange pull of the past.

And then Grey. I hadn't thought about him either, nor about the night we'd worked in Casualty together. Not that there was anything to think *about*, of course. It was his birthday, I'd wished him well, like any civilly minded person would. And if I'd used one of my precious free lunch hours to nip out and buy him a present, it was only because *Manners and Etiquette for the Young Lady* seemed to suggest that arriving empty-handed at a birthday party was as grave a breach as national treason.

In any case, by the time Saturday rolled around, it was looking rather unlikely that I'd be able to attend at all. Only the previous day, we'd been dressed down by Harry Jenkins, who had quizzed us on the tonsillectomy we'd sat in on and found our anatomical understanding so sorely wanting he looked like he'd quite like to remove a few tonsils from our group himself.

'By rights, you should not be sleeping or eating at all any more,' he'd announced, puffing himself up and rounding on all of us so fiercely that even Benedict had blanched. 'Especially since many of you have been given extra shifts this weekend to cover the staff shortage. Well, what are you still doing here? Go, go, for heaven's sake, stop dawdling.'

I'd been assigned an additional Saturday-morning shift on the ward, and by the time I'd finished all Sister Veronica's chores, it was so late it hardly seemed worth going to the party at all. In fact, I'd just decided that I'd go home and lie down, not getting back up until Monday morning, when I was overtaken by Grey on the stairs. With his overcoat balled up under his arm, he looked as dishevelled as I did and promptly overrode all my protestations.

'Grey, I look like I've murdered someone,' I said irritably. I'd spilled iodine over my hands earlier, and even rubbing alcohol hadn't been able to remove the stain. I gestured to the usual uniform of grey skirt and navy cardigan I always wore under my white coat. 'And I don't have time to go home and change.'

'You look fine,' he said impatiently as he hustled me through the hospital gates, 'and if I walk in with you, Mum won't be cross that I'm late and badly dressed. Come, the weather's held up beautifully, and she'll be so pleased to see you.'

Clarke did a very visible double-take when we walked in, but gamely stood aside to bow us towards the garden.

'I suppose I don't have time to change, do I, Clarke?' Grey said, pushing his fingers through his hair and trying to smooth it down.

'You can't change now.' I was horrified. 'You said we were in this together!'

'Perhaps just a quick tidy.' Clarke plucked Grey's coat from his arm. 'And some hairpins for Miss Isobel?'

Grey chuckled slightly as he sagged at the knees in front of the mirror to straighten his collar and smooth down his jacket. 'You know,' he said when I gave my reflection a sceptical glance, 'I didn't actually know it was possible to have that much hair. You certainly hide it well at the hospital.'

'It's not a blessing.' I tried to neaten my curls at the back. 'I'm thinking of cutting it all off, really short.'

'Oh don't,' he said, so quickly I turned and looked at him. 'I don't think it would suit you,' he added, more measured.

'Like Mabel's hair. Hers is so chic.' I was careful to look into the mirror and not at him.

'She's a whole different person,' he said. 'It does suit her, of course. I was just thinking – you look like you've worked hard. In a good way,' he qualified, 'one that made your hair stand on end.' He towered over me to put on the tie Clarke had just handed him, and I dragged a hairbrush through my curls before picking up a hairpin from the table.

'How long have you been together?' I kept my eyes on my reflection, ignoring the warmth rising from my collar.

He picked up some pins and jumbled them into his palm. 'Not all that long, actually,' he said, evasively. 'A few months.'

I nodded. 'Can I have my pins back, please?'

'We sort of fell into it, we've known each other for ages.'

'Of course. And she's so lovely.' I finished my hair.

'She is,' he said, giving his reflection a nod.

'I've told Mrs Carlisle you've arrived.' Clarke was back. 'They couldn't wait any longer to open the buffet, but they've waited for the speeches. If you'll step through here.'

Strains of string music and what sounded like the voices of many, many people floated in from the garden.

'Grey? Didn't you say this was just a picnic with friends?' I turned in time to see him shifting guiltily. 'Didn't you?' I repeated.

'Yes, friends certainly, although not all mine, and some of them probably rather fancy.'

'You said I was fine dressed like this,' I hissed. 'You said—'

'Kindly remember that you're not always the centre of attention.' He propelled me down the corridor. 'Mum's bound to have gone a tad overboard, that's all. She was still working on some of the sponsors for the Bonfire Ball, so she might well have decided to kill two birds with one stone.'

'I certainly know who I'm going to kill at the next possible opportunity,' I said furiously as he pushed me through a small door at the back of the house.

'We'll try to sneak in unnoticed. Just do your best to blend in,' he whispered.

The garden was a riot of bunting and balloons, the colours clashing cheerfully with the bright foliage and autumn blooms, and it was positively heaving with people. Standing or sitting in small groups or hovering around long trestle tables gorgeously decorated with garlands and holding platters of delicacies the likes of which I had certainly never seen in a picnic basket. The huge ancient gramophone had been wheeled out from the drawing room and fed tinkling string music into the late-afternoon warmth, and off to the side, another table was piled high with presents.

For a moment I was frozen, then, out of the corner of my eye, I caught Grey inching backwards. 'Oh no.' I clamped a hand around his wrist and pushed him in front of me. 'Under no circumstances are you leaving me here alone.'

'Everyone,' a voice suddenly announced above the din of the crowd, 'the birthday boy has arrived!'

Murmurs and laughter swelled as heads turned and the guests parted to reveal Grey and me seemingly holding hands. I sprang back immediately, hoping to melt into the edges of the group – and preferably scale the back wall and disappear altogether – but already Mabel and Lulu were rushing up.

'Grey!' Mabel exclaimed. 'Where have you been?' Her gaze fell on me, and something cold and assessing glinted in her eyes. 'Harry said your shifts ended at the same time, and he's been here an hour and doesn't look like he's been to the slaughterhouse. Oh Grey, honestly, wasn't there a minute to change?' She shook her head, her eyes still on me, and opened her mouth again, but her words were lost in the surge of congratulations and questions.

'We're so sorry, we're so sorry!' Grey finally managed to make himself heard. He pushed through the crowd, looking left and right. 'Mother, where are you?'

'I should be quite cross,' Ella held out her hand to draw him in, 'but God knows I'm used to it. Isobel, it's so lovely to see you.' I could see the corners of her mouth quirking up a bit when she saw my hands. 'Make sure you get tea and cake, and I'll come and find you a little later.' She was as impeccably dressed as before, and her skin seemed smooth and even, until a ray of sun caught her face from the side and I saw the heavy layer of powder keeping the foundation in place.

'Please don't worry about me.' I stepped back. 'And I'm ever so sorry we're late, it was very busy at the hospital—'

'Which is exactly why we so appreciate your generous donations,' she cut in smoothly, turning me and Grey towards a couple who'd been whispering to each other and eyeing my iodined hands with some concern. 'Once we get the Tomeyne Wing up and running, the hospital will benefit from the new facilities and the extra space to accommodate staff and patients.'

She gestured for a maid to hand round glasses of champagne as I smiled and nodded at the grey-haired couple. I noticed that Ella drank half her glass in one gulp, her hands trembling slightly, but then Mabel was next to Grey, smiling charmingly at the pair and producing perfectly calibrated snippets of delight at their generosity. Glad to be out of the limelight, I drifted away until I found myself next to the gift table. Turnbull & Asser seemed to have been divested of most of its stock, and pulling out my own gift, I wondered if there was any way I could make my wrapping paper a little less brown, the string a little less obviously rescued from Mrs Schwartz's last grocery delivery.

I glanced over at Ella and Mabel, who were still talking to the older couple. I could just pop it back in my bag, give it to him another time. I had come straight from the hospital after all – it would probably seem odd that I had the gift with me. As I pushed it into the bag, I suddenly caught Grey's eye. He cocked his head enquiringly, and I took the package back out and set it defiantly on top of a box of cufflinks, twitching the string into a jaunty figure-of-eight bow before moving away and fetching myself a plate of goodies from the buffet.

'Isobel!' Lulu was waving wildly from a nearby table, where she was holding court among some young men I remembered from the Vanderbilt. 'Come sit with us. James, move over. Sorry we didn't see you leave the Vandy the other night, but we won't let you out of our sight tonight, will we, boys? Ooh, can I have one of your ginger fancies?'

Lulu was dressed in a dress and matching coat of eye-watering lime tonight, and my tired brain had a bit of trouble remembering the names of the young men, who were all identically dark-suited and crisp-shirted and were no doubt the givers of the Turnbull & Asser presents. But their cheerful chatter and buoyant mood was infectious, and I suddenly realised that I'd walked into the party without any anxious thoughts whatsoever about someone questioning who I was. There was no need to worry any more, I thought, feeling something loosen in my shoulders, as long as I let the past be and kept on my path.

I leaned back and watched a young man ribbing Lulu about being a fashion diva, which she accepted as a compliment while she polished off most of my pastries. There was something so familiar about her, that air of cheerful defiance, her penchant for colour, the way she embellished every story. With a sharp squeeze of my heart, I recognised that she reminded me of my mother. But a different version of her, one that might have happened if she'd been allowed to be free. If I hadn't been there and things had been different.

I took a mouthful of my cold cup of tea and laughed a little too loudly as Lulu dived under the table to puff on her cigarette because her uncle was among the guests and didn't like ladies smoking.

'Good to know someone still thinks you're a lady,' one of the boys joked, and she gave me an owlish wink from under the table. 'Your hem needs fixing, Izzy, did you know? You should find someone to do it for you.'

Twenty-Five

Music and chatter wove into smells of autumn leaves, coffee and freshly baked cakes, which emerged at a steady clip from the kitchen. It was chilly and crisp, but the sun had come around and found our table, warming my back as I listened to the others' easy banter, feeling pleasantly drowsy.

'Sorry, what?' I sat up when I thought I'd heard my name.

'Mrs Carlisle said you lived in York when you were a girl,' Lulu repeated. 'I just wondered, did you know Molly Ashford?'

I blinked away sunshine and contentment as fast as I could.

'Lulu, that's like saying do you know my uncle Mo in Chicago,' one of the boys laughed, but she shrugged, turned back to me.

'The world is tiny. What school did you say you went to?'

I hadn't, actually. 'Aberforth School, on Cheshire Road.' I was relieved that at least my voice sounded nonchalant even if my heart had started a slow thumping of fear.

'But that's where Molly was!' Lulu clapped her hands together in delight. 'Oh, I do love connecting the dots. Do you remember her? Lots of brown hair, quite cheeky. Younger than you, though.'

Pretending to try to recall her gave me a few more precious seconds to collect myself, as I summoned the names of girls Isobel had been friendly with at Aberforth. 'Well, I was good friends with Maggie Healy and Liz Denton. Molly doesn't ring a bell, but then again, I was a day girl, because my father was a teacher there. And I only went there for two years.'

'Well, I'm seeing her in a couple of weeks, I'll have to ask her,' Lulu said. 'You know, I could invite her to the Bonfire

Ball – Uncle's bought a number of tickets. Ooh, maybe she had a secret pash on you. Younger girls always fall wildly in love with the older ones. I'm sure you were very popular—'

Just then, a fork was tinkled against a glass. I felt my sweaty back connect with the chair as I tried to imagine Molly Ashford turning up at the Bonfire Ball. It was Rose Bellerby all over again, with her *I can't wait to see you* and *so good to have a friend there*, forcing me to leave King's College. It couldn't happen here, not now, when it was all starting to go so well. I plastered a smile on my face and focused on Everett Carlisle who was standing on the upward slope of the garden with Ella and Grey.

'Thank you all very much for coming, and thank you to my wife for throwing such a splendid bash to celebrate our son. How exciting to be on the cusp of another year, especially one that will bring so many changes. Grey will be admitted to the medical register as a fully qualified practitioner, a supremely important point in his career after years of hard work and dedication. Not to mention the relief it'll be for Ella once he becomes more involved in my private practice. Who knows, I might even be home in time for supper – occasionally,' he added after a pause calculated to prompt a few titters of knowing laughter from the crowd. 'I only hope he'll find as worthy a helpmeet as I have.'

He didn't look at anyone in particular, but a little way away, Mabel flushed delicately. Her hair had fallen forward to hide her face. She seemed to be intent on Everett's speech, but from where I was sitting, I could see a small, thrilled smile playing around her mouth. Of course she would be a worthy helpmeet, wouldn't she? She was like Isobel. No dark shadows lurking in her past, no whiff of shame following her. No lies. It was only a matter of time before she became what Everett Carlisle was so heavily hinting at.

There was a smattering of applause, and Everett concluded, 'So please join me in a toast: to Grey in his success, and to all the other good news the year might bring.'

I looked away from Mabel and made my own smile bright, because I should be happy for the two of them, should most definitely not feel this horrible ache in my ribcage at the fact that Grey and I could never be anything other than friends. Not just because of Mabel, but because I was . . . well, exactly *who* I was was murky and complicated. And yet I couldn't resist glancing across to Grey and was startled to see that his face was stricken, even a little wild around the edges. He was leaning forward as if to interrupt his father when Ella held up her hand.

'Please, I'd like to add a few words of my own. No lengthy speeches, I promise.' She took a sip of champagne, then looked around at the gathering. 'Just my own very special happy birthday to Grey. He's been the light of our lives, always, and we couldn't be prouder of the man he's becoming.'

It was simply and honestly said, and even distracted as I was, I felt something inside me tighten. Around us there was a lot of throat-clearing and dabbing of eyes, but Ella held out her hand to Everett, put her other arm around Grey.

'I thank God every day that He has brought me into the lives of these two men, to allow me to be a part of their family.' Her voice was so quiet now you could barely hear it above the birds calling to each other and the leaves rustling and swaying in the evening breeze. 'And I will be a part of it for as long as I can,' she added suddenly, as if the words had slipped out in public when she'd meant them for Everett and Grey alone. Grey leaned into her. Everett kept his eyes on the ground, his face oddly pale. 'Anyway, I'm glad you are all here to celebrate today, thank you.' She finished in a rush, lifted her glass and drained the rest of it in one go.

Everett Carlisle stood for a moment, not moving, not looking up as people converged on them. Then someone else stepped up to say a few words, and something Ella had said snagged at my mind.

'What did she mean, she was brought into their lives?' I turned to Lulu.

'Oh, didn't you know? Grey is Mr Carlisle's son from his first marriage,' she whispered. 'It's a bit of a fairy tale, actually. They were neighbours, and Mrs Carlisle – well, Miss Lumley then, I think—'

'Neighbours?' I said. 'You mean, he lived . . .'

'Yes, over there.' I followed her pointing finger to the house in the middle of the row. 'Someone else lives there now, of course. Well, Carlisle's wife died tragically, so young, and he was alone for a bit with Grey, and it was an absolute disaster according to my aunt.'

'Poor Grey,' I said, shocked. 'That's awful.'

'Yes, it was, Grey was quite abandoned. Then one day, Doc Carlisle gets chatting with lovely Miss Ella over the garden fence, and next thing, he's married her. They moved in here eventually, because he couldn't bear to be in the house where his wife had died. Grey was, oh, I think four, maybe? It was the best thing that ever happened to them, my aunt says. To Grey.'

She broke off to join in loudly with the applause for the speaker, tinkling her fork so enthusiastically against her champagne glass that she broke the rim. I took it from her and set it back on the table, my mind a blur of dates, ages and people. If Grey had lived next door at four years old, like Lulu had said, then wasn't it possible that he might have seen my mother at some point? He might actually have met her, even; she'd always been so friendly, I could easily imagine her chatting on her way to run errands, trying to cheer up the sad little boy. The things he might be able to tell me – a child's memory, but still – if only I could ask . . .

I felt my hands trembling a little, struck by the strangeness of it all, that I was sitting in this garden as a guest, looking up at a house where only two decades before she might have hung out of the window to polish the glass, dusted knick-knacks, made beds, lugged coal scuttles. There was a thrill in it all at being close to her, and terror, too, at the nameless danger that seemed to be drawing near, like a noose inching ever tighter. And Grey, losing his mother at such a young age . . . It was awful to think about.

'Isobel!' I jerked upright when I saw Lulu's face right next to mine, her eyes round. 'You're bleeding.'

I looked down at my hand and saw that I'd cut myself across the ball of my thumb, smearing blood all over my palm.

'Bobby, give her your handkerchief,' Lulu ordered. Bobby, who looked a little reluctant to relinquish the snowy square of fabric, nonetheless made as if to hand it over, but I shook my head quickly. 'I'll just take this napkin and pop inside.'

Keeping to the edges of the party, my hand inside the bloody napkin tucked behind my back, I made my way slowly towards the house. It was quiet back here and, sidestepping a maid emerging from the kitchen, I saw that the glass door on the little terrace was ajar. That would take me to Ella's sitting room and from there straight to the downstairs loo.

Holding my hand aloft, I climbed the dainty wrought-iron stairs, pausing on the threshold to allow my eyes to transition from bright sunlight, music and excited voices to the quiet half-darkness inside. As I stood there, a shadow suddenly moved, and I gave a muffled yelp.

Everett Carlisle was sitting on the sofa.

'I'm ever so sorry, sir,' I said quickly. 'I didn't mean to disturb you. I was looking for . . .' My voice petered out when he didn't say anything, didn't even turn his head. The noise from outside suddenly felt jarring, and I quickly closed the door behind me.

At last he looked up, frowning as if it was taking him a moment to place me. He seemed unusually dishevelled, the buttons of his coat undone, his collar open. There was an open decanter of whisky on the side table, but although he was holding a full glass in his hand, it looked untouched. An envelope lay next to him, and I thought I could make out the hospital's name on it.

'Are you . . . I mean, are you all right, sir?' I asked after a moment. 'Should I fetch Ella, maybe?'

'No.' The word was so loud it cut across the silence. 'Not Ella,' he said more quietly. I glanced at the envelope, but he gestured to my hand.

'What happened?' he asked abruptly.

'Nothing, really. A glass broke. I was just going to clean it up.'

'Let me see.'

I hid the hand behind my back. 'It's just a cut, nothing you'd be interested in.'

But he gestured for me to sit, impatiently, much like he was on the ward, and I let the napkin drop away. He didn't touch my hand, and I didn't sit especially close, but with his ability to focus all his attention on one single thing, he always seemed to take up more space than the rest of us.

'Small enough,' he finally said. 'What are the first measures you take with a bleeding injury?'

'Pressure on the wound and elevation of the limb,' I said automatically. 'Stitches if necessary, ideally as soon as possible. Some success has been seen with a certain kind of tape holding the wound together.'

'And they say surgeons aren't good company,' he said wryly.

'On good days, we can clear the cafeteria in under five minutes.'

Voices drifted in from the garden, laughter, a shout, and then I thought I heard Ella's voice somewhere close by, perhaps talking to one of the kitchen staff.

'Are you sure you don't want me to fetch her?'

He had automatically looked towards the source of the sound, but his eyes seemed far away, and when he spoke, it was as if he hadn't even heard my question.

'Since we're doing question time, tell me, Miss McIntyre, what is your view on imparting a diagnosis to a patient?'

I blinked, a little startled at the sudden segue. 'Honesty,' I said. 'Isn't that what you always say, sir? That patients need to know everything?'

Out of the corner of my eye I glanced at the letter, the name of the hospital clearer now. He had picked up the glass again, swirling the contents round and round.

'I think it helps to talk about it.' I kept my eyes firmly fixed on the gently eddying liquid, the amber catching the light between his hands. 'It brings patients and loved ones closer together, it gives them the chance to use what precious time they have. However,' I added quickly, 'not all cases are so desperate, are they? For example, the recovery rate of some cancers can be a very positive message, perhaps even rallying the patient, thus aiding in recovery. Take cervical cancer—'

'Which has, what, a thirty percent chance of recovery?' His voice was harsh.

'That is something well worth knowing, though, isn't it?' I said. 'After all, line up a hundred women, and thirty of those will be fine. Thirty will walk away cured.'

'And seventy will die.'

I twisted the napkin tightly around my hand.

'Would it be wrong to want to see those other women walk to their deaths too in order to keep someone else alive?' He'd spoken so quietly that I had to lean in to hear him, and for a moment we were so close I could smell the heady fumes of the whisky, saw his fingers folded tightly around the glass.

'Wrong maybe,' I said, as quietly as he had. 'But it would be human.'

Silence fell; even the voices from outside seemed to quieten.

He set the tumbler back on to the side table with a small clunk.

'So, you've read Professor Whippet's piece in *The Lancet*,' he said abruptly. 'On the possibilities of surgical tape?'

'Yes,' I said, a little startled.

'It was quite a while ago, if I recall correctly?'

'Yes, well, I often read things and then seem to remember them. It's a bit of an oddity.'

'A useful one at that,' he said. 'I saw your exam results in your file.'

In an instant, the strange closeness that had pushed us together evaporated.

'My file? I mean . . . there's a file on me?'

'There's a file on all students.' He slipped the envelope into his pocket. 'Being a doctor carries much responsibility, and while the NHS is increasingly making it a meritocracy . . .' He held up his hand as if anticipating some kind of comeback from me. 'Rightly so in some respects; you're certainly doing your bit to show me that. But the old adage of needing to be of good character, well, it's still a vital component, particularly when it comes to the Royal College of Surgeons.'

'Of course,' I said guardedly. The earlier churn of fear was back at the thought of him studying my photo, my life story. Had *he* seen my mother, too, hanging out of the window polishing the glass? Would he detect similarities between me and the neighbour's former maid? Don't be ridiculous, I told myself urgently. He was a snob, he didn't *like* women, he never looked below his station. He wouldn't have noticed her, not enough to put two and two together after all this time. And yet . . .

'Well, go and put some iodine on it. There's some in the cupboard under the sink through there.'

'Of course.' I rose and made for the door, willing myself not to run. But when I reached it, he suddenly spoke from behind me.

'Miss McIntyre?'

'Sir?'

He jabbed his chin at the napkin wrapped around my hand. 'You should be more careful,' he said. 'The hands are the most important tools for a surgeon. If they're compromised, if you lose sensitivity in your fingertips, even the slightest impairment of mobility, it could derail your career.'

Twenty-Six

'Isobel? Are you in there? Are you *alive*?'

'Yes!' I shot up from the ornamental stool in the washroom, blinking sleep out of my eyes. Someone was hammering on the door.

'Whatever have you been doing?' Lulu's voice. 'All the old people have left and it's getting dark, but they brought out little heaters and the party's still going.' She almost fell into the washroom when I opened the door and stepped out into the corridor.

'I know it's only six o'clock, but I'm . . . well, I'm a little drunk,' she confided, then turned and danced ahead of me towards the little sitting room and the stairs to the garden. 'But Uncle's gone and I'm free!' She stumbled, giggled and suddenly ground to a halt. 'Shh,' she hissed loudly, putting her finger to her lips in an exaggerated way. 'Mrs Carlisle's sleeping.'

Sure enough, there was Ella, tucked into the corner of her sofa, fast asleep. The sitting room was dark, a muted half-light of dusky blues and greys, broken up here and there by bright orbs of colour from the lanterns strung up in the trees outside.

'Should we wake her?' Lulu asked in a round-eyed stage whisper.

'Let's not,' I said, noting that the glass that had been in Everett's hands before was now tucked between the cushions. I could smell the whisky, sharp and smoky, and the level of amber liquid in the decanter had significantly decreased. I thought quickly. 'Why don't you go back outside, Lulu. I'll stay here with her for a bit. But don't tell anyone, all right? She'd be so embarrassed.'

There was a raucous burst of laughter from outside and a

swell of music from the gramophone. Lulu lifted her head like a dog scenting a bone.

'Go, quick, before you miss all the fun.' I shooed her gently towards the door, waited for her lime-green dress to bop away and turned back to Ella. She was curled up, her skin flushed, hands tucked under her cheek like a child. Another sudden burst of laughter from outside made her stir, and she straightened drowsily and blinked into the half-darkness.

'It's me,' I said quietly, and she stifled a small, startled noise. 'I'm sorry, I didn't want to disturb you.' I sat down next to her. 'How are you feeling?'

'Bit tired.' She sank back against the sofa, winced and dug the tumbler out from beneath her hip, staring down at it as if wondering what had happened to the contents. 'It's just Grey's friends left now. They won't mind if I'm not out there.' Her voice was hoarse, the words a little fuzzy.

'Should I get your husband?' I asked. 'I saw him in here earlier.'

'No,' she said, a little sharply. Her eyes glistened in the gloom as she rubbed her cheeks in vigorous circles, smoothed back her hair. A lot of the make-up and powder from before had come off, leaving her blotchy and exhausted-looking. 'He'll just say I'm overdoing things. I'm fed up with it all, with them hovering and no one really properly spelling out what's going on.'

I thought back to the letter Everett had slipped into his suit. 'They're concerned,' I said cautiously. 'They want you to get better.'

There was a pause. Beyond the glass door, which Lulu had left slightly ajar, I heard a breeze rustle through the trees. The coloured lanterns swayed and danced in its wake and the dusky half-darkness inside came alive with coloured shadows. They flickered across Ella's face, reds and greens and purples that made her look strangely garish and overdone, like she was a made-up actress in a play.

'I won't, you know,' she said, and for a moment I had to blink to make her out properly amidst the colours playing across her features.

'You don't know that,' I said.

'Maybe not, but I can feel it. I can feel something waiting for me just ahead, some dead end that constantly reminds me that I need to fit as much as possible into that narrowing space between now and then.'

She reached across to the decanter, tipped it over the empty tumbler. Some of the liquid splashed across the side table, but she didn't seem to care.

'You said you still dream of your mum sometimes,' she said without looking at me. 'Do you think *they* will? Grey and my girls, and Everett? Do you think I'll be walking around up there somewhere and feel them dreaming of me? Or will life eventually take over and I'll just . . . fade away?'

'You won't fade away,' I said firmly. 'Don't think like that, Ella.'

'Just tell me, to humour me.' She drank from the glass.

'It never fades,' I said after a moment. 'It doesn't matter what life does, the memory of the people we lose will always stay.'

'The memory,' she repeated, as if she didn't entirely like the concept. 'I know a thing or two about that. Well, here's to memory, then.' She lifted the glass in a salute; then, unexpectedly, she smiled. 'That I met you, though, that we were able to spend time together, that I truly cherish. It is . . . it was so important to me.' She broke off, drank again, more deeply.

'Can I ask you something, Ella?'

She nodded over the rim of the glass. 'I like that about you, how you're so interested in people when everyone else just sits in awkwardly genteel silence. You'll make a good doctor; I know you will.'

I swallowed and felt a small twinge of guilt, because it was a compliment I didn't entirely deserve. I was interested in people, yes, but just as much of it was a defence mechanism. The more you asked people about themselves, they less they could probe into your life.

'Well,' I said carefully, 'it's lovely that you sought me out, and I've really been enjoying it, but I wonder . . . I mean, why was it so very important to you?'

She reached for the decanter again, splashed more whisky into her glass. 'Because my life is coming full circle. And this' – she jabbed the glass at her pelvic area and the amber liquid slopped on to her hand – 'is forcing me to look back. Because . . . well, because as I said, there isn't much to look ahead to. Only the end. And I had to come to the end to realise . . .' She fell silent, stared down into her drink.

'Realise what?' I leaned forward to see her face, no longer alive now with colour, but soft and blurry, the contours melting into shadow. Only her eyes glittered. I took the tumbler out of her hand and set it aside. 'To realise what, Ella?'

'It's your parents' anniversary today, you know,' she said as if I hadn't spoken. 'It was an autumn wedding, not warm like today, but the air crisp and clear enough that you could drink it. They were a good couple, Diana and her Henry. Your uncle Alexander – he was best man, because Henry McIntyre had no real family of his own. Alex always said we only ever have one perfect match in life. One true love. Do you think that's true? I hope it's not, because wouldn't we all be doomed if our first love was our one and only chance at true happiness? What if they left, what if they loved someone else, what if they *died*?'

I tried to keep track of her words, which were now sliding into each other, her voice slurring the consonants.

'You must be careful, you hear me? Guard your heart, it's your most precious thing.' She gripped my hand harder, and as I tried not to flinch at the hot, bony grasp, I saw to my horror that her eyes were full of tears. She was trying to pull away, but I held on.

'I will, Ella,' I said. 'I'll be careful, I promise.' I paused. 'Was Mr Carlisle your first love?'

Her eyes softened and the tears spilled over, ran down her cheeks and dripped on our joined hands. She didn't wipe them away. 'No, not Mr Carlisle. He was the best second love a woman could hope for. But mine was Alexander, of course.'

'Of course,' I repeated, and something slow and ominous started thrumming at the back of my mind.

'You couldn't not love him,' she said simply. 'He was magic, Alexander. Funny and clever. He went for life with a vengeance, took everything it offered. He was like Diana in so many ways, but where she could be a bit buttoned-up and strong-willed, he was brighter and warmer, the kind of person who lit up a room, you know, who made every conversation livelier, every game more interesting.'

She leaned back and closed her eyes, smiling to herself, but there was something off about the smile. I couldn't quite put my finger on it, but it made me uneasy. Diana had adored her brother. Ella had loved him. And Silkie – well, Silkie had been pregnant. The thrumming in my mind was pushing to make sense now, a rush of something urgent.

There was a rustle and movement next to me. Ella was groping, her eyes still half closed, for the photo album we'd looked at before the dinner party. But where before she'd handled it carefully, now she was dragging it towards her by a corner.

'Oh come on, you stupid thing,' she said crossly. There was a ripping sound as the spine got caught on the edge of the sofa, and before I could do anything, she had tugged it free, the impact sending loose photos, ancient invitations and other paper keepsakes flying.

'I'm sorry if this is making you sad,' she said defiantly as she spread the book open, started roughly leafing through it. 'But if I'm to die, and soon . . .' She reached for her tumbler again, drank deeply as she turned the pages, spilling a little across a photo of people standing in front of a boat.

'You really mustn't talk like that, Ella,' I said sharply. I took the tumbler and set it aside, then dropped to my knees to gather up stray photos and papers, my mind busy in the background, ticking through options, asking questions, starting to formulate answers.

'Someone has to remember them. You said the memory stays,' she looked down at me almost accusingly, 'but if no one is left to talk about them, then who is there to remember? *You* will have to, so I'm telling you. Diana's wedding was the last time we were together, all of us. Alexander in his suit, so glamorous, and Henry serious as always. Your grandparents were there, that was just before it all . . . went wrong. And my parents, and your mum in that dress – we were together, all together, it was still fine . . .' She'd been riffling through pages and tapping photos, but now her voice started to drift, fragments of sentences blurring into each other. She muttered something under her breath, but I had ceased to listen, frozen with my hand around a piece of paper.

It was a drawing of three girls: the bold, haughty features of Diana McIntyre, the birdlike grace of Ella Carlisle, and – I forgot to breathe – my mum, pretty in bright red in the middle. It was like seeing the dress photo all over again, only this time the shock was amplified tenfold, because where the photo had been little more than a static black-and-white shape, this sketch leapt with colour and brimmed with verve. And in the corner, a small, yellow daisy face winked out at me.

With a shaking hand I traced the sketched hem of Ella's dress swirling up brightly, remembered the way my mother had drawn. Constantly, almost carelessly, the pencil an extension of her hand the same way her needle had been. 'Never look directly at inspiration,' she'd sometimes said. 'If you act like nothing's happening, it always comes tiptoeing round. It's curious like that, you know.' She'd used bits of newspaper and the pages of an old exercise book, any old scrap she could find, had tacked them up on the walls around us, a gallery of dresses and hats and garments papering over the drab grey of the East End, rationing cards, blackout curtains, air raids.

'The party went on well into the evening. Even when Diana was in her going-away dress she was pulled back into the festivities.'

'Ella, what's this?'

'Anyway, off she went, and I would never have thought that—What?'

I sat down next to her on the sofa and laid the sketch across the pages of the photo album. Her eyes grew wide when she saw it and her fingers crept to the edges of the paper, curled around them as if she wanted to pick it up. Then she pushed it back at me.

'It's just one of her sketches. My mother used to scold her terribly, you know, always threatened to confiscate her sketchbook.'

'Her?' I prompted, when she broke off, her eyes on the sketch again. Her lips were pressed together, and I thought I saw them tremble slightly.

'Silkie. Our maid. Our . . . friend. She had this sketchbook, see, we'd given it to her for her birthday years before, Diana and I. Alex had given her a box of watercolour pencils, you know the kind that you use to shade and then you put a drop of water on it and it blossoms out like a—'

'I know the kind,' I said, my teeth gritted slightly. 'And?'

'And she filled it with all these dresses, so daring some of them, flirty and fun. Headbands and hats, and undergarments too.' She flushed a little. 'Such things she could imagine, Silkie, you have no idea. It was like she had a firework inside her all the time, going off in big bursts of colour.' Her voice was strangled by something that seemed angry – furious, even – but also wistful and longing.

174

'She hated her uniform, would secretly tweak it to fit her better, and she always had a project on the go. She altered our clothes, too. Mother didn't like it one bit. In those days maids were supposed to be like wallpaper, not seen, not heard, just *there*. And Mother *really* didn't like that we were friends.' Her fingers had crept towards the sketch again. 'But there was something between the three of us, you know, we just fitted together, maybe because we were so different. Diana headstrong, Silkie so creative, like a fairy, and me just happy to fit in between them.' She swallowed. 'Diana's mother hated our closeness even more than mine did, wouldn't have Silkie near their house. I'm sure she knew already, even when we were just girls.' Her words had become quieter and slower.

'Knew what?' At the sound of my voice, Ella's head snapped around and she looked at me almost as if she'd forgotten I was there. Seeing me seemed to suddenly tip her away from wistfulness and back towards anger, and she picked up whole handfuls of papers and photos, stuffed them back into the album, slammed it shut and shoved it at me.

'That it would all break, in that one night, and it was Silkie's fault. Alexander just took a ship and sailed away, never to return, and Diana left with her husband, and Silkie went too, and I was left here, in a place I would never leave, all alone.'

Without warning, she plucked the sketch from my hand, and before I could stop her, she'd torn it clean across, once, twice, tossed the pieces on to the floor. 'That's what was left of us, and all because Alexander never loved me.' She didn't look at me.

'He only ever loved Silkie.'

Twenty-Seven

I left without saying goodbye to anyone, walked as quickly as I could until the house was out of sight. Just a little way ahead, on the side of a small green, was a bench, and I sat down, hard.

Alexander only ever loved Silkie. I clenched my hands into fists, trying to wrap my mind around all the things I'd just heard, the biggest of them being . . . I felt my mind scurrying around frantically, trying to piece it together, and every way it turned, there he was. It had to be him.

Alexander Bellingdon.

Diana's brother, Hector Bellingdon's golden boy, Ella's first love. The missing piece in this strange story I'd come to discover about my mother. Sailing off into the sunset, cruelly dead before his time, and . . . could it possibly be my father?

I funnelled the word out softly into the evening air, said it again, tried to feel something for the man who must have abandoned my mother before I was even born. But it was devoid of meaning, a strangely empty concept, as if he was nothing more to me than a grinning face in a photo, holding a vase like a rugby ball; a stilted portrait on Diana McIntyre's mantelpiece. At that, something hot and awful pushed forward. Mrs McIntyre had treated me like a maid, like I wasn't really one of them, when all along I'd been her niece. All those moments I'd been secretly, sickeningly jealous of their family, desperate to belong somewhere after my mother had died. Had slipped my hand into Mrs McIntyre's at church because I'd been lonely and lost, and she'd pushed me away. If Alexander felt like an abstract concept to me, then Diana McIntyre filled me with a rage so tangible that I hunched over myself, trying to breathe through memories of her coldness and indifference, her distaste.

Fast girls. Free spirit. Trousers.

The yellow light of the street lamp wavered in front of my eyes as I sat clutching my satchel – no, Isobel's satchel. Isobel, my cousin. Somehow that, at last, calmed my mind. Isobel had never looked at me with distaste or condescension; she had been like a sister to me. She hadn't abandoned me, like Mrs McIntyre and Ella Carlisle had my mother. Even in death, she had tried to help me. And she was here with me now, wasn't she, would always be with me. I let my fingers brush across her initials, and for a moment I thought I felt her warmth, saw her delighted smile as we danced the polka, which my mother had taught me using a dressmaker's dummy – Mum, who'd been Isobel's sort-of-aunt, who'd been a part of the family.

I opened the satchel and pulled out my notebook, extracted the pieces of the sketch. They gleamed palely under the street lamp, the edges already curling slightly. The middle rip had narrowly missed my mother's face but had severed her arm, which had been flung around Diana's waist. I moved the fragments together to line up the ripped edges, whole and yet not whole, connected and yet making no sense at all, just like this strange tangle of family I seemed to suddenly be a part of. The fact that I had been impersonating Hector Bellingdon's granddaughter when I had actually *been* her all along. That medicine really *was* in my blood, that Diana had wanted Isobel to continue the Bellingdon legacy, which *I* then went on to do, unwittingly and with no one left to witness it. Why had my mother sent me to live with Diana McIntyre after their friendship had fallen apart, and why had Mrs McIntyre taken me in? Perhaps I had reminded her enough of her brother that she couldn't let me go to an orphanage or the workhouse, but she could never forget that I was his bastard child with the neighbour's maid. Who was also – and at this I gritted my teeth again – supposedly her friend.

I stuffed the other pieces of the sketch back into the notebook, leaving only Mum's piece out on top. On closer inspection, I realised that the bottom half of her dress was really a pair of wide-legged trousers, cleverly designed to flare out like a skirt. It was pretty, a bit outlandish, very cheeky, and suddenly whatever Diana had done and why ceased to matter. All that mattered was that I missed my mother, missed her so much . . .

I don't know how long I sat on the bench. The crisp October dusk deepened into early evening and the darkness outside the yellow circle of light became a velvety blue, punctuated only by cars or bicycles occasionally passing the green. I pulled my coat more tightly around myself and thought how Mum had managed to build a whole new life with me, without dwelling on the unfairness of it all, without ever letting on how hard it must have been. But also without sharing her story with me. I wanted that story. I wanted to know *everything*.

I opened the notebook to tuck the sketch back inside and found myself looking at my pages of notes on surgical procedures. I stared down at them, marvelled at the neat way they parcelled knowledge into sections and facts, connected arrows and lines to form a perfect whole. They seemed to belong to another life altogether, a whole other person, not someone straining to jumble together pieces of her mother's life as if they might provide some kind of answer. And to what question? Who was I, then and now? Where did I belong?

Startlingly, I saw my own life and Mum's line up alongside each other, running almost parallel. Like me, she had been alone, then was taken into a family and become part of a friendship, yet never truly belonged there. Like mine, her situation had suddenly fallen apart, and she had disappeared, re-emerging eventually to become a different person. Like me, she'd followed her passion, had tried to carve out a place for herself in the world.

But this was where our paths diverged, I realised with a small lurch of discomfort. She hadn't cared about fitting into someone else's world, *she* had not taken on someone else's life in order to make something of herself. She'd always remained defiantly, often infuriatingly, herself. The discomfort grew as I wondered what she would think of me now, the daughter she'd raised to be daring and different and independent sitting on a bench pretending to be someone else.

At that, I closed the notebook with a loud snap. Look at where her uncompromising independence and her defiant free-spiritedness had taken her. A doomed love story, a hand-to-mouth life in the East End, dying because she didn't go down to the shelter, because she only ever followed her own rules. I shoved the notebook back into my bag, remembering all those other moments that had also been a part of our lives, moments when I'd wished she might have tried, just a little bit, to fit in, and when her constant insistence on standing up for oneself had felt exhausting rather than empowering. When she'd introduced us to people exactly as we were, not only not trying to gloss over the fact that I didn't have a father, but defiantly, proudly flaunting it. When I'd eventually realised how much harder that kind of independence was to carry through on my own, at the McIntyres', at school, in my new life away from her, where not fitting in wasn't really an option.

I closed the bag and stood up, straightening my cramped, cold legs. In the end, figuring out who she had been and what she'd think of me now didn't matter, simply because it couldn't. The only thing that mattered was who I would be going forward.

'Isobel!' A car screeched to a halt next to me, making me jump. Grey leaned out, jabbing his thumb at the back door. 'What on earth are you doing here? Hop in, I'll give you a lift. I'm driving Mabel home anyway.'

Mabel turned to give me a long, cool look through the passenger window.

'I'm all right walking,' I said quickly. I might be calmer now, but I wasn't quite ready to put my masquerade back on, nor deal with the whole Mabel-and-Grey situation. 'You go on, have a good night.'

But Grey opened the door and made as if to get out of the car, and I sighed and climbed into the back next to a large parcel of what looked like leftover pastries and cakes. Mabel nodded at me briefly, then leaned into Grey as he drove on, murmuring things I couldn't hear.

'You can let me out there.' I pointed to the right, but Grey had already turned left and was speeding towards Belgravia.

'Watch out,' Mabel suddenly gasped, and he slammed on the brakes. 'You almost took out that bicycle,' she said accusingly.

'Sorry. Bit tired,' he said. He had deep shadows under his eyes and was gripping the wheel, peering out of the window as elegant mansion blocks came into view. 'Here's you, then.'

Mabel waited in her seat until he got out to open her door. Their faces were above the roof of the car, but out of the corner of my eye I could see her leaning in a little. Quickly I looked away, wishing I was anywhere but here, and disliking myself for the stab of relief when I caught Grey moving backwards as if distancing himself.

'Will I see you tomorrow?' I heard her ask, and I could tell she was working hard to make her voice sound casual. 'Remember we're going down to the river to watch the rowing with Sophy and Rupert. We were going to take a picnic lunch, make a day of it.'

'Can I ring you tomorrow morning? There's still such a backlog from that stomach flu, and I've got a mountain of case files to catch up on.'

'Oh Grey, we've planned it for ages, it was all arranged around your work.' A note of petulance had crept into her voice, and despite myself, I did feel a bit sorry for her.

'I know, I'm sorry. I just have so much on at the hospital at the moment.'

'The hospital,' she said angrily. 'I tell you, I'm getting a little—' She suddenly seemed to recall that I was still in the car and caught herself, smoothed out her voice. 'Of course. Make sure you get some sleep and feel better in the morning. We can talk tomorrow, yes? Once you're through with this year, things should calm down at bit, shouldn't they?'

Wondering if she knew that house officers worked, if anything, even harder post-registration, I watched them walk to her front door. Her dress slithered along her legs as she turned and squeezed his hand before disappearing inside. He made his way slowly back to the car, looking more tired than before. Seeing him weave a little, I quickly got out of the back and slid into the driver's seat.

'Hey,' he said. 'Are you stealing my car?'

'I'm driving,' I said firmly. 'In your current state, you're a public hazard.'

'So are you,' he said belligerently. 'Shove over.'

'I caught a small nap in the downstairs loo.' I gave him a grin. 'I can highly recommend it, it's very peaceful in there.'

'You didn't?' He sounded impressed despite himself. 'During my birthday party?'

'Well, it means I can get us home in one piece,' I said loftily. 'Now, are you getting in before Mabel gets worried and comes back to check on you?'

This, along with a small twitch of the curtains in the second-floor flat, seemed to galvanise him. Grumbling slightly, he got in on the passenger side. 'Do you even know how to drive?'

'Iso—' I caught myself just in time. 'Mother said it's one of life's basic skills. Now be quiet so I can remember which knob does what. Just joking, calm down.'

Twenty-Eight

We didn't talk any more after that, because I really did have to concentrate – I'd only driven a few times before, and had had hardly any practice. Mercifully, the roads were emptier now; even more mercifully, by the next street corner Grey had slumped against the window fast asleep, leaving me to manoeuvre my way through Pimlico in peace.

Mrs Schwartz's house was unusually bright against the dark sky and through the open drawing-room window I saw people moving and gesticulating. Bicycles were chained to fences and lamp posts; an ancient Vespa belonging to Jakob was parked at a rakish angle at the front.

Of course, Mrs Schwartz's musical soirée. She held them once a month, raucous affairs where people played and sang and danced until late in the night. It was only down to Katia's constant supply of baked goods that the neighbours hadn't rallied round to have us evicted. I smiled when I saw that old Mrs Fisher from next door had pushed her armchair right up to her window, a plate of *knishes* in front of her, knitting needles flashing as she listened to the strains of a clarinet.

A trumpet joined in and, perhaps roused by the sound, Grey murmured and sighed, resettled himself. His tall body was folded against the inside of the door, his face relaxed in repose. His lashes feathered across the deep shadows smudging his cheekbones, the sweeping curve of his mouth softening the angles of his face. I sat back and pulled my coat more tightly around me, wondering if I might somehow engineer a conversation about his childhood, something that led to—I pulled myself up short, because of course I could never ask him. Just as

I could never sneak back to Chelsea Row to look for more sketches or get Ella to tell me about Alexander. I watched Grey sleep for a while, feeling a creeping desolation, as if my mother was hovering close by and yet out of reach.

'Are you always in the habit of staring?' He smiled without opening his eyes. His voice was hoarse and croaky, but he seemed more alert when he sat up. 'Ah, the joys of being a doctor.' He rolled his shoulders with a small groan, cracking what sounded like every vertebra in his spine. 'The torture of sleep deprivation.'

There was a sudden burst of applause, along with a loud cheer. He peered through the darkness towards the house, where the drawing room was a haze of cigarette smoke and noise. '*This* is where you live?' He sounded incredulous.

'It's not usually this loud,' I said. 'My landlady is having a musical soirée for her friends.'

'Goodness. I'm sorry to have kept you, you must be wanting to get inside. You really should have woken me.'

'You looked like you needed your sleep,' I said firmly. 'And I'm just going to sneak past and go up to my room. I've had my fill of parties tonight. Sorry,' I added hastily, 'it really was ever so nice of you to invite me to yours, such a lovely do.'

He nodded appreciatively. 'You're a good liar. It was . . .'

'A bit much?' I suggested.

He sighed and laid his head back against the top of the seat.

'The private practice,' I said. 'I didn't know it was already so set in stone.'

'It's not,' he said quickly, with the slightly wild look from earlier. 'I mean, it's the plan, but . . . well, you know. Who knows what the year will bring.'

'You're lucky, I guess.' My thoughts had gone back to all the things I'd discovered that evening. 'To be a part of people who love you and plan for you, who understand you. I know you don't want that,' I added quickly, when he made an impatient noise. 'I just . . . I'd love to be—'

'A surgeon, I know. Like him.' He looked at the lit windows, from which the sounds of a string trio were now emanating.

'Yes,' I said after a moment's pause. But it was more than that. To be part of a family. To know – unarguably, unequivocally – who I was supposed to be. Not piecing together my mother's story while trying to figure out my own, all the while pretending to be someone else altogether.

We watched two women walk towards the house and disappear through the door. Across the road, old Mrs Fisher had fallen asleep in her chair.

'I didn't know about your . . . your first mother,' I said, unable to resist the temptation to go back in time after all.

He looked down at his hands, and I felt a twinge of guilt at making him sad just to satisfy my own need to know. 'It's nice of you to put it like that,' he said, without looking up. 'It leaves room for both of them.' He sighed. 'Mum – Ella – she saved us, you know. Father had taken care of my mother while he was still in training, working himself into the ground really, because he couldn't bear being helpless. I think – from what I can piece together now – her case became hopeless very quickly, but the doctor treating her held back a lot of information. Perhaps he was trying to be kind, but it made it all the more devastating when she died so quickly. My father was so angry, that's mostly what I remember, him shouting and ranting and knocking about the house, the servants all in terror.

'Ella . . . well, you know how she is.' He smiled at me and I nodded. 'I will never forget when we moved in with her. It was just next door, but the relief at being away from our house . . . Father had kept my mother's room exactly the way it had been the moment she died; he only shrouded the mirror, and no one was allowed to turn on the light. It was horrifying for me to think that she might still be in there, trapped behind the cloth on the mirror, not allowed to rest in peace. It was like a dark hole, her room.' He paused. 'Like death itself was squatting in there, holding her prisoner, and I should be fighting for her and dragging her back out. But I couldn't bring myself to even go in there. When we left, it was like a release, like she was finally allowed to be free.' He made an awkward sound. 'I'm sorry, I don't know why I'm even telling you this, it's silly really.'

'It's not silly at all,' I said through the lump in my throat.

'In Ella's house, the lamps were kept on, and Cook was down in the kitchen. There was a piano, too. Mother had played the piano,' he added, stumbling slightly over the words, 'really well, too. She'd tried to teach me, but I was too little, really, and after she died, Father wouldn't even hear of me getting lessons. He . . . I think he loved her playing, actually, and, well, I suppose it was complicated after that. Ella was so good for him; they've been good together. But something about me and him never quite healed. We both seemed to be a replacement that could never quite measure up to the real thing, and a constant reminder of what was lost. And he became this new person, with this uncompromising, obsessive focus on his work, always a bit impatient and often angry, even in his best moments.'

He threw me a look. 'And now, with Mum's *cancer*,' he pushed out the word reluctantly, 'it's happening all over again. That feeling of helplessness and inevitability. We've become good at rubbing along with each other, keeping our distance when needed, but I wish now . . .' he groped for words, his voice a little unsteady, 'that we knew how to be more . . . together, you know, so we could help each other. Not treading on eggshells because we're both terrified and yet unable to talk to each other.'

His words died away and the silence grew and expanded. It wasn't awkward, however, and I realised with a small start that we'd somehow passed that stage of guarded conversation, that it felt entirely natural for us to sit here talking like this.

'Do you still remember much about your first mum?'

'I do.' He wove his fingers together tightly. 'But it's only an image of her, I think, snatches of what I think must be her voice, a song maybe.'

'A scent sometimes,' I said, 'a feeling of déjà vu, something that pushes in unexpectedly and seems to come from a different world altogether.'

'A squeeze when you see a picture and wonder who that person was. Straining to remember . . .' The sound of his voice faded, but the echo lingered inside the car. 'I hate not knowing for sure whether a memory really does belong to her or whether I'm making up a story from a photo or someone else's recollection. It must be a small consolation for you,' he added, 'that you have so much more to remember of your mum.'

I stared at him, heat creeping into my cheeks, when I realised he was talking about Diana McIntyre. 'Of course,' I said hoarsely, 'easier in a way, yes.'

'Not easy,' he amended quickly. 'I'm sorry.' Hesitating, he touched my clenched fingers. 'Never easy.'

I looked down at his hand still lightly touching mine, and wished I could talk about Mum properly: recall her little quirks, her laugh, somehow describe her to Grey, with whom it was so easy to talk, who understood the enormity of such a loss and something falling apart for ever. But then things were different for him. He kept his first mum alive by cherishing the memories he had, while I had let my own fade away when I'd become Isobel, almost relieved sometimes to be someone new and shiny. And not just that; I had replaced her with Diana McIntyre, which meant that I could never connect with her openly without my life falling apart all over again.

'I'm glad you had Ella to take care of you.' I rushed out the words, just to fill the inside of the car with something.

He took his hand away and fidgeted with the edge of the seat. 'She's more important to me than anyone in the world,' he said, gruffly, as if he didn't want to part with the information but wanted it said all the same. 'But sometimes I feel . . . guilty about

186

my own mother. I think it's also why I love the piano so much. It connects me with her, it's like she's talking to me, you know.'

I pictured the sketch in my notebook, the colours zinging, the bold strokes of my mother's pencil jumping off the page.

'I do know,' I said, and across the shadowy inside of the car he found my eyes and held them for a long moment.

'I knew you would,' he said with a half-smile. 'It's odd, because we only met so recently, but you seem to . . . well . . .' He broke off, and I looked back at him as loss and grief, the joy of memory, the pain of having forgotten pushed back the outside world, the world in which we were doctor and student, Carlisle and McIntyre. In its place was something more urgent, something vulnerable and deeply unsettling that made my heart beat faster as tentatively, slowly, he moved closer—

There was a boom of laughter and someone hit the keys of the baby grand in a clanging volley of sound. Commands like '*Quiet*' and '*Sit down, Kurt*' could be heard, then someone was tuning a violin, playing swirly phrases and chords, until it was in harmony with a darker string instrument.

'What is it like to live in a house like that?' Grey said hastily, back in his seat and sitting quite straight.

'Like living above a concert hall,' I said breathlessly. 'With lots of hearty Jewish food. But you look a lot more perky, so you're probably fine to drive without wrapping yourself around a lamp post on the way home.' I tossed him the keys and quickly climbed out of the car. 'Thanks again for . . . well, for all of it. It was good.'

But he'd got out too and was looking up at the window.

'What are you doing?'

'Shh,' he said impatiently as the viola picked up the violin's tune, weaving in and out, the piano rushing to support them. He opened the back door and retrieved the parcel.

'Mabel forgot her cakes,' he whispered, then gestured to the house. 'Lead the way.'

Twenty-Nine

It was a marvel how many people Mrs Schwartz managed to fit into her drawing room. People sat on every available chair, perched on windowsills or leaned against the walls.

'Over there.' I pointed to the far corner of the room and set off, Grey behind me.

An older man slid courteously off the windowsill when he saw me coming, and I clambered up. Grey, hugging the cake parcel, stood half in front of me, his back braced against my knees to keep me from falling off the sill, and then he didn't move at all any more, just stood and listened.

It wasn't a formal concert as such, more of a salon where people came together in ad hoc ensembles, pieces were requested and encores demanded. Fiddles seemed to be plentiful, but several people shared the two clarinets and one ancient double bass. Sometimes two people played the piano, sometimes just one in accompaniment of a singer or another instrument. It got louder and jollier as they went, until the rush of performers slowed at last and a young woman was propelled towards the piano seat, firmly instructed in a mix of Yiddish and English that it wasn't polite to answer back to one's elders and she should just play.

It was a simple folksy melody, not something I recognised but obviously well remembered and much beloved by the others, because a sigh went through the audience as she played. Two women in front of us had tears in their eyes, others mouthed words along with it. The lodgers crowded close to Mrs Schwartz, her presence solid and broad next to Jakob's pale, narrow elegance. There was Marek, who was still hoping for news of his brother ten years after he'd last seen him in Lodz, and Irina, who had skilfully avoided handing her sister over to the authorities for the last few years so they wouldn't be separated. They all gathered here each month, perhaps to try and replace a little of the family they'd lost.

The girl's hands slowly climbed up the keys, lingering over the last few notes, as, across the room, Mrs Schwartz caught my eye. She looked at me for a long moment, then nodded and smiled slightly, as if she was offering me what *they* had, a cobbled-together family, a place where you could belong and be truly yourself. Surely it wasn't this easy, though, you couldn't just . . .

There was a small movement next to me and I saw that Grey had turned to watch me instead of the piano. His hand touched mine, not tentatively any longer, and he slid his fingers into mine as if it was the most natural thing in the world. There was a beat of silence in the wake of the girl's song, as if the entire room was drawing breath, but when she lifted her hands, the spell was broken and she was pulled up from the chair amidst much cheering and clapping.

Grey didn't let go of my hand; in fact, he was pulling on it, pulling me off the windowsill and bringing our clasped hands together to close the distance between us. Details sprang into focus at random: the cake parcel bumping into my hip, a gust from the open window lifting my hair. But I didn't look away from his eyes, saw them crinkle at the edges as he smiled slightly, opened his mouth, his face now inches from mine, so close I could see the tiny golden flecks around his irises, the smooth plane of his jaw—

I pulled back abruptly, because as utterly lovely, utterly right it felt to be this close, this easy, it wasn't possible, and it certainly wasn't right. He was with someone else, someone perfect and real, and I was . . . My lie was getting ever bigger . . . I wasn't—

'A new guest.' Mrs Schwartz had made her way through the crowd. Her sharp gaze flicked from Grey's narrowed eyes to my warm cheeks, and then down to our hands. I flushed more deeply as I imagined what she must think, and quickly tugged mine free.

'Mrs Schwartz, this is Grey Carlisle, a . . .' I swallowed, avoided looking at Grey, 'a friend. I hope you don't mind that I brought him.'

She inclined her head gravely, fixing Grey with a long stare, and then said, 'I'm very glad you had someone to escort you home safely. I wouldn't want you to come to any harm.' She enunciated the last word carefully, and my flush receded a little when I realised that she wasn't disapproving but – in her own inimitable way – standing guard over me.

'It's a pleasure to meet you.' Grey executed a perfect bow over her hand, then straightened up and added, 'The concert was wonderful. So beautiful. I'm honoured to be here, thank you.'

Running out of words, he offered the cake parcel instead, now bent out of shape and a little squishy with cream at one corner. 'And we brought pudding.'

After that, the party got started in earnest.

'My lodger, Izabella, and her friend,' Mrs Schwartz introduced us to the guests, but Grey didn't seem to mind that he had been reduced to my add-on. I lost him at some point, when I was roped into handing out pieces of cake while Mrs Schwartz kept sternly instructing people to *Be nice, she will be a doctor,* although what one had to do with the other, I didn't know. A little later, I ended back up by the window, talking to Irina, the girl who'd played the sad song earlier. She waitressed at a Lyons tea house during the day and played the piano in a hotel lobby at night, and was trying to put her sister, a stocky girl being lectured by a diminutive man with an oversized moustache, through school.

'Proper English education, that's what I want her to have.' Irina's accent made all her words fierce, but these ones particularly so, and I smiled to myself because this was a sentiment I understood.

Across the room, Grey had taken off his jacket and rolled up his shirtsleeves, his face flushed with warmth. He wasn't remotely bothered by the mix of English, Yiddish, Polish and other languages. He listened the same way he'd listened to the music earlier, stood next to the piano and watched as someone played in emphasis of a point. And when they finally realised that he too was a musician, there was much exclaiming and clapping on backs. Someone produced bottles of Marek's home-brewed schnapps and poured it into whatever receptacles people had in their hands.

Above Marek's head, Grey looked up and gave me a happy wave. In all the weeks I'd known him, I had never seen him like this, so loose and unbuttoned. Like himself, I thought with a start, like the person he was meant to be, away from the role and the path his father wanted him to take on.

'I could help your sister a bit,' I suddenly heard myself say to Irina. 'If you like, that is?'

She opened her eyes wide, clapped a hand in front of her mouth. 'That would be . . . oh, an honour,' she said in a choked voice. 'A doctor helping my sister!'

'I'm not a doctor yet,' I said, a little alarmed. 'In fact—'

But she shouted across the room, 'Henryka! Henny. Come here. Hurry now, don't dawdle.'

The girl trod dutifully through the crowd towards us, Mrs Schwartz nodding as if she'd expected nothing less of the evening. More schnapps was poured to toast me, more exclaiming about my educational prowess, then Grey's when it was revealed he was a doctor *and* a musician, until someone picked up a clarinet, someone else grabbed a fiddle and the bass player was pushed behind the enormous instrument. They played once more, a wild, fiery sort of music that cleared the middle of the room and brought everyone to their feet. I felt my chest widen as if I was expanding in all directions, my heart free and unfettered, twirling at the hand of the moustached man, then doing some kind of waltz with Irina, and then with Jaroslaw, who'd abandoned his typewriter for the night. And through it all, Grey kept catching my eye again and again, until finally the crowd washed us both into the same corner.

He gave a happy sigh and fell back against the wall next to me. 'This is the best birthday party ever.' He shook his head and I gave a small huff of laughter, thinking about the pretty cakes, expensive presents and nicely dressed friends his mother had organised. He didn't seem to notice, just turned his head and looked sideways at me. 'I opened it, by the way. Your gift.'

'It's probably a bit small compared to all the other things you got,' I said. 'And I'm not sure if you could see it properly in the frame, but it's a record sleeve, signed by Billy Mayerl himself. Mr Bennet at the charity shop has heard him play and says he's an inspiration. Maybe,' I shrugged a little self-consciously, 'maybe it can be a reminder that there are many paths in life.'

'That I'm certainly beginning to see,' he said happily. 'I actually talked to Jakob about piano lessons.' He sounded almost a little shy. 'He says to come by next week and he'll listen, and if I'm not an utter embarrassment then he might help me improve. *Might*,' he added humbly. 'He says there's nothing worse than amateurs thinking they're professionals. And if all works out, who knows, maybe I'll have a chance at the conservatory audition next year. Or whenever.'

'You'll have to tell him, though, won't you? Your dad?'

His expression fell. 'Yes,' he said after a moment. 'I suppose I will.' He looked over to where Marek was holding forth, waving his clarinet around. 'There are a few things I need to talk to him about, actually. Like the fact that they seem to think I'm moments away from being engaged to Mabel, which is absolutely not true. It's what *they* want, because it makes the most sense to them. But it doesn't to me, or not,' he gave me a quick glance, 'any more.'

I stared at him, something hard and painful lodged in my

throat. Nothing about us made sense, really, I knew that. Just like I knew that I should smile and give him a friendly pat on the arm, change the subject and keep things simple between us. A friendship at a distance. Only I didn't. I wanted to forget all the things the evening had brought, I wanted to forget everything that was complicated about me and about the two of us.

So I leaned in. There was a melee of noise and shouting as another toast was drunk across the room, accompanied by a flourish from the baby grand. Grey and I were buffeted gently by the crowd of people and pushed even closer together. His hand reached for mine, and for a moment, a long, glorious moment, he was all around me, his scent, the whisper of his breath against my cheek, my hair curling into his neck, fingertips touching. And then he kissed me.

'I loved your gift,' he breathed into my ear. 'It was my favourite. Thank you.'

Thirty

It couldn't happen again; it was as simple as that. Not the close-ness, not the thrill, not the kiss that felt like a promise of something utterly lovely. We'd both been drunk, on brown schnapps, music and euphoria. I had been feeling a bit raw and vulnerable after finding out the truth about my parents. He was exhilarated with the prospect of lessons and that conservatory audition. But there was no way I was going to risk everything I'd worked so hard for. It had been a momentary rush of feelings, brought on because we were so very different and yet seemed to share so many things, too.

And maybe, if I made it clear that there could be nothing between the two of us, he would remember all about perfect, poised, peach-complexioned Mabel. I felt itchy and uncom-fortable at the thought of them together, then reminded myself firmly that Mabel would be the perfect human shield between us, between me and the way he had looked at me at the soirée: warm and challenging and tender all at the same time.

I knew I wouldn't be able to avoid him completely, but at least I could make sure I never stood still long enough to be drawn into a private conversation. Already I found it a little difficult to forget the look on his face when I'd seen him the Tuesday after the party. He'd lit up and mimed something that looked like a hangover, or dancing, or both. I'd given him a friendly, neutral wave and hurried away, but not before I'd seen his smile slip and his expression turn uncertain. I put it out of my mind resolutely, working flat out all week, volunteering extra time wherever possible or else hiding in the back of the library to read up on cervical cancer, radical hysterectomies and radiation treatments.

At home, whenever I had a spare minute, I fixed up Lily Collier's dress. Cutting away the threadbare bits, I merged the remainder of the skirt with a length of gleaming red and gold satin I'd bought at a street market. I had propped the piece of the sketch showing my mother next to Katia's sewing machine, and at some point, Lily's skirt became something else entirely. Something that suited a smiling, cheeky girl with irrepressible curls, who held her head high and was impossibly free-spirited, her dress so beautifully swingy, so very *fast*, that Mrs McIntyre would have turned in her grave.

Now well into our clinical course, we had evidently been on the ward long enough for Everett Carlisle to decide that we were no longer a waste of his time. He began to include the new students during rounds, firing questions at random the way he did with the more senior ones.

'Correct, Miss McIntyre,' he said after I'd identified the differences between a gastrectomy and a gastroenterostomy for duodenal ulcers. 'This one is first on tomorrow's list, so make sure you're in the gallery bright and early. Mr Mertins, enlighten us on the rate of recurrence after the procedure, please.'

Ella had sent me a note after the birthday party, apologising for getting a bit *swept up in things* and asking if I'd made it home all right, and would I like to pop by again for tea. *Nothing stronger*, she wrote, *I promise*.

I'd smiled at that. I still liked her, even with the way she spoke about my mother – she couldn't know, after all, who I really was. She hadn't said any more about her health, and I couldn't ask Grey, not when I was so studiously avoiding him. I had been watching Everett Carlisle covertly for any signs of what might be happening to his wife, but he never allowed the personal to interfere with his work, and outwardly his demeanour towards the patients – and indeed, the staff – seemed unchanged. Still, I couldn't help but think that he looked strained, more obsessed than usual with the cases on the ward, more obviously relieved with every patient he could discharge as healed.

Two days later, he came across me at the top of the stairs, gathering up a stack of notes and notebooks I'd dropped when rounding the corner too fast. Even after our strangely cosy chat in Ella's sitting room, he wasn't in the habit of directly addressing me outside rounds. But now he did stop.

'You look dead on your feet, Miss McIntyre. I've seen you on the ward and in the gallery at all hours. Do go home at some point. You're no use to anyone if you keel over.'

'I'm not going to keel over, sir, I promise.' I shuffled together handfuls of notes.

'What's that?' He nodded at a book in my hand.

'Oh, just some extra reading, to be more informed, you know.'

He looked at *Understanding Obstetric Surgery* for a long moment, and I thought there was something strangely bright in his eyes.

'I should go,' I said quickly, and nodded in farewell. But just as I turned to leave, he said my name.

'Yes?' I turned back.

'Your rota on Surgical III is coming to an end, you know.' The brightness in his eyes was gone, his voice back to its usual impatient growl. For the first time, I noticed that he seemed to be on his way somewhere special, because he was unusually formal in his black coat and hat. 'You'll move on to the gynaecological and antenatal wards. It'll be good for you.'

'Because I'm a woman?' I said, before I could stop myself.

He regarded me through his spectacles. 'Because it will broaden your experience,' he said. 'You'll see surgical cases from a very different angle. Mr Hughes is an excellent obstetrician; he's been around for so long, he has seen everything there is. You'll need it in your portfolio. And they . . .' he gave me a smile, for once not mocking or impatient, but oddly vulnerable, and all of a sudden, I thought I could see the man that Ella had fallen in love with, 'they could do with someone like you over there.'

With a curt nod, as if he was embarrassed by his own softness, he turned on his heel and stalked away, leaving me to stare after him, feeling a pleasure so overwhelming I thought I was going to levitate straight back into the ward.

I was so preoccupied with my elation that I didn't watch where I was going, and when I turned down the small corridor towards the private ward, I ran straight into Grey.

'Sorry,' I said, a little breathlessly. 'I . . . Oh, you're all dressed up.'

He'd changed from the white coat he'd worn earlier into a dark suit and tie, looking smooth and glamorous against the sterile white surroundings. His hair was still standing up in stubborn ruffles at the back, though, and I looked away quickly, not wanting to remember how it had felt touching it. 'Going anywhere nice?'

'Attending a function at the Royal College with my father. Lots of starched shirts rabbiting on about cataract surgery and joint replacement.'

'Sounds lovely,' I said automatically, trying not to notice the green of his eyes, the generous sweep of his mouth, twisted in a half-smile that was both superior and unguarded.

'I wanted to ask you, actually,' he bit his lip and flushed a little, 'if you'd like to come to the Bonfire Ball with me.'

My effort not to think about him was gone in an instant rush of memory. It seemed to push my body towards his, desperate to be back where we'd been at the soirée, to take his hand and run out through the door and into the sunny London afternoon to talk and laugh and drink tea and . . .

'I've got a lot of things to finish up, I'm afraid.' I took a step back and folded my hands firmly behind my back.

'Is it just me, or have you been avoiding me this week?'

'I've been busy.' My voice sounded harsh, sharpened perhaps by the willpower it took to rebuff him, and I saw the light in his eyes solidify into something hurt and confused.

'Too busy to talk about what happened?' The smooth skin of his throat moved as he swallowed, and I took another step back, hitting the wall.

'Could we discuss this later?' I craned my head to look towards the ward. 'I think someone is . . .'

'You seem too elusive for "later",' he said angrily, closing the distance between us in one stride. 'I want to talk now.'

'Grey, you're with Mabel.' I squirmed sideways. 'There is nothing to talk about, and even if there was, this isn't the place. Just leave it, Grey, please?'

For a moment, he towered over me and I had to tip up my face to see him properly, bristling and annoyed and yet seemingly unable to stop moving his hands towards mine, here in the hallway in the middle of the day, on full display. It had to stop, right now. *I* had to stop it.

'I broke up with Mabel,' he said abruptly.

I went still and stared up at him. 'You did?'

'Yes. After I left the soirée.' He paused, and the air between us whispered with the dancing and laughing that had happened that night, the kiss. He looked at me and I couldn't look away, saw the tiredness creasing the edges of his eyes, a dark, troubled green now.

'I never went to sleep. I went and waited in front of her house until she woke up, and I made it very clear that—'

'Grey! Are you still here? We need to go.' Everett Carlisle's voice was suddenly between us, somewhere close. Too close. I tried to duck away, and Grey was straightening, but it was too late. Carlisle had rounded the corner before we were fully apart, and I knew, instantly, that he'd seen everything. Just like on the ward, where he spotted the first invisible signs of infection before anyone else, where he seemed to be looking right into the body he was examining, he saw Grey pressing his lips together, the rigid set of his shoulders, my red face, my body straining away; he saw the tension, the frustration, the hum of our closeness still hanging between us.

There was a moment's silence, then he said, 'We need to go. Mabel and Ella will be waiting.'

Grey had flushed, but at this he shook his head defiantly and, avoiding my eyes, said, 'Mabel isn't coming, Father. We're not . . . we're not together any more.'

For another long moment Everett Carlisle said nothing, then he nodded slowly and turned to me. 'Miss McIntyre.'

It wasn't a question or a command, it wasn't even harsh or dismissive. Perversely, I wished it was, that he'd shout and bully and order me around instead of looking at me like he was now: wistfully almost, as if after weeks of being forced to take me seriously – against his better judgement – he had been right about me all along, right about female students on his ward. I was behaving exactly as he'd always known women to do, involved in a dalliance, sidetracked by emotions, taking up room that should go to someone more committed – and worse still, a dalliance with his *son*, whom he never in a million years would accept being with a working woman, who was supposed to be with someone like Mabel.

It was all happening right there, in front of my eyes. His expression became hard and unforgiving, until he looked at me like he had on my first day on the ward, and I hated it.

'We should go.' Dismissing me with a last glance, he moved between us and gestured for Grey to walk ahead. 'And I'm sure you are needed on the ward, miss.'

'Wait,' I said desperately. 'Please, sir, it's not what it seems. Not at all.' I avoided looking at Grey. 'We're not . . . That is, *I'm* not . . .'

I couldn't possibly have said the word 'not' more often or more emphatically. But Everett Carlisle was already opening the door and didn't turn back; perhaps he hadn't even heard me. Instead, it was Grey who looked back at me, his eyes as flat and hard as his father's. 'It seems I've been mistaken then, miss.'

Thirty-One

'Mr Hughes wants you down in Casualty.' Nurse Mavis stuck her head into the sluice room.

'Really?' I immediately tossed the metal kidney dish I was holding back into the sink and started tugging off my apron.

The gynaecological ward was on the same floor as Surgical III, along with the antenatal and maternity wards, utility rooms, side wards and private rooms in between. I had arrived a few days ago to find Mr Hughes in charge, acknowledging my presence with a narrow-eyed look of scepticism, as well as – rather unfortunately – Sister Veronica, who was temporarily filling in to supervise Gynae IV alongside Surgical III and was all the sharper about it. I was pleased to see Mrs Smith, who, I'd since learned, was a bit of an institution around here, now working at different London hospitals after a long stint as a community midwife.

'You're a bit keen, aren't you?' Nurse Mavis observed as I made for the door, barely pausing to give her a farewell wave. I couldn't very well tell her that yes, I was indeed a bit keen because the moment I stopped thinking about work, anxiety started seeping in. Anxiety and regret and a horrible ache I didn't bother identifying but was trying hard to get rid of. Partly to do with Everett Carlisle's disappointment and disapproval, which I couldn't see a way to rectify now, the gratifying interest he had taken in my career soured by our most recent encounter. Partly to do with Grey and the way we'd left things. I was livid that he'd put me in such a compromising position at work, and yet I couldn't forget the hurt look on his face at the haste with which I'd denied that there was anything between us, that Everett Carlisle had nothing to worry about.

There *was* nothing between us, but – and at this, the ache in my chest always took a particularly vicious stab in the direction of my heart – he was no longer with Mabel. He'd waited in front of her house to tell her. I wrestled with the glow at imagining this, because it didn't change anything at all. I was living a lie, and being with him would risk everything falling apart. So ironically, Everett Carlisle really *did* have something to worry about, were he to know the truth about who I was, in particular the fact that my father was Alexander Bellingdon. That part I still hardly believed myself, constantly questioned and wondered if it would ever catch up with me properly.

'I'm here, Mr Hughes,' I said breathlessly, when I found him in one of the back rooms in Casualty. 'What can I do?'

'Flying Squad.' He nodded for the orderly to wheel the trolley down the ramp.

I stopped short. 'Flying Squad, sir?' I repeated. 'Out to the East End?'

'That's the general idea.' He gestured for me to follow the orderly. 'We're a student short. Pick up your feet, Miss McIntyre, if you please. It'll be a busy night.'

'I knew we'd get you out with us one of these days.' Mrs Smith rushed past with a smile. 'Take that stack there, will you? Quickly now.'

I hurried down the ramp to the idling lorry. The nurse I'd met last time, Nurse Reeds, jumped forward to relieve me of my burden. 'We're in here, miss.'

She climbed into the back, waggling her fingers for me to follow. I looked at the small, windowless space she was crouching in, and turned to Mrs Smith. 'I've only just started in Gynae IV this week. I wonder if I'm quite the right—'

'Absolutely. Students shadow and lend a hand, help clean and make cups of tea.'

'All things a girl should be good at anyway.' Mr Hughes flung open the passenger door, ignoring the combined looks of outrage from the nurse, Mrs Smith and me. 'Now let us get going, and Mrs Smith can try yet again to achieve with her driving what centuries of fatal illnesses have failed to do: kill us all.'

I couldn't go back there – I was meant to be *dead*, for heaven's sake – but more than that, I didn't *want* to go back to the place where my mother had fled after everyone had abandoned her, where our rainbow flat had gone up in flames. Without her being there, without her waiting for me, how could I possibly—

I was back. I fell out of the van as the doors opened, and almost instantly the East End rushed at me: the familiar streetscape of narrow, crooked houses, laundry strung out to dry, big-wheeled prams outside front doors. Piles of rubble everywhere, broken buildings left over from the war and covered in bombweed. The burr of conversation from the women gossiping in the street and two men walking past swinging metal lunch boxes. It was all exactly the same, as if I only had to blink and I'd be running home, my book bag hitting the backs of my knees.

I could feel myself scrabbling for my Isobel shell, to pull my bright new life around me, as I ran to follow Mr Hughes and Mrs Smith into the nearest house, my arms full of equipment; to block out the faded wallpaper, the worn tread on the stairs, the two mugs on pegs, exactly like in our shop. Mum shaking out a piece of fabric while I perched on the table and read to her . . .

Hold her arm like that, Miss McIntyre. Yes, blood group O rhesus negative. Untangle that. Remake the bed with clean sheets. I boiled water, I made tea, I fetched rags, mouthing the familiar patient questions alongside Mr Hughes like a reassuring mantra, and slowly the shock of being back, the pull of remembering lessened. I was back to being Isobel, I was in control.

*

Our next stop wasn't the Flying Squad's usual type of call-out. A neighbour had rung the hospital, alarmed at the noise issuing from the flat. The community midwife had been inexplicably delayed, but the mother-to-be, Mrs Callender, had not been particularly pleased when we arrived. She refused to lie down, bellowing through her early labour pain, forcing a slightly irate Hughes to examine her in a half-crouch. 'Madam,' he said loudly, 'you need to lie down and calm yourself. You'll be a while, and in the meantime, you're not helping the baby like this.'

Mrs Smith tried to guide her into a lying position, but Mrs Callender threw herself about and hunched over the kitchen table. It was hot in the room, with water boiling on the hearth, and Hughes had just pulled out an enormous handkerchief and was mopping his forehead when Nurse Reeds came panting up the stairs. 'I rang the hospital, there's an emergency on Ashbury Lane, number 12 . . .'

Hughes got to his feet, snapped his bag shut and motioned us toward the stairs.

'Midwife, midwife!' A girl suddenly shot into the room. 'My mam's had a bad fall on her bump, there's blood, I saw the van, come quickly . . .'

Mrs Smith gathered up her things and made for the door, where the girl was hopping up and down making flapping motions like a distraught bird. Within seconds, they had vanished down the stairs.

Hughes waved the two Callender children forward. A girl who was no more than ten or eleven dragged her little brother by the hand.

'The community midwife should be here any minute. If anything happens before then, I'm at 12 Ashbury Lane.' He looked around for his stethoscope. 'Fetch the neighbour from downstairs until then and stay in the other room.'

'Not her,' Mrs Callender ground out.

'Yes, her.' He turned back to the girl. 'Your mum'll be all right, I promise. Miss McIntyre, quickly now.'

The girl's eyes were huge as she eyed her mother hanging sideways across the kitchen table, her bump heaving. 'But you can't leave her like this, Doctor, please,' she said, a little breathless at addressing him directly. Her eyes flicked to my white coat and the bag I was holding. 'Please, miss.'

'Mr Hughes?' I held him back. 'Why don't I stay here and keep an eye on her?'

'No,' Hughes said, already halfway out of the door. 'You're only meant to be with patients under the supervision of myself or Mrs Smith. Mrs Callender still has time, the neighbour'll be plenty.'

'I wouldn't do anything medical. I'll just help her lie down and be calm. I'll send . . .' I looked at the little girl.

'Alice,' she said eagerly.

'. . . Alice to fetch you if needed, and as soon as the community midwife arrives, I'll come over to Ashbury Lane.'

He looked at me. The front of my coat was wet where Mrs Callender had upset a bowl of water and I'd dived to catch it, my pockets were stuffed with torn-up sheets, and my hair, I knew without touching it, was escaping its pins and writhing madly in the humidity of the room.

'All right,' he said reluctantly, 'but make sure—'

'I will,' I said, all but shooing him out of the door. 'Don't worry.'

Silence fell in the wake of his departure, then Mrs Callender moaned and shifted on the table, holding on to the back of a chair for support.

'All right, we'll just get you lying down—'

'I don't want to lie down,' Mrs Callender pushed out. 'Lying down was what got me here in the first place. Bloody Matthew.'

'My da,' Alice said helpfully.

'I don't want him,' Mrs Callender said mutinously. 'I don't

want to lie down ever again, I just want to—' She doubled over with another bellow and the little girl sprang back in alarm.

'It's all right,' I told her. 'Mums often get angry during labour, it's a way of coping with the pain, redirects it to something else, see. But they don't really mean it.'

'She probably does,' Alice said. 'She's been on at my da with every sleepless night and every twinge of pain.'

'Don't want,' Mrs Callender squeezed out.

'That's fine,' I said firmly. 'But you will have to move soon, for the sake of the baby.'

I waited until the contraction passed, then took hold of her arm and peeled her off the table. 'Alice, take her other arm. And you . . .' I looked at her brother.

'Lucas,' Alice said.

'You look like a strong lad. Move those chairs out of the way as best as you can, and the table too.'

Relieved to have something to do, Lucas noisily proceeded to clear a space for us in the middle of the small room.

'What now?' Alice enquired.

'Now we walk. Walking is good in early labour, makes the baby more comfortable, distracts the mother.'

We walked. Round and round, supporting Mrs Callender, who stopped every so often to double over in pain before she started shuffling again. Despite my earlier confidence, I was starting to worry just a little. Each time we passed the small clock on the shelf, it was becoming more and more apparent that it had now been quite a while since Mrs Smith and Hughes had left, and there was no sign of the community midwife. Lucas had wrestled more water on to the hearth to boil, and the room was even hotter, making sweat run down between my shoulder blades and settle at the small of my back.

'I wonder,' I said to Alice, trying to make my voice sound as light as before, 'should we maybe fetch your neighbour after all? Give us a bit of a break?'

If she was here and seemed capable, maybe I could slip down and find Mrs Smith. And I didn't really want the children in here for the birth.

'Mam hates Hazel,' Alice informed me.

'She's dirty,' Lucas added. 'Her fingernails are always black.'

All of a sudden Mrs Callender dug her fingers into my arm, and the low, ongoing grumble of pain turned into a louder bellow, then a scream as she doubled over, arms reaching to hold something.

'It's coming,' she hissed, and I felt a surge of horror. 'I can feel it *coming*. You have to do something, it wants out, I want it out, I want it *out*...' She was wild-eyed now.

'Alice. Run fast and try to find Mrs Smith.'

Mrs Callender wrenched her arm out of mine, dropped to her knees next to the bed and started grunting. I stared down at her, my mind racing.

'No, Alice. Stay,' I said shrilly, scrabbling for the birthing kit sitting on the kitchen table. My hands were shaking so hard it took me three tries to rifle through it. 'Lucas, you go. Ask anyone you can see for the midwife, anyone at all, you hear me? And if you can't find her, rush to 12 Ashbury Lane for the doctor. Send whoever you find first back here.'

He shot out of the door so fast I thought he would vault straight down the stairs.

'We need her on the bed, there's no other way,' I said. 'But first, water, in that clean bowl over there.'

'Should I get Hazel?' Alice fetched the water.

'With the black fingernails? No, thank you. Anyone else in the house?'

'Two old men downstairs, and Mary Allen on the second floor, but she's on night shift.'

'Just us then,' I said grimly.

*

We were both dripping with sweat by the time we had the bed covered properly and persuaded Mrs Callender on to it. She absolutely refused to lie down, so I compromised by letting her kneel, her upper body braced against the top of the headboard, hands pressed against the wall and eyes squeezed shut. It was a far cry from the positions in my textbook, which had mostly been nice, compliant women with snowy cloths draped across their pulled-up thighs, but it would have to do.

'I need to wash my hands very, very thoroughly,' I said to Alice, who nodded solemnly and held out a clean towel. 'Now fetch that bottle from the kit and pour it over my hands. Just a little . . . a little more . . . that's it. Now roll up your mum's dress, very neatly, and tuck it in up there.'

I talked her through what we'd do as I cleaned Mrs Callender's thighs and leaned in to feel her belly, and with each word my voice became less shrill and my hands steadied. Images started lining up neatly in my mind, like the slides on old Professor Harbinger's projector. The womb, viewed sideways and across. The umbilical cord. The foetus curved around its own belly, legs tucked up. I'd observed a woman being examined internally several times but had never done it myself, and was fairly certain it fell under *not touching a patient without supervision*.

'Can you look out of the window and see if you can spot the midwife?' I asked desperately.

Mrs Callender let out another bellow and a contraction tightened her belly. Alice abandoned her lookout and rushed to hold her mother's hand. I'd have to do it, there was no other way, I'd have to check her properly, and if I was struck from the register before I'd even had a chance to be on it, then so be it.

'I can feel the baby,' I said through gritted teeth.

I could feel the baby all right, but not what I thought I should feel, the round shape of its head, and not the way Professor Harbinger had shown us in the plastic model – he'd prodded it down quite forcefully, I remembered, reassuring us that contractions were nature's way of helping. Well, nature didn't seem to be helping here all that much. Mrs Callender groaned as I continued to examine her and felt . . . oh God, a shoulder. The baby's body was angled slightly, and facing forward rather than backward. Horror made my hands start shaking again, and I forced them to stop only with an enormous effort.

'Wash your hands exactly as I showed you,' I instructed Alice, 'for a long time and between your fingers, then use the brown bottle—'

My words were lost in another contraction. 'It's coming,' Mrs Callender screamed, 'Mary and Joseph, please help me . . .'

And then it all happened very fast. I let go of what I thought was the shoulder just as another enormous contraction came. Mrs Callender bellowed, Alice dropped the bottle of antiseptic, and the door burst open to reveal the community midwife along with Mr Hughes.

'It's in posterior,' I shouted. 'I had a shoulder, but it's gone. I'm sorry, I'm so sorry . . .'

Hands pushed me out of the way, the smell of antiseptic from the broken bottle was overpowering, and for what seemed like an eternity all was noise and grunting and voices as I brought more water, scrabbled for towels, until finally . . . a thin, reedy wail.

'It's a little girl.' Mr Hughes got to his feet.

'It is?' I stared at him, noticing his red-rimmed eyes and the deep lines around his mouth, the smudges on his spectacles. 'Is it . . . is she all right?'

He frowned down at me for a long moment, then his face broke into a grudging smile. 'She is all right, yes.'

'Can I . . . I mean, can I see her?' I started towards the bed, where the midwife was tending to Mrs Callender.

'Miss McIntyre,' Hughes held me back, 'you—'

'I'm sorry,' I cut in breathlessly. 'I know I'm not allowed, but it all happened so fast, and no one was coming and—'

'You did well,' he said.

Thirty-Two

Mrs Smith caught up with us as we made our way towards the truck.

'I'm so sorry, Doctor. I ended up having to call an ambulance. There was no chance to come and fetch you, and by the time—'

Her eyes fell on my blood- and fluid-covered coat, and she stopped in mid sentence. 'She's never had the baby already? She was miles from it. Oh goodness.'

She gasped as Hughes related the whole story, but I wasn't really listening as I helped Nurse Reeds load the equipment back into the truck. The street felt different from before, the familiarity not needling me with darts of pain. Instead, I felt fluid and light, inhaling deep lungfuls of night air. If you'd set me down anywhere around here, I'd have been able to find my way home by smell and sounds alone: a bell tolling a few streets over, a foghorn drifting up from the river, the smoke from too many chimneys weaving through wet fog.

'Sounds like you had quite a night.' Mrs Smith had come to stand next to me.

'It was fine.' I smiled at her a bit ruefully. 'I didn't think it was fine halfway through, but it turned out all right.'

She nodded approvingly. 'I knew you had it in you. You're seeing it all tonight, Miss McIntyre. It's not usually quite this mad, I promise. Now, we're almost done. Just one last stop.'

We drew up in front of a narrow building in one of the streets off the river. The brackish smell was stronger here, the houses shabby, with big gashes where bombs had taken out whole terraces that hadn't been rebuilt. Hughes had fallen asleep, despite Mrs Smith's attempt to hit every pothole between here and Limehouse, and only grumpily awoke when the van came to a stop.

'What's happening?' He clambered wearily out of the truck. 'Weren't we on the way back?'

'I spoke to one of the midwives from the Convent of the Holy Sepulchre earlier today; she said there was a problem with a patient we treated in Casualty a few weeks ago, asked if we could look in on her on our way. Remember Lily Collier, the girl with the bruises, Miss McIntyre? She hasn't been seen in a while, but the landlady swears she's in her room.'

It was close to midnight now and the street was dark. The curtains in the front room were pulled closed and there was no light. Mrs Smith rang the front doorbell a few times, then, when a woman emerged from the opposite flat, ducked past her into the narrow hall and knocked on Lily's door.

'You'll not have any luck with that one,' the woman said. She had a dressing gown over her nightdress and her hair was in chunky pin curls. 'Hasn't been seen in more than a week. I know they've been by to collect the rent. Wouldn't be the first time someone's tried to get out of paying.'

I'd been peering through the window to make out any movement, but there was something about the woman's voice, the cosy gossip laced with a whiff of disapproval, that made me look at her.

'Well, it's all good for *some*,' she said defensively when she saw my eyes narrowing.

'Clearly not for her. Wouldn't it be more appropriate to see if she needs help rather than accuse her of dodging her rent?' My voice was hard.

'Miss McIntyre, please,' Mr Hughes said briskly. 'Why don't you go and get my bag.'

He knocked on the front window, but I didn't move, staring

the woman down until she backed away a little. 'I meant no harm,' she said. 'I was only saying—'

'Maybe don't,' I snapped.

Hughes turned, scandalised. 'The bag,' he ordered.

I went back to the van and snatched it down in time to hear the woman say, 'Since you're here, Doctor, could you come and have a look at my mum's leg? It's huge and I don't think I'll be able to get her to the clinic tomorrow.'

It was a good thing that she was already going back into the house, or else I might have swung the bag at her.

'Mrs Smith, I think we'd better ring for the constable to open the door.' Hughes stepped back from the window. 'You have a quick look at that leg, Nurse, see what's amiss, while I find a telephone. And then you and I will have a little chat about how to comport ourselves on duty, Miss McIntyre.'

With a mammoth effort I swallowed back all the other things I had wanted to say to the woman. I could feel them churning around at the back of my mind, though, where they met skirts twitching out of my way and whispers at church when my mother and I walked in, girls chasing me home from school – *bastard, bastard* – and Mrs McIntyre's moue of distaste, until I found myself rapping on the window to Lily's room again, so hard the lead frame gave a little. I pushed at it, felt the vibration of the panes, and a rattle where the latch met the window.

'Miss McIntyre?' Mrs Smith appeared next to me.

'I'm just going to speed things up a bit.' I dug my fingernails into the gap by the latch, then extracted my mother's knife from my pocket and slid it next to my fingers, jiggled it up and down until I finally heard a click. I turned to find Mrs Smith and Hughes staring at me, their mouths open.

'And here I was ringing the constable, when we already have a criminal in our midst.' Hughes reached past me to swing the window open. The curtains billowed out into the night, and with them came a smell so fetid and stale that all of us fell back, gagging slightly.

'Oh no,' Mrs Smith said, her voice for once not calm but full of horror. 'Miss Collier,' she parted the curtains, 'can you get up and open the door? It's the doctor and the midwife, we've come to check you're all right.'

But the shape on the bed seemed altogether too still. I felt nausea rise. Surely, *surely* someone couldn't just decide to lie down on a bed and die. I blinked, saw the blanket move.

'She's alive,' I said breathlessly. I whirled round, spotted the box containing bandages and first aid supplies, dragged it over and set it down beneath the window.

'Good girl.' Mrs Smith grabbed my legs and pushed up until I was perched on the narrow windowsill, shredding my knees on two sticking-out nails before finally rolling down on the other side.

I crossed the distance to the bed in three big strides, pulled the covers down and almost fell back again, clapping my hands in front of my mouth to keep myself from retching. Lily Collier was lying on her side with her eyes closed. Breathing shallowly, I crouched next to her, felt for a pulse. There, a faint flutter beneath the paper-thin skin, enough for me to jump up and hurry to open the door.

Mrs Smith pressed past me without a word and knelt by the bedside.

'Holy Mother of God,' Hughes choked out at the stench, but he advanced on the bed and ordered me to fetch his second bag from the van, along with an extra bottle of antiseptic, and by the time I was back, they had turned the girl over so she faced them.

Lily Collier looked and smelled like she hadn't washed since we last saw her. Her hair was tangled around her face, her bruises faded yellow and green against her white skin. Her arms and legs were so thin and brittle I was afraid they'd break, her belly grotesquely big and swollen in comparison.

Mrs Smith was speaking to her urgently, but Lily didn't open her eyes.

Quickly I knelt down and opened the bag to hand Hughes his stethoscope. After his earlier treatment of Lily in Casualty, I thought he'd be brisk and impatient, but he seemed intent on the task at hand and gentle in his handling of her. Outside, I could hear voices, people poking their heads out of doors to investigate the commotion.

'Severely malnourished and dangerously dehydrated. And one of the gashes she had at the hospital is infected. She'll need constant supervision. Have another look at the baby, Mrs Smith.' He stepped back to give the midwife space.

After a few minutes, Mrs Smith got to her feet. 'It's alive, but who knows in what state . . .' She broke off, and we all looked down at Lily Collier, who had preferred starving herself and her baby in a slow and agonising death to living in the world around her.

'She can still make it,' I said urgently. 'If she gets help, if she feels there is support, she could still find it in her to fight.'

Nurse Reeds came in, and behind her, the neighbours, led by the woman from across the hall, whose mouth opened in an O of fascinated horror when she saw the bed. I flew across the room and pushed the door closed behind the nurse.

'You've rung for the ambulance?'

'Yes. And the constable's here, Mr Hughes.' Nurse Reeds gave a meaningful look at the door. 'I haven't said that she . . . I mean, how exactly we found her and all, but . . .'

Mr Hughes exchanged a long look with Mrs Smith.

'Don't report it quite yet, Mr Hughes,' she said quietly. 'Let's see if we can sort her out at the hospital. She'll never get out of it otherwise.'

He grimaced, rubbed his hand over his forehead, then

nodded curtly. 'I'll speak to him now, Nurse. Give her a little of the sugar-salt solution and stay with her. I'll be back.'

'I know I said I'd try and find something for her,' Mrs Smith said ruefully when he'd left. 'I'm ashamed to say it got away from me. Though most of what would be available wouldn't be all that much kinder than that.' She jabbed her chin at the window, where the petulant, eager voice of the neighbour could be heard.

'I hope Mr Hughes . . . I mean, when she was first brought in, he wasn't . . .' I nodded emphatically, hoping she'd get my drift.

She gave me a long look. 'Mr Hughes was the one who helped launch the Flying Squad, you know.'

'He did?' I was so surprised I took a step back. 'Really?'

'He might be old-fashioned when it comes to women's morals, but not where poverty, abominable living conditions and lack of education are concerned. I've been working with him for a long time. By rights he should report Miss Collier's suicide attempt to the police; she could go to prison, at the very least in front of a judge.'

'But he won't.'

'No. He might be a man of many contradictions, but he's a good one at heart.'

The nurse returned to help with the transfer into the ambulance, and I pulled out a few clothes and a nightshirt and packed them into a threadbare carpet bag I found underneath the bed. There wasn't much else in the flat, little in the way of food or extras. It was as if she'd arrived here with the contents of her bag and nothing else, evicted from her former place, perhaps, or kicked out of her mum and dad's house.

'Miss McIntyre, are you coming?'

I almost ran from the room with that carpet bag, so keen to be gone that I realised only as we rattled away through the night that there had been no baby clothes either. No place for it to sleep, no pram or nappies or anything else that showed a child would soon be coming into the world.

Thirty-Three

I dreamed I was running down the road, away from Lily's room and Mr Hughes, pressing the small flyers we'd made up for Mum's business on passers-by. She'd sketched a little drawing on each of them: a blouse, a dress, a pair of wide-legged pantaloons, a flurry of familiar images. In my dream, people took them and smiled, and I smiled back, flying through the streets towards home, fleet-footed and happy. Warm light spilled through the open door; I heard the sound of her voice. I was free. I was home.

Music wove into my dream memory, making it blur at the edges, become hazy and indistinct. And then it dissolved, leaving me all alone in my tower room, wet face pressed into the pillow, the edge of my stupid etiquette manual, which had slid into the gap by the wall, digging into my cheek. Late, I thought, struggling up from the bed, I was late, because Mrs Schwartz never got stuck into Brahms until breakfast was over. Then I sank back on to the bed. It was Saturday, and I wasn't due at the hospital today.

My head was still full of all the happenings of the previous night as I made my way downstairs a little later, and it took me a moment to realise that actually the music didn't sound at all like Mrs Schwartz's usual repertoire. It was more of a stop-start and – yes – two people. Playing, then talking. A strange tingling swept up my spine. When I passed the drawing-room door, I heard them again. And now I didn't need my spine to tell me that Jakob was instructing someone. There was the sound of a chair shuffling, footsteps . . .

'Oh Izabella,' Jakob said delightedly. 'Look who is here. He is promising. With a lot of work, that is,' he added to Grey, who was nodding humbly behind him. 'Now, Katia has gone to the market and we were just about to find some coffee in the kitchen. And you must have breakfast, you were very late coming in. Maybe it's warm enough still to sit in the garden.'

'I'm not sure,' I said, a little overwhelmed by the onslaught of information, and the fact that Grey Carlisle was here, in *my* space, where I was used to being me rather than being on my guard. 'Actually, I was on my way out.'

'I'll walk with you,' Grey said. His voice was cool, his face expressionless, but his body was already moving towards me.

I took a step back. 'Coffee first, then.'

The kitchen smelled sweet and homey. There were small whorls of flour on the countertop where Katia had been baking, and a fat braided challah loaf sat on the counter, glazed and shiny, exuding comfort. I was grateful that Jakob kept up a polite patter, asking Grey about his studies, setting out a dish of jam, cups and plates. The smell of coffee filled the kitchen.

'Would you like some challah?' I asked as I fetched a breadknife from the drawer.

Grey looked bemused, and I realised that he probably wasn't used to being in people's kitchens. Oddly, it seemed to give me an advantage of some kind, and my voice sounded more normal when I explained, 'It's a sweetish kind of bread. And,' I gave a small flourish towards the dish next to it, 'Katia has our butter rations under lock and key, but there's jam. Heaven on a plate. Here.' I handed him the knife and gestured towards the loaf.

'Isn't there always jam?' he asked, bending over and beginning to saw at the bread in a concentrated way, perfectly even slices falling away from his hands.

'Sugar wasn't rationed in Chelsea?' I shared an amused look with Jakob, who chuckled as he filled a coffee mug and, inviting Grey to come back to practise whenever he wanted, started bowing himself out.

'Wait, Jakob, surely you don't need to leave already?' I said, suddenly loath to be left alone with Grey. 'Jakob!'

When I turned back to Grey, he had poured two cups of coffee and was pushing a plate towards me. By some unspoken agreement, we didn't sit, but leaned against the countertop, the coffees steaming gently between us.

'So,' I said, to fill the awkward silence.

'So,' he repeated with a small sigh, then took a deep breath. 'I wanted to apologise. It was unforgivable of me to accost you like that at the hospital. I just . . . I wanted to talk to you, I guess, and you had been ignoring me. I forgot myself, and I'm sorry.'

I opened my mouth, closed it again, because I had expected him to discuss, to argue even, but not this, a genuine, disarming apology.

'I know you couldn't have let on to my father, I understand why, but . . .' He paused, then added in a rush of words, 'But how quickly you said it, how emphatically it came out. I don't know, it made me feel foolish somehow.'

He picked up his coffee cup, perhaps to have something to do with his hands, took a deep sip.

'I'm sorry about that. It's only . . . I had just about reached a level of grudging acceptance with him, and then he catches me doing exactly what he always thought a woman in my place would do. So I had to say it like that, though to be truthful, I wish I could have the chance to tell him again, explain that it's . . .'

Grey slowly set down his cup, spilling a little on the counter. His face was lit up by the sun that came through the back door, his eyes intent on mine.

'. . . that it's complicated.' My voice was hoarse and my heart raced inside my chest. I reached past Grey for a cloth to wipe up the spilled coffee, but it dropped from my hand to the floor. Without a word, he picked it up and cleaned the countertop, returned the cloth to the sink.

'Maybe we can keep it separate.' He leaned forward to look at me. 'Be together and still be entirely professional at the hospital. We could be open and honest about it.'

'No.' I shook my head. 'It won't work. You know as well as I do that I'd have to leave the hospital.'

'Then I could find a job elsewhere, and you could come and meet me . . .'

'No.'

'. . . and eventually you'll be on the register, by which point you'll no doubt be running the place and no one will dare dismiss you out of hand.'

'Grey. You're not listening to me.'

'Maybe you don't get to decide this one all by yourself. And we're quite alone here, no one to see.' Slowly, unhurriedly, he reached for my hand, pulled me closer until my body was flush against his.

'We're too different, Grey. I'm sorry. We're just not suited.' Even were I to find a way to tell him the truth about who I was, which I could never do without sacrificing everything, the fact remained that Everett Carlisle's only son could never be with the girl who was actually behind the masquerade. Bastard Agnes, the good-for-nothing Crawford girl.

I tried to pull away, but he refused to let go, and bit by bit, his clean peppermint scent forced back the sour taste in my mouth, the sun warm on my back. His eyes were the same greeny-blue they'd been when I first saw him, and he stroked my hand gently, his thumb running up the soft underside of my wrist until my mind calmed and my heart stopped racing, and from somewhere joy bubbled up. Clear and warm and utterly right, it made me sigh and close my eyes.

'I don't understand why you're so worried about being suited, whatever that means,' he whispered, running his hand down my back now. 'You're smart, your grandfather was a well-known surgeon, you're my mother's old friend's daughter – how on earth could we not be suited? Just give it a chance, please, Isobel.'

I snapped upright so quickly that I felt the counter connect painfully with my hip. Isobel. Of course. With her perfect family and her unquestionable situation in life, yes, *they* were well suited, weren't they? I couldn't possibly argue with that. All I knew was that if he said her name like that again, in that lovely caressing way, I would die.

'It's not what I want,' I said loudly. 'I'm sorry. Please go.'

Out of the corner of my eye, I saw that his face had gone white. 'I don't believe you,' he said slowly. 'I know that you feel it too, what's between us, when we're together like this – "it fills all of you until nothing matters but doing the thing you love most of all", remember?'

His words came in fast and relentless, met that bubbling joy inside me, and for a brief moment I wondered if maybe this *could* somehow be untangled. Almost immediately, though, I pushed the thought away. How could I ever love someone, let myself be loved, when I had no idea who I really was? Because it wasn't Isobel who wanted to reach for Grey, it couldn't possibly be that shy, reserved girl I was pretending to be. So it had to be Agnes who was desperate to take his hand and lean in and kiss him on and on, Agnes who wanted to figure out a way to take on the world. But it *couldn't* be Agnes either, because Agnes had worked too hard to be Isobel to risk it all now. Being Agnes wasn't an option. Being Agnes in love even less so.

I blinked furiously, tried to situate myself back into Isobel's story, but all I could think about was my mother loving Alexander, being abandoned by him. For the second time, I felt my life slide alongside hers. The way we'd both fallen in love with someone we weren't supposed to, the way our love stories were complicated, different and ultimately doomed.

He saw it on my face, I could tell, because his eyes changed and everything that had been loose and happy about him a moment ago drew in on itself.

'I was talking about medicine, being a doctor. Not about us,' I said, looking away now because I couldn't bear to see the expression in his eyes. It was *my* doing, that hurt, it was because of *my* lie. 'I'd like us to be colleagues, maybe friends again in time, but that's all.'

I kept my eyes on the floor, methodically cataloguing the cracks and chips in the ancient flagstones, until I heard the sound of footsteps, then the door closing with a soft click. When I next looked up, I was alone in the sunny kitchen that smelled of coffee and freshly baked bread.

Thirty-Four

'To monitor pre-eclampsia effectively in hospital, you'll need to . . . Anything interesting happening outside, Miss McIntyre?'

Quickly I turned away from the window. The small group of people I'd been trailing through the antenatal ward had fallen silent, and Hughes was giving me a piercing look.

'Of course not,' I said quickly. 'I was just listening intently.'

'Then maybe you can tell us how to monitor pre-eclampsia effectively.'

'Bed rest. Vitals observed closely. Sedation. A special diet. No salt, low fluids. Or was it salt and sugar?' I faltered, trying to remember.

'No salt, low fluids.' Hughes peered at me over his spectacles. 'Foetus needs careful monitoring as well.'

He turned and continued his pilgrimage down the line of beds. I gripped my notebook and vaguely jotted down *no salt*. What was I doing staring out of the window? I had everything I wanted now. A successful stint on the Flying Squad, culminating in rare praise from Hughes. I'd been back in the East End and weathered all the complicated emotions that went with that. I had nipped things in the bud with Grey. I was free to charge ahead full steam; I was *safe*.

And yet I found it harder and harder to squash down all the other things that had also happened. After years of distancing myself from my past, it was suddenly more present than ever, pulling me further away from Isobel's bright and shiny future. There was the brief glimpse of how lovely things could have been with Grey if only . . . well, if it had all been different. And then my past and the knowledge of what had happened to my mother when she'd fallen in love had collided with Grey and who I was now, and I knew that even if the lie part could somehow be forgiven, the reality of who I was behind the lie couldn't be changed.

The gynaecological and antenatal wards were full to capacity. Two new patients had been brought in when I'd arrived after a morning lecture, and Sister Veronica had immediately dispatched me to take pulses, blood pressures and temperatures, so that I hadn't yet had a chance to check on Lily Collier. There were so many patients to visit that we moved slowly, and it wasn't until we got closer to the end of the row that I noticed a bed hidden behind a yellow folding screen. Not at all unusual in wards where people might need shielding from illnesses, but with space at a premium until the Tomeyne Wing was finally open to house all of gynaecology and maternity, the use of screens had had to be abandoned unless absolutely necessary.

Hughes had stopped by Bed 14. I studied the screen, then sidled backwards until I was level with the narrow gap between the panels and peered in. Lily was lying on the bed, her enormous bump lifting the sheets. Her eyelids flickered briefly at my approach but didn't open. She looked a little better, no doubt thanks to the fluids I saw on a side table next to a chart monitoring her intake. Someone had bandaged her wounds and washed her. And yet there was a slightly menacing feeling about her space. The screen was closed almost completely, and the bed had been made so tightly that she was practically pinned against the mattress, looking like she'd been inserted into the bed in the middle of the night and hidden from sight.

Glancing over my shoulder at the crowd around Bed 14, I slid the screens apart just enough for me to squeeze through. Swiftly I loosened her sheets a little, then felt her forehead, murmuring to her all the while. At some point I realised her eyes were open and following me, and I smiled at her.

'It's you,' she whispered faintly. 'What are you doing here, miss?'

'My name is Isobel,' I whispered back, mindful of Hughes's voice a few feet away. 'How are you feeling?'

She bit her lip uncertainly and her eyes, huge in her thin face, slid away from mine. She fidgeted with the edge of the sheet. 'I'm all right,' she mumbled, flushing faintly. 'And I'm right sorry for all the trouble.'

'You needn't be,' I said, spotting a bedpan that had been forgotten beneath her bed. 'It's what we're here for. You look better already. And maybe they can find you a bed by a window, put a bit of colour into your cheeks.' I picked up the bedpan. 'I'll be back,' I whispered.

Trying to widen the gap in the screen with my foot while balancing the bedpan, I made the metal leg screech loudly against the floor. All heads turned towards me, then parted to reveal Hughes, looking immensely irritated.

'Miss McIntyre, this is the second time you've interrupted rounds today,' he huffed. His eyes fell on the screen behind me, then the bedpan in my hand. 'And whatever are you doing?'

I opened my mouth, but Sister Veronica stepped forward, her lips set in a thin line. 'It's the new patient brought in last night, sir,' she said, quelling me with a look.

'Lily Collier, sir,' I added. 'I just wondered . . .'

Heads swivelled. Even the women in the beds close to us leaned in to listen.

'The screen, surely it's not necessary?'

Sister Veronica drew herself up to her full height so as to better bristle down at me. 'State she was in, we thought it would be better.'

'Enough,' Hughes said curtly. He parted the screens and took in the small scene. 'Nurse Mavis, we'll have a look at the gash on her right arm now. This is the fluids chart? And *you*, do something about that bedpan.'

He disappeared through the gap and bent over Lily's bed, waving the nurse forward, and there was nothing else for me to do but disappear into the sluice. By the time I returned, the screen was firmly closed and Hughes had moved on.

I knew better than to interrupt him again, but I kept looking back at the screen, imagining Lily lying there in the half-darkness, the yellow folds rising around her like a prison cell.

At the very end of rounds, I lingered. Hughes always instructed the ward sister on special cases before leaving.

'Please see to it that Miss Collier has her bandages changed regularly, and have someone check on her constantly. She's due any time, so really do make sure to keep a special eye on her, Sister.'

'Yes, sir.'

'There's no need to remove the screen; the others in the ward might be distracted by—What on earth are you lurking around there for, Miss McIntyre? Don't you have work to do?' He deposited a handful of case notes on Sister Veronica's desk.

'I wanted to talk to you about the screen,' I said, making my words as firm as I could. 'I understand why, but it's giving her the impression that she's done something wrong.'

'She's getting all the care she needs. The screen is for her own good. In other circumstances,' he turned away from Sister Veronica and added in a voice so low only I could hear him, 'she'd have a police officer sitting by her bedside right now. She's lucky to be here, so please, Miss McIntyre, kindly remember that you're not in charge. Sister,' he said more loudly, 'find this student something to do. She clearly has too much time on her hands.'

'We can't just leave her in there, Sister Veronica,' I said as she swept me back into the ward in a rustle of starched skirts.

'She has peace and quiet and medical care, which is a lot more than others have.'

'You're forcing her to lie there while people judge her,' I said furiously. 'She's not some kind of dirty blob on your precious ward. She needs—'

'*You* need to do what you're meant to be doing here, which is assisting us and following orders for the time you're assigned to work here.' Her gaze swept the room, searching for something for me to do. 'Please go and see to the bandages in Utility 4.'

Sister Veronica had me scurrying back and forth past Lily Collier's screened-off corner with trays of bandages and gauze. She kept her eyes on me throughout, and I didn't gratify her ostentatious suspicion with even a glance at Lily's cubicle until she was called back to Surgical III to attend rounds with Carlisle. The moment she was gone, I slipped into the cubicle, where Lily was lying on her side now, looking down at her bump as if it was a wholly separate thing from the rest of her body. It was surprisingly big for her small form, and the baby seemed active. Here and there a bulge showed where a foot or an elbow was pushing and squirming.

'Dancing a jig in there?' I asked softly.

She looked up, then back at the bump, gave a small shrug. The bedsprings creaked a little as I sat down next to her. Outside, Nurse Mavis's footsteps squeaked on the linoleum. I waited until she was past.

'I'm sorry about the screen,' I said. 'I tried to get them to remove it. I'll—'

'Please don't,' Lily interrupted me. 'I prefer it this way. Thanks all the same, Miss . . . Isobel, you said? You're very kind.' Her shoulders drooped a little, as if the exchange had exhausted her.

'But maybe seeing the other mums will make you feel a little more settled, part of the hustle and bustle.'

'Miss, I'm not the same as them. Please. I'm fine in here, really.'

I looked at her for a long moment, then nodded. 'All right, peace and quiet it is. I wonder, though, have you anyone helping you at home at all? I could ring a friend for you, or go and fetch—'

'No. My parents threw me out when . . . And the father, well, he gave me these.' She nodded at one of the faded bruises on her arm. Involuntarily I touched the one closest to me. She flinched, before cautiously relaxing against my fingertips.

'Why didn't you say that when Mr Hughes saw you in Casualty? He thought you'd tried to . . . to do something.'

She coloured a little and didn't look at me. I took my hand away from her arm and waited.

'Wouldn't have been much better to say I was beaten up by the father of my bastard baby, who has no plans to marry me.' She pressed her lips together and flushed more deeply.

'But someone could—'

'No!' She looked up at me. 'Please, Miss Isobel. I don't want anyone tracking him down and making trouble. It's bad enough as it is. I don't need to draw attention to it any more than I have to.'

'So when you left hospital, you just went home and lay down on your bed and . . . I don't know, what did you think would happen to you?'

She fidgeted with the edge of the sheet, worrying at the seam, until I tugged it out of her hand. 'Sister will not be pleased if you ruin her linen,' I said with a wry smile.

'I was so tired, miss,' she said softly. 'It's such a struggle, every hour, every minute of the day. Heaving this great big belly around and everyone looking at me, everyone *knowing*. I thought my parents might have done me a favour kicking me out, that leaving home would be better for me, I could blend in somehow. But now I have no money at all. I can barely scrounge up enough food. And once this' – she gestured towards her belly – 'is here, it'll only get worse. No one will hire me, and anyway, how would I work if I have no one to look after the baby? I just want to sleep, miss. And maybe . . .' her voice was very quiet, 'maybe when I wake up, all this will be over.'

I stared at her, unable to say anything. For a moment I thought of my mother, wondered if she'd ever thought about giving up, if she'd ever wished for *all this* to be over so she could have the life she wanted. But before I'd even finished the thought, I knew the answer. She had fought for me; she had never allowed me to feel unwanted. *You and me, always.* I looked away from Lily's small, pinched face so she couldn't see what I was feeling, the warm glow inside me at the certainty that my mother would always have stood up for me.

With some effort, I smiled. 'I saved your dress. The pretty red one? Well, what was left of it. I'm making . . . I'm making you something new from it.'

'Really?' She turned her head eagerly, and I suddenly saw the spark of a young and lively girl. Then she sagged back again, her face twisting a little. 'That's kind of you, but to be honest, I don't want it. It'll always remind me . . .' She paused, a frown knotting her brow. 'Why are you doing this?' she said. 'Being in here with me, talking to me like I'm normal and everything, fixing my clothes?'

The nurse's shoes squeaked back by.

'Because you *are* normal,' I whispered fiercely. 'And I think you can have a life – maybe not the one you always thought you'd have, but a good one. All you need is a little help. What would you have done if you'd . . . I mean, if it had all gone to plan?'

'I would have liked to be a cook,' she said. 'Apprentice in a fancy house and—' She broke off. 'They would never take me now, of course. Being in service with a bastard hanging about?'

'Don't say that.' I swallowed, then rallied. 'Maybe you won't be a cook, not right away, but you could work elsewhere until you find your feet. Let's think about this. You'll be here until the baby comes, then you get to stay for two weeks' lying-in – that's the usual. You'll be nice and warm, with lots of food, all paid for by the National Health Service. And after that, there are places where you can get help. We could find someone to look after the baby during the day. There's local clinics, and soup kitchens . . .'

She didn't say anything, but her eyes were fixed on mine and there seemed to be a glimmer of hope in them.

'Everyone's a bit frightened of being a mum,' I went on, encouraged, 'but you learn on the job, just as you'll learn to ignore the hateful people out there and find some you like, who will help you. I know you can do it, Lily, I know that as long as the two of you stay together, it'll be all right.'

I stopped. She was still looking at me, and had just opened her mouth when the screen scraped loudly across the floor.

'I thought Mr Hughes's instructions were clear.' Sister Veronica stood between the panels, hands on hips, vibrating with indignation.

'The bandages are finished, Sister.' I got to my feet. 'As is my shift. I was just visiting my friend here.'

Lily turned her head a little and gave me a small smile. Sister Veronica was tapping her fingers against the side of the screen, and beyond her voluminous skirts, I could see the nurse approaching with the tea trolley.

'I have to go,' I said to Lily. 'And I have a seminar next week, so I won't see you for a bit. But I'll be back as soon as I can, all right?'

'Bye, miss,' Lily said. 'And thank you. For everything.'

Thirty-Five

A pathology seminar kept me away from the ward, and the day before I was due to return, Hughes dispatched me to Casualty to shadow one of the house officers for the remainder of the week. I went gladly, relishing any opportunity to stay busy.

I continued working on Lily's dress, too. I knew she'd said she didn't want it back, but it seemed crucial somehow to keep at it, like it was an omen of hope for a better future, urged on by the curly-haired girl in red who was smiling at me from the sketch still propped next to the sewing machine.

I arrived at the hospital early on Friday, hoping to snatch a quiet cup of tea down in the cafeteria, but instead was greeted by an inordinate amount of hustle and bustle. People were carrying boxes and crates into the front hall; others ferried stacks of logs towards an enormous pyre skulking off to the left, halfway built.

Of course. The Tomeyne Wing would be unveiled tonight, at the Bonfire Ball. I ducked past a weary-looking crew of builders heading towards the scaffolding and was pondering the complicated process of relocating patients and reshuffling wards when, across the front hall, I spied a familiar face. Small and a little wispy, Ella Carlisle was standing to one side, surveying the erection of a small stage.

I stopped in my tracks, wondered if I could sneak away without being seen. She had written a few times more, asking me to drop by, inviting me to tea at the house, but I had declined on the grounds that I was – yes – busy. It wasn't just the awkwardness with Grey and Everett Carlisle, or the fact that I really was rushed off my feet. The truth was that it was becoming increasingly hard to field conversations about my mother and not be able to ask all the things I really wanted to know. I liked Ella, very much, and was anxious about her illness and desperate for her to get better, and yet every minute I spent with her, I lied to her about the very thing she said was giving her such comfort – spending time with Diana's girl. It was better to just avoid her altogether for the time being.

'Isobel, how lovely.'

It was too late. She was walking slowly towards me, and I felt another stab of guilt when I saw how drawn she looked.

'How are you, Ella?'

'Oh, you know,' she said, a little evasively. 'I have another appointment upstairs today, a final check on . . . well, options, but I thought I'd come a bit early and see how they're getting on.'

We watched the workmen discuss the edging of the stage.

'I can't believe the ball is here already.' She sighed and shook her head.

'Will you be there?' I pulled her out of the way as two men carried in a long piece of wood.

'Yes. By the grace of God and the Carlisle men.' She gave me a small smile. 'They've never been so united as in their quest to get me to stay in bed and rest. But I simply can't miss tonight, so I'll just come for a little while. After all the planning and fundraising I've done, and it's the last time they're having it, so . . . Anyway, you're coming too, aren't you?'

The nurses had been discussing the ball ad nauseam: plans for dresses, and hair appointments fitted carefully around shifts and duties. But with all that had been going on in my own life, it had been little more than a vague background melody these last few days.

'Yes,' I said, so as not to encourage further probing into my attendance, or worse, an invitation to join the family.

She fidgeted with her handbag. 'Would you . . . I mean, would you like a cup of tea in the cafeteria? I could do with a warm drink and a quick sit-down. Or are you busy?'

'I am, actually.' I looked at her pale, pinched face. 'But I'm early. Tea would be lovely. My treat.'

We'd come between shifts, so the cafeteria was quiet, a couple of workmen leaving as we walked in. The tea urns gurgled softly, the place was warm, and I felt my shoulders unclench as we settled at a small table in the corner, a metal teapot and a plate of iced buns between us.

'I know it's not the Ritz.' I smiled. 'But the buns are good. Here, have this one, it's nice and plump.'

She nodded, picked at a few crumbs, dabbed up a flake of icing with her fingertip, then took a sip of tea. 'I haven't seen you in a while,' she said, a little awkwardly. 'I'm sorry about that. I feel . . . I mean, did something happen between us?' She gave a quick glance over her shoulder, but the only other people in the cafeteria were two residents yawning over coffees in the far corner. 'It wasn't our conversation last time, was it? I'll be honest with you, I'd had too much to drink. I saw the photo album the next day and had a feeling I'd spoken out of turn somehow.'

I fiddled with my spoon, trying to think of a neutral subject, something that would deflect attention away from me, keep me safe. Ask a question, Agnes, something about her appointment today, or Grey, even, or—

'What did you and my mother fall out over? Why did she leave?' It had come out just like that, not neutral and certainly not safe, as if I had no control over my voice at all.

'Oh.' Ella clearly hadn't expected this either, and two red spots bloomed on her cheeks. 'Well, she had just got married, and Henry had a variety of teaching posts lined up . . .'

I frowned, then realised that she was talking about Diana McIntyre. Of course. Always Diana.

'No, I mean the rift that broke your friendship,' I cut in.

She took a large gulp of her tea, and when she set her cup down, I saw that her mouth had twisted a little.

'I've been thinking about that a lot, since we last talked,' she said haltingly. 'Since *I* last talked, I should say,' she added with a pained half-smile. She fell silent again, then took a quick breath. 'It's not easy to explain, or maybe it's too easy and just hard for me, because . . . well . . .' She swallowed, then said, with some difficulty, 'Because it was my fault. My fault that Alexander left, that he never came back, that he died out East without any of us ever seeing him again. And Diana never forgave me for that.'

I stared at her. 'How can all of that be your fault? You said it was to do with Silkie.'

Ella looked up, and I realised that the name had slid too readily off my tongue. After a moment, though, she nodded. 'You see, for the longest time, I didn't know about Alexander and Silkie.' The two red spots had diffused into a faint flush, and her mouth was trembling a little. 'I was so silly, gushing about him to Diana and Silkie at every opportunity, making up all these stories and scenarios in which we might be together, interpreting every look, every glance. Like you do when you're seventeen and in love. And all along, Silkie never said, she never let on with a single glance what was really happening. And then the day after the wedding, I caught them. Embracing. Kissing. And not just a little bit, but passionately, like they never wanted it to end. It was one of those moments when clarity hits you over the head so hard you actually feel like you're being knocked down. It all fell into place, all the inconsistencies, the strange moments I'd not noticed in my infatuation. Once I knew, I couldn't believe I hadn't seen it before, that it was like a light was turned on when they were together. He loved her and she loved him back, and it felt like she had stabbed a knife right into my back while I was down.'

I opened my mouth, my mind pushing out more questions – about how they had fallen in love, what they were like together, what he was like – but she was still talking, and with an enormous effort I held back.

'He was supposed to leave for the Far East, some kind of posting to be a doctor with the military, I can't remember. Once I knew about them, of course, I understood that he must have planned it that way so he could take her with him. People mightn't care so much in some far-flung outpost of the Empire, and they could be together, get married even. So they were just going to leave, both of them, *my* Alexander, and Silkie, who wasn't supposed to be in love with him, let alone have him, who was . . . who had been my friend.' Her voice, unsure and quiet at first, had become firmer with the telling.

'What happened then?' I said urgently. 'What happened to Silkie?'

She frowned at me, confusion weaving into the anguished expression on her face, and I remembered that it was still Diana I belonged to, not Silkie.

'What happened?' I asked again, forcing myself to be calm.

'I answered the door one night. Alex had come to drop off a note for her. Something about a change of plans, that he had to leave earlier and was enclosing a passage for her to follow. He would be waiting for her . . .' She paused, and the faint flush deepened.

'You read it,' I said, and it was not a question.

'Every word,' she said, and then she sighed, a long-drawn-out exhale that sounded almost like relief. 'I read it over and over again, his endearments, his promises, and then . . .' she dug her knuckles into her mouth, muffling her breathing, 'and then I . . . I hid it. I never gave it to her.'

I swallowed. 'He left and Silkie never knew about the passage?' My voice had risen slightly, ringing out across the cafeteria, but when I glanced over her shoulder, I saw that we were quite alone now. Even the residents had left. From the back came the noise of dishes clattering, something metallic being dropped.

Ella's shoulders had slumped forward, and she bent over her folded hands on the table with another long, shuddery breath. It sounded so horrible I involuntarily put my hand over hers to stop it.

'There's more,' she said in a cracked voice, her fingers twisting around mine. 'I have to tell you, tell someone, before it's too late. I've held on to it for so long, and I'm so ashamed, Isobel, so very ashamed.'

Images unspooled before my eyes. Alexander – still absurd to think of him as my father – and Silkie, shining with light when they were together. My young mother, seemingly abandoned by him, but really betrayed by Ella. I wondered suddenly whether Ella had actually known that Silkie was pregnant, whether she'd ever known about me, Alexander's baby.

'When I went to tell Diana, I . . . I realised that she already knew. Of course, she wasn't at all happy that he'd decided to go so far away, start a new life with Silkie. But she adored him, much more than me or Silkie, and that hurt, too, that when pushed, she would always be on his side. And Alexander . . .' she pressed her knuckles harder against her mouth, and her face was wet, 'Alexander left thinking Silkie would follow, but she didn't, and it was only a short while later that the news came that he was missing, presumed dead. Diana's father killed himself, and Diana . . . well, she was devastated. She blamed Silkie, of course, but when she found out I had kept the letter, she was furious with me for interfering and driving Alexander away. She never spoke to me again.' Her voice cracked.

'But Silkie?' I said, my voice choked. 'What happened to Silkie? What did *she* do?'

Ella lifted her head, and through the strange haze in front of my eyes, I saw her expression change, saw her frown as if trying to figure something out.

'What happened to her?' I forced myself to repeat it more quietly, and Ella sagged back, the puzzled look slowly giving way to one of shame and misery.

'I told my parents the whole thing. They sacked her on the spot and she left that day. It was the last time I ever saw her.'

Thirty-Six

My feet must have found their way to the ward of their own accord, because I couldn't really remember leaving the cafeteria. All I knew was that I had to be away from Ella Carlisle's pinched, anxious face and from all the things she'd told me.

I had left her at the ladies' room, where she said she was going to tidy herself up ahead of her appointment. 'We'll talk more, Isobel. Not tonight, obviously, but soon. A lot more. I'm so sorry about all this, I should have made more of an effort to talk to Diana, and I'm sorry about your uncle, that you never met him, because of what I said.'

I had backed away then, mumbling words of farewell, and had almost reached Gynae IV when the door to Surgical III opened and Grey emerged, frowning down at a sheaf of papers in his hands as he walked. He looked the same, tall and impatient, hair standing up at the back, and for a moment I forgot that we weren't on speaking terms any more and willed him to lift his head and smile at my approach, to walk a few paces with me, to talk again like we used to.

The door opened again. Grey looked up at the sound, spotted me. And for a brief, wonderful second, he did smile, as if he too had forgotten that everything was different now. But then Everett Carlisle came into view, and instantly Grey turned away.

Mr Carlisle gave me a brief nod in passing, and after a moment's hesitation, Grey did the same. 'Let's just quickly go over the file again before Ella's appointment,' I heard Everett say as they walked on. 'I wondered what you thought about . . .'

Momentarily blinded by the sun that flooded the hospital corridor, I listened to their voices fade. From somewhere came the sound of Hughes talking. He was on the ward, and I should be too, in that blank white space where I could be Isobel again, feel clean and good and stop thinking about what I'd just heard: my parents' love for each other destroyed with just a few words. How different things might have been if Ella, this young, angry girl used to getting what she wanted, had held back:

It was like a light was turned on when they were together.

Horror and sorrow chased each other around my mind, and I stood with my hand braced on the door, then pushed through. I was late. I needed to be inside, fall in step with everyone, quickly . . .

Rounds hadn't started yet, but doctors were in attendance, so the ward was quieter than usual, with Hughes and a houseman discussing the ovarian cyst in Bed 11, Nurse Mavis assisting Mrs Smith, who was bent over one of the antenatal patients in the far corner. Hughes acknowledged my arrival with a nod, but didn't break his conversation, and I suddenly noticed that something had changed. There was no screen around Lily Collier's bed any more, and when I squinted to bring it into focus, I saw that there was no need for a screen.

Lily was gone.

I shook my head to clear some of the strange fuzziness inside it. Hughes had left the houseman with the patient and was now over at the desk, writing something down. I took a deep breath and approached him.

'Excuse me, sir, where is Lily Collier?'

He looked up, over at where she had been only a week ago, then immediately back down at the paper in front of him.

'Ah yes. Well, you'll be pleased to hear that the baby arrived a few days ago.' He kept his eyes on the notes. 'Birth was straightforward. She was discharged yesterday, early, at her own insistence.'

'She's gone already?' I asked, confused. 'And the baby?'

'A bit jaundiced, being taken care of in the nursery, but otherwise fine. A wonder, really, after all the mother's efforts to the contrary. There's nothing for you to worry about, Miss McIntyre, I assure you. Now, if you'll kindly let me finish these notes, we'll start rounds in a moment.'

But I didn't move. A few beds down, Mrs Smith looked up from her patient. She seemed to sense something was amiss, because I saw her exchange a look with the nurse.

'I don't understand,' I said, even though my mind was well ahead of me and had already grasped exactly what had happened. 'She—'

'Enough.' Hughes cut across me. 'She made her choice.' He made as if to shoo me away, but I didn't move.

'You sent me to Casualty so I wouldn't be here when she had the baby, didn't you?' I said, moving until he was forced to look at me. He had the grace to look abashed, but quickly rallied.

'What I do or don't do is none of your concern. I don't need to explain myself to you, Miss McIntyre. A family will be found for the baby and that is that.'

'I don't believe it.' I shook my head. 'She was going to give it a try, she just needed a little help, it was going to be *all right*—' I suddenly remembered the lone carpet bag, the absence of anything to do with the baby, and broke off.

'She's not been forced into it, if that's what you mean,' he said. 'Mrs Smith, there you are. I beg you, help me get through to Miss McIntyre.'

Mrs Smith looked from me to Mr Hughes, then to Sister Veronica, who had spotted our little group and was advancing like a wrathful angel.

'Look, Miss McIntyre. Isobel,' Mrs Smith said urgently. 'You saw the state of the flat, the state of Miss Collier herself. We *must* think about the baby. The little girl will have a chance at a different life, a better life. And it's what Miss Collier wanted. Here, she gave me a letter for you. She said you were kind to her, she wanted to write to thank you.'

The note contained only a few lines.

Dear Miss Isobel,

I didn't get a chance to see you again to say goodbye, but I wanted you to know that I thought about all you said. I know you mean well and I appreciate your kindness, I really do. But the thing is, miss, I'm not like you. I'm not strong and properly independent with money of my own and people around to help. It's different for someone like me, it's not easy. I hope you won't think of me too badly.

Yours,
Lily Collier

Heat prickled up the back of my neck and into my cheeks. *I'm not like you. It's different for someone like me.*

The words swam in front of my eyes, and for a moment I couldn't breathe.

I had failed her. I hadn't done enough, hadn't done anything, really, but give her empty words. How could I expect her to believe that a future was possible when my own was based on a lie? Who was I to tell her to stand tall and build herself a better life when I had stolen someone else's because it had seemed to me the only way forward in this world? And who did I think I was to rail against Hughes and Sister Veronica, Lily's neighbour, Mrs McIntyre, Ella even, when I was no better than any of them?

Lily was right, it wasn't easy, it was bloody hard, and yet my mother had done it. My beautiful, funny, dancing mother, the person I had loved most in the world, who'd been betrayed and abandoned, who'd been there when I got up in the morning and there at the end of the day, the other half to my whole. She'd held on to me against all odds. And I? I thought of the day three years ago when I had pushed her photo into the lining of Isobel's suitcase, and felt a burst of shame at who I had become and how far I had moved away from the girl she had raised, the girl I had obviously felt wasn't good enough. I had been ashamed of that girl, that was the truth of it, and by implication, ashamed of Mum. I was no better – worse, in fact, because I wasn't even honest with myself – than all the rest of them.

I looked up, saw Mrs Smith's homely features, Hughes, who had inexplicably lingered, perhaps unnerved by the expression on my face. Sister Veronica, for once, was quiet, and Nurse Mavis hovered anxiously.

'It's best for Baby, miss,' Nurse Mavis suddenly said softly. 'We've seen it before.'

I looked at her for a long moment. 'Maybe so. But the mother needs to be given the same chance at a better life. One that includes her child. You might not have forced her, Mr Hughes, and you might want what's best for the baby, Mrs Smith. But none of us allowed Lily to make her choice, free and clear of prejudice. We gave her no hope for a better life if she chose a different path, no hope for anything at all.'

Mrs Smith opened her mouth, then closed it again, while Mr Hughes spluttered a few things. But when I didn't say anything else, Sister Veronica bustled away on her usual swell of outrage, and eventually rounds began.

I followed Mr Hughes from bed to bed, taking notes in Isobel's small, neat handwriting, and thought of my mother, and when my shift was over, I slipped out the back before Sister Veronica could throw any more chores my way.

I took the stairs two at a time, through the entrance hall domed by the beautiful cupola, then the big glass doors, striding down the road until I drew level with a bus, glanced sideways, saw the words *Stepney Green* on the front.

It was packed to the gills, but I stood at the very edge of the platform, leaning out to feel the cold air on my face, the rumbling of the bus beneath my feet.

I would go back. I would knock on the door of what was left of my mother's shop, now rebuilt perhaps, step across the threshold into the space that now belonged to someone else, selling different things. Too dangerous, a small voice tried to say, too risky; was it really worth it just to see what I'd feel when I was there?

It didn't matter. I was going back. I was going home.

Thirty-Seven

I got off the bus at Edgeley Street, made my way down Armoury Lane and turned the corner. I realised I was holding my breath expectantly, as if waiting for some kind of revelation, or relief at feeling my mother more acutely than before. Instead, I found myself dispassionately scanning the warren of little streets I'd known so well, reality overlaid with memory.

There was the street down to the school, there the butcher's shop, which had given way to a shoemaker. The grocer two doors down was still there, and the steps were swept as always. The streets seemed narrower, however, the houses closer together; more claustrophobic than I remembered, but less threatening as well. Just a crumbling, slightly ramshackle assortment of homes belonging to people like the woman hurrying along, a girl clutching one hand, a basket in the other; two men arguing by the corner, then parting ways; someone cycling by, slowly so as not to slip on the wet cobblestones. I found that I wasn't nervous of discovery any more. Somehow I no longer had anything to do with the schoolgirl who'd rounded the corner with her books towards . . . there it was, number 10.

And now I did feel something; a great many things, in fact. The back of the building and the floors above were still gone, jagged pieces of masonry like broken teeth in a gaping mouth. Only the shopfront stood, exactly as it had after the raid: a horseshoe of walls topped by a piece of ceiling, looking – a breath caught in my throat – as if no time had passed at all. The brass doorknob my mother hadn't polished nearly enough for the neighbours' liking, the low sill below the window where she had sometimes kept flowerpots. As if maybe there had been a mistake, maybe, if I walked slowly, never took my eyes off it, the door would open, just like it always had. *Darling, come on in out of the rain.*

I knew I was being stupid. No one could possibly live here, even though the step had been swept clean and someone had stacked bricks tidily in the entryway. I lifted my hand and—

'Can I help you?'

It was a young woman, early twenties maybe, fine fair hair framing a red-cheeked face, pushing an enormous double pram. Puffing a little, she'd come to a stop next to me.

'I . . . Oh, not at all, I was just looking.' I stepped back quickly and scanned her face. But either she'd been younger than me at school, or she wasn't from round here, because I didn't recognise her.

'Bit of a mess still, isn't it?' She pushed the pram against the side of the house and came to stand next to me, peering through the window, obviously glad of a break. 'We're meant to be moving in in January, but I can't see that happening.'

'You . . . I mean, you'll be living here?'

'Not living. Running a shop. It's been empty for ages. The state it was in, I can't tell you, droppings and rubbish and things. But we'll have it spick and span soon, just waiting for some more building materials.'

'What kind of shop?' I asked.

'Electrical goods, of all things.' She smiled. 'As if anyone around here could possibly be in the market for a television. But my husband is obsessed with it all, hoovers and hairdryers, says it's the way of the future.' She pushed her hair out of her face and chuckled, but fondly.

'You've been renovating it, then?' I asked.

'Oh no, not us. We're both terrible at that sort of thing. My brother-in-law's been doing it, at the weekends when he's got time. Which is why it's taking an age.' She observed me. 'You're not local, are you?'

I flicked my eyes back to the shop window to avoid her frank curiosity. 'I used to know the seamstress who was here during the war,' I said. 'I was passing by.'

'Oh, you did? I moved here from Kent, so I didn't know her, but I tell you, the things we found in there . . .'

I swallowed and flushed. 'You mean the sewing things?' I said. 'I think someone was meant to collect what was salvageable. I did wonder what had happened to it all.'

'I don't know about that. I don't think a whole lot survived, to be honest. The only thing there was . . . Oh, it was just lovely. Some walls were still intact, see that one facing us, and they had all these drawings on them, from floor to ceiling.'

I stared at her. 'Really?' I managed.

She nodded. 'Most were ruined and fell apart when we unpinned them – it must have been years since they were put up, I suppose. A few survived, though. There were layers and layers of them, like wallpaper, and the ones at the bottom did better. I kept those; thought maybe we'd frame one to put in the new shop. There was one with such a sweet house dress. I told Olly, my husband, that it would go nicely with his hoovers.' She gave me a wink, and even though my eyes stung when I remembered that wall – all the walls in the place, and the space in between – I had to smile.

'Would you show me the ones you kept?' I asked suddenly. 'I was ever so sorry to hear that she'd . . .' I swallowed, 'that she'd been caught in a raid back then.'

'Sure, we're just down the road here. I'm afraid I can't ask you inside. It's all topsy-turvy with the babies' clothes – twins, you know – and I'd be embarrassed to let anyone in, but I know where they are. Do you want a quick look inside the shop?'

I looked at the closed door, pictured the bare concrete inside. For a moment I could have sworn I heard a snatch of a song, and laughter, then I shook my head. 'I'll come back when you're up and running,' I said, my voice only a little bit breathless. 'I'll buy a hoover from you.'

'Oh, please do.' She reached for the handle of the pram. 'We're anxious to do well. The seamstress, was she successful?'

I fell in step alongside her. 'Not particularly,' I said eventually. 'Times were hard, you know, with rationing and the war.'

'Of course,' she said sympathetically.

'But she was very, very good. And . . . a lovely person, too.'

'I'm sure.' She patted my arm, then resumed her chatter as we walked down the road, telling me about who lived where and what the nurse at the clinic had said about her twins.

'How old are they?' I leaned forward to peer into the pram.

'Only a few months,' she said. 'Feels like a lifetime, though.'

'Did you have an easy birth?' I asked, only just refraining from scanning her midsection. 'I mean, twins can be difficult.'

'Tell me about it.' She shook her head. 'It was a bit of a nightmare, actually. They were early and it ended up being a very messy, very long affair, with a midwife, and then a doctor, and my husband carrying on like an idiot outside.' She shuddered.

'Were they breeched?' I asked. 'Or in distress?'

'I don't know, they just wouldn't come out.'

'Narrow pelvis, perhaps. You're quite slender.'

She huffed a slightly awkward laugh. 'You're awfully specific, aren't you?'

'Well, I'm . . .' I paused, wondering if I should part with the information. 'I'm studying to be a doctor. At Thamesbury Hospital.'

'A doctor?' she said, a little doubtfully, then nodded. 'I would probably have preferred you to the old codger who ended up pushing and prodding at me, ripping my best quilt in the process. Are you going to be a midwifey kind of doctor?'

'A surgeon,' I said.

'Ah.' She sounded impressed. 'Well, then I wouldn't see you, I suppose. Not many surgeons around here. We barely have enough doctors to cover the clinic; waiting time is ages.' She gestured to a row of terraced houses. 'Let's cross the road, I'm just down there.'

I helped her manhandle the enormous pram across and up on to the footpath and waited as she disappeared inside the narrow house.

It took her a little while to emerge, but eventually she returned holding a thin sheaf of papers in her hand. I recognised them immediately: patches of wallpaper, pages snipped out of exercise books and catalogues. She held them out one by one, commenting as she carefully leafed through them. She'd been right: most had been ruined by water or fire or just general decay, some images partially obscured or faded away. A few stood out, though, the ones drawn in full colour on good paper. The colours on those were still vibrant, the strokes clearly visible, a few deliberate brushes with water creating lovely patches of colour. *Alex had given her a box of watercolour pencils, you know the kind that you use to shade and then you put a drop of water on it and it blossoms out like a . . .*

My hand was shaking slightly as I took the last page. So they were both here in my hands now, my mother's drawing and my father's gift. Slowly, gently, I exhaled the breath I seemed to have been holding since I got off the bus. The sketch was of a woman and a girl. They were looking at each other, the woman fanning out her dress, the girl dipping down into a playful curtsey, splashes of violet and yellow and blue, as if they were about to launch into a dance. I held it in my hands for a long time, remembering rainbow hour and the Singer whirring away; stories and songs and the day righting itself as I hoisted myself up on the long table to watch my mother work.

'Lovely, isn't it?' she said. 'Is it very much like you remember her? Your friend?'

'Yes,' I said softly, 'it is exactly her.'

I felt her shift next to me, knew she was going to want it back any second now, that I'd have to part with it, the precious rendering of Mum and me together. Not quite yet, I wasn't ready . . .

'Would you like to keep it?' she suddenly asked. She smiled a little uncertainly when I lifted my head and she saw that my eyes were too bright, my face flushed. 'I have all these, see, more than enough, and it's not like they were really mine to keep in the first place. I can see you knew her well.'

I nodded wordlessly, slid the drawing into my bag before she could change her mind, and just as I finally managed a thank you, there was a mewling squawk from the pram.

'Well, that's me,' she said with a sigh. 'It was lovely talking to you, er . . . I'm sorry, I never caught your name?'

'Oh, I'm . . .'

But a second cry had joined the first now, more insistent, and she was already fluttering back towards the door, waving both hands in farewell. 'Lovely to meet you, don't forget to come back and see us for your hoover.' The door slammed shut behind her, leaving me standing on the footpath.

'I'm Agnes,' I said, very quietly, to the empty street.

Thirty-Eight

Mrs Schwartz's house was dark – they'd all be at the synagogue – and I didn't turn on the lights when I came in, but slipped quietly up the stairs and down the corridor to my room. Light came in from the street lamp outside, and as I looked around the space bathed in jagged shadows, it felt like I'd been away for years.

My clothes hung neatly in the wardrobe, the bed was made, medical books stacked on the little side table. Katia had set a covered plate in the middle of my desk. She had dusted too; I could smell the piney wood polish, noticed that she had re-arranged the papers and knick-knacks on the mantelpiece. The postcard of Prague sent by a former college friend, the portrait of the McIntyres in its silver frame, the sketch piece of my mother.

I lifted the cover off the plate and saw in the glow of the street lamp a piece of cake dusted with icing sugar. On top, knowing they were my favourite, Katia had stuck a small candied cherry.

An ache closed my throat at the sight of that lone cherry – a rare treat with sugar only just being freely available again – and intensified when I noted the careful way she'd set the plate well away from my papers and notebooks so as not to spoil them. How could I possibly tell this lovely, kind woman what I'd done? How would I find it in myself to stand up – after dinner, perhaps, or in the evening when they were all together – look them in the eye one by one and say the words out loud? That I was a fraud. A liar.

Panicked, my mind skittered away from the enormity of what would happen then and jumped backwards instead. To me leaving London as a child, my mother's death, the McIntyres', then Isobel's, the hours spent in the vault. Moments of overwhelming loss when my life had threatened to dissolve into nothing, when I was going to be cut loose without an anchor, without a place to belong.

I heard a strange noise in the half-darkness, a harsh, rasping sound of despair. I realised that *I* was making it and pushed my knuckles into my mouth to force it back. I stood there holding on to the mantelpiece, my eyes tightly shut, and wished with everything I had that I could find a way to make this all right and stay here among the music and the cheerful clutter, the smells of food and the unconditional companionship. Here where I had always felt like I could be me. But – and at this I dragged my hands across my cheeks and through my hair – that was exactly it, wasn't it? I *hadn't* been me. Even here, where I'd felt so at home, I hadn't ever been fully myself.

I washed my face and pulled a brush through my hair, deciding on impulse to leave it loose, even though it curled a bit madly around my face. Stepping in front of the wardrobe, I reached for the dress I'd finally finished the day before. The fabric slithered joyfully off the hanger and pooled across my hands as I shook it out and put it on, pausing every now and then to snip off a loose thread, fix a hanging hem with a discreet safety pin. I wasn't nearly as accomplished at sewing as my mother had been, but I did all right for myself. Finally I straightened, smoothed the dress down one last time and lifted my head to look at my reflection.

I had cut the trousers as wide and flared as I could. Standing still, they looked like a skirt, classy and shimmering, simple. But the moment I moved, they became trousers, swirling and swishing around my legs in brilliant reds and golds. I felt a smile break out across my face at my mirrored self: my hair a halo of curls, the trousers making my legs look as though they were dancing.

There was one last thing I wanted to do before I left. Kneeling carefully, I reached into the back of the wardrobe and pulled out Isobel's suitcase. Using my mother's little knife, I quickly unpicked the lining and slid her photo out from beneath the satiny fabric. It had been a cheap one to begin with, and the contours looked washed out and faded next to the sharper image of Mrs and Mr McIntyre. I took that one out of its frame and fixed my mother's picture inside instead, then set it next to the sketch on the mantelpiece. I looked at the two images for a long time, wishing my mother could be standing here with me wearing her creation, her smile bright and happy. I reached out and touched the photo one last time, then turned, the fabric slithering gently against my legs as I walked back through the dark house and out into the street.

I'd never seen the hospital look so impressive. The Tomeyne Wing had emerged from behind its scaffolding, and now swept out to the side of the main building with its vaulted glass dome shining brightly into the evening sky.

People were walking up to the front doors in twos and threes, pausing to admire the new facade and calling out greetings to others. A short distance away, the huge wooden pyre of the bonfire hulked in the darkness, workers moving around it like shadows to add the finishing touches before it would be lit after the opening ceremony.

I made my way up the brick path alone, smiling a greeting at a staff nurse I knew from Casualty, nodding at a professor who was helping his wife up the front steps. When I reached the glass doors, which only a few weeks ago I'd sped through on the way to Theatre 4, my heart gave a great lurch at the memory of my first sighting of Everett Carlisle and then, shortly after, Grey.

A couple of people passed me, eyeing me a little curiously, and the last one held open the door for me. I gripped the handle, the metal cold between my fingers as I tried to push back the panic lapping at the edges of my mind, the fear of losing it all. What would Grey say? What would Everett Carlisle do to me?

An ambulance rumbled past on the street beyond the gates, its white paint glowing faintly as it turned the corner towards the back of the hospital. It was heading to Casualty, and later, the Flying Squad would be going back out into the East End.

Limehouse, Stepney, Mile End. Wapping, Poplar. I said the names softly to myself, wondered if some of Mum's old friends were still around. Maybe I could go and see the shop rising again, buy a hoover from the friendly woman with the twins. I thought of the sketch she'd given me of the little girl dancing with her mother. There would be places for me to belong, wouldn't there? There were still things I could be and do. I just had to go through with it now. I needed to find Ella and tell her, and then, in quick succession, tell them all: Everett Carlisle and Mr Hughes, Mrs Smith, and – for a moment the panic swelled again, but I pushed it back resolutely – Grey.

The foyer was barely recognisable. The upper floors had been walled off with screens and blankets so as not to disturb the patients and the unlucky staff who'd remained on duty. The door to the ground-floor corridor to the Tomeyne Wing was open but barred with a ribbon, which would later be cut, so guests could see where exactly their generous donations had gone. It was a crush already: doctors, sisters and nurses, professors and students, distinguished older men and their wives, all chatting and laughing, familiar colleagues unfamiliar in their finery.

Fixing a determined smile on my face, I picked my way through the crowded hall, craning my neck for Ella. At first my shoulders were rounded, my hands gripping the little clutch bag I'd made to match the dress. But as the trousers swirled and eddied around my legs, I could feel the relief of my resolve growing stronger behind the dread, and drew myself up, nodding regally at Mr Tallard, Carlisle's registrar, then at Staff Nurse Willow and Nurse Baker from Ward III.

'Miss McIntyre.' It was Hughes, unusually tidy in a black jacket and white shirt.

'Good evening, Mr Hughes.' I spoke quickly, keen to be gone. Ella had to be the first one I told; I didn't want to be held back now.

'My wife Jacqueline. Jacquie, this is one of the medical students working on the ward.'

Mrs Hughes's eyes had been locked on the bottom half of my dress, obviously trying to figure out its intricacies. She smiled. 'Nice to meet you.'

'And you. I hope you have a lovely evening.' I hesitated, then said, 'Mr Hughes, if you don't mind, could I have a word with you first thing tomorrow?'

He raised his eyebrows, but nodded. 'I have a rare morning off, to spend with my daughter, but I'm on duty in the afternoon.'

'McIntyre, over here!' Benedict, sharp in a dark suit, and Iain, equally impressive but a little rumpled, were waving me over. Mrs Hughes smiled at their enthusiasm. 'Charles, we'll let her go, shall we? Enjoy, Miss McIntyre.'

'You scrub up all right,' Benedict said when I drew level with them. 'Although you might need to wear a name tag. No one'll recognise you.'

'You look wonderful,' Iain said staunchly.

'That's what I said!' Benedict protested. 'Lulu is over there, come on.' He pointed across the hall to where Mabel and Lulu were surrounded by the usual crowd of sharply pressed young men. For once, Harry Jenkins wasn't in Mabel's vicinity. Instead – I did a small double-take – he had Nurse Jameson hanging off his arm, pretty in mufti and chattering cheerfully.

'I can't now, I'm sorry.' I was already moving away. 'I might see you later.'

'What do you mean, might? Where are you going? McIntyre? All the fun's over here.'

Music wove through the swell of voices and laughter, a familiar warm, honeyed voice crooning softly around a string ensemble. Ducking away from Benedict and Iain, I turned to see Solly standing on a little dais towards the back, he and his band handsome if a little sombre in black suits. A man was carrying an extra microphone to the front, where, I realised, speeches would soon begin. I suspected that Ella would leave right after that, and was breaking into a hurried stride when a hand on my arm held me back. Mrs Smith, unfamiliar in a stiff dark gown, accompanied by a woman.

'Miss McIntyre, I'm glad to see you here.' She gave me a sharp, searching look. 'I wanted to talk to you this morning, but you disappeared before I could do so.'

I frowned, trying to remember what felt half a lifetime ago.

'I'm sorry, I had to leave,' I said. 'I hope Sister Veronica wasn't—'

'Not Sister Veronica,' she said dismissively. 'It was about Lily Collier.'

I sighed. 'I think all was said.'

'Actually, no. What I *wanted* to say was . . .' she fidgeted, looking slightly uncomfortable, 'well, that you made me feel a bit ashamed of myself. I still think, given the circumstances, it was best for the baby to go to a new family. But that doesn't mean we should stop trying to help women make the right choice – to do what's best for *them*.' She glanced briefly at her companion. 'I know you said you wanted to be a surgeon, but I wonder . . . Well, I think you should seriously think about doing what you're really good at. Which is talking to women, understanding them, fighting their corner. Meeting them where they are – not in the wards or the operating theatre, but out there. You seem to be at home there; it would be invaluable to have someone like you on the ground, as it were.'

She turned to her companion. 'Marie, this is the student I was telling you about. Marie Gladwell teaches over at the London School of Medicine. Or the Royal Free Hospital School of Medicine, as we're now supposed to call it.'

'Oh,' I said. I knew this was a medical school for women, although under the NHS it now admitted men as well. It was affiliated with the Royal Free Hospital, which had been the first hospital to admit female students to its wards. 'Lovely to meet you, Mrs Gladwell.'

'And you.' Marie Gladwell had seemed slight at first glance, but as she moved closer, I saw that she looked quite tough and no-nonsense. She glanced around at the glamorous couples still pouring into the hall. 'What a fancy do, and the music is quite nice. I expect the patients are all up there longing to join in.'

As we exchanged pleasantries, I was momentarily diverted by Benedict striding past, hanging on to Lulu, who was giving me an enthusiastic thumbs-up, mouthing, 'Fabulous dress!'

I turned back to Mrs Gladwell to find her studying me intently. I was fidgety with nerves at the prospect of facing Ella, and trying to think of how to extricate myself from the conversation, when I heard a familiar voice. Hoarse and a bit growly, it drifted across from the left, where Everett Carlisle was holding court among a small group of distinguished men. Next to him – my breath caught in my throat – was Ella.

After fighting so hard to be here tonight, she seemed subdued and tired, a slightly forced-looking smile on her face as she listened to her husband.

'It really was good to meet you,' I told Mrs Gladwell. 'I hope you have a lovely evening.'

'You and I should have lunch,' she said abruptly. 'I'll be in touch.'

'Oh, I . . . Yes, that would be nice.' Another surge of panic winded me momentarily. It was unlikely I'd be having lunch with anyone in the medical community once it became known what I'd done. But maybe I could explain, maybe they'd understand some of it.

They were already moving away, Mrs Smith turning once to smile at me over her shoulder. From my left came Everett Carlisle's voice again.

It was time.

Thirty-Nine

The crowd had swelled and I made slow progress. I was still several yards away from the group – Carlisle had his back to me – when a gaggle of nurses moved aside and Ella suddenly spotted me, raised a hand in greeting, waved me over. Her smile seemed as inviting as ever, but as I walked towards her, the trousers flaring and swishing, my curls loose and rising around my face, a small frown suddenly appeared on her face. Slowly her gaze travelled down my dress and locked on to my evening bag. It was just a simple reticule, but into the corner I'd stitched a bright yellow daisy. She narrowed her eyes, her face changed, her mouth opened in an O of sudden realisation, and then I watched all the other things unspool on her face that I'd been dreading for so long. Confusion. Disbelief. Horror.

My stomach was heavy with dread and for one mad moment I wondered if I could turn and run, but I tipped up my chin instead and kept my eyes on her as I crossed the last few feet. She pulled her arm out of Everett's and came towards me, slowly at first, then more quickly.

'In there,' she said, her voice sharp as she pointed to the open door leading to the Tomeyne Wing.

She barged past the post holding the ribbon and I followed her. We came to an abrupt stop just inside the archway, then turned and faced each other. Her eyes were roving across my face, taking in my hair, the trousers, then locking on to that daisy again. She gestured at the bag, made a choked sound.

'I don't believe it,' she said finally, and her voice was so strangled I could barely make out the words. 'I thought, when we last talked . . . I had the strangest *feeling*, but I couldn't put my finger on it. Why – and *how*?' Her voice rose until she clapped her hands in front of her mouth, trying to push the sound back in. And then suddenly Everett Carlisle was there too, striding through the archway, his eyes flashing.

'Ella, the speeches are starting soon, what are you—'

'She was pregnant . . .' Ella's voice was faint, but it cut across Everett's as if he wasn't even there.

I felt my fingertips coast across the stitched daisy. 'She was my mother,' I said. 'I'm Alexander and Silkie's daughter.'

It was the first time I had said the words out loud. And oddly, after guarding my secret so fiercely for so long, after all the fear and dread at what would happen if I was found out, something inside me seemed to suddenly come loose at the sound of them. I wasn't nothing at all, I wouldn't fade. I was someone's daughter, suspended between two people who were my parents, and my path would take a new shape from here onwards.

'She was your mother,' Ella repeated, then seemed to catch on something. '*Was* . . .'

'She died in the war. An air raid,' I said.

She took a small step back. 'Silkie is dead,' she whispered.

'Ella, what is this about?' Everett's composure faltered a little when he saw the expression on her face, her eyes wide and stricken, hands shaking. 'Come, love, let's go home, I'll take you . . .'

'Mum? What is going on?' A tall figure had ducked through the door and was hurrying towards us. He shot me a brief look, unsmiling and almost fierce. My heart gave a hard, painful squeeze and for a moment I couldn't bear giving it up after all. 'Isobel?'

'I'm not Isobel.' My voice was choppy with determination. 'I used to . . . I was evacuated from London during the war and sent to live with the McIntyres.' Silence. 'I was ten years old. I stayed on, worked as a maid after the war. Until three years ago.'

I took another breath, the enormity of the story I was about to tell momentarily making me feel winded.

'What happened?' It was the first time Grey had looked at me directly, his eyes troubled and dark, but strangely, I found I could go on more easily.

I told them everything. At the beginning, I spoke haltingly, feeling the need to justify what I'd done, apologies tripping over themselves. But the more I talked, the easier the words came. I stopped apologising and stumbling, until it was like a deluge, like I was purging myself of my secret the way Ella had in the cafeteria. And in the wake of it all, a strange vacuum started forming, room perhaps for all the other things I could now finally say out loud too. Who I had been all along, the real me, who had pushed her way through medical school and made a go of working – and doing well – at one of the best hospitals in the country. Who my mother had been and all the things she had done.

'Her real name was Daisy.' I lifted the bag, smoothed out the fabric and let my fingers rest on the flower. 'She was a seamstress in the East End, and she was so good. She was never meant to be a maid. If she was still alive, she would have gone on to do amazing things.'

Finally I stopped, let the awful, deafening silence wash over me. They were staring at me, all of them: Grey and his father; Ella, who'd sat down on one of the chairs lining the wall halfway through my story. Lulu, who must have seen us and slipped in through the door, her mouth open in a cheerful greeting that had almost instantly died on her lips. Now her eyes were wide and round as she turned towards Benedict and Iain hovering behind her uncertainly.

'You pretended to be her.' Everett was the first to rally, and his voice rang across the corridor so loudly Lulu winced. 'You let us all believe you were Diana Bellingdon's girl. You came to my *house*.' He took hold of Ella's elbow and tugged at her. 'You're an imposter,' he hissed, 'a criminal. You infiltrated my family, preyed upon Ella's weakness. Grey, I think it's time to call the police. We'll keep her here until—'

'No one is calling the police,' Ella said sharply. She wrenched her arm out of her husband's grip and turned back to me.

'Did you know who I was? Did you do it because you wanted revenge?' She bit her lip.

'No,' I said quickly, 'I had no idea of Mum's life before me until you showed me that picture of Mrs McIntyre's dress.'

Ella exhaled a long, careful breath and nodded. 'Did Diana know?'

'She must have. I can't imagine how else my being there would have come about. She was always a bit strange around me, to be honest. She didn't seem to actually like me very much, and yet she couldn't let me go either.'

Ella swallowed. 'I saw you at the funeral,' she said slowly. 'I saw two girls there; I just never got a close look at you. It was . . . hard, all the memories. I told myself I would write afterward, explain.'

'Ella.' Everett's voice sounded almost pleading now. 'I don't understand what *you* have to do with all this.'

Ella was silent. Then she said, 'I did a terrible thing. I couldn't bear them being together, so I destroyed them both.'

Grey moved in her direction, seemingly involuntarily, but Everett had become completely still, looking at his wife, not blinking, the only evidence of what he felt a flush spreading across his cheeks.

'I knew I shouldn't have done it; deep down I could *feel* how wrong it was. But it was like a freight train in motion. Things just kept happening, awful things that brought more pain, more loss. And when Alex died, I didn't think I could go on, for the longest time.'

'And then we met,' Everett said. He didn't sound angry, but tentative almost.

'We did. That was a good day,' she said softly, smiling at him. But when she looked back at me, her eyes were sombre again. 'All the time I told myself that it was Silkie's fault. I focused my misery and hatred on her, all these years. Eventually I moved past it, but when this,' she swallowed and gestured below her stomach, 'started, the memories returned and I wanted so desperately to turn back time and make things different. It became this fixed thought that if I took you under my wing, I could somehow make things right, in however small a way. And then,' she gave me a faint smile, 'I found that I liked you, too. You were so gutsy and clever, so funny, so interested in everything. And you know, I always did think that maybe it ran in the family – that you were a bit like him,' she whispered, flushing.

'Mum waited for him for a long time,' I said, after a moment's pause. 'And even when she must have known he'd died, she never looked at another man.'

Ella's eyes were shiny with tears. 'Oh Isobel,' she choked out.

'My name is Agnes,' I said. 'Agnes Crawford.'

'Agnes,' she said, trying it out. Everett made a convulsive movement, but Ella took my hands, tentatively, as if she was afraid I'd shake her off.

'I'm so very sorry,' she said quietly. 'I should never have let her leave like that. I should have helped her.' She looked at me for a long moment. 'I've spent so much of my life blaming her that I somehow forgot that I loved her too. Loved how funny and different she was, how warm, how single-minded. I'm sorry for what I did, for the way your life turned out, I'm sorry . . .'

I blinked away tears, felt them fall as I tried to find words. 'You didn't do it to me. I just wish that things had been different.' I pulled my hands free and suddenly I found I was shaking. Something settled on my shoulders, and I saw that Lulu had given me her evening jacket.

'I always knew you were a woman of mystery,' she whispered. 'I just didn't quite know that that mystery extended to . . . Well, let's just say you keep things interesting.' Her smile faded and she shifted a little uncertainly. 'I just don't know what happens now.'

She didn't look at Everett, who had his arm around Ella and was talking to her in a low voice. Ella appeared impossibly tired all of a sudden, swaying a little on her feet, but she shook her head firmly.

'No, we're not going to call the constable,' she told him. 'We won't say anything at all to anyone. Do you hear me? All of you. This is between me and Iso—Agnes. No one else.'

She looked around the small circle of people, and it was then that I noticed that Grey had gone.

Forty

The air was cold outside, and I shivered as I looked around for Grey.

The orderlies were just lighting the pyre, I saw. Flames licked up along the sides of the enormous wooden structure, throwing a reddish glow against the facade of the hospital. Other, smaller fires had been lit in a wide circle around the main pyre, with benches for people to sit.

No one was out here yet, everyone still inside for the speeches, but all the way on the other side of the fire I thought I could see a tall outline standing close to the flames. Dodging two men who were walking back and forth with more wood, I circled the pyre until I reached him.

His face was set, his mouth a thin, hard line. The only life in his features came from the flickering glow of the fire. When I touched his arm, he started and pulled away.

'I think everything's been said.' He spoke coolly. 'Don't you, Agnes Crawford?'

'No, everything *hasn't* been said. I never meant to deceive you. Well,' I amended when I saw his incredulous expression, 'I hated having to deceive you.' I put my hand on his arm again, forced him to turn. 'Just listen until I'm finished, that's all I'm asking.' I paused. 'After this, you'll probably never see me again anyway.'

He made a small involuntary movement at that, then looked down at my hand. 'Talk, then.'

'It was a matter of a second, taking Isobel's name.' I spoke slowly, trying to feel my way back into my story. 'I'd never known my father; my mother had died just a few years before.

Then the McIntyres were gone, and Isobel was all I had. We were really close. She was lovely; her telling me to take her place at university was so much like her, thinking of others even as she was dying. We were buried below that bank for hours, not knowing whether we'd ever be found, and then she was gone, and I was alone in the awful darkness. I had no one left, I had nothing at all. In that moment, I didn't know how I'd go on, who I was, what life to live. Taking hers gave me one; it gave me a person to be, a place to belong. Not who I had been as Agnes, but someone proper who made sense to the world that I wanted to belong in. It wasn't right,' I added quickly when he didn't say anything, 'of course I knew then that it wasn't the right thing to do. But it felt at that moment like it was the *only* thing, and once it was done, I gave it all I had. I studied and worked and did everything she would have done. I'd like to think I made her proud.'

He opened his mouth, but I shook my head. 'At first it was glorious. It worked, I think, because I wasn't close to anyone, not anyone who mattered. But then I met Mrs Schwartz and Jakob, I met you and your mum, and it started feeling a little uncomfortable. Nothing I couldn't move past, however. Until I saw the photo of my mother in Ella's photo album, and that's when everything suddenly got very complicated.'

The fire was roaring now, and the warmth reached for me, dispelled the crisp air that smelled of wet leaves and smoke. I looked at Grey across the small space dividing us. He looked tired and drawn, and on an impulse, I gestured towards the benches grouped around one of the smaller fires. 'Could we sit for a moment maybe?'

Without a word, he gestured for me to lead the way. Once we were sitting down, he sighed and held out his hands towards the flames. 'You were saying it was complicated.' He didn't look at me.

'Yes. Because after all the years of hiding inside Isobel, I suddenly wanted more. My mum had been in your house, she'd lived there. I wanted to know more about her. And my father – there was an enormous missing piece that by rights belonged in my life too. Not my new life, the one I was trying to hang on to so desperately, but Agnes's. I couldn't leave it, much as I tried, and the more I went in search of that, the more the real me came out.'

He turned a little, and maybe it was the fire, the flames an illusion of warmth, but his face was no longer quite so hard and cold.

'At the same time, I wanted more from the people around me. I started hating having to lie to them. And all the while, I was trying to keep things going, to hold on to what I'd achieved. You were especially hard,' I gave him a slightly lopsided smile, 'because, well, I liked you. I liked talking to you and spending time with you, but it got more and more difficult to pretend and to keep up my guard, and—'

'So that's what you meant when you said we weren't suited?' he interrupted. 'That day in the kitchen.' My face flushed with more than the heat from the fire as I remembered that morning. Fingers lacing into mine, the fizzing happiness, the horrible things I said to make it stop. I looked up into his face and could see that he was remembering it too, and not just the horrible things, but the joy of it, how easy and right it had felt. Involuntarily, he moved, as if wanting to reach out to me, then changed his mind halfway through and let his hand rest on the bench between us.

'We *weren't* suited, Grey. And not just because I was lying about who I was, but also because of who I *really* was. This no-name East End girl, a bastard with a murky past who on top of everything else was related to your family in a sad and horribly complicated way.'

'I can handle complicated,' he said mutinously, then sighed and shook his head, looked back into the flames. 'I just wish you had told me the truth,' he said. 'I'd like to think that I wouldn't have been deterred by a no-name East End girl. But when I look back now to all those moments when I thought you and I . . . that we shared something special, I can only see the lie. Like nothing is real, like *you're* not even real.'

We sat for a long time, side by side, watching the fire crackle against the midnight-blue sky.

'The ironic thing is,' I finally said, 'that the girl you met and talked to, I think she was more me than any other version. You drew her out, the real me, and she started pushing against the fake me, and that's when it all started coming apart.'

'So you're saying it's my fault, eh?' He raised his eyebrows in mock indignation, perhaps trying to inject something light between us. But his eyes were sad.

'Essentially, yes.' I tried to smile, but found that the flames wavered a little in front of my eyes. I drew in a slightly shaky breath. 'You know, more than anything else, it was those moments that made me want to be who I really was. In the car, when you talked about losing your mum as a child, I had this sudden urge to talk about my real mum, and about all the things you and I really shared. That devastating loss and the feeling of being lost as a child. You would have understood that, you knew how it felt.'

He nodded. 'I think I did understand,' he said softly.

We fell silent again. The flames on the main pyre grew and intensified, the smaller fires bouncing and crackling cheerfully around us. From inside came the sound of clapping, then the doors were flung open and people started drifting out. Briefly I wondered whether Ella was still there, or whether Everett had taken her home. It hurt to think about them, about never seeing Ella again, and about my life at the hospital ending. I looked away from the doors and back towards Grey, and unexpectedly found him watching me.

'So what happens now?' he asked, his eyes still on mine.

'I don't know.' I looked away and twisted my fingers in my lap. 'Do you think that maybe, one of these days, we could . . .' I broke off helplessly. Too much had happened. Too many lies sat between us.

There was a small rustle next to me, and I turned to see Grey holding out a handkerchief. I took it, but my hands were shaking so much I couldn't grip on to it. He took it back, folded it up. Gently he dabbed at my cheeks, his cold fingers pushing curls out of my face, and I remembered the end of the soirée. He was as close now as he had been back then, but the air wasn't crackling with something dangerous or forbidden. It was looser somehow, free and warm. Oddly it made me feel stronger, this feeling of rightness that wasn't full of possibility and heady with freedom, but real and solid.

When I took the handkerchief from him, he grasped my fingers for a moment, then twitched away as if it had been an involuntary gesture he didn't mean. I didn't let go of his hand, though, but rested it against my cheek, and slowly he relaxed. Even when I released him, he lingered against the curve of my jaw. His fingers were warm, his face close, as the promise of what might have been – and maybe could still be – filled the space between us. With a small smile, he tucked a last curl behind my ear, then let go and put the handkerchief back into his pocket.

'Will you try and stay here?' he asked.

I shook my head. 'I don't think so. I have a lot of things to sort out in my mind, and somehow I have a feeling that they might not include being a surgeon any more. Or if I'm going to be a surgeon, then one that is closer to real people. Women. It took me a while to see it, but, well, you know, maybe I should play to my strengths.' Briefly I thought of Mrs Smith and the enigmatic Mrs Gladwell from the London School of Medicine. 'Even if your mum persuades your father not to turn me in for, I don't know, fraud or whatever; even if he has it in himself not to make a public scandal, I think staying here would push him over the edge.'

He nodded. 'Although he's changing too, you know. A few months ago, I was convinced he'd bully you out of his ward within days. Next thing I know, he's taking Mum to Dr Fatima for a second opinion – a woman *and* a foreigner.' He imitated his father's impatient growl, and I had to smile. We'd moved a little further apart, but I found I didn't mind as much. I was breathing more freely now, and his voice sounded more natural.

'And you? What will you do? Will I one of these days be walking past a poster advertising Grey Carlisle, concert pianist? Sold out, of course.'

I'd meant to make him smile, but he just gave a strange little grimace. 'Mum's operation and radiation treatment is coming up, and everything is up in the air until . . .' He paused.

'Until she comes out of it all right,' I said firmly.

'Yes. And it's only a few months until my registration.'

'And the conservatory?'

He hesitated. 'Was a bit of a pipe dream. A good one,' he added fiercely, as if I was going to argue. 'But just that, a dream. Take Billy Mayerl, for example. He started studying music when he was seven. I'm decent, sure, and I'll keep playing as much as I can, but I've not had enough training for the kind of life I'm thinking of. There's no real chance I could make it. And anyway, somehow I found myself agreeing with a certain someone that it would be a shame to throw all this away.' He jabbed his chin in the direction of the hospital.

'I do believe in dreams, though,' I said defensively. 'It's just that you're good at this. You can *do* good.'

'Yes, sure,' he said. 'But rest assured that whatever good I'll be doing, it won't be in my father's practice.' He gave me a half-smile. 'We talked, you know, *I* talked most, if you can believe it. I sat him down, far away from case files and patients, and we talked about Mother and Ella for a long time. I think we're a bit better together now. Once we're through the operation, he's gradually going to dissolve his private practice altogether. Partly because Mum'll need him home more, and also because—'

'Private practice catering to the rich is an obsolete concept?' I suggested.

He laughed. 'Quite. Either way, I'll be applying for jobs elsewhere, away from Thamesbury Hospital, pretty much anywhere but where he works.'

'So you two are very much better, I can see that,' I said drily.

'Well, we're talking. And I played the piano for Mum, with him in the room. Baby steps, eh?'

'So, will we see each other again, do you think?' I said after a small pause.

'Who knows. If anything, tonight is a testament to the kind of unexpected things life throws at you.'

'Yes.' I looked down at my hands. 'I'll hope for unexpected things, then,' I said in a rush. 'Because I wish things had turned out differently, Grey. I want you to know that.'

'I think I do now. And I'm glad we talked. It's always been . . . it's always been so easy with you.' He got to his feet, abruptly, as if he'd said too much, then held out his hand to help me up. For another moment, his fingers were in mine, then he bent and gently kissed me on the cheek. 'All the best to you, Agnes Crawford.' He smiled down at me, then turned, shouldered his way through the crowd and was gone.

I had known it was going to happen, had been trying to brace myself for that feeling of loss and lost-ness with every day that had brought me closer to discovery. And yet as I stood there, my eyes tracking Grey's tall form until it dissolved into darkness, there was hope there too. Maybe he would keep remembering the things that had been real about us; maybe he'd miss the girl that had been Agnes and would look out for her.

I turned back towards the fire, breathed in the wet, smoky air and the brackish scent of the river drifting across on the breeze. For now, though, I had no one else to fall back on; I could be no one but myself. And that would be enough.

Forty-One

Eight months later

'Up here!' I had spotted the ambulancemen from Great Ormond Street Children's Hospital down in the tenement courtyard and hung over the railing to urge them on. 'Stairs are over there. Quick!'

A gaggle of children had already helpfully surrounded men and equipment and, laughing and chasing each other, were chivvying them towards the stairwell.

'Ambulance is here,' I said breathlessly when I was back in the small flat. 'And one of the girls rang the Flying Squad for blood. How is she doing?'

Sister Margareta was bending over the bed, where a young woman lay quite still, her eyes closed, arms around a tiny, squirming baby on each side. 'Placenta's been delivered.' She nodded at the side table. 'Mum's in and out.'

I peered into the dish. 'Looks all right, doesn't it? Now, once we get some blood into you, Mrs Stopes, you'll feel much better. Shall I take this little man from you, Sister?'

I knelt next to Sister Margareta to take the third bundle, wrapped tightly and shockingly light in my arms. 'I'll keep him warm for you,' I told Mrs Stopes. Her eyelids drifted open, tracking her baby anxiously, and I smiled at her, nodding at the two babies in the crooks of her elbows. 'Seeing as you have your hands full.'

I tucked the woollen shawl more carefully around the baby until all that was visible was two eyes and a tiny, pinched face. I was careful not to look at Sister Margareta. Normally stout and unflappable, she looked tired and a bit grim, her habit smeared with the detritus of a long, protracted labour. The whole tenement had been privy to the births, complete with shouting, bellowing and the most colourful cursing I'd ever heard. The babies had come early, not uncommon with multiples, and the moment the last one had been born, a boy, who was tiny and blue next to his sisters, Sister Margareta had dispatched a neighbour to ring an ambulance for immediate transfer to the children's hospital.

In the kitchen, two older women were minding a gaggle of tow-headed children, all girls. One of them, Betty I thought her name was, inched towards the bed, then fell back when Sister Margareta got up to examine the placenta.

'No children, please,' the nun said, scrutinising the metal dish. But Mrs Stopes, her eyes still closed, had turned her head in the direction of Betty's footsteps. Throwing Sister Margareta a quick look, I nodded for the girl to come closer. 'Don't touch the babies, mind, and scarper the moment the doctor arrives,' I told her. Betty nodded seriously and took her mother's hand.

And then, all of a sudden, the door was flung open and the small flat was ringing with voices and the clattering of equipment. An incubator, a ventilating machine and oxygen cylinders were carried in; the paediatrician swiftly plucked the baby from my arms to examine him, someone else checked over the other two babies. I moved all the way back to kneel by Mrs Stopes's head, Betty, still holding her mother's hand, now wedged between me and the bed. I knew Sister Margareta would disapprove, but Mrs Stopes was shifting restlessly, and I thought she could do with some reassurance as the men prepared her baby for transport. Questions were asked of Mr Stopes and his mother-in-law, cups of tea offered to anyone who wanted them, and half the tenement seemed to be congregating outside in the corridor, chattering and whispering and calling in encouragement.

'It'll be all right, I promise,' I kept saying to Mrs Stopes in a low voice, more to drown out the hubbub than anything else. Over by the door, I heard Sister Margareta urging the crowd to please let the doctor through, and when I next looked up, some-one new was bending over the bed, someone tall, with dark hair that stuck up at the back, and I found myself looking straight into the greeny-blue eyes of Grey Carlisle.

'You're in need of a little fortification, I hear?' Grey gave me a swift smile, then bent down to Mrs Stopes. 'You look like you've been through the trenches, if you don't mind my saying, but no fewer than three beautiful babies, all in one go – very efficient. May I have a look?'

He examined her quickly, talking all the while. 'You must be worried about your little boy, but there's no need, the doctors at Great Ormond Street will take good care of him.'

Her breathing was shallow and her eyelids flickered, but she nodded.

'Miss . . .' Grey threw me a look, 'Miss Crawford, if you could help get the transfusion ready?'

Later, Sister Margareta and I packed up the last of our things. Mrs Stopes looked a little better, and the aunties were monitor-ing the introduction of the other two babies. 'Careful or they might break,' one of the aunties was telling Betty.

'He'll come back, won't he, miss?' Mrs Stopes kept asking me anxiously.

'How about we telephone the hospital for you, and the sister coming to check on you later will let you know?'

I knelt to scoop up the remains of a jug that had been broken in the melee, and one of the aunties bustled up disapprovingly.

'That's not midwives' work, miss.' She gestured for a child to bring a broom.

'I don't mind.' I smiled at Betty, who was holding one of the wrapped-up babies. 'She won't break,' I mouthed.

'All the same, you'll have places to be. For all your troubles, miss.' The woman held out a loaf cake wrapped in a piece of paper, then shooed me towards the door, where Sister Margareta was talking to someone on the landing.

'I'm heading back to the convent now,' she said when I joined her, 'but you're free to go. It's been a long night. I'll see you tomorrow?'

'Yes, of course. I'm not leaving for another six weeks. Here, they gave me cake, would you like to take it with you?'

'Sister Anne made some last night, but thanks all the same. You have it.'

Holding the cake carefully against my ruined cardigan, a forgotten stethoscope slung around my neck, I trudged down the stairs after her, thinking about Grey's surprise appearance. Who'd have thought he'd be on the Flying Squad—

'I did tell you our paths would cross again, didn't I?' Grey slowly detached himself from the entryway and held the door open for me. Sister Margareta was already strapping her bag on to her bicycle, chatting to a woman unpegging some washing. She gave me a quick wave and set off towards the archway that led out on to the street, circling the rag-and-bone man just coming in with his cart before speeding up and veering around the corner.

'Didn't you have to go with the Flying Squad?' I looked around for the car, but he shook his head.

'They're heading back to the hospital, but I'm done for the night and thought I'd make my way home from here—Hey, that's mine.' He pointed at the stethoscope.

'Of course.' I smiled and flushed, flustered for no reason other than that he was here, with me. He'd rolled up his shirtsleeves and taken off his jacket, his hair was standing on end, and he was smiling as if it was perfectly normal for us to meet in an East End tenement courtyard filled with early-morning light and the smell of cooking.

I pulled at the stethoscope, managed to get it tangled in my hair, and he laughed.

'I'm glad to see that a few things haven't changed,' he observed, batting away my hands and deftly disentangling the rubber handles of the stethoscope before sliding it into his pocket. 'Quite a few have, though.' He gave me a sidelong glance. 'Mum says you're a midwife now.'

'Not entirely. Part training, part volunteering. I've been shadowing the midwives at the convent, picking up loads of useful bits and pieces. It's been great, actually.' I paused, because I still couldn't quite wrap my head around the glorious enormity of it all. 'I've been accepted at the Royal Free. I'll be starting my clinical studies all over again this autumn, a completely clean slate.'

Grey's jaw dropped. 'But that's brilliant news. Mum never told me.'

'That's because it's only just happened and I can't quite believe it myself,' I said, hugging myself happily. 'I'm a bit worried, actually, that I'll blink and it'll not be true somehow.'

I had caught up with Mrs Smith at the Bonfire Ball, told her the truth as baldly as possible. To my surprise, I'd heard from her the following week. The Convent of the Holy Sepulchre would be glad of an extra pair of hands if I felt able to donate my time there. A few months later, she'd suddenly appeared in the clinic, accompanied yet again by Mrs Gladwell, who informed me that should I be so inclined, she'd be happy to recommend me to the London School of Medicine for the clinical part of my degree. I'd not cried at all since the Bonfire Ball, but at this, to Mrs Gladwell's uneasy astonishment and the alarm of an entire clinic filled with women and children, I'd burst into tears. 'Yes, please. I'll do my best,' I'd choked out, trying to dry my face with my shift. 'I will, I promise.'

Mrs Gladwell had handed me a handkerchief so starched it was more like a crisp board. 'I know you will,' she'd said, and for the first time, her severe face had cracked into a faint smile.

'I think you'll do really well,' Grey said now. 'I did always picture you turning the Thamesbury on its head, but maybe that's wishful thinking.'

'There's still time.' I grinned. 'One of these days I'll be coming for Sister Veronica, mark my words.'

'Please ring me first, so I can be in the gallery for that.'

'And how *are* things at Thamesbury?' I asked. 'How is your father?'

He gave me a wry half-grin. 'Miss him, do you? From what I hear, he's his usual self, taking on disease one patient at a time, terrorising nurses and housemen—'

'And housewomen,' I threw in.

'Especially those. I've left, though, took a post at Guy's,' he added when I looked at him questioningly.

'Good for you! I bet you're doing brilliantly well.'

'I muddle along all right, I suppose,' he said bashfully. He gestured toward the exit. 'Shall we walk a bit? I can push your bicycle if you like.'

'How's your mum?' I asked as we set off.

His smile faded. 'I think she's finally doing a little better with the radiation treatment. Although Dad's still not fully convinced, they managed to contain the spread.'

'What a nasty, nasty illness,' I said soberly.

He nodded. 'She's been enjoying your letters, though.'

Ella and I hadn't seen each other since the night of the Bonfire Ball. I had written after her operation, just two lines asking how she was, and an equally short note came back, in someone else's handwriting. The notes became longer, and she started writing them herself, a little less formal each time, until they were proper full-length letters that eventually turned into a conversation. From time to time her stories seemed livelier; there was mention of an occasional outing into the garden. Other times she was more sombre and her fear shone through clearly. Very occasionally Grey flitted through the lines, and here and there was a mention of her husband. But most of our correspondence was about my mother and their time together, about Alexander and Diana, as well as my own childhood in the East End. Slowly, bit by bit, we filled in all the little cracks and gaps of the last few decades. In fact, I had her latest letter in my bag. It had arrived the day before, but I hadn't got around to opening it before the call-out.

We'd been walking more and more slowly as the corner came into view, as if we were loath to go our separate ways.

'I'm heading in that direction,' he finally said, then hesitated. 'Actually, I wondered, if you fancy it . . . I mean . . .' He started rifling through his pockets, handing me the stethoscope to hold, before extracting a flyer. It was covered in jaunty writing and musical notes. 'I put together a band at the hospital. A handful of doctors, a porter on the drums, a nurse who sometimes plays the violin.'

'How very democratic.' I grinned at him. 'I love it.'

'We . . . well, we're playing our first gig on Saturday, a dance over at a church hall in Clapham. I thought maybe you'd like to come.'

'Me?' I stared at him.

'Yes. We don't play all night, in fact we're opening for another band, so there'll be dancing. I seem to remember that you loved dancing. And were rather good at it.' He was holding on to my bicycle as if he was trying to keep me from making my escape, but I wasn't going anywhere.

'But I thought you wouldn't . . .' I collected myself quickly. 'What I mean to say is, it sounds wonderful and I'd love it. The listening *and* the dancing,' I added a little breathlessly. 'And whatever else.'

A group of workmen jostled past, causing me to stumble, and Grey grabbed me around the waist before I could fall. It was an awkward sort of embrace, which I thought he would break the moment they were gone. But he stayed where he was, his hand in the small of my back, the faint hint of aftershave and mint and cigarette smoke in the air between us, his eyes green as they smiled down into mine.

'I can't wait.'

I cycled home carefully, feeling the long night catching up with me with every push of the pedals. Here and there people recognised me or waved good morning. So Grey was at Guy's. Grey was on the Flying Squad, and he had a band. I would go and watch him.

I smiled to myself as I turned the last corner and dismounted, tying my bicycle to the lamp post. Above me, the windows were open to let in the warm air, and as I extracted the big key from my pocket and stepped across the threshold, I could hear strings being tuned, then the cheerful pitter-patter of a clarinet weaving into piano and bass melodies.

'Agnes?' The piano broke off and Mrs Schwartz appeared on the landing above. 'We were wondering where you'd got to. Irina said her sister is coming by later for studying. Katia's saved you some breakfast in the kitchen. Go have it out in the garden. Sunlight first thing, it is very good for the constitution.'

I took the tray out to the garden, where I sat listening to the bees buzzing around Katia's vegetable beds and the music coming from above, interspersed with the clacking of Jaroslaw's typewriter. I needed to go to Fleet Street a little later, because I had finally decided to check whether anything had remained of the McIntyres' safety deposit box, wondering perhaps if there was unfinished business Diana McIntyre might have wanted taken care of in there, or some important heritage from the Bellingdons. But for now, I had a few minutes' peace in which to read Ella's letter.

Dearest Agnes,

You'll be pleased to hear that I'm sitting out in the garden with a dirty trowel next to me and soil on my dress. After being very tired these last few days, I suddenly felt more energetic today and went outside. However, Everett has the gardener in such a terror to keep things looking nice so I don't worry about the state of it that there isn't much for me to do. I've abandoned my digging and am sitting in the sunshine with a cup of tea to write to you instead. Please do come by soon, it's so peaceful at this time of year and I'd love to see you.

Now, have I told you yet about the time we dragged your mother to Beatrix Humphreys' masked ball? Really, we shouldn't have; she would have been in SUCH *trouble, but of course she was thrilled. The theme was Carnival of the Animals, and she and I made the most gorgeous face masks. If I recall, I wanted to be a cat and she a butterfly. Diana I don't remember, but I'm sure it was something respectable, like a swan or a lioness. I lent Silkie a dress and a plan was hatched how exactly to smuggle her in and keep her cover intact. It was elaborate to say the least, involving complicated signals and many diversionary tactics. That's seventeen-year-old girls for you, a menace to society, really. We'd have been better off in some strict boarding school. Or prison, maybe. But instead, there we were, on a lovely June evening, sauntering into Beatrix's bash of the season, ready to introduce your mother as Comtesse de la Rouge, a distant cousin from France . . .*

'Comtesse de la Rouge, is it?'

Silkie had been nodding at a young man from behind a large fan, decorated to match her butterfly mask. Now, she turned.

'*Oui.*' When she dipped her head gravely and sketched a small curtsey, Alexander made a low sound of amusement.

'May I, er, Comtesse?' He indicated the dance floor.

'Oh, *oui*,' she said again, and although there was a suppressed choke of laughter from behind her mask, the *oui* sounded distinctly heartfelt.

'Is that the only French word you know, Silkie?' Alexander enquired as he led her away from her hopeful suitor.

'It's a grave flaw in our plan is what it is.' For the flash of a second, Silkie's laughing face appeared from behind the profusion of feathers and paint. 'Please, Alex, can we go out on the terrace for a moment? It's infernally hot in here. But you know, we were so busy working out my story – and you must admit, we've been very clever with everything, the French cousin was Diana's idea – that somehow it didn't occur to us that I'd actually have to *speak* French. I've been a very shy, taciturn mademoiselle so far.'

He grinned and stood aside to let her pass through the glass doors on to the terrace. 'How fortunate that I was here to rescue you, then, because I'm not sure how you could have kept *that* up.'

'Are you saying I'm forward, *monsieur*?' She struck him on the arm with her fan, then led the way to the left. From inside came the strains of jaunty music, and a group of young people broke into a noisy waltz, carousing and laughing in the middle of the terrace.

'Not at all,' he said quietly. 'Irrepressible, maybe. Cheeky, certainly.' He reached around her and gently tugged on the strings holding her mask. 'And very lovely, as always.'

'Alexander, no, someone will see,' she whispered urgently. 'I'll be in such trouble, honestly.'

'They're all watching Tom Courtenay and Beatrix Humphreys making fools of themselves over there,' he said. 'And if this is to be our first dance, then I'd really like to see your face.'

Silkie checked over his shoulder to make sure they were unobserved, then smiled and looked up into his eyes.

'All right.' She put her hand on his shoulder and he drew her close.

They looked at each other for a long moment.

'Let's dance.'

Historical Note

The late 1940s saw one of the most fundamental and widely celebrated changes in the medical landscape in Britain: the birth of the National Health Service. Before the Second World War, patients were cared for by a patchwork of family doctors and private specialists, charitable and teaching hospitals, local and municipal clinics. As of July 1948, literally overnight, medical services became free to all and were based on need rather than the ability to pay. For the patient, this was nothing short of a miracle. For the government, it meant a huge administrative effort of reorganising and planning, especially in the early years, in which *The Life I Stole* is set.

Women's roles in healthcare had historically always congregated in the areas of nursing, midwifery, education and philanthropy. For a long time, it was almost impossible for women in England to gain creditable qualifications in medicine, acquire training or be admitted to hospital staff. Very early pioneers such as Elizabeth Garrett (1836–1917) and Sophia Jex-Blake (1840–1912) were forced to obtain their qualifications outside England or use loopholes in the system to enter the profession. (It's important to note that the situation in Scotland and Ireland was somewhat separate from this and, throughout the decades, provided more opportunities for women.) Early attempts to formalise women's medical education eventually led to the establishment of the London Medical School for Women in 1874. In 1877, the Royal Free Hospital was the first to admit female medical students for clinical training.

However, despite ongoing efforts to champion possibilities for young women, obtaining a medical education continued to be difficult, as was pursuing a career and securing choice posts. It wasn't only official rules that stood in the way, but the male suspicion of academic women in general. Why would a girl need a higher education, it was argued, when their main role was ultimately inside the home?

Change came with the National Health Act in 1948, the same legislation that brought Britain the NHS. From here on, medical schools were obliged to admit female students, at minimum a quota of around 15 to 20 per cent.

In theory, the way was open for women to take the medical profession by storm, and many amazing women did: Dame Hilda Lloyd (1891–1982), who became president of the Royal College of Obstetricians and Gynaecologists in 1949, the first woman ever at the helm of a royal college; Dame Sheila Sherlock (1918–2001), who was Britain's first female professor of medicine, at the Royal Free; Professor Dorothy Russell (1895–1983), the first woman in Europe to hold a senior university position in pathology.

But for many young women, the day-to-day reality of gaining a medical qualification – or indeed any other traditionally male degree – was fraught with challenges. The availability and quality of education at secondary school level, though by then officially based on aptitude and available to all, still differed widely according to social class, wealth and family support. And while the war might have shaken things up for working women, the 1950s – a decade of rigid respectability and male-dominated hierarchy – all but closed ranks against them again. Women were supposed to be wives and mothers first. Typically female jobs – nurses, typists and teachers, for example – were not really designed for career advancement, not least because newly married women were generally expected to stop working, if not immediately after the wedding, then at the latest when the first baby was born. As women married young and the Pill had yet to make its debut, this posed an additional challenge for women trying to get through six to eight years of medical education and training before starting to vie for staff positions with their male counterparts, all of them free and unfettered from societal expectations and restraints.

It is this world that Agnes enters when she begins her clinical training at Thamesbury Hospital in 1953. This was a time when patients were still cared for in Nightingale wards, long rooms with beds lined up on each side, overseen by a beady-eyed staff nurse and ward sisters. Staff shortages were a major issue as hospitals tried to keep pace with the restructuring of the health system, and yet the coveted consultant positions at the top of the career ladder were like gold dust (and yes, for the most part firmly in the hands of men). Casualty was often 'round the back' and in dire need of a more cohesive structure.

It was also a decade of archaic morals and lace-curtain respectability across all social strata. Any deviation from the norm was anathema to upstanding society and the situation for unmarried mothers and illegitimate children was appalling. I explore this in detail in my first novel, *My Mother's Shadow*, but suffice it to say that girls who found themselves 'in trouble' – raised without any kind of sexual education on the one hand but held solely responsible for the outcome on the other – had very few options. At best they had family willing to support them and absorb the baby amidst their ranks. At worst, they were stuck in the workhouse, the baby given up for adoption, the mother marked for life.

I've read extensively across all areas covered in the novel, but here and there some creative licence was taken, most importantly with Thamesbury Hospital. Although based on the workings of a big teaching hospital in London, Thamesbury is fictional, as are obviously all the staff, not just at Thamesbury but other places as well. Any similarities to real people are entirely accidental.

If you'd like to dive deeper into Agnes's world, here are some reading recommendations:

Women's lives in the 1950s

Perfect Wives in Ideal Homes, the Story of Women in the 1950s (Virginia Nicholson)
The Last Curtsey: The End of the Debutantes (Fiona MacCarthy)
Hidden Lives, A Family Memoir (Margaret Forster)

Britain in the 1950s

A 1950s Childhood (Paul Feeney)
Family Britain 1951–57 (David Kynaston)
British Society Since 1945 (Arthur Marwick)

Nursing

Sixty Years a Nurse (Mary Hazard and Corinne Sweet)
When the Nightingale Sang, A Nurse's Life in the 1950s and 60s (Cynthia O'Neill and Rosalind Franklin)
Any books by the 'Queen of Hospital Fiction', Lucilla Andrews

Medicine and midwifery fiction and memoirs

Call the Midwife (Jennifer Worth)
My Life as a Woman Doctor (Beulah Bewley)
The Citadel (A. J. Cronin)

Return to Night (Mary Renault)
Yeoman's Hospital (Helen Ashton)

Medicine non-fiction

Women and Medicine (Joyce Leeson and Judith Gray)
Medical Practice in Modern England (Rosemary Stevens)
The Surgeon's Craft (Hedley Atkins)

Acknowledgements

Writing a story might be a solitary endeavour, but turning it into a book is always a group effort.

I'm particularly thankful to my wonderful agent Caroline Hardman for keeping me sane, and keeping me writing whenever the going got tough; my brilliant editor Marion Donaldson for all her sage advice, endless patience and countless rereads; and the amazing team at Headline, who put all the pieces together in the end and made the magic happen.

I love my little corner of the writing community, which has kept me company throughout with beta reads, encouragement and virtual high-fives. Many of these authors are part of the Romantic Novelists Association, of which I've now been a happy member for almost eight years. A special shout-out to the lovely Jenny Oliver, for her words of wisdom, sharp eye and the occasional much-needed glass of wine.

Closer to home, I feel endlessly buoyed by the combined might of the Scott-Schaefer clan. For four books they've cheered me on, fed me chocolate and generally been the best champions a writer could wish for.

Much love and thanks to my boys, and of course to the most wonderful and staunch ally in all things life and writing – my husband Paul.

Writing and publishing a story is only half of the equation, however. The other half is the person on the other side – you, the lovely reader out there. Connecting with a reader over one of my stories is probably the most special magic of all, and getting a note from someone to ask a question or say hello always makes me smile. So please get in touch if you fancy a chat. I'm at nikola@nikolascott.com.

For the last five years I've been sending out a monthly newsletter, in which I talk about all things writing and reading, with giveaways, short story freebies and lots of pictures. Please sign up and be a part of it all. I'd love to have you.

Nikola

Sign up for my monthly newsletter:
www.nikolascott.com

Why not try Nikola Scott's unputdownable

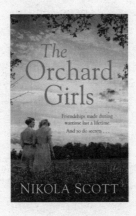

'A clever, wonderful, expertly woven story'
Lorna Cook

London, 2004. Frankie didn't always have it easy. Growing up
motherless, she was raised by her grandmother, who loved her –
and betrayed her. For years, the rift between them seemed irreparable.
But when their paths suddenly cross again, Frankie is shocked to
realise that her grandmother is slowly losing control of her
memory. There is a darkness in her past that won't stay
buried – secrets going back to wartime that may have a
devastating effect on Frankie's own life.

Somerset, 1940. When seventeen-year-old Violet's life is ripped apart
by the London Blitz, she runs away to join the Women's Land Army.
She wants nothing more than to leave her grief behind. But as well as
the terror of enemy air raids, the land girls at Winterbourne
Orchards face a powerful enemy closer to home. One terrible night,
their courage will be put to the test – and the truth of what
happened must be kept hidden, for ever . . .

Available to buy now in paperback and ebook

REVIEW

Don't miss Nikola Scott's unforgettable

'Beautifully written' *Daily Mail*

August, 1939

At peaceful Summerhill, orphaned Maddy hides from the
world and the rumours of war. Then her adored sister
Georgina returns from a long trip with a new friend, the
handsome Victor. Maddy fears that Victor is not all he seems,
but she has no idea just what kind of danger has come into
their lives . . .

Today

Chloe is newly pregnant. This should be a joyful time, but she
is fearful for the future, despite her husband's devotion. When
chance takes her to Summerhill, she's drawn into the mystery
of what happened there decades before. And the past reaches
out to touch her in ways that could change everything . . .

Available to buy now in paperback and ebook

And discover Nikola Scott's gripping

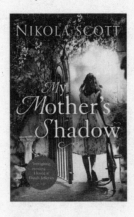

'A well-written, intriguing read full of family secrets . . .
Brilliant' *Fabulous*

Hartland House has always been a faithful keeper of secrets . . .

1958. Sent to beautiful Hartland to be sheltered from her mother's
illness, Liz spends the summer with the wealthy Shaw family.
They treat Liz as one of their own, but their influence
could be dangerous . . .

Now. Addie believes she knows everything about her mother
Elizabeth and their difficult relationship until her recent death.
When a stranger appears claiming to be Addie's sister, she is
stunned. Is everything she's been told about her early life a lie?

How can you find the truth about the past if the one person
who could tell you is gone? Addie must go back to that golden
summer her mother never spoke of . . . and the one night that
changed a young girl's life for ever.

Available to buy now in paperback and ebook

REVIEW

Keep in touch with the world of

NIKOLA SCOTT

For up-to-date news from Nikola, exclusive content and competitions, sign up to her newsletter!

Visit her website <u>www.nikolascott.com</u> to sign up.

REVIEW